Gabriel Stuart MacWalter

Life of Antonio Rosmini Serbati

Founder of the Institute of Charity. Vol. I

Gabriel Stuart MacWalter

Life of Antonio Rosmini Serbati
Founder of the Institute of Charity. Vol. I

ISBN/EAN: 9783744694674

Printed in Europe, USA, Canada, Australia, Japan

Cover: Foto ©Raphael Reischuk / pixelio.de

More available books at **www.hansebooks.com**

LIFE

OF

ANTONIO ROSMINI SERBATI

FOUNDER OF THE INSTITUTE OF CHARITY

BY

GABRIEL STUART MACWALTER

IN TWO VOLUMES—VOL. I.

LONDON

KEGAN PAUL, TRENCH, & CO., 1 PATERNOSTER SQUARE

1883

PREFACE.

To WRITE the Life of a truly great man is a formidable undertaking. To write a suitable Preface to such a Life is a task of very great difficulty. The formidableness of the undertaking and the difficulty of the task are, for obvious reasons, rather increased than diminished if the personage who is the subject of the Life be of the writer's own time. Yet such is the undertaking, such the task, assigned to us who are so unequal to either, and whose only qualification is an earnest desire to do our best to set before the public a faithful picture of one, every feature of whom—as boy, youth, and man—and every phase of whose whole career we have for years studied closely.

Antonio Rosmini was not only a Priest who had led a life of singular holiness, a life heartily and heroically devoted to the love of God and the good of his fellow-men; but he was also a

profoundly learned writer commissioned by the
highest authority on earth to do battle for Christian
Philosophy. Herein is to be found the key to
his biographer's greatest difficulties ; for, generally
speaking, men are now as little disposed to appreciate properly a true Philosopher who happens to
be their contemporary, as men of old were to
credit a Prophet who happened to be their country-
man. But the simple history of such a man's life
ought to establish his claims to just appreciation :
what if the historian's incompetency should stand
in the way ? This is our fear.

It has been said of St. Ignatius of Loyola that
'his mission was to restore the principle of authority
ignored by the innovators, and to give back to
Christian Obedience its glory and beauty.'[1]   In like
manner it may be justly said that the mission of
Antonio Rosmini was to restore the principles of
Truth trampled on by the innovators, and to give
back to Christian Philosophy its unity, harmony
and prestige. The story of his Life should prove
this claim. But what if we have failed to tell that
story rightly ?

A distinguished modern historian assures us

[1] Meyrick's *Life of St. Ignatius*, preface, p. xvii. (London, Burns
and Oates, 1871).

that 'if we would discover the real rulers of mankind, we shall find them rather in their philosophers and literary men than either their statesmen or their generals. The only difference is that it is a posthumous dominion in general which the author obtains : his reign does not begin till he himself is mouldering in the grave.' [1]

History is so full of evidence to the truth of this remark, in more than one form, that no student can fail to find testimony in abundance to suit the form he prefers. It may, then, be superfluous to suggest any examples ; yet we venture to use a student's privilege and indicate, *en passant*, the few which first occur to us touching only one form of the fact.

All the valour and all the wars of Philip of Macedon or of his 'invincible son' Alexander were utterly powerless to conquer that perpetuity of sway which the Philosopher's pen easily secured to Plato and to Aristotle.

The ages in which the persecuted Fathers of the Christian Church struggled with the mighty Cæsars (Pagan or Christian) are rich in a nobler evidence to the same fact, but all may be summed up in this :—The despotic and haughty Cæsars

---

[1] Alison's *History of Europe*, &c., vol. i., preface.

and their greatest statesmen have left hardly a name behind, while the despised and oppressed Fathers still reign through their writings.

The rule of Genseric the Great Vandal ended for ever soon after the capture of Hippo, fourteen hundred and fifty years ago ; but the reign of St. Augustin, the great Christian Doctor, who died there during the siege, began then and still continues ever increasing in authority and power.

Who now cares to know anything of the generals and statesmen, or even of the crowned Fredericks and Conrads, in whose hands were the destinies of the Western Empire during the life-time of St. Thomas of Aquin, six centuries ago ? Their sway perished with their bodies ; whereas St. Thomas, when he lay down to die in the Cistercian abbey of Fossanuova, commenced his reign over the intellects of men—a reign which is daily putting forth fresh activity and gaining brighter lustre.

Coming nearer home and to far inferior names, we all know that, while Lord Bacon the statesman was forgotten almost as soon as the grave closed over him, Lord Bacon the author then took a new lease of power, and his dominion still continues. We also know that, while the military

exploits and statesmanship of Frederick the Great
bore fruit that withered before it ripened, and,
at best or worst, affected merely a small section
of Europe, the Voltaire whom he used and then
thrust disdainfully aside holds a too-potent influence
to-day throughout all Europe, and far beyond it.

Thus, for good or for evil, great writers on
philosophical subjects have always won, over men,
a dominion that has long outlasted the utmost ever
achieved by the greatest generals or statesmen.
But though a great Philosopher usually begins to
reign when 'he is himself mouldering in the grave,'
his claims to dominion are seldom undisputed. It
is a remarkable fact that the greater the Philosopher is, and the nearer he approaches to *perfect
truth*, the more surely and bitterly are his claims
resisted and his positions assailed; more remarkable still, they who oppose him with the greatest
insistence, and often with the greatest animosity,
are generally 'of his own household,' so to say—
men who should have been his supporters from the
start, and who (as represented by the schools of
thought they leave after them) ordinarily end with
becoming his champions.

In what concerns the 'System of Truth' identified with the name of Antonio Rosmini we have

a forcible illustration of all this. But, as there are older and even more suggestive illustrations to be found in ecclesiastical history, it may be as well to note one or two of them as furnishing the best explanation possible of Rosmini's true position, and of the value to be set on the unseemly controversies aroused by his masterly vindication and restoration of Catholic Philosophy.

No less an author than St. Augustin, 'the Eagle of the Latin Fathers,' becomes our first illustration. When his wonderful books on *Divine Grace* were published no one questioned the doctrines they expounded. They opened up depths of thought which had not been explored before, but the learned saw nothing in them which was out of harmony with the Christian Faith. However, when, in the course of time, the Pelagians and Semi-Pelagians attacked those doctrines as novelties in the Church, St. Augustin was openly reproached, by prominent Catholics, with having imprudently raised questions too abstruse for ordinary minds, and calculated to mislead many.[1] Even such celebrated scholars as the monks of St. Lerins joined in the outcry against him, and others of

---

[1] See St. Augustine *De dono perseverantiæ*, c. xx.

hardly less influence took up the assault, adding insinuations that the works thus assailed had caused the loss of numerous souls. These insinuations have more than once since then assumed the shape of distinct charges.[1]

This, however, was a petty warfare compared with that in which, surprising to say, St. Jerome, the *doctor maximus*, took a part against the Saint. He went so far as to formally accuse the great Bishop of Hippo with having, in his comments on the Psalms, gone against the interpretation of the Fathers; with having said things which the Christian sense could not justify; with having sown, in one of his books, heresies which competent authority should oblige him to retract.[2] St. Jerome, though misled for a time by a false alarm, was not an unreasonable opponent, unready or unwilling to examine calmly for himself the matters in dispute. No sooner had he done this than he discovered his mistake, and acknowledged that the productions in question were entirely free from error.

St. Augustin, however, was less fortunate with less important and less competent opponents. He

---

[1] A list of his opponents, especially those of last century, will be found in the *Vindiciæ* of Cardinal Noris.

[2] See *Epistolæ* lxxii. et lxxv., in the second volume of St. Augustine's works, edited by Migne.

wrote more than thirty short treatises to satisfy these, but, for the most part, in vain. Some, indeed, who had declared against him in good faith, and desired only the truth, allowed their eyes to be opened and their minds and hearts to embrace the doctrine he explained. Others, unwilling to be convinced of the truth, were in no way persuaded but much annoyed by the clearness of his expositions. In fact, the more manifest he made the truth which he taught, the more exasperated they became and the more virulent their hostility. His personal friend St. Prosper, alluding to the work _De correptione et gratia_, says : ' The perusal of this new book of your Beatitude has had the effect that while those who followed the authority of your apostolic doctrine have grown very much enlightened and instructed, those who, on the contrary, had their minds hindered by the darkness of prejudice (_persuasionis suæ impediebantur obscuro_) have become more hostile to you than they were before.' [1]

All the explanations of the holy Doctor were unavailing, since they for whom he wrote them were resolved to insist that he must be wrong. For more than a century after his death there came

[1] _De corrept. et grat._ cap. xxxv.

those who kept up the assaults, and though there were long periods of quiet, the antagonism was renewed again and again, until the Church made his triumph complete and he now reigns unchallenged.

We find our next illustration in no less an author than St. Thomas of Aquin, 'the Angelical Doctor.' A few years ago Cardinal Zigliara (an author whose words carry peculiar weight) published an important work, in which he says : ' Many persons who, with perhaps a good intention but with the most wicked action (*sed actione pessima*), had persecuted the most meek Doctor while he was yet living, opposed him with much greater virulence after his death.'[1] In corroboration of this his Eminence quotes the following passage from Eckardt : ' Both during his life and after his death St. Thomas was opposed by persons who, whether from jealousy or envy, sought a paltry celebrity by impugning his doctrines ; and amongst them were men eminent for dignity and for talent.'[2]

We all know that the *Summa Theologica* is now the standard work of all Catholic seminaries—

---

[1] Zigliara, *De Mente Concilii Viennensis in definiendo dogmata unionis animæ humanæ cum corpore*, &c., p. 155 (Rome, 1878).

[2] *Scriptorum Ordinis Prædicatorum*, &c., T. i. p. 436.

that it has won the highest eulogies from Sovereign
Pontiffs and from theologians generally. Nevertheless, on its first appearance, it was fiercely
attacked, especially by a certain William de la
Mare, a noted Catholic writer of the time, who
criticised it in a very censorious spirit, branding
many of its propositions as heretical in theology and
absurd in philosophy.[1] He did not or would not
understand the author, and, misrepresenting him,
became without difficulty a leader of those who
were too ready to accept his distortions for truthful
representations.

But a more painful phase than this in the
hostility to St. Thomas is, we grieve to say,
associated with our own country. Still availing
ourselves of Cardinal Zigliara's work,[2] we find
that in two Provincial Synods held at Oxford
(the one in 1277 and the other in 1286), 'an
anathema was pronounced against the doctrine of
St. Thomas on *the unity of the substantial form*,
and against other doctrines taught by him.' The
first of these synods was presided over by Archbishop Robert Kilwarby, who (strange as it may

---

[1] About ten years after the death of St. Thomas, this De la Mare
wrote a work under the title of *Correctorium Fratris Thomæ*, which
title, in the course of time, came to be known as *Corruptorium Fratris
Thomæ*.

[2] *De Mente Concilii* &c., pp. 158, 206, 208.

seem) was himself a Dominican, and therefore a *confrère* of the Angelical Doctor. The second was presided over by Archbishop John Peckham, 'a Franciscan, who in 1284 had confirmed the sentence of his predecessor against Brother Thomas'; but, as many learned men in England as well as abroad continued to defend him against the two Archbishops, it was deemed expedient to convene this second Synod in 1286. The condemnation which it pronounced against the Saint began thus : *Hæreticæ quædam opiniones per Dominum Archiepiscopum Cantuariensem declaratæ et damnatæ in nomine Domini, Amen.*[1]

Not content with this severe blow, the adversaries of the holy Doctor brought against him influential members of the renowned Theological Faculty of the Sorbonne, and with these formulated thirteen articles the condemnation of which they demanded—a condemnation designed to damage seriously if not fatally the good fame of St. Thomas. So successfully did these people push their efforts, that the then Bishop of Paris, Stephen Tempier, was induced to issue the condemnation under his episcopal seal !

[1] See Labbé's *Collectio Conciliorum*, T. xiv. col. 1533-34 (Venet. 1731).

When this condemnation was made public a
learned Dominican remarked : '*Condemnationem
illam nequaquam mare transisse*,' meaning that it
had not been adopted by Rome—*the* Rome of
the Christian world, the Apostolic See. It sig-
nified little what Provincial Synods and Bishops
decreed in matters of this sort so long as Rome
did not confirm their proceedings ; and Rome
did not approve the condemnations which had
been persistently hurled against St. Augustine
and St. Thomas. On the contrary, as in the
case of Rosmini similarly assailed, ' Rome at last
threw around them the mantle of her official protection.'

There is one significant passage in the work
from which we have been quoting—a passage which
very properly stigmatises as ' wicked ' a custom that
is even more prevalent in our time than in the days
of St. Augustine and St. Thomas ; for Antonio
Rosmini (as Cardinal Zigliara was and is in a
position to know) has had to endure more of this
kind of injustice than they had. ' There prevails
nowadays,' says his Eminence, ' a wicked method
by which obsolete difficulties against a doctrine, in
itself worthy of respect, are reproduced again and

again, and greatly magnified, *while no notice is taken of the answers already given and oft repeated.* Thus it comes to pass that simple-minded people are led to regard as erroneous, opinions which are highly approved of by theologians of the foremost rank.'[1]

Misconceptions and misrepresentations thence arising, or thus fostered, generally lead to persecution. But persecution has ever been the lot of Saints, and the greater the Saint the more violent the persecution. Whether he be a great author, like St. Augustine and St. Thomas, or a great 'Restorer of the principle of authority,' like St. Ignatius, it is all the same: persecution is his portion, and alas! this persecution in its most afflicting form comes, as we have just seen, not from outside the Fold but from within it. 'And a man's enemies shall be they of his own household.' Unfortunately it often happens that those who inherit the bitterest memories of persecution so little profit by its lessons of charity that they, in turn, become persecutors, generally with the best intentions. Thus it is that some *few* representatives of an Order which has done and still does glorious work in the service of the Church—an Order which, from its birth, drank to the dregs of persecutions spring-

[1] *De Mente Concilii,* &c., p. 232.

ing from misconception—were amongst the foremost
to revive and continue against St Thomas an opposition based on misconception. No wonder, then,
that some few of these should be the first, and
remain the chief, assailants of Rosmini, who became
the Restorer, Defender, and special Exponent of the
Angelic Doctor's teachings.[1]

However, we who write his Life are not so
much concerned in the great Philosopher as in the
Saintly Man ; but, as the qualities proper to either
character are so interblent in Rosmini that they
seem to be inseparable, we could hardly have
avoided the few remarks we have made, especially
when we remembered that his opponents, like those
of St. Augustine and of St. Thomas, and even of
St. Ignatius, have striven, and still strive, to
separate the Man from his Mission—the great
Catholic Priest from the great Catholic Philosopher,
the Founder of an Order devoted to the practice
of Christian Charity from the Restorer, if not the

---

[1] See chap. xiv. pp. 224-6, vol. i. of this work. From his boyhood
(as the history of his life will show) up to the close of his career,
Rosmini was a diligent student and enthusiastic admirer of St.
Thomas. In the first edition of his ' Philosophical Essays,' published
at Milan in 1827, he took delight in declaring that he walked ' *Sulle
orme di S. Agostino e di S. Tommaso*,' and he never lost an opportunity of recommending the study of St Thomas to all who sought a
sound knowledge of Catholic Theology.

Founder, of a scientific system devoted to the vindication of Christian Truth.

The biographers of St. Ignatius claim that 'the secret of his greatness lay in his power to discern the wants of the age, and in that genius which foresaw the dangers certain to accrue to the Church from the rise of a heresy which was to deny the very basis of her authority.'[1] Now, the greatness of Rosmini lay in the power to discern the wants not only of his own time, but of the times that were to follow, and in the genius that not only foresaw the dangers of the misleading philosophies that were sapping the basis of Christianity itself, but provided a sure method of resisting their subtle assaults on the Church, and of strengthening the bulwarks of Truth against aggressions that threatened to destroy its very foundations. As St. Ignatius was misunderstood, slandered and persecuted for what he did or attempted to do in furtherance of the Mission for which such greatness as he had was given to him, so was Rosmini. More fortunate, however, than St. Ignatius, Rosmini was never brought before the Inquisition to rebut charges of heresy and other vile

---

[1] *Life of St. Ignatius*, &c., translated by Rev. T. Meyrick, S.J. M. Sainte-Foi's preface, p. I.

a 2

accusations. But, as unfortunate as the other, his adversaries have sometimes been, like those of St. Ignatius, excellent men, heartily devoted to the interests of the Church.

It is very sad to think how much suffering good and great servants of God, like St. Augustine, St. Thomas, St. Ignatius and Rosmini have had to endure from being misunderstood by other servants of God who were also good, and, in some cases even great. History is overladen with testimonies to this infirmity of poor human nature. How often our Saxon Saints were persecuted by other Saints! St. William of York suffered many tribulations at the hands of St. Bernard and other holy men. St. Wilfrid was 'misunderstood by Saints persecuted by Saints, deposed by Saints as unworthy of the Pontificate. Truly, a very fertile theme for the shallow criticisms of the children of the world: while to a Christian its lesson is that earth is not our home, that the balance of things is not righted till the judgment, the Church militant is not the Church triumphant.' [1]

Although the harsh treatment which St. Ignatius met with from the many zealous Catholics, some of

[1] *Lives of the English Saints.* St. Wilfrid, Bishop of York, by F. W. Faber (London, Toovey, 1844).

them in most exalted stations, who misunderstood his acts, words or motives—although this and the misrepresentations that constantly harassed him, in the work to which he was called, bear a marked resemblance to the harsh treatment and misrepresentations which Rosmini and his work have encountered, especially at the hands of those who are heirs to sobering traditions of harsh treatment and misrepresentations, we have no desire to lay much stress on the parallel. But there is visible another and much more agreeable parallel between St. Ignatius and Rosmini—a parallel of character.

Considering the great difference between the nature of their talents and acquirements, to say nothing of the great difference between their early training and their intellectual pursuits, this parallel could hardly be, were it not for the one thing which was with Rosmini from his childhood onward, and came to St. Ignatius in his manhood—that intense love of God which is the soul of sanctity. M. Charles Sainte-Foi has, in a few sentences, drawn an admirable picture of the character of St. Ignatius. So striking is the likeness to the character of Rosmini that, if we had read it without knowing to whom M. Sainte-Foi specially applied it, we should have taken it to be the character-portrait of him whose life it has been our privilege to describe in these volumes.

'The idea we would represent of him,' says M. Sainte-Foi, 'is that of a man who in all his life, and even in his least actions, is perfectly master of himself, always self-possessed, always keeping nature under control and never for one moment letting it loose. He does not act until he has deliberated long and maturely; he takes no resolution until he has weighed and balanced carefully the reasons for and against it. You would say that he is a man who counts only upon himself, and yet he reckons on nothing but on God. All his deliberations and mental labours were sanctified, assisted and elevated by prayer, to which he never failed to have recourse in the least difficulty, recommending the matter to God and putting all his confidence wholly in Him. His letters and conversation exhibit the same character; they give evidence of the same ruling and sober reason, the calm wisdom which knows always how to keep between the two extremes, and when directing others, the watchful care to guide in the way most suitable to the given nature, taking account of the dispositions of mind and of the affections, so as to draw these out and develop them to the best issue for the glory of God

—that being the sole end which he had before him in all his actions.'[1]

The illustrious Father Genelli, S.J., when writing the Life of St. Ignatius, took occasion to express his regret that so little use had been made of the Saint's letters in all the earlier biographies of him ; 'for it cannot be disputed that every man is the best painter of his own portrait, and this more especially in his letters.'[2] Mindful of this fact we have freely used the correspondence of Rosmini and thus enabled himself to 'give us, in some sort, his photograph.' As the class of letters which best illustrate character are those called 'familiar,' it is this class and this alone that we have laid under contribution. Considering that Rosmini's correspondence (now preserved in the archives of the College at Stresa) on all manner of subjects would fill twenty volumes of printed matter, it must be evident that we have not, after all, drawn heavily upon it.

Had we been dealing with the Theological or Literary Doctor merely, or with the Philosopher

---

[1] *Life of St. Ignatius*, &c., translated from the French by Rev. T. Meyrick, S.J. ; Preface by M. Charles Sainte-Foi, pp. xviii.–xix.

[2] Genelli's *Life of St. Ignatius*, Author's Preface (translated from the French edition by Father Meyrick), p. 1 (p. xxii. of the English edition. London, 1871).

merely, or with any particular phase of the many
aspects in which his versatile genius and vast erudition presents to us an individuality strongly marked
in each and all, we should have no difficulty in
selecting a volume of admirable letters to illustrate
his greatness in that special character. But our
object was to show all the features of *the man*, to
show them fully and not after the manner of a
colourless profile. However much we might extend
the outlines of such a profile, it would still remain
a dim, partial, sectional representation; whereas the
picture we attempt to draw is meant to be a full-
sized and life-like portrait, carefully preserving
every feature of the man. For this purpose his
every-day familiar letters were indispensable and
sufficient.

Familiar letters are generally unstudied compositions, written off-hand without attention to literary polish. Those of Rosmini are hardly an exception. But, though the manner often seems to be
deficient in elegance or to betoken hurry, the matter
is never wanting in point, never at fault in giving
adequate expression to his meaning; for, however
hurriedly he wrote, he always considered carefully
what he had to say. Graces of style had to yield
to the necessity of replying promptly and fully to

so many letters that, if he paused to frame his sentences in accordance with the set classical rules which purists insist on, most of his correspondence and much of his ordinary work would have to be set aside. The letters we have selected may be regarded as, in some sort, written echoes of his habitual conversations, as colloquial rather than formal; and in translating them we have aimed at retaining the form as well as the sense.

We are so sure that we possess none of the many gifts necessary for a successful historian that we should never have undertaken this work had not the task been imposed upon us as a duty. Circumstances, not of our own seeking, brought us in contact with most of the scenes and many of the persons intimately associated with Rosmini in his lifetime. A fondness for that kind of research called 'biographical' led us to make many special inquiries touching his life and its incidents, and to note carefully all we heard, read, or saw that had any connection with him. An earnest attachment to the very name of one who had done so much, and been so much traduced, gave a zest to our investigations, which were brought to a close when the *Life of Rosmini*, by Don Francesco Paoli, appeared in Italy, and its translation into English was proposed.

Now, Don Paoli, who had served for more than twenty years as private secretary to Rosmini, and had been constituted his executor, possessed exceptional facilities, with the requisite talent, for writing a complete history of his life. The elaborate memoir which he published will always bear witness to the good use he has made of his opportunities.[1] The proposal to translate it was, however, abandoned, mainly because the work had been composed with special reference to affairs in Italy. It was, therefore, in its actual form, not well adapted to English readers, who know little or nothing of the controversies and local circumstances that led to the course Don Paoli felt bound to take. But, as the work teems with authentic information essential to any Life of Rosmini, Don Paoli's memoir must continue to be the *thesaurus* from which every biographer of that illustrious man will have to draw. We have drawn from it so fully and freely that, to avoid constant references to the fact in the text, we make this general acknowledgment here.

[1] *Della vita di Antonio Rosmini-Serbati, Memorie di Francesco Paoli pubblicate dall' Accademia di Rovereto* (Rome, Paravia & Co., 1880).

The other authors, such as Niccolò Tommaseo, whom we have had occasion to consult, will be found duly credited wherever we have used the information got from them. Besides the material obtained from these principal sources there were many little details which neither Don Paoli, nor Tommaseo, nor any of the many Italian writers who have discussed the Life of Rosmini, saw fit to note, but which seemed to us worth gathering up from the recollections and memoranda of humble people who had well known Rosmini at his original home in Rovereto, or during his residence in Padua, Milan, Domodossola, and Stresa. Such 'unconsidered trifles' can add nothing, perhaps, to the substantial value of any narrative ; but they help to tint the picture and give it those indefinable little lights and shades which go so far to finish a likeness and make it more and more natural.

G. S. M.

St. Etheldreda's, London,
October, 1882.

CONTENTS

OF

THE FIRST VOLUME.

——•◦•——

INTRODUCTORY CHAPTER.

ROVERETO AND THE ROSMINIS.

(A.D. 1442–1797.)

CHAPTER I.

BIRTH AND BOYHOOD OF ANTONIO ROSMINI.

(A.D. 1797–1813.)

CHAPTER II.

ROSMINI'S EARLIEST COLLEGE DAYS.

(A.D. 1813-1815.)

His personal appearance at sixteen—His dislike of novelties in dress—His conversations—His first scholastic thesis—How

CHAPTER V.

ROSMINI ENTERS THE UNIVERSITY OF PADUA AS A
THEOLOGICAL STUDENT.

(A.D. 1816-1817.)

CHAPTER VI.

ROSMINI CLOSES HIS SECOND SEASON AT THE UNIVERSITY,
AND RECEIVES MINOR ORDERS.

(A.D. 1817-1818.)

CHAPTER VII.

ROSMINI'S EVERY-DAY LIFE AT THE UNIVERSITY.

(A.D. 1818-1819.)

CHAPTER VIII.

ROSMINI LEAVES THE UNIVERSITY AND RECEIVES
THE SUBDIACONATE.

(A.D. 1819.)

CHAPTER IX.

ROSMINI AN HEIR AND A DEACON.

(A.D. 1819-1821.)

CHAPTER X.

ROSMINI A PRIEST.

(A.D. 1821.)

CHAPTER XI.

ROSMINI'S 'PASSIVITY' AS ILLUSTRATED BY THE FIRST YEAR OF HIS PRIESTHOOD.

(A.D. 1821.)

CHAPTER XV.

ROSMINI'S FIRST VISIT TO ROME.

(A.D. 1823.)

CHAPTER XVI.

ROSMINI'S PANEGYRIC OF PIUS VII. THE BEGINNING
OF TRIBULATIONS.

(A.D. 1824.)

CHAPTER XXI.

CHAPTER XXII.

CHAPTER XXIII.

ROSMINI RECEIVES THE EXPECTED MANIFESTATION OF
PROVIDENCE.

(A.D. 1827.)

LIFE

OF

ANTONIO ROSMINI.

INTRODUCTORY CHAPTER.

ROVERETO AND THE ROSMINIS.

(A.D. 1442–1797.)

Olden and modern days of Rovereto—Its chief attractions—How the
Rosmini family came to be connected with Rovereto—Genealogy of
the Rosminis of Rovereto, with a brief account of the heads of the
family for three centuries—How the Rosminis took the name of
Serbati—Short sketch of Antonio Rosmini's uncle, parents, and
only sister.

IN olden days, when the favourite highway from
Germany to Italy led through the Tyrol, along the
picturesque valley of the Adige, there was a little
village, some sixteen miles south of Trent, which
became a popular resting-place on the road. This
village had grown around a fortified castle that stood
in the midst of an oak forest, from which it took
the name of Rovereto, or 'oak plantation.' Travellers tarried there, partly because of the protection
the castle gave, but mainly because, in those days,

even ordinary wayfarers liked to have more than a
passing glance at the 'disparted hills' and 'frowning
rocks' immortalised by Dante as—

> . . . . That ruin which Adice's stream
> On this side Trento struck, should'ring the wave,
> Or loos'd by earthquake or for lack of prop ;
> For from the mountain's summit, whence it moved
> To the low level, so the headlong rock
> Is shiver'd, that some passage it might give
> To him who from above would pass. . . .[1]

In modern days, the fine old coach road through
that mountain gorge is merely a well-preserved
memorial of the slower past, and travellers care less
to loiter amid magnificent scenery than to 'outstrip
the wind' and dispense with wayside resting-
places. The route, however, is much the same as
in olden times, for the railroad which connects the
Tyrol with Italy closely follows the ancient track
by the left bank of the Adige, touching at Rovereto
(now a considerable town), in the charming vale of
Lagarina. There a smiling prosperity—wrung from
nature's ruins by ages of patient culture—has come
to soften the rugged grandeur and awful chasms
that were without any such relief in Dante's time.
Then the attractions of the village were, as for ages
they had been, exclusively associated with the wild
majesty of the surrounding scenery, and with the
strategical importance of the castle as the most
southern and not least formidable of Tyrolese
frontier posts. *Now*, the village has become a
town, stripped of military pretensions and vested in

[1] Dante's *Inferno*, c. xii. 4-10 (Cary).

the more palmy garb of thrift and industry. Those add constantly increasing charms to the encircling Alps—the Trentine—at the base of which a steady extension of the town goes on, just near enough to the famous Adige to enjoy its benefits, but far enough away to escape its dangers. The gushing waters of the Leno, flowing through the centre of the municipality, supply the Roveretans so abundantly with ' fluvial blessings ' that they can afford to forget how nigh they are to the mightier river.

Long busy with the production of silk and wine, Rovereto is fitly embowered in mulberry groves and vineyards, as in the natural emblems of its commercial life ; while on every side, beyond the municipality as well as in it, are visible other emblems sacred to the faith which has never once, ' through weal or woe,' been separated from the place or people. Amongst those ' other emblems ' English tourists may see such significant memorials of the far past as the ruins of a church, built on the Leno in 1250, to the honour of God, through St. Thomas of Canterbury ; there also they will find the memory of St. Oswald[1] more honoured than in his beloved Worcester or York, and the fame of St. George more reverentially preserved than in the land which emblazons his glory on heraldic shields and standards.

But it is not of its natural beauties or business attractions, not of its marble mansions or quaint

---

[1] The pretty little church of St. Oswald (erected in 1791 by Ambrogio Rosmini) is close to the site on which the church of St. Thomas once stood.

streets, not even of its churches and chapels, whether
of the past or the present, that we have now occasion
to speak, unless in so far as they say something
special of a name which sheds a bright halo over
them all—a name that has lifted Rovereto from
the obscurity of a simple wayside town to a lofty
and abiding dignity which makes it already more
famous, and far more revered, than many an opulent
and pretentious city in that part of the world. This
name is Rosmini ; for ages it has been most intimately and honourably blent with the well-being of
Rovereto. A Rosmini was of those who bravely
defended the castle and its dependent village in
1487, when ' bombs ' were for the first time used in
war, and the Archduke Sigismund satisfied himself
that, without this new projectile, he could not have
soon vanquished that gallant little outpost of the
Venetians. The walls of the battered old castle can
still speak of its Rosmini commandants. The
courts of justice preserve traditions of the Rosmini
magistrates, whose decisions and virtues are held up
to the veneration of modern judges. Many of the
singular old edifices which dot the valley beyond
the town, or adorn its streets, still bear witness to
the business enterprise or the architectural skill of
some Rosmini. So, too, all the religious shrines
have much to say for Rosmini generosity, taste, and
piety ; while schools and charitable institutions bear
living witness to the enlightened munificence which
at all times distinguished this most faithful Catholic
family.

All these, however, have less interest for us than a certain monument which stands at the top of a noble avenue that was opened, not many years ago, through the Rosmini gardens down to the railway station.[1] It is a magnificent statue in white marble, erected close to the Rosmini mansion, overlooking the Rosmini Infant Asylum, and bearing 'mute but eloquent' testimony to a goodness and greatness far surpassing all that had ever before been associated with the name of Rosmini or Rovereto. It represents the homage of the municipality to its grandest, most gifted and saintly son, ANTONIO ROSMINI-SERBATI. Of him, and him only, have we any desire to speak here ; but, as we sympathise with that propensity of our race which craves to know something as to the pedigree of eminent men, we shall attempt to satisfy this natural inquisitiveness by briefly setting forth the lineage of the great Priest, Founder, and Philosopher, whose holy life we are about to sketch.

Long before the Tyrol became a dependency of Austria the Rosminis held an honourable place among the patrician families of northern Italy. That branch of the stock from which the subject of our memoir sprang became connected with the Tyrol while the Venetians held sway there, and before Austria had recovered the domestic quiet so rudely disturbed by the noxious principles of Huss. It was in those tempestuous days, when false philo-

---

[1] See *note* Chap. 1, pp. 30–32 of this volume.

sophy was furiously struggling to overthrow the order of Christian society, that one of the Lombardian Rosminis founded a home in Rovereto which became the nursery of a distinct line. From the *Monografia* of Don F. Paoli, the *Araldico Geneologico*, and other trustworthy sources, we learn how this nursery answered its purpose, and how the descent of the children reared in it passed on from generation to generation.[1] The record, though scanty and in itself dry, as genealogies usually are, derives much interest and importance from the subject to which it directly leads and the lessons to which it indirectly points.

ARESMINO, who had been Lord High Constable of Verona in 1456, was the founder of the Rovereto Rosminis. In 1464 he left Verona to establish a family residence in Rovereto. Some twenty-five years before, while serving in a military capacity at Rovereto Castle, he was required to act as magistrate of the Lagarina district—a circumstance which probably led him to choose Rovereto for a permanent abode when he decided on retiring from public life in Verona. At all events, there is reason to believe that during his official stay in Rovereto he bought a house (sometime in 1442), which remained his property while he filled the elevated post to which the Veronese had elected him. On leaving that post he returned to this Rovereto home, and, re-invested with judicial authority, spent the rest of

---

[1] *Antonio Rosmini e la sua Prosapia*, Rovereto 1880.

his days there, 'universally loved and esteemed as the noblest of its citizens.'

Aresmino was a man remarkable for probity and prowess at a period when both these qualities seldom met together in the same person. In 1469 he died, leaving to his heirs high patrician rank, with such a good name as brightened afresh the family escutcheon. Of his four sons, the second (Picenino) founded the family of Rosmini di Volano, and the two youngest (Pamfilo and Carlo) served God and their country as exemplary Priests. One of these (Pamfilo) was so popular that, in spite of his efforts to escape all such honours, he was elected Podestà of Rovereto, a dignity which he declined as inconsistent with his priestly duties. He then became Vicar-General of Verona and afterwards of Mantua (under Cardinal Gonzaga), where he died in 1543. His brother Carlo was a learned canon and Rector of St. Mary's, Verona.

GUSMERO I., eldest son of Aresmino, succeeded to that public confidence which soon secured for him, as it had for his father, the elevated post of High Constable of Verona. This, however, did not interfere with his family establishment at Rovereto, where he and his kindred gallantly battled against the Teutonic invaders during the war of 1487. He was married to Anna, daughter of the noble Mattia de' Seni, of Verona, and their union was blessed with three sons—Gusmero, Rosmino, and Pietro.

The second of these (Rosmino de Rosmini) was destined, as we shall see, to continue the regular succession of the family in Rovereto. Rosmino espoused Cristina Pilati, a highly-gifted Roveretan lady, who practically seconded his efforts to promote the moral and commercial welfare of their native town. They had four sons—Antonio, Alberto, Zaccaria, and Cristoforo. Through Antonio was preserved the lineal descent of the Rovereto Rosminis. Alberto and Cristoforo became eminent citizens and founders of two other branches of the Rosmini family; while Zaccaria, who had been given to God's service, ministered for many years as the zealous Rector of St. Mark's, Rovereto. ˙

The youngest of Gusmero's sons (Pietro) lived permanently in Verona, where he filled with credit responsible municipal offices, and earned the right of honourable mention in Torresani's *Elogi Storici* of noble Veronese.

GUSMERO II., eldest son of Gusmero I., served with distinction under Charles V. of Germany at a time when he probably had for a near companion in arms the chivalrous Ignatius of Loyola, then also in the military service of˙ the same monarch. This Gusmero took for wife a daughter of the Dolfini, a Venetian family of considerable note in those days. The alliance resulted in five sons :—Francesco, Pietro, Pamfilo, Giorgio, and Carlo. The eldest son (Francesco) chose the Church for his spouse, and became Rector of St. Mark's in 1566; he died in 1575. The second son (Pietro) embraced a military life, and won some of its brightest honours under Philip of Spain against the Mussulman Amurat in

1576. During the following year he accompanied
Cardinal Andrea of Austria to the court of Rome,
on a special mission to Pope Gregory XIII., and
returned to die at home in 1578, 'leaving a noble
memory' but no children. His younger brother
(Pamfilo) devoted himself to commerce in Bergamo
and Verona, as well as in Rovereto, leaving in all
these places 'memorials of his piety and charity.' In
Verona he took a foremost place amongst the patricians eulogised in Torresani's ' Veronese Nobility.'
His descendants came to be known as Rosmini-
Pamfili. Giorgio, the fourth son of Gusmero II.,
made Verona his home, where he died ' full of years
and honours.' Carlo, the youngest, like his eldest
brother, embraced the ecclesiastical state.

In 1574 the Emperor Maximilian II. conferred
the privileges of imperial nobility on all Gusmero's
sons, as a special mark of consideration for their gallant
father, and the patent extended the rank to all their
descendants direct and collateral. As all the immediate heirs of Gusmero II. soon died away without
direct descendants, the headship of the Rovereto
Rosminis regularly passed to the heirs of his younger
brother Rosmino de Rosmini.

The succession thus derived came down in this
order: Antonio I., nephew of Gusmero II. and eldest
son of Rosmino, continued the Rovereto line through
his only son Francesco Antonio, who in turn was succeeded by his only son Cristoforo Antonio, born in
1573. To this Cristoforo were given two sons,
Nicolò and Antonio. On the former devolved all

the rights of succession vested in the Rovereto
descendants of Gusmero II.

NICOLÒ I., great-grand-nephew of Gusmero II.,
on succeeding to the family heritage, obtained from
the Emperor Leopold I. a formal confirmation of
the rank and privileges hitherto conceded to the
Rosminis of Rovereto. The concession, 'in perpetuity to the descendants of both sexes,' was given in
1672 by a patent which mentions the services and
virtues of the Rosmini family in the highest terms
of praise. Count Nicolò added much to the family
wealth and importance by taking an active part in
extending and perfecting the silk culture, which for
a long time afterwards was to contribute so largely
to the prosperity of the Tyrol. As he was not
blessed with children, he took the necessary steps to
secure the right of succession to Cristoforo, the third
of his brother Antonio's sons, the others acquiescing
in the arrangement.

CRISTOFORO, the favourite nephew of Nicolò I.,
duly succeeded his uncle. He married a Turinese
lady of the Perretti family. As they had seven sons
and one daughter, it was not thought likely that the
transference made by Nicolò I., giving the right
of succession to a younger son, would fail for want
of heirs. Two of the seven sons (Ferdinando and
Francesco) were dedicated to the service of the Sanctuary, where they well represented the intellectual
vigour and religious zeal of a family which never
failed to acknowledge that its glory and greatness
came from God. The other sons of Cristoforo having

left Rovereto in quest of military glory—some honourably battling for the Venetians and some for the
Emperor—made themselves homes elsewhere; and
so it came to pass that the succession, after all, re-
verted to Nicolò the heir of Antonio's eldest son and
the direct representative of Rosmino de Rosmini.

Nicolò II., nephew of Cristoforo, was born in
1656 and married in 1678 to Cristina, only child and
heiress of Count Ambrogio di Pietro Parolini. By
this marriage the other most noble and ancient family
of Rovereto was merged in the house of Rosmini, and
thus the palatial residence of the Parolini came to be
the Rovereto home of Aresmino's heirs. The offspring
of this happy alliance—two sons, Nicolò Francesco
and Ambrogio—were greatly esteemed for wisdom,
benevolence, energy of character, mental culture, and
sterling piety. Nicolò II. was an active citizen, who
applied himself energetically to the commercial interests of the town, in which he was repeatedly called
on to hold high offices. He died wealthy, but, what
was far more to him, universally honoured as one who
had faithfully discharged all his public and private
duties and never neglected those he owed to God.

Nicolò Francesco, eldest son of Nicolò II., was
a man of considerable ability and high culture, the
author of some learned disquisitions published in
1689. He also published in 1733 a collection of
Latin and Italian poems, supplied, at his request, by
the most popular contemporary poets in Rome, Florence, Bologna, and other literary centres. The
volume was intended to honour the first Mass of his

nephew, Nicolò Ferdinando, who had just been ordained Priest, at Trent. Not the least valuable composition in the book is a sonnet by the compiler himself. Nicolò Francesco resolved that he and his only
brother should continue their noble line in Rovereto
somewhat after a patriarchal plan. He, as the elder,
had the heir's right to the Parolini mansion, but, being
wealthier than his brother, he affectionately surren-
dered it to him, with other property which of right
belonged to the headship of the family, as though he
would anticipate what Providence decreed in making
Ambrogio the real stem of the Rovereto trunk. Meanwhile, he built for himself, at a convenient distance
from the óld mansions, a new palace, which is said to
have been 'splendid.' He was chosen to fill many
responsible offices, such as governor of Rovereto
Castle, controller of the city, and chief magistrate
of the Lagarina, with its dependent districts. In 1702
he wed Egeldina de' Baroni Pizzini. They had seven
children. The eldest son (Ambrogio) gave himself
to the special service of God. The fourth-born (Angel-
antonio) also dedicated himself to religion, and became a distinguished divine, Vicar-General of Trent,
and in 1762 the Capitular of the diocese. The second
son (Francesco) was known as the 'learned.' He
was the bosom friend of the famous Girolamo Tartarotti, and stood high amongst contemporary men of
letters. His love of books was so great that he spent
a fortune in collecting a large and very select library
—then a rare and princely private possession. In
connection with Tartarotti and others he started, in

1733, the *Accademia degli Agiati*, which was not,
however, definitely founded until 1750. The other
sons of Nicolò Francesco were no less worthy ; and
so of their children's children—intellectual superiority,
religious merit, and state dignities seemed to have
been their natural portion.[1]

AMBROGIO I., younger brother of Nicolò Francesco, more immediately interests us, because to
him was confided the headship of the family in
Rovereto, and from him sprang the greatest of all
the Rosminis. This Ambrogio was born in 1680,
and at twenty-four years of age espoused Cecilia
Teresa, daughter of the illustrious Dr. Orefici of
Rovereto. Charles Philip, Duke of Bavaria and
Prince Palatine of the kingdom, conferred many
privileges on Ambrogio by patent, dated Innsbruck,
April 6, 1710. The dignities of nobility inherited
under the patents of the Emperors Maximilian and
Leopold were also recognised as 'belonging to him
and his descendants.' Greater dignities than human
sovereigns could bestow on him were given by the
King of kings, who favoured him with the virtues
that distinguish the faithful servant of the Most
High. Besides blessing him with the personal quali-

---

[1] Some of them were advocates and some authors, who won a
fame that passed far beyond the borders of the Tyrol, or even of
North Italy. Not the least of these was the learned Chevalier Carlo
Rosmini, whose numerous works—embracing many fields in the broad
domain of literature—were very popular at the beginning of this
century, and whose ' History of Milan ' is still a standard work. This
gifted author was distinguished not merely for deep and comprehensive learning, but also for the earnest piety which marked the whole
course of his life. (See Chap. xxiii. of this volume.)

ties that endeared him to his fellow-citizens, God
gave him six excellent children—three sons and
three daughters. The daughters chose to live and
die virgins. Of the sons, the eldest (Ferdinando)
devoted himself to religion and learning. He is
known as 'the annalist of the family.' He became
a Franciscan, and died 'the death of the righteous'
on August 26, 1753, in the convent of his Order at
Trent, where he was secretary to the Provincial.
It was in honour of his first Mass that Nicolò Francesco compiled the volume of poems mentioned in
connection with his name. The youngest of Ambrogio's sons (Felice) went to God while his baptismal robes were still unspotted. For the other son
(Gianantonio) was reserved the privilege of continuing the noble line it was God's will to termi-
nate in his saintly grandson.

GIANANTONIO, who was born in 1714, applied
himself very successfully to revive, by commercial
enterprise, the drooping prosperity of his native
country, and at the same time to keep up the
literary spirit which his father, uncle, and brother
had done so much to foster in the Tyrol. He was
a man of earnest piety, an upright magistrate, and
an open-handed friend to the poor. He married
Margherita, daughter of Count Bossi-Fedrigotti—
that being the second time in which these noble
families were thus allied. Two sons (Ambrogio and
Pier Modesto) and two daughters were born of this
marriage. The two sons call for separate mention
in this genealogical record, and of the daughters it

will be sufficient to say that, like their aunts, they lived and died virgins.

Gianantonio was the first of his family to use the added surname of Serbati, derived from his mother, and assumed in compliance with the express terms of a 'deed of trust.' By this legal instrument the estates, etc., of the Serbatis (failing male heirs) were passed to the female line, on condition that the name of Serbati be added to the surname of the family in which this female line should prove to be directly represented. It came to be thus represented in the house of Rosmini through Cecilia de Orefici, the mother of Gianantonio, and thenceforth the family adopted the name of Rosmini-Serbati.

AMBROGIO II.—the artist and architect—elder son of Gianantonio, never married, but from an early age attached himself to intellectual and art pursuits with an ardour which, for a long time, refused attention to aught else—his religious duties excepted. Having studied philosophy under the Jesuit Fathers at Innsbruck and Bologna, he turned to jurisprudence at Urbino, where the spirit of Raphael so completely swayed his thoughts that thenceforth he directed his attention to the fine arts and architecture. He travelled through Italy in quest of all that could improve his taste and knowledge in a profession he practised for love and without any expectation of pecuniary returns. During these journeys he collected, at great expense, the finest specimens of engraving, represent-

ing every style known : the samples number twenty
thousand, and are still preserved in the Rosmini
house at Rovereto. The best of his own paintings
are sacred subjects. Some were presented to
churches and some to friends ; but the family mansion retains most of his productions; the walls of
many spacious rooms, of several large inner courts
and corridors, as well as of all the principal stair-
ways, are covered with admirable paintings by himself, or by those Old Masters whose works he used for
the purpose of study, or by young aspirants to art
honours whose talents his purse nourished. As an
architect he held an honourable position in the
estimation of his cotemporaries, and has left some
admirably-planned and well-executed edifices, ecclesiastic and other, to attest his skill in that profession. More than once his fellow-citizens chose
him to preside over the Municipal Council, and
during his long life he merited a fame far better
than all which the utmost triumph in any human
science or art could bestow—an unblemished fame,
which tells us how he, learned and rich as he was,
led the life of a self-sacrificing Christian, practising
charity, purity, humility, and patience to a degree
rarely met with in secular society. Mantled in this
bright fame, he passed to God in 1818, having lived
here below for seventy-nine years.

To meet the wishes of the Tyrolese generally,
Giuseppe Telani wrote a life of the good Ambrogio,
which was published soon after his death. From it
we gather that this illustrious and accomplished man

was, in a special sense, the tutor of his nephew Antonio's delicate appreciation of the beautiful; and to his cultured taste in other respects 'no little was due by that young mind which, even in the uncle's lifetime, gave many signal evidences of its giant powers.'

PIER MODESTO, brother of Ambrogio II. and younger son of Gianantonio, had reserved for him a more abiding distinction than any which can be claimed for the most renowned of his ancestors ; for he was chosen to be the father of the saintly philosopher whose genius should carry the name of Rosmini beyond the confines not only of the Tyrol but of Italy and Europe.

Pier Modesto was born in 1745, and lived so long unmarried that people began to think 'the grand family was about to end' without leaving a representative who should let its name and merits be known to distant nations and ages—a result contrary to Alpine folk-lore, which taught that every 'noble house' that had been founded in goodness combined with glory, and had maintained for centuries unbroken loyalty to Faith and Fatherland, was destined to have, as a reward, some child whose greatness and goodness might reflect 'far and wide and for aye' the lustre of the house, when the family should cease to have heirs. There were, indeed, many illustrious sons of the Rosmini race certain to be remembered for ages in their own country, but none of a fame great enough to meet the folk-lore conditions.

However, without regard to rural superstitions, Pier Modesto, before passing away from middle age, gave hope to legendary prophets, for he resolved to share his domestic happiness with the Countess Giovanna Formenti de Riva, a lady of vigorous intellect and considerable acquirements, who, like her spouse, was full of genuine piety, and partial to the quiet charms of home life. This marriage, in all respects happy, was blessed with four children— Margherita, Antonio, Giuseppe, and Felice—all brought up to specially honour God, but one above all specially called to bear the standard of truth and justice as firmly, as bravely, as faithfully, and as perseveringly, as ever it was borne by servant of God—' He will take equity for an invincible shield' (Wis. v. 20). Of him we have much to say, and shall proceed to say it presently ; but of the others, meanwhile, let us make a passing mention.

The youngest son of Pier Modesto, like the youngest of Ambrogio I. (another Felice), left the world while an infant. The second son, Giuseppe, whose health had never been good, married the amiable Baroness Christina de Rallo, and in 1863 closed an honourable life, leaving no children to continue a name which had then, in another and far nobler way, secured a perpetuity and pre-eminence such as no mere family succession could have ever given it.

Margherita, the only daughter of Pier Modesto, was the feminine counterpart of her great brother Antonio. Like him, from the first dawning of reason to the last moment of her mortal existence, she devoted her mind and heart to God. Through love of Jesus Christ she directed all her energies to the caring of 'the little ones for whom is the kingdom of Heaven.' She was one of the first to co-operate with the venerable Marchioness of Canossa in extending the great work that holy lady had begun in North Italy by means of her Daughters of Charity.

But long before the pious Margherita Rosmini permanently joined this admirable Order she had distinguished herself by kindred labours in Rovereto, where she had for many years zealously applied her time and means to the education of little orphans. On taking the vows as a Daughter of Charity, she founded, at her own expense, a convent of the Order in Trent, where its services were urgently needed. There she toiled so indefatigably and unselfishly in the cause of Christian charity, that her health gave way under the weight of incessant labours fondly endured for the love of God and the benefit of His little poor. It was thought that a change to Verona and some repose might restore her physical strength ; but all in vain. God took her to Himself on June 20, 1833—' Being made perfect in a short space, she fulfilled a long time.'

Her accomplishments, even in the social sense, were very numerous, and included such a familiarity with modern and ancient languages as entitled her to be deemed a linguist. In short, so good and gifted was she in all respects, that Italian poets, as well as Tyrolese, have made her the theme of song. Her great brother, whom she venerated most profoundly, summed up her whole history in these few words: 'The faith of Jesus Christ, which she deeply studied and on which she constantly meditated, lifted her high above the prejudices of the world, and made her impervious to its vanities and its wickedness. Her mind intently fixed on God, she became all through life, to those who knew her, a mirror of heroic virtue, by the continual performance of the most humble and toilsome works of charity. To these labours her life at last succumbed—a victim not so much to be mourned as envied and blessed.'

Pier Modesto, the father of these saintly children, lived to know the choice of life they had solemnly made, but not long enough to see them fully vested in it. He died in 1820, at the age of 75, soon after Antonio had taken Minor Orders and the Subdeaconate, but before he was ordained Priest, and before Margherita had formally associated herself with the Daughters of Charity. The young ecclesiastic, much to his own surprise, was made 'the heir general.'

The Countess Rosmini, who died in her 84th year, survived her husband twenty-two years, and so was spared to see her son more than fulfil the highest expectations of her heart—a happiness which, alas! like all human joy, had its bitter mixture of sorrows in the clouds of persecution she could notice gathering around him, and some of which showered their assaults upon him even while she lived. But she well understood the consolation contained in the words, ' The Apostle is not greater than He that sent him.'

CHAPTER I.

An eventful epoch and a portent-bearing birthday—His baptism, precocious infancy, and studious childhood—The Bible his first
reading-book—Is sent to a public elementary school—His juvenile
charities—His singular and suggestive amusements—Is sent to the
Roveretan High School — His great meekness, industry, and
humility—Why his teachers thought him wanting in talent—How
he eluded his mother's efforts to moderate his ardour for study—
His popularity with other children the result of respect for his
goodness—He prays and studies while his companions play—What
he thought of theatrical amusements.

ANTONIO ROSMINI-SERBATI was born in the palace of
his ancestors at Rovereto early on the morning of
March 25, 1797.

What stirring memories that date calls up! It
was a terrible epoch. All Europe was just then
convulsed by the horrible triumphs of a pernicious
philosophy, which found its practical embodiment
in the frightful atrocities of the French Revolution.
The Tyrolese Alps had hardly ceased to re-echo the
thunder of Bonaparte's artillery, so recently triumphant at Lonato, Castiglione, Arcola, and Rivoli;
while the wonted quiet of Rovereto had not yet recovered from the shock of battle at its own gates.
Mantua had fallen on the feast of the Purification, in

the previous month, and from there to Trent the
revolutionary invaders commanded every post. But
it so happened that on the Feast of the Annunciation—when the future apostle of a saving, godly
philosophy was born—these armed champions of
a godless, destroying philosophy were resting from
the work of slaughter, during the short-lived lull
following the treaty of Tolentino. That treaty,
which dealt so shamefully with the Pontifical States,
had just been signed, as though to give the modern
Sennacherib time to readjust his military tactics to
the anti-Christian philosophy of the day, that he
might the better recommence the march of carnage
and spoliation which enabled him to practically
apply the hideous principles of such philosophy.

   To our thinking, there was a something very
portentous in the circumstances which thus sur-
sounded the birth of the last heir born to the house
of Rosmini-Serbati on that eventful March 25, 1797.
This something does not lose in significance when
we remember how it was amidst the turmoils produced by the false philosophy which gave revolutionary champions to the tenets of Huss, three centuries before, that Rovereto itself was chosen to be
the cradle of this child's race.[1] So there, amidst the
terrors and abominations generated once more by
false philosophy, was he born who was to be the last
of that race, but nevertheless destined to leave behind
him a numerous family and a priceless legacy that
should make his name imperishable. That family·

---

[1] See Introductory Chapter, p. 5.

was to be a Religious Order, and that legacy a Philosophy at all points fitted to be a lasting and effective barrier between Christian civilisation and revolutionary barbarism—between the Church of God and the Synagogue of Satan.

Was it not meet that he should have been thus born amid the din of a furious war waged against religion in the name of human progress and philosophical enlightenment ?—Was it not meet, since he was chosen to be the teacher of a philosophy that should weld together all the armour of God's Truth, so as to make it proof against every weapon modern science or sensism might invent on behalf of human error ? The Providence which had so arranged the time and circumstances of his birth had, as it were, built around his infancy and boyhood a school of startling events that passed into history before his eyes, and filled his young mind with facts and lessons that were in some way to fertilise all the studies of his riper years.

But, whether seen from these or other points of view, that was a memorable 25th of March on which Antonio Rosmini was born. It was his double birthday, and often, while he lived the life his first birth gave, did the return of this Feast announce to him some new favour of Heaven or mark an event in fulfilment of the promises of his second birth.[1] The second birth took place within a few

---

[1] Tommaseo notes how many of the important events in Rosmini's life were associated with the Feast of the Annunciation :—' It was on that Feast he began the special retreat for the Priesthood ; on that Feast he first entered Rome ; on that Feast he commenced his

hours of the first; for on the same day he was baptised in the parish church of St. Mark, where in after-years he was to do so much as Rector. Teresa Tachelli, the nurse who bore him to the baptismal font, often declared that 'something about the babe made her feel he was to be a great and holy man.'

Nurses are, indeed, prone to indulge in flattering predictions as to the future of the little ones intrusted to them; but their vaticinations are almost invariably uttered for the ears of fond parents, and seldom, like those of nurse Tachelli, kept silently 'treasured in heart,' or merely whispered in solemn confidences to the Parish Priest. While Teresa watched the marvellous calm of the child's face, as he was born again of the Holy Ghost, she wondered much why there was no wincing when the regenerating water fell on his little head; she wondered more why this unruffled solemnity gave way to a sweet angelic smile when the ceremony was over; she wondered still more why little Antonio smiled not again for months, but, like his sister Margherita, 'preserved an extraordinary gravity and quiet for half a year or so, as if in mute thanksgiving all the time.'

This affectionate nurse, who tenderly watched over him during the years of his infancy, felt so sure

greatest philosophical work; on that Feast he founded the Order of Charity; on that Feast he began to write out formally the Constitutions; on that Feast he and his first associates took their solemn vows as members of the Order,' &c., &c. 'We,' says Don Paoli, 'often witnessed the sublime sentiments of religious piety with which Antonio Rosmini commemorated that anniversary of the Incarnation of the Word and of his own regeneration.'

that he would become 'á great and holy man,' that she carefully put away in her own trunk all his disused playthings, as relics 'to be prized in other days.' The trifles thus religiously preserved bear no traces of the rude treatment children are wont to bestow on such articles, and so far confirm the nurse's description of him as 'the most careful child that could be.'

Teresa Tachelli spent a long life in the service of the Rosminis, having survived for many years the child and benefactor whom she was never weary of calling 'the little angel'—'always so gentle,' she used to say, 'always so thoughtful, always so generous : even as an infant his charity was extraordinary, and he cared to keep nothing for himself if he fancied another wanted it. It was delightful to see him at his prayers, which he said voluntarily and with great feeling.' [1]

His mind set itself to study almost as soon as his little limbs were trained to walk. A fact which he himself in after-years mentioned to his life-long friend, Don Paoli, shows that his intellectual faculties must have begun to work at an astonishingly

---

[1] Nurse Tachelli had such a love and veneration for the child that she preserved not only the playthings associated with his infancy, but several articles of dress, her fixed notion being that he was 'going to be a great saint or something else wonderful.' In 1862 she disclosed the secret to Don Paoli, and at the same time delivered to him, with much ceremony, the various relics as 'sacred treasures.' These interesting little memorials are now kept at the Rosmini mansion, in a glass case, with sundry other objects of 'personal contact' belonging to his maturer years. All are sorted and classed according to the different periods of his life, beginning with the gorgeous baptismal robes of the babe, and ending with the sombre cassock of the Priest.

early age : while lying in his cradle at night, being
then only two years old, he used to reflect and
wonder why the nurse regularly placed the light in
a position which prevented him seeing it, and why,
when he chanced to see it, his eyes were pained
and his imagination affected in a peculiar manner.[1]

He was, in fact, as Don Paoli puts it, a reflecting
child at two years of age, an almsgiving boy at five,
a most studious youth at seven, a practical ascetic at
twelve, a brilliant moral essayist at sixteen, and such
a proficient in philosophy at eighteen that his professor became his disciple : marvellously gifted all
his days, from the cradle to the grave.

He commenced his elementary studies under a
private tutor named Runck, who thought so highly
of his little pupil's capacity, or ' tone of mind,' that
he gave him the Bible for a reading-book. So well
did the experiment answer M. Runck's expectations that before Antonio Rosmini was five years
old, he knew more Holy Scripture than boys of
fifteen in the grammar schools of a land which
claims Biblical knowledge as ' the leading feature
of its Christian enlightenment.'

[1] The cradle, a heavy wooden rustic cot, with other equally simple
furniture of the nursery, still occupies its place in the room wherein he
was born, and the room itself (a plainly-furnished chamber facing
the gardens) is said to be much as it was when he first vacantly gazed
on the homely objects around him. On a marble tablet in the wall is
the following inscription :--

IN HOC CUBICULO

NATUS EST

ANTONIUS ROSMINI-SERBATI

VIII KAL. APRILIS

A. MDCCXCVII.

In his sixth year he was sent to a public primary school, as his illustrious family were desirous of supporting and encouraging by example those useful institutions which, through their influence, had just then been established, in a greatly improved form, at Rovereto. The motive met with the reward it merited ; for the presence of the patrician child attracted many boys who would else have stayed or been kept away, while his charming manners and angelic character not only won their hearts, but swayed their conduct in a marked degree.

Even at that tender age, when the natural generosity of childhood is so capricious and impulsive as to be often a kind of churlishness, and at best a fitful, disorderly, thoughtless liberality— even at that age he gave remarkable evidences of the settled, thoughtful, orderly spirit of charity which possessed his soul and became the shining characteristic of his whole life. When setting out for school in the morning, he made it a point to be always provided with some pocket money, as well as a lunch, with the fixed purpose of applying neither to his own use, but to the wants of the poor people he was sure to meet on the way. In distributing the alms, he took care to select the objects so prudently that the neediest and most deserving were almost invariably chosen.

We all know how children delight in anything new, and how tenaciously even those of them who have the most generous nature cling to the least article of dress while it is, or seems to be, new. Little Antonio Rosmini was an exception to this rule ; for his great delight was to share with the poor the best he had, and he was always ready to part with his newest garment if he found anyone in need of it. When warned that it was an extravagance to give to poor children costly articles of dress that they would rather sell than wear, he confined his gifts to things free from such an objection.

One chilly morning, on seeing from his room a poor woman with a little boy whose sockless feet looked very cold, he threw to her from the window a new pair of warm stockings, which his mother had just left for his own use, contenting himself with an older and less comfortable pair. As the shivering child instantly put them on, that fact was his defence against a suggestion of extravagance—
'they are not too good for a little one dear to our Lord.'

The very amusements of his boyhood bore the impress, deeply marked, of that earnest yearning for 'doing good' which produced such beneficial fruit through all the years of his manhood. For example : A popular pastime among the Tyrolese children in his juvenile days was 'playing at policeman.' He liked the sport, since he always contrived to secure a post—not that of captain, nor of director, but of magistrate—which gave him an opportunity of conveying some good moral lesson through the sentence he might have to pronounce. He was partial to any games which tended to benefit the mind as well as the body, or enabled him to give or receive some instruction.

On the other hand, he had no liking for recreations that were of less apparent advantage, or that did not afford distinct means of edification. Hence, he had no relish for the 'accomplishment of dancing,' although when he went, with his brother, to acquire 'the personal polish' it is supposed to impart, his dancing master, judging by the youth's graceful bearing, thought he had a most promising disciple. The hopeful professor, however, found him an unwilling pupil, who very soon withdrew from 'social exercises' that clashed with the strong bent of his mind.[1]

This strong bent was made unmistakably clear in his favourite amusements—playing at monk and studying the Lives of the Saints. To ordinary children either would seem less entertaining than irksome, rather more of a drudgery than a relaxation. But for him there was no pastime so precious. The extensive gardens attached to the family mansion afforded ample space for playing at hermit or monk, his sister Margherita and their cousin Leonardo being his only partners in the game.[2] The sister, who was three years older than

---

[1] This personage, who bore the apt name of Angelico Festi, was so greatly disappointed that Count Ambrogio felt bound to console him by painting his portrait—a compliment that soothed him for the rest of his life. The picture is now in the Rosmini mansion, where good old Festi still smiles on every visitor ascending the grand stairway.

[2] The Rosmini gardens are now comparatively small, but still fairly kept and well stocked with fruit, flowers and vegetables. Originally

Antonio, having pious sentiments closely resembling his, entered heartily into the spirit of the recreation ; but Leonardo enjoyed it less, though he willingly conformed to the rules. These rules suited the circumstances of the juvenile recluses, who carried them out in cells constructed, after an approved model, at distant parts of the garden. The 'play'

they were very extensive, and at the rear of the mansion (formerly known as the Palazzo Parolini), which then faced the town, walled off from the streets within a fine court-yard, having a noble arched stone gateway with the family arms boldly carved on the outside. As the town spread around the gardens, municipal improvements called for the surrender now of one portion, and now of another, until at length, the grounds dwindled down to the dimensions of one of the larger London squares. This process of contraction was materially assisted by cessions of land for the use of two charitable institutions, one being the Rosmini Infant Asylum, erected on the spot where Margherita used to have her cell when playing at monk with her brother. Near this asylum, on a stone tablet in one of two handsome little sheds at opposite corners of the present garden bounds, along the new street, there is this inscription :—

IN HOC HORTO
AMBROSIUS ROSMINI
JAM SENEX ARCHITECTABATUR
EIUSQUE EX FRATRE NEPOS
ANTONIUS
ADHUC ADOLESCENS
DE ORIGINE ET NATURA IDEARUM DISPUTABAT
HOC NE POSTERIS PEREAT
FRANCISCUS PAOLI
A.D. MDCCCLXXV. P.C.

Although the frequent grants of ground seriously diminished the size of the gardens, this did not, for a long time, impair their sequestered character as delightful appendages of a secluded mansion. A few years ago, however, a public avenue, the noblest in Rovereto, was opened through them close to the rear of the palazzo and straight down to the railway station. This changed all. The rear of the mansion became forthwith its front, and the gardens took the character of a public square cut off from the palazzo, a tunnel beneath the road now connecting the house with its once beautiful grounds. The old main entrance through the baronial court-yard remains still in use, but the consisted in holding conferences on sacred subjects and relating anecdotes of Saints, now at one cell, and then at another ; the rule obliged each little 'monk' to read alone the life of the Saint of the day, to meditate on it, and connect it with our Lord's life and teachings, and after that to meet at a given place and time to interchange thoughts on the subject; they then. prayed together, and separated to pray apart in their different cells ; the whole 'entertainment' often taking up about two hours

true grand entrance to the palazzo is now through either of two massive iron gates, some fifty feet asunder, forming part of an ornamental metal railing which separates the new front of the house from the new street. These gates open on a floral plot having a paved carriage way into two enarched halls—one at either end of the façade, beneath the dining and ball rooms (now picture galleries) and passing on to the old court-yard. On a marble slab in one of these passages is the following inscription :—

HASCE ÆDES
IN QUIBUS
ANTONIUS ROSMINI-SERBATI
NATUS EST ANNO MDCCLXXXXVII
RESTAURATIONEM PHILOSOPHIÆ
AGRESSUS EST A. MDCCCXVI
SOCIETATEM A CARITATE NUNCUPATAM
PRIMUM MENTE CONCEPIT A. MDCCCXXI
FILII SPIRITUALES ET DISCIPULI
IN ANGLIA ATQUE IN ITALIA LEGATIONEM PRO CHRISTO FUNGENTES
RENOVARUNT
AC
NE ULLA UNQUAM ÆTAS
DE TANTI VIRI LAUDIBUS CONTICESCAT
P.C. A. MDCCCLXXX.

Although the palazzo has no longer its old aspect of baronial seclusion it retains much of its ancient stateliness. The style of architecture is simple and unattractive ; but Don F. Paoli (as executor of Rosmini's will) has done much to make it elegant. It is very large, containing more than a hundred rooms, most of them very spacious and all of them lofty.

in the morning and two in the evening. Tommaseo, speaking of these saintly amusements, tells us how little Antonio, only seven years old at the time, 'used to be moved to tears of admiration and tenderness while reading or listening to the Acts of the Martyrs.'[1]

Thus, 'like true young Saints,' these pious children whiled away the time of recreation in a manner most agreeable to themselves, but little likely to win others of the same age. We quote the phrase 'like true young' Saints as a stereotyped expression ; for when we read the memoirs of great warriors, or navigators, or statesmen, or despots, or even criminals, they are usually described as having been, during boyhood, 'like true young' soldiers, or sailors, or politicians, or tyrants, or rascals ; prone to sports that mirrored, more or less clearly, their course in manhood. It is certain that the favourite pastime of the Rosmini children foreshowed their future, as both afterwards solemnly adopted and nobly adorned the Religious Life they loved to practise as a juvenile solace.

The other strong bent of Antonio's mind was study ; but this too, like his amusements and charities, had God for its object. To please 'Our Father Who art in Heaven,' and to carry out all the promises of the Lord's Prayer—which he said fervently not only every night and morning, but frequently during the day—was the set purpose of his young soul in all he did. What he preferred to study, even as a boy,

---

[1] *Rivista Cotemp. di Torino,* 1855, No. xxxv., art. 'Rosmini.'

had reference to God, and to whatever might give glory to God.

The good example for which he had been sent to the public school having been most effectively given —in a far higher and wider sense than his parents thought of when sending him there—he was withdrawn to enter a classical seminary, or *ginnasio*, similar to our grammar schools. At the same time, his home studies were entrusted to Don Guareschi, a pious Priest retained in the family mansion somewhat in the quality of a domestic chaplain. None of his fellow-students at the public school was so diligent as Antonio, none so docile, none so pious ; yet his progress in grammatical studies did not seem to correspond with such promising qualities, and he allowed others to carry off the school prizes. The best his teachers could say of it was, that he went on creditably, but not as brilliantly as his great talents and marked application led them to expect. Don Guareschi at first blamed the system of the teachers ; but, finding his own method at home produce no brighter results, he soon concurred with those who assumed that, after all, the boy's intellect was rather dull ; and so he bluntly told him.

Antonio meekly accepted this sentence without attempting to explain why he appeared to make slower progress than the professors thought within his power. In his uncle Ambrogio, however, he had a warm defender ; for this vigilant observer of the little student's course knew that other and graver studies so occupied his mind that the ordinary school

exercises were more or less distasteful, while to keep
up with them as creditably as he did was, under the
circumstances, to do a great deal. He knew, moreover, that although this might prevent such technical
evidences of progress as a zealous pedagogue looked
for in a most promising pupil, it did not interfere
with a studious boy's real progress, even in those
branches of study with which he seemed to be less
familiar than his teachers wished.

St. Thomas of Aquin, at a riper age, but for
kindred reasons, was denounced as a mere dunce
—'a dumb ox'—though his mind was then brood-
ing over the most subtle questions in Christian
philosophy. So, when his tutors decided that Antonio Rosmini was slow of intellect—'a sluggish-
brained boy, too much given to prayer and too
little to the conjugation of verbs'—he was actually
mastering the contents of such works as the
Summa of St. Thomas. This he was doing with
the full approbation of his accomplished uncle,
whose authority in the matter was to him as
law. Therefore he felt that, so long as he remained
dutiful to all his instructors and kept well up with
his class, he was disobeying no one, but rather practising humility, if he allowed an idea to get abroad
that his intellect was, after all, no brighter than that of
others. Had he been consulted by those who ex-
cused him, he would have requested them to offer
no explanation whatever ; but the affectionate uncle,
without seeing into the depth of piety whence this
self-sacrifice sprang, continued to defend him, and to

supply him with the books he chose to have for his private study. These were books which modern students of more than double his age would look upon as 'intolerably heavy reading.'

There was one other who shared with uncle Ambrogio the pleasure of defending Antonio. This was his mother, who knew that he studied for a duty, a work, and a pastime, and who feared that he so studied too incessantly. She used to relate, with a natural complacency, how her beloved boy tried to overcome the fatigue caused by the labours he thus imposed on himself, and how he managed to elude her maternal solicitude. She frequently found him in the library (a large and valuable one) with several tomes 'of the Fathers and of Latin classics,' opened on the long table, so as to fringe it at all sides. He applied himself now to one, now to another, until he had carefully read a set number of pages in each, within a given time every day, changing his book and position as best answered the relief his body or mind needed. If she entered with a reproachful look, as sometimes happened, he would anticipate her remonstrance by exclaiming, ' O beloved mother, these beautiful things ! O the holy teachings which these books give me ! Let me enjoy myself, as it is good to be in such company and thus entertained !' Such appeals usually called forth the desired smile on the anxious mother's face, and she would then retire, agreeably conquered ; leaving him to 'kill time,' not as children, but as sages do.

His teachers, however, knew nothing of all this.

Even Don Guareschi remained for a long time ignorant of the real condition of things. Although he noticed his pupil going often to the library, and found him sometimes poring over volumes which seemed in no way suited to his age or capacity, he had no suspicion of the extent to which his studies were thus carried ; for the library being the special cabinet of Ambrogio, the chaplain seldom stayed there longer than was necessary to procure the book he wanted. One day he chanced to enter while Antonio was intently reading the *Summa* of St. Thomas. With mixed surprise and scorn he tapped him smartly on the head, saying, ' What have you to do with such books ? ' The answer was a mild reference to the sanction of his uncle. Forthwith, the astonished Priest began to discover that such books were not beyond the capacity of that boy, who, like St. Thomas, while appearing to be only on a level with his class, was in many things farther advanced than his teachers.[1]

Although young Rosmini's intense love of study, earnest, systematic piety, and lofty sense of decorum in all he did, was little calculated to win popularity with those of his own age (who generally prefer less staid qualities), nevertheless his society was much courted by his school-fellows ; and the youths who could claim him for a companion in recreation, or as a visitor during the holidays, made a boast of the fact. One of those who did boast of the fact—the

[1] Mons. Andrea Strosio, *Difesa della Fama e della Vita di Antonio Rosmini*, Cap. I. Tommaseo, *Rivista cont.* 1855.

Baron Simone Cresseri di Castelpietra—tells us how Antonio used to ' amuse himself' when on a summer visit to the princely castle of the Cresseri, in the magnificent valley of the Folgaria, near Trent.   Thither Rosmini and his brother sometimes went for a few weeks during the ' long vacation,' to enjoy the sports there provided for themselves and some other patrician boys.

On these occasions Antonio made study, as usual, his principal amusement, but without damping the spirits of the others, who, respecting his every wish, were content to know he was near enough to see and hear them.   So, while all his companions sported at ball, or ' hide and seek', or any other of the diversions which delighted them, he betook himself to some adjacent pine shade or creviced rock, where he read and prayed as if he could never weary of such entertainment.   When any of his more frolicsome companions, through sheer exhaustion, sought repose, it was always near his retreat, but not close enough to disturb him, unless he invited them nearer, which he did if he thought the opportunity suitable for imparting some edifying or instructive information.

His constant companion during these visits to the splendid hospitality of Castelpietra was the Parish Priest, a learned man, in whose conversation he took more delight than his young friends found in their boisterous mirth.   But though he liked to thus amuse himself in his own way, he never disapproved of the way preferred by the others.   On

the contrary, if they could not have enjoyed themselves thoroughly unless he took an active share in
their games, he would set aside his own preference
to ensure them the full benefit of their holiday. He
never waited to be asked when he saw a chance of
throwing a moral or some special instruction into the
sport, as when he played 'magistrate' and 'monk' in
his still more juvenile days.[1]

It was during these school vacations that Tyrolese parents usually indulged their children with
visits to the theatres. Antonio went now and then
with his uncle and brother, but cared very little for
the spectacles ordinarily represented. Comedies he
disliked because they appeared to exhibit what was
trivial, vulgar, and coarse, without bringing into
effective relief the moral which should compensate
for these inherent blemishes ; but to tragedies he
was more favourably disposed, because it seemed to
him that, at the worst, they more directly lifted his
soul to God. Boy though he was, he ventured to
tell his uncle Ambrogio that the stage, unless
managed with the greatest care, had little to commend it to thoughtful minds ; while, as commonly
directed, it had much to charm and debase the
thoughtless.

Thus, even in his tenderest years, the lineaments

[1] That he highly approved of manly field sports is made evident
by an essay which he wrote on the subject of ' Public Amusements,' as
forming or showing forth national character. This essay, though
written in his youth, and read to the Rovereto Accademia, where it met
with ' marked approval,' was not published till after his death, when it
was deemed important enough to be incorporated with his *Filosofia
della Politica.*

of the man's character were distinctly visible. His
fervent piety, his studious habits, his generous and
orderly charities, his precocious spirit of Christian
mortification, his sound judgment, so far above that
which men usually associate with persons even of
ripe age, were all such as to foreshow the vigorous
growth of those solid virtues and that intellectual
greatness which distinguished his still more saintly
manhood.

CHAPTER II.

ROSMINI'S EARLIEST COLLEGE DAYS.

(A.D. 1813-1815.)

His personal appearance at sixteen—His dislike of novelties in dress —His conversations—His first scholastic thesis—How he bore his college triumphs—Elected member of the Rovereto Academy, its first and only boy-Associate—His first essay, and how he took the applause it won—Why he established a domestic Academy—The 'dignity of the Priesthood' the subject of his first public discourse—Sage counsels of his earliest letters—Virtue the only reward worth having—His country retreat—His love of solitude— His first important literary production—His desire to be a Saint— Correspondence of a boy with veterans—How he valued Christian friendship—Dedicates himself to Religion—Leaves Rovereto College.

WHILE the moral and intellectual qualities of Antonio Rosmini were systematically developing themselves, day by day, into sterling virtues, his physical growth gave evidence of such a hale constitution that, at sixteen, he was one of the most blooming and comely youths in Rovereto. Don Paoli gives us a description of his person which sets the indefatigable student before us as one upon whom incessant brain work, relieved by a very moderate share of bodily exercise, had no ill effects whatever. ' He grew up robust and healthy,' says Don Paoli, 'and although his appearance presented a development which betokened some excess of the cerebral organs, for the most part favourable to natural talent but not to health, he was a hale, handsome youth, as may be gathered from a portrait which his mother preserved.[1]   He was of middle height, slender form and well proportioned, except that his head was remarkably large. He had a high, massive forehead, an abundance of dark brown hair, an aquiline nose, a somewhat projecting chin, a softly blooming complexion, sprightly eyes, which were always in subjection to a sensitive modesty.' The sweet smile of an affectionate heart 'constantly played around his finely-chiselled lips.' His manners were exceedingly affable, and his intercourse with others was always marked by a winning condescension most felicitously adapted to all manner of persons and circumstances—'the result,' adds Don Paoli, ' of a kind nature properly developed by most refined home culture.'

Although neat in his dress, and careful to observe the proprieties of external appearance, he was little disposed to countenance the caprices of 'fashion.' During his boyhood, the Napoleonic dominancy in Northern Italy brought French styles into vogue ; but, while Roveretan society pretty generally affected the new mode, the Rosminis resolutely adhered to the old, and Antonio preferred to bear the scoffs of his companions rather than to op-

---

[1] A photograph copy of this finely-finished likeness adorns the first page of Don Paoli's *Monografia.* On the death of the Countess Rosmini the original painting was given to the Marquis Benso de Cavour as a souvenir ; but on his death it was claimed by the representatives of Rosmini, to whom it now belongs.

pose the taste of his parents, or sanction what seemed
to him uncalled-for innovations. Moreover, he thus
entered a protest against the principles of the Revolution, which had imported these novel costumes.
But, however he dressed, his bearing was always
the same—always gracious and gentle—always
showing forth that 'exquisite virginal modesty'
which remained his life-long characteristic. To robe
the soul in virtue, the heart in prayer, and the mind
in knowledge, was to him of first importance ; the
rest troubled him little.

Towards the termination of his course at the
Rovereto Preparatory College he was required to
compose a thesis on 'The Encouragement of
Studies.' The subject was selected for him on
account of his own great love of study, but without
any hope that one so young would be able to treat
it in a profound or practical manner. However, to
the surprise of all assembled on the Exhibition Day,
he acquitted himself so well that few were ready to
credit a mere lad with such a polished and well-
reasoned essay. Foremost amongst the few who,
without hesitation, believed it be the boy's own
unaided production, was Don Pietro Orsi, a frequent guest of the house, who had taken more
pains than the others to know his capacity. But
though the keen-sighted Priest admired and esteemed him much for what he already knew of his
moral and intellectual character, the signal success
of the theme and the charming modesty of the
young orator gave this esteem and admiration a

new direction, and an intensity which soon led to a
more intimate connection between them—that of
devoted pupil and devoted master.

His collegiate triumphs and conspicuous virtues
won for Antonio an extraordinary distinction before
he had completed his sixteenth year—a Fellowship
in the Academy of the Agiati. This institution,
which may be styled ' the Royal Society ' of Rovereto,
was founded in 1750 by the famous Tyrolese critic
Girolamo Tartarotti, and other literary celebrities of
the time and place, including more than one of the
Rosmini family. Active membership was confined
to local *literati*, who were selected with great care,
not only as to their scholastic attainments, but as to
their moral character and social standing. This last
qualification excluded the lowly, however worthy,
and was deemed a serious blemish in its organisation by the patrician youth who was invited to sit
with its sages as one of themselves.

He could not help thinking that, as it had for
the first time opened its doors to a boy in years,
it could afford to extend the exceptions to those
who had grown grey in quest of knowledge without
aspiring to social position. But to press his opinion
on the directors of the Academy would have been
inconsistent with the modesty of his years, and the
boy-Fellow never forgot he was a boy. As to his
own election, the sagacity of the Academicians was
proved by events. That boy soon became the
greatest of the Agiati, and was destined, ere long,
to be the perpetual honorary president of the

society : in fact, his genius still presides, and imparts to the Rovereto Academy a renown, if not a
stability, that will live through the ages.[1]

When Antonio Rosmini was thus winning the
peaceful laurels of college victories there was a lull
in the Napoleonic wars which had so long convulsed Europe. This lull promised something more
than an ephemeral peace ; at all events, such was
the general hope. The young Academician seized
this popular hope as a fitting subject for the literary
composition with which he was expected to acknowledge the high compliment that had been paid him.
' The Blessings of Peace ' furnished, indeed, a right
noble theme ; and he dealt with it so effectively
that his fellow-Academicians overwhelmed him with
eulogies, some of which found vent in printed poems.
One of these pieces, which was supposed to have
more than ordinary merit, styled him ' the hope of
Italy,' adding—

> Through thee, we trust, will Italy regain
> The golden splendour of her ancient reign.[2]

The hearty plaudits which thus greeted him on
every side, instead of elating, humiliated him.
Praise invariably caused him pain, and this pain was
always aggravated by such allusions as most of
these poems contained. In order to moderate the
enthusiasm of his more immediate associates he

[1] It was for this Accademia that Don Paoli published the elaborate
biography of Rosmini to which we are ourselves so much indebted.
[2] It was composed by Giacomo Barchetti, who came to be known
as the ' patriot and pietist.'

used to remonstrate with them in this manner :
'Youth should be cautious, and above all just.
Now, if you were just, you would not deem me
worthy of these extravagant commendations.' He
did what he could to make them understand that
emotions of personal affection are not the deliberate
outcome of calm justice; on the contrary, out-
flows of feeling were apt to be unjust, and therefore he who valued them at their real worth could
have no satisfaction in them, unless as a means of
humiliation. But as this implied the injustice of
his friends, he was forced to grieve for them as well
as for himself. Hence these gushing encomiums
were doubly annoying, and he insisted that they had
better be avoided altogether.

The spirit of justice and modesty thus evinced
led him to establish a little Academy in his own
house. Here he could be industrious without
being intrusive or appearing to do more than his
brother Academicians ; here his labours could bear
ripened fruit in abundance without exciting the
admiration he disliked ; here his active mind would
have the means of sifting and strengthening his
studies by the discussions which all similar institutions encouraged ; here religious devotions could be
made to precede and follow, and, as it were, per-
meate all the proceedings, without seeming to be
out of place ;. here he could set aside the invidious
distinction between rich and poor, patrician and
plebeian, college-bred and self-taught.

The members of this domestic Academy, unlike

those of the Agiati, were not chosen from the wealthy and aristocratic merely : poor but talented and pious students were preferred, and though some of the upper classes were soon amongst them, the young founder defrayed all the expenses out of his private allowance, backed by contributions from his uncle Ambrogio. The youths who were privileged to be his associates in this little Academy —at once a mutual instruction and mutual edification society—read their several compositions in turn, and each was expected to criticise whatever productions were thus read. When any of the papers were judged to be of sufficient importance, they were printed for piivate, and sometimes also for public, circulation.

'The sage of sixteen summers,' who had established and been chosen to rule this little Academy, took care that its members never wanted matter for discussion. Though they were all much older than himself, and some of them well advanced both in years and learning, it was their unanimous wish that he should read an essay or deliver an address at every meeting. To this, however, his modesty objected. He preferred to take his turn with the others ; but whenever any member failed to produce a promised paper or deliver an expected discourse, he consented to fill the vacancy if no one else present were ready to do so. The first letter in the *Epistolario*,[1] written to his cousin, Count

---

[1] *Epistolario di Antonio Rosmini-Serbati. Lettere Religioso-Famigliari.* (1813-1854.) 2 vols. Torino, 1857. More than 10,000 of Rosmini's

Antonio Fedrigotti, alludes to a discourse which he had thus delivered in his domestic Academy. The subject, 'Praises of the Priesthood,' shows not only the tendencies of this literary institute, but the leading quality of its founder, who directed all he did and said to God and His Church.

This short epistle, which very fitly opens the first volume of his published correspondence, affords us an excellent opportunity of knowing what sober and solid thoughts filled him at an age when youths are usually least sedate and most superficial. Count Fedrigotti was at the time considering what profession he should adopt, and taking counsel with his wisest friends as to the state of life for which he was best fitted, the ecclesiastical being his own preference. Signorino Antonio Rosmini, though only sixteen years old, was included amongst 'the wisest friends,' and here is how he gave the advice which his 'grown cousin' stood in need of :—

I think it due to you, because of the very intimate friendship so long existing between us, to say a few words to you on the subject. Nor can I do better, I think, than by sending you a discourse of mine which I wrote not long ago, and delivered at a meeting of young aspirants to learning, whose task it is to read, each in his turn, some little production in prose or verse. It is a eulo-

letters, on all manner of subjects, are preserved in the archives of the Rosmini College at Stresa. In 1857 Don G. B. Pagani, Superior General of the Order of Charity, caused 548 of them to be published (in two volumes) as a 'representative selection,' and it is from that selection we translate those quoted in this work as from the *Epistolario*.

gium of the Priesthood. Far be it from me to persuade you to enter that state, or even to suggest such a step ; since it is one that has been regarded by many illustrious men with feelings of serious apprehension. My intention is simply to give you a clear insight into the beauty of that state. Nevertheless, would to God that what happened of old to Chrysostom, in respect to Basil, were to be my case now in your regard ! Believe me, it is my love for you that prompts me to address you thus.

ROVERETO, *October* 22, 1813.[1]

When the day came for deciding as to his own 'state of life,' he forgot not the advice thus modestly tendered to his hesitating kinsman. As in all his juvenile pastimes he made everything tend to religion, so in all his letters, be the subject what it may, that is the prominent, the pervading idea.

A veteran rather than a boy seems to speak in this short note, written about the same time, to Simone Tevini, a friend who had worldly ambitions that suggested its terse exhortations :—

I have just received a letter from you, in Latin, which has given me unspeakable pleasure. It is not devoid of elegance, and leads me to hope great things from you. All men, it is said, are born equal ; virtue alone can ennoble. Let nothing withdraw you from the practice of virtue. Virtue is 'its own reward,' as one of the poets sang ; or, to speak more correctly, God is its reward, surpassing great.

I must be brief for want of time.

Accept the sentiments of a friend who wishes you well. Love God, in whom you will find your all. Love solitude and wisdom. Farewell.

ROVERETO, *December* 3, 1813.[2]

[1] *Epistolario*, Letter i. [2] *Epistolario*, Letter ii

VOL. I.   E

The essays and discourses that delighted the
Academies of his boyhood were never regarded by
Rosmini as worth preserving. But one literary and
scientific production of those days remains to bear
witness to the profound love of God, and earnest
affection for literature and philosophy, which had
then taken firm root in his soul. It is entitled a
' Day of Retirement,' by Simonino Ironta—the *nom
de plume* being an anagram of his name attached to
most of the papers he read in the Academy of
the Agiati, as well as in that founded by himself.
This charming little work was composed at a rustic
villa—a summer seat of the family—on the mid-
slopes of a mount overlooking Rovereto.[1] Thither
he was in the habit of going frequently, in quest of
a solitude which enabled him to write and contemplate and pray without the interruptions that beset
him overmuch in the town.

The subject of this little book is grave, and
thrown into a form evidently borrowed from the
once popular work of Boetius—*Consolatio Philosophiæ.* He skilfully sketches an imaginary contest
between two most beautiful virgins, who happen to
meet with a poor deserted boy, whom they desire
to adopt : each resolved to educate the forlorn

[1] The ascent to a popular sanctuary that is nestled in one of the
inviting natural terraces of this mount, and the splendid view of the
town and valley from that point, must have come vividly before his
mind when, in after-years, he ascended Monte Calvario, and stood
on the terrace there to contemplate the much smaller town of Domo,
in the much grander and vaster valley of the Ossola (see Chap. xxiv.
of this volume).

orphan in her own way. The virgins are Friendship and Philosophy. Friendship is arrayed in
snow-white garments and enwreathed with blooming roses; Philosophy in gracefully-folded russet
vesture, and well provided with books. While they
dispute, a third virgin, of sedate and love-inspiring
mien, steps in to restore harmony. This is Religion,
in flowing azure robes studded with resplendent
stars. She decides that all three shall take charge
of the child, but that their united purpose must be
to train his soul for God—the development of true
piety towards the Creator to be 'the supreme end
of their joint efforts.' The strife terminates in the
acceptance of Religion's counsel. Then Friendship
and Philosophy loyally set about doing the duties
proper to each, while Religion attends to all the rest;
the result being that the boy soon acquires every
quality that can fit him for effective work in the
service of the King of Kings, and consequently
becomes the best of men even for the purposes of
ordinary social and political life.

This production of Rosmini's sixteenth year may
be styled 'the literary prelude to all the works of
his after-life.' It is full of pious fancies, wholesome reflections, and evidences of solid learning.
Long before then he had, indeed, done and written
enough to demonstrate his thorough devotion to God
and the Church of God. In the very dawn of his literary
and scientific life one could see the man in the youth
—' the man whole and complete,' says Don Paoli ;
' perfectly harmonious in his formation and unfolding.'

But this little treatise revealed more of his powers than they who knew him intimately had yet seen. It proved that he had made marvellous progress in the Latin and Italian classics, that he had deeply studied the philosophers (especially Seneca and Plato), that he had become critically familiar with the Sacred Scriptures (which were, indeed, the constant source of his daily meditations), and that he had heartily absorbed ' the science of the Saints.'

Often before had he discoursed, with the skill and ease of a diligent biblical student, on the vanity of all things human ; but never before had he handled the subject with the profound insight of a Christian philosopher. Often before had he maintained that the sciences without God are useless ; but never before had he shown how much worse than vain they are when not centred on God, and not constantly pointing to Him. Often before had he urged the necessity of cultivating the sentiment and the intellect so that they should be sanctified by God's Grace ; but never before had he so learnedly insisted on this in the application of knowledge and the direction of personal conduct. Often before had he eloquently counselled devotion to the Holy See ; but never before had he so forcibly put it as an indispensable quality in an enlightened citizen and sincere Christian. ' In short,' as Don Paoli says, ' this juvenile work blends together and well harmonises the man of letters, the philosopher, and the ascetic, as the characteristics of each subsequently came forth, still together; but more majestically represented, in the works of maturer years, and in the whole course of his life.'

Although he gave so much time to study and to literary pursuits, although he dearly loved to spend hours meditating in solitude, although his religious exercises seemed to absorb all the time not devoted to the acquisition of knowledge, or to the duties of family and social intercourse; nevertheless, so orderly were his habits, so well regulated his hours, that he found sufficient 'spare time' to carry on an extensive correspondence with numerous friends, young and old, to whom he had some encourage-ment or information to give, or from whom he had some advice or instruction to receive. In this latter category strangers were frequently included, and brought within the circle of friends. Thus, when he decided on starting his domestic Academy, he put himself in communication with Fontana of Florence, from whom he obtained full information as to the system so successfully employed in the great Academy of that city. So, with the presidents of other similar establishments he held correspondence for a like purpose, gathering and utilising all the hints he could get. His own views were in turn sought by these, and this Roveretan youth, while consulting sages, was invited to be their counsellor.

All these letters, no matter what the special object of any, breathe the ardent spirit of piety which animated whatever he said or did. Here is how that spirit directed him to disguise in boyish sympathy the counsels of a prudent thinker bent on winning the confidence of a dear kinsman, Count Antonio Fedrigotti, who was then so placed that he might soon have been led aside from the regular path upon which they both, as boys, had walked together. It will be seen that he rather insinuated than expressed the wholesome admonitions he meant to convey, and that, thus early, he had the rare gift of putting his advice in a few words, and most delicately adapting it to the disposition of its recipient as well as to the circumstances of the case :—

Oh! how often have I not sighed for an opportunity of opening my heart fully to you in a long letter, and giving expression to those feelings of love which I so fondly cherish for you—feelings which are dictated by the most genuine and sincere desire for your well-being. The longed-for moment, however, has not yet arrived for discharging those duties which are enjoined by friendship, as well as by that charity which makes us all brothers, and welds us together in the closest union by its sweet and sacred bonds. Oh! the beauty of friendship! Oh! ever blessed and holy charity!

But to return to ourselves. Well, then, my dear Antonio, I must repeat that I do indeed wish you every good, and I trust that love, which brings the distant near, may evermore unite us. Methinks I see you engaged with me—now, in innocent recreation and amusements; now reading together and learning how inexperienced lads, such as we are, may reach the holy goal; now pouring forth earnest prayers to our good God that He may direct us and be our guide, that He may root out and destroy the ill weeds that perchance have sprung up in our hearts, and be moved to pity us, and our brethren, who are, alas! but too wretched, because bondsmen groaning beneath the yoke of sin. But, really, how do you employ your time? You are studying and cultivating wisdom, not merely for the sake of glory, which is vain and transient, but for the life to come, which is, in truth, eternal. Oh! how delighted I am to learn this from your own letter!

Continue, then, in the path you have entered on, and offer all to God ; have recourse at all times to Him, who is the beginning and end of all things ; speak to Him frequently, and when you are in the very warmth of your prayer, present to Him me, His needy and most wretched servant, and call aloud for mercy in my behalf.

ROVERETO, *August* 1814.[1]

That Antonio Rosmini had from his earliest boyhood given himself to God's service was made manifest in various ways. But until his seventeenth year this dedication of himself took no positive form. Hitherto it was only an expression of the general fact that everyone can and should give himself to God's service, in any state of life ; to do so was, therefore, a duty incumbent on all, and not necessarily implying the Ecclesiastical or the Religious State. True, he was often heard to say things which showed his own inclinations to be all in favour of the Ecclesiastical State. But, as a family tradition tells us, he rather hinted than freely spoke of a fixed intention to embrace that state ; for he had reason to fear that his father would dislike, and possibly oppose such a purpose. In his seventeenth year, however, he avowed it in terms that left no doubt of his determination to give up everything in order to follow Christ more closely than he could in any Secular State.

This determination was confided to his mother,

[1] *Epistolario*, Letter iii.

who gave him no encouragement, but allowed the matter to drop, thinking that as he grew older he might see reason to change his mind without her assistance. Meanwhile, the importance of his position and prospects as heir of a noble house were more frequently and conspicuously set before him. All this, however, seemed to be unconnected with him, for his mind and heart had long since been detached from merely human hopes or human desires. Time, therefore, only strengthened his intention, and he took the earliest occasion of 'putting it on record' in a letter to his friend Bartolomeo Menotti, who understood and sympathised with him. That friend, well knowing the various temptations which lay in wait for one of such brilliant talents, dreaded lest even he might, in time, be induced to think more of man's kingdom than of God's. Here is how young Rosmini reassured him :

Oh! how grateful I feel for the excellent advice you give me, *never to forget the Christian commonwealth,* for truly it is sweet and noble and just advice. Indeed there is no wisdom here below if it come not from the Father of all light. You may therefore rest assured that the pursuit of letters has of itself no charms for me.

I am resolved to become a Priest, and to part with all that I have to purchase a treasure *which* neither moth nor rust can fret away, and *where* thieves cannot break in and steal. What little learning I possess I mean to make use of, with God's help, in the work of education. (And what more pleasing task than to be useful to our fellow-men ?) Nor will I suffer my body to eat its bread in idleness—it must toil and labour ; my worldly substance I shall employ in advancing the sciences and relieving the poor. These sentiments are dictated, not by my intellect alone, but by my heart also.

Continue to be my friend, and recommend me to our Lord.

ROVERETO, *September* 22, 1814.[1]

' Continue to be my friend ' was an appeal which Rosmini's heart ever made to the good ; and all his actions prove that he never wearied of being their friend. They who knew him intimately during the last years of his life have spoken much about the earnestness and enduring character of his love for those worthy of love. It had always been thus with him. All the letters written in his youth abound with the gushing expressions that are often mean- ingless common-places in ordinary Italian corre- spondence. But with him they were never empty phrases. None of his warm assurances of friendship were without that solid foundation, that elevating motive, which gave substance to the cordiality ; and none of his friendships were unworthy of the affec- tion he bestowed. Evidence of this may be found in the following letter, pithily setting forth the nature of Christian friendship. It was sent to his cousin, Count Antonio Fedrigotti, as a continuation of some remarks he had occasion to offer in a former letter :—

Make haste and come, for I have long eagerly expected you, and your delay in coming seems an age. You are, it is true, always with me. But such is the nature of friend- ship that, although its seat is in the heart, still its votaries long to meet and pass their time together occasionally

[1] *Epistolario*, Letter iv.

in familiar converse ; the result, perhaps, of that wondrous
union which exists between soul and body. The love I
bear you, my dearest Antonio, is unalloyed by aught that
is mean or common ; it is a love more than ordinary, being
pure and noble in its aim, and having for its sole object
your real good. Indeed, I love you as I love myself, and
those very blessings which I desire for myself I pray and
wish also for you. Be then persuaded that love like this
is unimpaired by separation ; it wanes not, nor languishes
with lapse of time ; but is lasting and unchanging. The
reason is, that it comes not from man but directly from
God, Who *is* everywhere and is everywhere the same. You
understand well what I mean, especially now that you are
engaged with syllogisms, and are deeply engrossed in the
subtle investigations of philosophy. How often I have
reproached myself with tardiness in writing to you !
But you already know how my time passes without my
telling you. However, I was determined, at all hazards,
to steal away this evening and spend it thus with you. I
have done so in order that you may see how you are always
present to my mind.

Farewell.

Be ever mindful of our good God, the most loving of
Fathers, the wisest of Masters, the dearest, and surest, and
truest, and sweetest of Friends that can be found. Yes !
recommend yourself to Him, and recommend me also
earnestly. I embrace you and long to see you. Meanwhile, apply yourself to study. How beautiful and how
precious a thing is wisdom.

ROVERETO, *October* 27, 1814.[1]

The 'study' and the 'wisdom' to which the
young writer was himself so zealously devoted he
had, about this time, to seek outside the walls of the
local college, in which he had been thus far educated.

[1] *Epistolario,* Letter v.

At the close of the school term of 1814 the Rovereto *ginnasio* parted with him as a student who had advanced in knowledge far above its level. In so parting with its most brilliant *alumnus*, the Provost of the College (as its archives for that year attest) confidently predicted that Antonio Rosmini would become the great teacher he did become. Provost, professors, and students took formal leave of him as one whose collegiate career left, for all alike, a model on which to shape their course, if they sought to be truly learned and truly good.

CHAPTER III.

ROSMINI'S CALL TO THE ECCLESIASTICAL STATE.

(A.D. 1815-1816.)

His first affliction—The whole family opposed to his choice of the Ecclesiastical State—How he met the opposition and disposed of all
objections—The call unmistakably from God—His motives for
embracing that state—Yet another affliction—Selects humility
as the safest road to Heaven—Continues his home studies—Typical
character of this period of his life—Contempt for worldly pleasures
—Yearning of his heart for a perfect state—Living up to a
religious rule and nursing the inspiration of a religious Order—
His friendships, wishes, and designs all for God—Arts and sciences
nothing without God—One drop of morality and religion worth an
ocean of human learning—His undesigned noviciate for the Religious State.

THE first real affliction of Rosmini's young life came
with the open avowal of his resolution to embrace
the Ecclesiastical State. No sooner had he announced
his determination to closely follow Christ than he
had to bear the cross. All had hitherto been domestic
serenity of an exceptional kind. Between him and
his parents there had ever been that blissful peace
which comes from 'loving the law of the Lord,'
and to them, says the Psalmist, 'there is no
stumbling-block.' This peace had never yet been
disturbed by any breeze strong enough to ripple,
even slightly, the still waters of Antonio's home

happiness. But on a sudden all was changed, and the stumbling-block seemed to be there. For Antonio it was a severe trial, because he had ever loved his parents fondly and ever obeyed them loyally. That they were zealous, practical Catholics, heartily devoted to the Church, only added new perplexity to his position.

It was made still more embarrassing when he found himself opposed by the considerate uncle on whose aid he had confidently counted. But the affectionate Ambrogio, who had been ever ready to cheer him on the course that pointed to this vocation, was unable to withstand 'the logic of lineage.' He, too, instead of encouraging, besought him to remember that the continuance of the Rosmini family depended on him ; that his only brother was too delicate to be thought of as heir ; that his only sister already contemplated representing the family in the ranks of Religion ; that he was, after all, too young to choose ; that, before deciding, he should see more of the world than he had yet seen ; that a brilliant future awaited him ; that, with the great wealth, great talents, great acquirements, and great piety which were undoubtedly his, he could do more effective battle for country and creed as a lay leader than as a Priest.

All these appeals, urged as they were in every form, and by those whom he most loved, distressed him much, but left his resolution unshaken. The voice that said deep down in his heart ' Follow Me ' held him enlisted beyond the power of human suasion. He would not desert the Cross, around which every impulse of his soul had been twined more and more closely, day by day, since his childhood. Bitter, indeed,. was this first taste of what its true followers had to endure ; but without such bitterness where would be the sweetness of following 'The Man of Sorrows?' Nerved by this thought, he calmly met all the entreaties by counterentreaties. He recalled the advice he had given to his cousin Fedrigotti, repeated what he had written to his friend Menotti, reproduced in all forms the arguments of his juvenile discourse on the Priesthood, and finally besought his affectionate tempters to remember that no one is born merely for this life, but for life everlasting ; no one should prefer the service of man to the service of God.

The whole of this struggle between young Rosmini and his parents bears a remarkable resemblance to that which, under circumstances exactly similar, formed an important episode in the life of St. Francis of Sales, the story of whose boyhood and youth, to say nothing of manhood, is in many other respects strikingly like that of Antonio of Rovereto's boyhood and youth.

Every friend, whose influence or eloquence stood a chance of having some effect on his mind, was induced to employ it against his resolution ; but all in vain. Amongst the friends who were requested to act in this way Don Luigi Sonn held a high place in young Rosmini's estimation ;' and therefore, when home influence failed, he was one of the first

intrusted with instructions to assail the youth's purpose. He did so from points of view that were
intended to alarm a very sensitive conscience, which
was called on to dread lest inexperience, or the nature
of his favourite studies, or close association with
religious persons might have led to the resolution.
The task was an ungracious one, but Don Luigi none
the less earnestly besought his young friend to
pause and fear lest his heart had been decoyed
into a determination which, after all, might not have
sprung from sufficiently considered or sufficiently pure
motives. Antonio promptly met all the objections
in a very complete way, and went so far as to
supplement his spoken replies by the following
letter :—

Dearest friend,—Do you for a moment suppose that I
dissent in any way whatever from what you say concerning the office and duties of a Cleric? With what other
end in view, think you, have I chosen that state of life (so
dear to me for many reasons), unless it were to devote
myself entirely, and in a special manner, to the service of
my good Lord and God. Once consecrated to Him, I shall
be in a position to sing His praises in the sublimest
manner that is possible to man ; in a position to learn and
to preach His most holy law, which gives light unto little
ones, and is, to the ignorant and unlettered, wisdom passing
great ; in a position to enrich with this treasure—more
precious than gold or gems, and sweeter far than honey—to
enrich with it, I say, all my brethren, whom I strive to love
tenderly in Jesus Christ.

This, my dear friend, *this* is the sole aim and desire of
my heart, if our Lord will only help me ; and surely He
will do so, for He is good. May all my studies and all my
talents be directed to no other end ! In truth, how fasci-

nating soever may be the pursuit of learning in itself, it involves, none the less, such intense fatigues as to make man feel sensibly that he was born a sinner. But, for my part, I am ready to renounce for His sake even life itself, at any moment; aye, and, if He make the demand, to sacrifice it, too, in the most unheard-of and painful manner. Believe me, my dear Luigi, I speak from my heart and open my mind to you fully; nor lies there a corner within it to which you have not free access. Insipid—mark what I say, for I say it emphatically—insipid, nay, quite unbearable, would seem to me the most sublime learning, were it not seasoned with the love of God and a pure intention.

ROVERETO, *August* 8, 1815.[1]

When all the local advocates of earthly interests had failed to entice Rosmini from his holy vocation, Padre Cesari, the distinguished Oratorian of Verona, was persuaded to try his fervid eloquence to that end. Young Antonio had a great regard for this estimable Priest, whom he sincerely admired as an author and revered as a friend. For some years it had been the custom of Padre Cesari to spend his Autumn vacations in Rovereto, where his society was much courted by the noblest and the best, who appreciated his virtues and his learning. During one of these visits he happened to be present at a meeting of the local Academy when an oration of Rosmini astonished all there, and won the warm admiration of the illustrious Veronese. Then began a friendship that ripened into cordiality, and gained for the venerable Cesari a strong hold on the young Roveretan's mind and heart. If anyone could divert

[1] *Epistolario*, Letter vii.

him from his purpose, with the best arguments that could be suggested by a deep knowledge of the human soul and a long experience of the weak and strong points of youth, here was the man.

The task was accepted, for Cesari earnestly espoused the view of the parents. Having taken the earliest opportunity for a private interview with the son, he employed all his skill and eloquence to turn 'the called of God' from the resolutions to which love of God had so long been forming his mind. The venerable Oratorian went as far as he reasonably could; but he desisted on finding that he had exhausted all his arguments and all his inducements without making any impression on the strong positions taken by the other. On the contrary, his young friend's logic not only resisted but overthrew his own, and Cesari retired from the contest, not merely to report his discomfiture, but to advise the parents not to oppose any longer so manifest a call from God. In this appeal he was more successful than he expected ; for, already weary of the struggle, they began to fear lest their opposition might after all be sinful. The failure of the eloquent Oratorian confirmed this fear, and they decided on recognising God's evident Will in the matter. Forthwith, the first dark cloud that had flecked the bright calm of Rosmini's young life was dispelled. Although his family at first consented somewhat grudgingly, they afterwards submitted with devout heartiness to God's decree.

It may seem strange that his parents, on seeing

from his earliest days how their Antonio's heart and soul were set on whatever belonged to Religious Life, had taken no steps to detach his thoughts from it, so far, at all events, as to ensure 'a worldly vocation.' But, apart from the fact that the Eternal Father's designs could not be thus easily altered, there remains this reason : Tyrolese parents, usually pious themselves, looked upon a fervent spirit of religion as an ordinary and desirable quality of a good child, and never as an unmistakable sign that when the time for making a choice should come, such child would choose the ecclesiastical or religious state, rather than some secular profession.

In Rosmini's case the choice was made in childhood, assented to in boyhood, and ratified on the threshold of manhood. At last it was approved by his earthly parents, as it always had been by his Heavenly Father.

When this greater cloud disappeared a smaller rose up to cast some shadows on his holy joy. His parents were eager to direct their son's course towards the Prelacy—towards the ecclesiastical dignities to which their wealth, social standing, and family history led them to look with much confidence and no small share of natural vanity. Little did they know of the severe but wholesome religious training to which Antonio had continually subjected his heart. They knew not, therefore, how firmly he had enthroned humility within his soul. Hence they were surprised to find him resolutely, though modestly, opposed to their pardonable aspiration after 'a privileged grade' in the Priesthood. He assured them that the honour of serving God in the lowest rank was a privilege beyond his merits, and the only one he could permit himself to aim at.

Like St. Philip Neri, he silenced all entreaties to put himself on the path to lofty 'position' by exclaiming 'Paradise! Paradise!' That to him was the loftiest position, and he knew well that the straightest road to it was by the lowly rather than the high posts of this life. This induced Padre Cesari to make an effort at securing in him an exemplary disciple for the Congregation of the Oratory. There was no need to expatiate on the advantages which association with the Oratorians presented. Cesari's young friend would himself willingly have said more in their praise than their representative did say. But that voice within, which had never ceased to whisper 'Follow Me,' had not yet said more; and until it distinctly said more he would bide his time. Therefore this proposal of Padre Cesari fared no better than that for the Prelacy. Young Rosmini would neither enter the Roman Academy of nobles nor the Verona Oratory. As yet God's Will did not seem to ask more than the quiet continuation of his studies at home.

These studies were subordinate to the sanctification of his soul—means to that one end of which he never lost sight. The more he studied, the more he saw the need of study; the more he prayed, the more he felt the power of prayer. Attachment to both increased with his years, but his greater love

for prayer soon made all his studies so many
channels of praise and supplication to the God for
whose glory he thought, worked, and lived. Love
of practical charity in every form kept pace with his
love of prayer and study ; but as the generous
deeds which continuously proved this love 'were to
him an unfailing source of great spiritual solace, he
used to say that he alone was benefited by them.

Before the completion of his seventeenth year
an incipient Society of Charity grew up around him.
Its members consisted of a few intimate friends—
the more piously disposed students of his domestic
Academy. He framed for their use a rule, by which
they were held to attend before all things to their
own spiritual interests, and then to provide for the
spiritual and temporal wants of their neighbours.
Some of those who belonged to this forerunner of
the Order to which all the training of his earlier days
tended, became in after-years Prelates of the Church ;
others were destined to fill important municipal
posts ; while all bore through life the pious impress
of their early association with Antonio Rosmini.

Don Paoli considers this period of Rosmini's
youth to be the most typical—the most abounding
in those 'coming events that cast their shadows
before.' At earlier periods the lineaments of the
man could easily be traced in the boy, but not the
special features of development which were now
becoming visible. His soul was, as it were, more
aglow with God's Grace, and all he said, or wrote,
or did, faithfully reflected its beams. The call to

follow Christ was promptly, joyously, and resolutely
obeyed, because Grace gave it. Other calls, which
seemed to be in keeping with this, if not its direct
outgrowths, were set aside, because man gave them
and human motives urged them. But coincident
with the distinct call to follow Christ was another
call which, as yet, he could not so clearly understand.
All his familiar letters of this period allude,
in some way or other, to 'the mysterious graces'
that were vibrating within him, and 'unfolding
the bloom of his future.' Here is one written
to his cousin Leonardo Rosmini, then at the University of Padua, where he had to encounter temptations deemed likely to withdraw him from close association with Antonio in that 'undeveloped something' for which he was daily preparing himself,
without knowing it, or rather, to which he was
being led on sweetly by Grace :—

You ask me for news. I have just read two sonnets in the
Academy, one of which you have not seen. I therefore
forward it to you, that you may give me your opinion upon
it. You would be astonished if I were to tell you how
many verses I have written since your departure. But I
have no time for such matters now ; so let us to business.

Your letter has somewhat reassured me. Oh! never
trust in your own strength to accomplish great things,
especially when external and internal foes conspire for our
destruction. The combat is a weary one, and St. Paul
lamented it too, in that beautiful passage which he thus
concludes : ' Unhappy man that I am, who shall deliver me
from the body of this death?' (Rom. vii. 24). And we—
what must *we* say after this ?

My dear cousin Fedrigotti informs me that he is no longer beguiled by amusements—such, for instance, as dances. Indeed, during the entire Carnival he would not be even an eye-witness of these pastimes, although Don Pietro made no objection to his going, and everyone else was urging him to do so.

If you write to him (and he is anxious that you should), I beg of you to congratulate him, on my part, for the victory he has gained over himself, and which is no inconsiderable one. Let him see that you take a lively interest in his welfare, and encourage him to persevere. Oh! my dear friend, who knows? Who knows? In one of my sonnets I have written these three lines, and perchance to this end adapted :

> A shapeless block, disdained by workmen's hands,
>   Was that same pillar, object of Thy choice,
>   Which, smooth and bright, now in Thy temple stands.

'The foolish things of the world hath God chosen that He may confound the wise ; and the weak things of the world that He may confound the strong ; and the base things of the world, and the things that are contemptible, hath God chosen, and things that are not, that He might bring to naught things that are, that no flesh should glory in His sight ' (1 Cor. i. 27–29). . . . .

ROVERETO : *February* 18, 1815.[1]

The cousin whose meritorious self-conquest is so skilfully commended to Leonardo's imitation was one of the well-beloved few on whose co-operation Antonio counted in that 'undeveloped something' which could, as yet, be only indicated by a significant, 'Who knows? who knows?' Beyond doubt, this enigmatical, 'Who knows?' concealed the germ of that

---

[1] *Epistolario*, Letter vii.

vine of charity which subsequently expanded into the Institute. For a long time he had reduced to personal practice the principles, and, as far as circumstances permitted, kept the rules of this Institute, though it was yet but as an idea, a germ of the vine Grace had planted in his soul. Day by day the vine grew, and as it grew its tendrils sought to attract and attach themselves to the most exemplary of his friends, old and young.

The following letter to Don Luigi Sonn, while giving us a special glimpse of how young Rosmini spent his time in those days, shows with what earnest yearning his leading idea drew him to those whose lives were devoted to God, and who heartily sympathised with any project having in view the attainment of perfection. Don Luigi was known to be one of those, and the idea hidden beneath the phrase ' Who knows ? '—an idea which sometimes felt the blight of surrounding coldness, — received fresh strength when this good man decided on coming to Rovereto, where he was likely to assist in the development of his young friend's plans :—

I have been obliged to go to Ala, to spend some days with a gentleman of that place. Time passed away drearily enough, I can assure you, and it seemed an age ere I got home again. Far away from all I hold dear in life, with my wonted regularity ruthlessly trespassed upon, I became almost a prey to melancholy ; my only comfort the while being to snatch to myself a few hours, when I could, now and then, that I might spend them all alone in my chamber, reading or in prayer. At last I have returned, and read your letters with the greatest eagerness. They furnished most delicious nourishment, and were well calculated to refresh the weary wanderer.

Having thus explained my silence, I proceed to answer your kind letter of the 21st instant. It has afforded me one of the greatest consolations I ever experienced in my life. To learn that you mean to strain every nerve in order to make Rovereto your home is indeed delightful news, and the more I think of it the greater is my satisfaction. It fills me with a new life, new hope and buoyancy of spirits. Oh! how our Lord smiles on my efforts and prospers my every wish, my every design. Be firm and resolute, then; and since you are yourself persuaded of the desirability of the move, I will content myself with giving you, on my part, a warm-hearted and earnest encouragement. The friendship which is common to both of us urges me to this. It is a friendship which exists for God and for virtue's sake alone, whence it derives at once its being and its strength. Finally, I will add words of prayer and entreaty. You know from whom they come, and I know to whom they are addressed. I will now say no more, although the mere mention of *the plan* which I have proposed to myself, wholly for the *honour and glory of God*, would furnish you with some very cogent reasons for adhering to the resolution you have made.

ROVERETO : *August* 1815.[1]

The 'plan' thus dimly hinted at was no other than a formalisation of the thoughts apostrophised in the pithy 'Who knows?' of a former letter. More than once before, he had constructed, on a small scale, the framework of a religious society designed to carry out the principles of orderly charity. This leading idea was strong within him while he drafted rules of life and horaries as long ago as when

[1] *Epistolario*, Letter ix.

he 'played at monk' with a relish which he never had
for any other amusement of his childhood. These
at best were immature and rudimental plans, com-
pared with what he could now produce; but these,
such as they were, invariably set his own sanctification as the first thing aimed at. Even his ardent
love of philosophy and of literature, in all forms that
tended to cultivate the mind or elevate and charm
the taste of man, were as nothing in the way of this
one predominant thought—his own sanctification.
Human learning he prized, in so far as it led man to
know God better and love Him more; but he valued
it not at all for its own sake. The subjoined letter to
Don Pietro Orsi, on the ordinary topics of familiar
correspondence, will make this sufficiently clear :—

On learning from yourself how much you take to heart
our separation, I feel grateful indeed to you; at the same
time, confused. From your own grief you may measure
mine—at least you may form some conception of it;
for how much *more* reason have I to cherish and augment
those sentiments of pure and holy love which I treasure up
in my heart for you. The bonds of an intimate friendship,
such as ours is, keep us thus inseparably united. Who
knows that in the councils of our good God a time may not
come when I shall be able to convince you that these sentiments are not mere empty words? Meanwhile, I feel sure
that in speaking as I do to you my words will find a ready
acceptance, and will of themselves suffice. As to the
future—it is idle to speak of *that.*

I am delighted with the news of Cobelli, although not
much has accrued to science from his work. *One drop of
morality and religion is, in my estimation, worth more than
an ocean of human learning.*

Padre Cesari has been to see me—that celebrated man, whom I consider the most elegant Italian writer of the day. I regret that I have not been able to enjoy his company as long and as familiarly as I should have wished, for there were many strangers present. I regret it, indeed, very much ; but I must submit patiently to circumstances. The painter Udine, who has just come from Florence to see his friends, has also been with us for a considerable time to-day. We conversed at some length : his knowledge of the fine arts is very good. As he is considered one of the best painters, I feel proud of the reputation he enjoys, for we are fellow-countrymen. If I had two or three hundred lives, I should cheerfully give one to painting. I am passionately fond of this art, and at times imagine myself a Raphael. How enraptured I am when I think of his paintings, of his cartoons, of the countenances of his Madonnas, and those of Jesus—of his angels and his saints ; and, when I consider his powers of invention and the grouping of his figures. But it is better that my enthusiasm should cool. We who die on the morrow of our birth cannot hope to accomplish much. We must therefore choose the better part. ' It is folly to learn superfluous things in such a dearth of time.'

Ah ! if instead of running after vanity, I were to strive earnestly to please God and walk in his sight peacefully and hopefully ! Could I but help my brethren in any way, oh ! what a happy lot were mine ! My dear Don Pietro, intercede for me with God, without whom we can do *nothing*—intercede for me that my *wishes* may be fully realised. Yes, this it is which makes my heart throb violently. It is this which sweetens and alleviates fatigue. Without this the acquirement of all the arts and sciences, however beautiful and sublime in themselves, would appear to me distasteful, dull, and even repellent.

ROVERETO : *September* 28, 1815.[1]

[1] *Epistolario*, Letter viii.

His wishes were indeed to be realised, but not yet. The process of undesigned preparation had to go on until every monition of Grace should meet with complete and continuous response. Then Providence would open the way to the will thus fully formed by Grace—then ' the plan ' which had been taking shape for years would assume the perfect form that God designed for it. But until then he must continue the long and unperceived noviciate within which Grace held his soul as though spellbound. In this noviciate Grace was, as it were, the Master, and Prayer the Socius. With him prayer had ever been a habitual, solid, deliberate outflow of the mind, and not a mere impulsive gushing of the heart. ' It had ever been,' says Don Paoli, ' the grand means he employed to discover and do God's Will, and to become great in Christian philosophy.' The light of reason and that of faith were so blent in him that they formed only one luminary. This luminary showed him God in everything, and he cared to see nothing which did not refer to God.

Such was Antonio Rosmini when he left Rovereto College, a polished Christian student, well versed in human lore, but still better in divine science—such was he when he responded so heartily and firmly to the voice that said within him ' Follow Me.'

CHAPTER IV.

ROSMINI'S EARLIEST PHILOSOPHICAL STUDIES.

(A.D. 1816.)

Why a private Lyceum, under Don Orsi, was established for Antonio
Rosmini—The student soon outstrips his master—How the professor bore the superiority of his pupil, and how the pupil tried to
conceal it—The humility of both protects their intercourse, and
makes their friendship life-long—What each thought and said of
the other—Rosmini's ascetic and literary studies go hand in hand
—His correspondence on scientific subjects with experienced
critics—Wonderful extent of his philosophical knowledge and
wide range of his general reading at this time—His desire to be a
Saint—Suffering and sanctity inseparable—Warns a friend of the
dangers surrounding University life—His enquiries as to the moral
and scholastic character of Padua—Exhorts his brother to be
studious and virtuous—When and how the grand principle of
Ideal Being took possession of his mind—Religion the ground-
work and shield, and God the object of all his philosophical
studies.

As soon as Rosmini's family formally sanctioned
the choice he had made, and abandoned their efforts
to direct his steps towards the Prelacy, they allowed
him to obey, as he deemed best, what was so plainly
a Divine call. But his parents were still anxious that
he should remain near them. There being no philosophical school in Rovereto, he would have had to
continue his studies elsewhere, if the eager wish to
keep him at home as long as possible did not find a
means of deferring the separation. To further this

affectionate design, some of the principal families in the town and district agreed to unite with them in establishing a private Lyceum, over which Don Pietro Orsi should be invited to preside.[1]

Don Orsi had such a high respect for the Rosminis, and such a sincere regard for their son, that he was soon persuaded to undertake the task. In a short time he was enabled to form a class, which included about a dozen of the noblest youths of Rovereto, Antonio Rosmini being their acknowledged leader. Discarding the system of pedantic teaching then in vogue, Orsi adopted sometimes the method of the old Academicians, and sometimes that of the Peripatetics; now giving his lessons while seated in a delightful garden belonging to the family of one or other of his pupils, and now while rambling over the Tyrolese Alps, or strolling along the banks of the Adige.

It was not long before the professor discovered that the philosophical knowledge of his chief disciple was far in advance of his own; at all events, that he was more conversant with the works of the Schoolmen. Antonio was himself more slow to perceive it; but on at length noticing what was already clear to all the others, as well as to the master, he scrupulously avoided contradicting the amiable teacher or perplexing him with difficult questions, and took great care not to say or suggest anything likely to

---

[1] This Don Orsi (a distinguished graduate of the University of Vienna) was at the time engaged as tutor in the family of Rosmini's cousin, Count Fedrigotti-Bossi. He afterwards became headmaster of the Rovereto High School, and died at Recoaro in 1837.

embarrass him. When replying to questions he occasionally found it necessary to differ from the solutions of their text-book—that of Samuel Karpe[1]—but in showing the shortcomings of the author, he cleverly diverted attention from those of his expounder, who, like Karpe, followed the system of Locke.

As Don Orsi's main strength lay in mathematics, Antonio took refuge from a limping philosophy in a diligent study of the exact sciences; not that he ceased, or even diminished, his philosophical studies, but that he applied himself to them apart from his class, and so as not to be in conflict with his master. Ere long, however, the professor and pupil were fellow-students in philosophy, and all the others looked for information as much to young Rosmini as to the venerable Orsi, and this without displeasing the teacher or disregarding the humility of the student.

It is a remarkable fact that these relations, which in ordinary cases so often beget enmity on one side and contempt on the other, left not a trace of either sentiment in this master or pupil. On the contrary, Don Orsi had the good sense to discern in this real superiority, so modestly borne, sound reason for loving his disciple the more; while Antonio was equally ready to recognise in the professor's patient self-control and sturdy humility fresh bonds of union. Their mutual esteem, thus enhanced,

---

[1] Karpe was 'Imperial Professor' of Philosophy in the University of Vienna.

was sincere and lasting. More than once in after-life Rosmini gave noble evidence of this ; as, for instance, by specially dedicating to Orsi his grand philosophical work, the *Nuovo Saggio* on 'the Origin of Ideas.'

So, too, in the *Introduction* to the philosophical system he speaks of him in these kindly terms :— ' While I was yet a boy, and my mind was but poorly equipped for the effort, I ventured into philosophical questions with a daring somewhat characteristic of youth. My guide was Pietro Orsi, a man little known to the world, but never to be forgotten by me. Day and night I roamed through flowery paths, as it were, in the vast demesne of philosophical lore, feeling all that joy which the first scientific aspect of truth infuses into the soul, feeling that security which borders on hardihood, feeling those indefinite hopes peculiar to youth when for the first time turning, with elevated and conscious reflection, to the universe and its Creator, thinking to absorb the one and the other as easily as we breathe. No difficulty daunted me ; nay, difficulties but inflamed my ardour, because in every difficulty I saw a secret calculated to arouse my curiosity, a treasure to discover. I noted down daily the results of that artless and as yet inex-perienced liberty to indulge in philosophical specula-tions, knowing that I thus stored up seeds which should bud forth in all the after-labours of my life on earth. In truth, all the productions of my maturer years were the outgrowth of those seeds.' [1]

[1] *Introduzione alla Filosofia,* ' Disc. agli Am.,' p. 116.

Although Rosmini devoted himself most assiduously to philosophical and kindred studies during the
two seasons (1815–16) that he remained under the
guidance of Don Orsi, he never found it necessary
to curtail any of his devotional exercises, nor to
abandon his ascetical readings, nor to interrupt the
correspondence which he held with various persons ·
on religious or literary subjects.   It was during this
period that he wrote to his friend Scrinzi the profound reflections on Dante's *Divina Commedia*
which were so highly esteemed by his contemporaries, and the comments on the *Monarchia*, which
they deemed beyond the powers of one so young
and so little acquainted with actual politics.   It was
then, too, that he discoursed so learnedly on mathematics and literature, in letters to Beltrami, that it
is very difficult to understand how he contrived to
master such an extensive range of reading in such a
short time.

The difficulty is increased by a perusal of the
erudite letters he was all the while writing to Tevini
and others on his favourite theme, philosophy, treating especially of 'the division of the knowable into
objective and subjective, intellectual and material;'
meaning in the first division the ideal and the real,
and in the second the experimental and the rational.
He has himself thus explained how he could do so
much, or rather so well do so many things together
—'When things are done methodically and perseveringly, a short time yields a great deal of profitable work.'

Whatever the subject on which he wrote, there was always thrown around it a halo of religion ; but this was so skilfully done that it never seemed forced or out of place. In all the letters of his youth, as in those of later days, his heartfelt desire for sanctity can be easily traced ; but it is only in those to his special religious circle that the feeling comes forth strongly expressed. Indeed, he managed to disguise it somewhat when writing to strangers or to casual correspondents ; for he did not wish that more than a select few should have the means of penetrating within the sanctuary of his heart. The reason of this may be found in the closing sentence of the following letter, written while he was detained at home by a slight illness, and meant to console a fellow sufferer—his religious confidant, Don Luigi Sonn :—

As I am an invalid myself, and cannot go to see you, I must write, and so we shall derive mutual comfort from each other's words. I mean to speak briefly to you of what should be a source of consolation to both of us. Our infirmities, viewed in a proper light, are rather blessings than otherwise. Ah ! to one who loves God, as *we* are seeking to do, the evils of the present life are nothing short of real favours. How much of the debt we owe to our Lord may we not liquidate, while still on earth, by a few moments of suffering, endured with resignation, humility, and love of God ! How much pain and suffering we may thus spare ourselves in the life to come ! The Saints longed and sighed to suffer, and besought God to this effect, with tears in their eyes, as I have read in their lives ; nor could I myself refrain from weeping while doing so. And when their prayers were heard, it seemed as though they had become more humble in the sight of God ; and it seemed as though

He, at the same time, had drawn so much nearer to them that He appeared to be by their side, administering words of sweetest consolation as a friend and a brother. Oh! the words of soothing comfort that come from God!

And when the Saints raised their thoughts to Jesus Christ, their master, pattern, and exemplar, what ineffable sweetness filled their hearts! They saw Him to be so great and humble and patient in His sufferings, and then saw that their own afflictions were as a shadow when compared with those endured by their Redeemer and Brother. Hence it was that they ever gloried in their sufferings for Jesus' sake. The heavier and the more painful the cross, the more closely did it seem to them that they followed Him and the more perfectly that they copied Him.

I once read of a poor woman who was afflicted with a dreadful cancer. She had been for a long time in a state of despondency and wretchedness, when a holy man came one day to see her, and spoke to her of Jesus Christ. From that one visit she derived the greatest consolation and strength. Although she had been in the most abject poverty, and had lain on a bed of sickness for more than thirty years, where she was tormented by the most heart-rending sufferings (from which she afterwards died) this poor creature always maintained her cheerfulness and serenity of mind, and used to say that no one could persuade her that she was less happy than the great and mighty ones of the earth.

True, *we* are not Saints; really, when I hear this objection made I feel much grieved, and am wont to reply confidently that God can make us Saints, and I sincerely trust, in the merits of Jesus Christ, that He will do so, for we have a right, every one of us, to become Saints, and the path to sanctity and glory is open alike to *all.* Yes, this is my hope, and we shall attain to it if we pray without ceasing, and recommend ourselves to God and to Jesus Christ and to His Holy Mother and all the Saints. Do you pray for me, and I will pray for you.

I beg of you not to show this letter to such as entertain sentiments different from our own, ' lest truth should be evil spoken of.'

ROVERETO : *January* 29, 1816.[1]

With another friend, then at the University of Padua, he thus held counsel more like a venerable pastor than a youth of eighteen ; but his friend— Demetrio Leonardi—would have been surprised, and even shocked, had the good Antonio written in any other strain ; for he was known to them all as having ' the head of a sage on the shoulders of a boy.'

You do well to lay aside all formality between us. Formality only serves to dim and shroud sincerity, that brightest ornament of all friendship. Hence, I claim and insist on cordiality as indispensable to our friendship. As for the other matters of which you write, I clearly perceive that you maintain the sound judgment and good sense which have ever characterised you. And though I always felt persuaded that such would be the case, yet it is consoling to have proof of it. This renders me more and more attached to you. For, alas ! far different are the customs which prevail where you are now residing. But such is the condition of all large cities ; nor can we apply a more fitting remedy than you yourself suggest, when you say we should form around us a little world of our own. This we may do by eschewing the crowd of fast young men ; by not admitting to an intimate friendship any of those who, perhaps, only follow us as the vultures do their prey. Let us be courteous and affable towards all, lovers of solitude and retirement, as far as circumstances will permit, and earnest in treading the path of sanctity.

Application and labour are also efficacious means for

[1] *Epistolario,* Letter x.

enabling us to live securely. We thus remove the occasions of sin ; we live happy and contented with ourselves and are free from the inquietude of remorse, which is nothing else than our own concience unceasingly upbraiding us. Doubtless, you make use already of such efficient means. You are pious, and you love your religion. You frequent the lectures, and, what is more, you take a pleasure in them ; and hence, for your recreation, you choose what is profitable and instructive.

I shall be glad to hear from you, at your convenience, an account of the state of the University, of the Professors who fill the different chairs, and especially of your own Professors. Let me also hear again from you about your studies, and about the morality of the place. Meanwhile, believe me to be your sincere friend, desirous only of your welfare.'

ROVERETO : *February 7,* 1816.[1]

The inquiries with which the letter finishes were for no idle purpose. Preparations were already in progress for sending Antonio himself to Padua, and he desired to have that sort of information which parents, rather than children, usually seek. Most youths who are about to enter a University are mainly interested in knowing something as to com fortable chambers, academic costume, popular sports and pleasant society; or something as to the salubrity of the place, the quality of the food and the temper of the college dons ; or something with reference to the best means of avoiding severe study, and spending the time gleefully; or something as to the countless small matters which never troubled him. He craved to know only how the University

[1] *Epistolario,* Letter xi.

maintained its repute as a great public school, and how well the purity of its moral atmosphere was preserved.

His brother, still in a discouraging state of health, had just gone to complete a college course in Verona, and thither Antonio's prized exhortations speedily followed him. These were full of the sedate sense and solid counsel which would have been 'passing strange' in any other of his years ; but, in him, they were perfectly consistent. Though older friends knew the special requirements of that brother on whom the family now depended for the continuation of its line, no other would have touched them so effectually, or been listened to so attentively. Giuseppe Rosmini was virtuous, but his weakly health made practical piety a burden and study less agreeable than irksome. Here is how Antonio stimulated and directed him.

I have to reply to your welcome letter, from which I learn your satisfaction at finding yourself where you are. This is, indeed, joyful news for me, and comes to sweeten the bitterness of our separation, which I must confess I feel exceedingly. It seems as though our Lord were assisting you in an especial manner, and thus answering the prayers I have always poured forth and still continue to offer up in your behalf. Yes, it seems as though that little corner of Verona were marked out especially for you. There you will advance in piety and learning, provided you have the proper dispositions. And may God grant that you become the man I so ardently wish you to be, a pattern to your fellow-citizens—a pattern to all—humble, charitable, kind ; —in a word, moulded on virtue and Christian piety, while, at the same time, a lover of all that is beautiful and good, a man of letters devoted to study, especially to the literature of Rome.

Oh! how sweetly and profitably the life of the diligent student passes away! In his silent occupations he is a lively image of contentment and of the happiness it is permitted man to enjoy here below. How hard of heart are those who, while immersed in Tullius and Horace and Virgil or other classical writers of our own Italy, taste none of their pure delights, and fail to be touched by any of the beauties which such authors breathe. It appears to me almost impossible that there should be students so unimpassioned, so insensible, so utterly indifferent to the charms of the classics, regarding them as matters of no moment. Do not *you* be of their number I entreat you, but, on the contrary, seek to drink deeply of the classics and to cultivate a great esteem for them, as well as a refined and delicate sense of whatever is beautiful in literature, as did our own Clementino, and also Casa, Bembo, and nearly all the best writers of the fifteenth century. In short, next to Religion, let your first care be study and Literature. Read and re-read the classics (oh! that I had time to do so, too!); let your every thought, your every affection and desire be to advance in all knowledge.

I rejoice to hear that good discipline reigns in the college, and am especially pleased to learn that you write a good deal ; for writing much is, as the rhetoricians say, the best preceptor of the art of writing well. I do not dislike emulation as we see it in children ;—however, let it be confined to children. On your part study with earnestness and zeal ; but let your motives be far nobler than mere emulation ; let them be as they ought to be, for the glory of God, your own profit, and for the beauty and sweetness of the studies themselves. Then let your amiable and intelligent master direct you in everything.

I am much obliged to you for answering the questions I put to you about Cesari, and am delighted that he is so friendly to you. Hold fast to him, and especially to the

counsels he gives you in all that regards morality and religion. And, speaking on this subject, you can do nothing
more agreeable to me than to tell me something, in your
next, as to your spiritual director, &c. ; for, as I wish to
know everything about my friends, how much more do I
desire and expect to be informed about you, who are not
only the dearest of my friends but also my brother.

We and our studies are getting on well in this quarter.
Philosophy and the contemplation of nature (the latter
made, as now it is, in the cool hours of these lovely morn-
ings), far from wearying us, form such an agreeable recreation that I should not be disposed to sacrifice it for any
other. Thus wandering about, like the disciples of Aristotle,
we always find in this our picturesque neighbourhood new
and delightful retreats. To me everything is new, owing to
the retired life I have hitherto led at home ; everything
appears to me of singular beauty, and gives me intense
pleasure.

With regard to my private occupations :—Having dis-
patched my literary correspondence with some friends and
finished the little pamphlets of which you are aware, I
resumed the composition of a discourse on the ' Utility and
Necessity of Cultivating the Faculty of Reason.' The more I
advance the more new matter I find, so that when I fancy
myself to be approaching the end I discover that I have still
a great way to travel.

ROVERETO : *May* 11, 1816.[1]

Giuseppe already well knew how eagerly his
affectionate brother pursued the studies he looked
upon as holding the key to all human knowledge ; but that hurried glimpse of what he was
doing had a home charm which linked Rovereto
with Verona and made the exhortation to study
more effective. About the very time that Antonio

[1] *Epistolario,* Letter xii.

was, himself, thus laboriously groping his way to 'the end,' a sudden flash of genius, if not a revelation, so illumined the course that he could clearly see 'the open portal of philosophical truth.' The incident is very noteworthy, though destitute of all the dramatic attractions which give startling effect to the 'biographical episodes' of worldly heroes.

Stirring events hardly ever usher in the birth of a grand discovery in knowledge, which is ordinarily brought forth under circumstances as tame and unromantic as those that found Newton catching at the law of gravitation, or Watt solving the problem of steam. But these discoveries none the less bring stirring events in their train, and sometimes wholly revolutionise human systems of science and industry. Rosmini's mind seized the grand principle of *Ideal Being* under circumstances partly in keeping with those that have produced the most important discoveries known to science, and partly with those that had the qualities of a Divine Revelation. Let the reader judge ; for we shall record the incident as he told it himself to Don Paoli, many years after it had taken place.

One of the least frequented streets in Rovereto in those days was an avenue called *Terra*, in which persons of wealth and rank had residences carefully railed in or walled off from 'noisy business.'[1] While

[1] Before Rovereto outgrew its village dimensions, and while it had but a few houses at either side of the road that ran through the Castle estate or *terra*, this road was known as the *Terra* or *Estate* road. When the Venetians, in the fifteenth century, took the castle and gradually enlarged the village, other roads soon stretched beyond the bounds of

passing homeward slowly, thoughtfully, and all alone
through this quiet street, one evening after a 'philosophical excursion' with Don Orsi and his pupils,
young Rosmini allowed his mind to speculate freely
on a variety of things. Now his attention was held
by one mental object, and now by another. Suddenly he perceived that each object was far from
being simple. 'On the contrary,' said he, when explaining the circumstance to Don Paoli, 'each
object appeared to me in itself a group of many
objects. But, on looking more closely into the
matter, I saw that these, instead of being many
objects, should have been called many determinations of one object, more universal and less determinate,—their common container. Then, by re-
peating on this object the very analysis I had
applied to the others, I found that it was itself
in the same condition, and that when divested,
by means of abstraction, of those less definite determinations, which it still retained, it appeared to
me as a new object, still more universal and less
determinate than the former. I say *new* in reference to my intuition (because I had not as yet
looked at its new aspect), but not as being new
in itself; for it was the container not only of the
object which my mind had under analysis, but
also of the others that had been previously ana-
lysed. By continuing this process I discovered

the garrison, and these received names that were changed from time
to time, but the original road always retained the name (Terra) which
had been previously given to the whole estate.

that, no matter what the point of departure might
be, I was invariably brought to the most universal object—*Ideal Being*—destitute of all determinations whatever, so that I found it no longer possible to abstract anything from it without annihil-
ating thought, and at once I saw that this object
was the *universal container* of all the objects on
which my mind had already rested. I then undertook the process of verification. This consisted in
seeking to discover which determinations of *indeterminate being* were the first possible, and then which
came next, and so on to the last. By these means I
discovered that synthesis brought up again before
my intellectual vision all those objects which analysis
had caused to disappear gradually from it. Then
it was that I became convinced that indeterminate
ideal being must be the first truth, the first thing seen
by immediate intuition, and the universal means
of all acquired knowledge, whether perceptive or
intuitive.'

Such were the profound cogitations of Antonio
Rosmini in his eighteenth year ; such the fruit and
the evidence of his intense application to the studies
that led him to know aright the works of God and
to worship Him the more ardently. In too many
instances abstruse speculations of this kind have
made sad havoc with the piety of old as well as
young hearts ; but, so far from diminishing Rosmini's
religious fervour they increased and strengthened it.
As Don Paoli tells us, it was the ardour of his religious spirit that suggested and sustained his philo-

sophical research ; and this in return brightened and fortified his religious spirit. Never did he apply his mind to discover anything from mere curiosity, and the bare suggestion of acquiring knowledge for the vain purpose of appearing learned would have horrified him. Pure love of God evoked and ever directed his love of philosophy, and if he thought that man—whom he loved in and for God—should derive no benefits from the truths he set himself to establish against the enemies of God's Church, he would have abandoned his efforts as no longer having an object worthy of the love that dictated them. As in the greatest things, so in the smallest, all he did or attempted had in view the glory of God and the good of man.

CHAPTER V.

ROSMINI ENTERS THE UNIVERSITY OF PADUA AS A
THEOLOGICAL STUDENT.

(A.D. 1816-1817.)

St. Francis of Sales and Antonio of Rovereto—Similarity of their
University life—What the students and professors thought of
Rosmini, and what he thought of them—His special companions
and their special qualities—Tommaseo—How to live in the
University with the regularity of cloistered monks—He tells his
mother how religion assuages grief—Takes the Bachelor's degree
and returns home for his first vacation—Resumes his course at
Padua with permission to wear the dress of an ecclesiastical student
—With what solemn earnestness he took the clerical habit—In-
tense love of purity and distrust of 'the world.'

TOWARDS the end of 1816 Antonio Rosmini was
sent to Padua, in order to study theology and complete his philosophical course. Although his parents
no longer sought to interfere with his vocation, they
were not without some lingering hope that residence
in the famous city, and close association with the
ambitious students of its old University, might lead
him to reconsider his resolution.

Just two hundred and sixty-two years previously,
a comely youth of the same age (and who was also
'the heir and pride of a lordly house,') had been
sent to Padua, with a like hope on the part of his
parents, who fancied that a course of jurisprudence,

in the great mediæval law school, might wean him from love of the Ecclesiastical State. That youth was St. Francis of Sales, whose virtues and even personal habits were so thoroughly reproduced in Antonio Rosmini, that the University life of the one bears a marvellous resemblance to that of the other. This resemblance may, indeed, be somewhat incomplete as regards the qualities of their studies, but it is perfect in whatever relates to an uninterrupted recollection of God's presence, and the unceasing self-control and prayerfulness which this necessitates.

Although Rosmini entered the University as a Theological Student, he did not wear the ecclesiastical habit. They who believed that there was yet a possibility of something occurring which might retain him in the ranks of the laity, supposed that all chance of this would utterly disappear if the clerical dress were formally assumed. These good people failed to see that his soul was already so vested in the robe of his vocation that it mattered little what garb his body wore. But he, knowing this, willingly humoured the desire of his parents, and consented to remain without the cassock as long as possible. Besides, their preference had its advantages.

The habiliments of a layman left him unembarrassed in the pursuit of knowledge, outside of the theological curriculum. Accordingly, he attended as many non-theological lectures as he could without loss to his regular course. This afforded him a more extensive opportunity of imparting, unconsciously, that edification which one so young, so noble, so engaging, so pious, so talented and so diligent could not fail to give. Among the classes thus attended was that of medicine, in which he took a profound interest. Dr. Baroni of Rovereto, who was then attached to the medical school in Padua, relates how learnedly Antonio used to converse with him on the mysteries of life, and what an advantage his theological readings gave him over those who could handle the subject only from the physician's point of view.[1]

His contemporaries have borne witness that no collegian, during his time, was so generally known and so universally loved in Padua as Antonio Rosmini. Every lecture-room had for him a place, and all the professors held him in the highest esteem. Students in every branch of study vied with one another to possess his friendship and do him honour. The exceptions to this rule would have enabled a Paduan of those days to discover the students who loved the gaieties of society more than their books, or the students who deemed indifference to religious duties an evidence of 'mental independence.' Between him and such as these there was nothing in common, but the fact of having been together at the

---

[1] 'He used to lament deeply that one of the principal evils of society, in the present age, is the false method on which so many study medicine, whence arise impiety and libertinism, and frequent ill success in the treatment of diseases. On this account he ardently desired a radical reform of this art, as may be seen in his *Antropologia* and *Psicologia*, and he desired that all its professors should be animated by a Christian spirit. For this purpose he maintained some medical students at his own expense at the University, with the intention of appointing them to attend the sick in hospitals that he designed to open.'—*An outline of the Life of Antonio Rosmini*, translated from the Italian and edited by Rev. W. Lockhart, p. 83. London, 1856.

same University. The most distinguished professors of that day and place spontaneously and cordially acknowledged the grandeur of his genius, the depth of his knowledge, and the solidity of his virtues. These professors included such men as Cappellari, Bishop of Vicenza, who taught him dogmatic theology, and Baldinotti, one of the most astute metaphysicians of the period.[1]

After Rosmini had been long enough in the University to form an opinion of men and things within it, he wrote to his father in high terms of his own masters and fellow-pupils, while to his uncle he sent 'a description of the place,' as 'the hotel of letters and of the Latin muses.' But it seemed to him, nevertheless, that Latin was not treated there with the homage it deserved ; for he found Italian so universally spoken as the language of the classes, that few students thought it desirable to cultivate a close acquaintance with the mother tongue.

Those of his own immediate circle were much given to the old language, and this, doubtless, was a bond of union between them. It was, however, the least of the ties that held them dear to him : he prized them most because they were estimable in character and decided lovers of God. Some of those who belonged to that 'immediate circle' have gained distinction in Italian literature, and some have won a place in his own published correspondence which has ensured their memories a long future. Amongst

[1] Tommaseo records this evidence in the *Cronica Contempor.* Torino, 1855.

them were Tommaseo of Sebenico (author of a
dictionary of synonyms and other standard Italian
works), Alessandro Paravia (afterwards a distinguished professor in the University of Turin), Appollonia of Cividale (subsequently a popular master in
the Seminary of Udine) and Uzielli of Livorno, a
young Jew of great talent and virtue, from whom
Rosmini obtained much useful information touching
Hebrew literature and customs.

For some time, Tommaseo was the nearest to
him of all who composed the ' immediate circle ' of
fellow-students. One can easily see why this preference existed, when told that Tommaseo, though
eccentric in many ways, was not only, like all the
others, very steady in his habits, very diligent in
his studies, and very learned, but also, unlike the
others, very ' little favoured by fortune.' Collegians
who were practical moralists, or lived in strict accordance with the obligations of the Church, thereby
earned a special right to Rosmini's esteem and
friendship. But they who loved to join him every
morning in hearing Mass, and every evening in the
recital of the Rosary, or in other devotions—they who
went with him frequently to the Sacraments of
Penance and Communion—they who liked to live in
the world with the regularity of cloistered monks—
these had the strongest claims upon his affection and
his confidence.

Tommaseo was one of these, with the additional
qualification of being poor and desiring to remain in
that condition. He so prized the privations which

attend poverty that Antonio could not induce him
to part with them, 'lest his humility might be endangered.' They lodged in the same house, Rosmini's apartments being such as the bounty of a
wealthy father insisted on his occupying, while those
of Tommaseo were not only comparatively mean but
unhealthily situated. Knowing this, Rosmini, with
hearty good will, repeatedly requested his friend to
share in the spacious accommodation provided for
himself; but he preferred to continue with what a
companion (Gozzi) described as ' the poverty that is
made magnificent by soul-felt resignation to God's
Will.'[1] In a letter to his mother, Antonio styled
Tommaseo 'a prodigy.' When their college days
were passed, this ' prodigy'—who loved his young
friend ardently—attached himself to Rosmini in the
quality of literary secretary ; but, for all that he was
regarded and treated as a member of the family,
he never abandoned his love of personal lowliness,
though he more than once resented, whimsically, the
notion of being dependent on others.

Before Rosmini had well settled down to his
studies, a letter from home informed him that the
air of Verona brought about no marked improvement in his brother's health. This news was all
the more affecting, as he felt that the choice of
life he himself had been inspired to make, would
cause his brother's state to weigh the more heavily.
on his parents' mind. He at once wrote to his
mother offering no mere boyish sympathy to soften

[1] *La Giovine Età di Rosmini.*—J. Bernardi.

her grief, but that loftier and sturdier condolence
which points to religion as the only true sweetener
of what human nature deems bitter :

Lo ! just at this moment a long letter brought to me
from home by three Roveretans. I open it on the instant
and recognise my dear father's handwriting, and find enclosed another from my dear mother. A precious gift
indeed for me. But alas ! the tidings of my brother's ill
health cause me the deepest and sincerest sorrow. Nevertheless, blessed be God in all things ! He from Whom
springs every blessing knows well why He sometimes min-
gles evil with good. Let us repose confidently in Him.
The heart that looks to God and leans on Him finds there
such comfort and such strength that not only the multitude,
but also those who pass for philosophers, regard it as a
marvel not to be credited.

Let men say if they will, aye let them boast that it is
characteristic of human nature to feel and smart under
affliction ; meanwhile, he who is conversant with the pro-
digies of religion knows how the Christian finds in his God
not only medicine to alleviate his sorrows but ineffable
consolation. Thus, when the clouds of bitter anguish have
passed away, a clear and bright serenity ensues, accompanied
by an inexpressible sweetness which often finds a solace
even in tears. However, the wise and virtuous conduct of
our Giuseppe would of itself be sufficient to soothe my grief.
If all have reason to feel contented with him (as my father
assures me ye have), I not least have cause for the completest satisfaction. For my part, I shall not fail to recommend him to God ; nay, I have him always present to my
mind when I go to prayer, praying for myself and for him
as for one identical person. God is very good and will hear
our prayers.

The news that Lorenzi is coming amongst us is joyful
beyond measure. I request you to congratulate this worthy
friend of ours most warmly on my behalf. With what joy

will he not be hailed here in Padua, by the students of the
University. It will, doubtless, be in a manner that can
leave him little cause for dissatisfaction. Their esteem for
him is very great. And who could do otherwise than vene-
rate the rival of Cornelius. Oh! good Lorenzi (suffer me
to apostrophise thee, while my enthusiasm is aroused and
carries me away!) O good Lorenzi, come amongst us!
Mayhap the honoured shades of the illustrious men of last
century who, treading the path of glory, addressed the citizens of Livy in the pure language of Tullius, will silently
exult in their tombs at seeing thee thus grace with thy presence the city that gave them birth.

PADUA: *January* 29, 1817.[1]

The Abate Lorenzi, who is here so fervidly
alluded to, was formerly one of his professors in the
Rovereto College, and stood so high amongst the
Latinists of the time that they who longed for a
healthy revival of Latin learning in Padua set
much store on his co-operation. In the efforts he
subsequently made to restore the old classics, young
Rosmini was one of his most efficient supporters.
The aid thus given in no way impeded the progress
of Antonio's theological course; for, though he
studied in every branch of learning, and set apart
much time for correspondence and for literary productions of various kinds, he did all with such admirable
order, both as to the division of work and hours, that
he was never much pressed for time or forced to do
anything in a perfunctory manner. And never did
he begin a task or a duty of any kind—never did he
turn from one study to another, or go from one

[1] *Epistolario*, Letter xiii.

lecture-room to another, or change his labours in any form, without saying aloud or mentally a short prayer. To God he offered everything he did or attempted to do, and from God he expected whatever success attended his efforts ; but, when no success followed, or when it was less than he hoped for, the failure, too, was accepted as from God.

Six months after young Rosmini had entered the University he took the Bachelor's degree 'with honour.' The event so little elated him, in the way that worldly usage made popular, that he would not permit his friends to celebrate it, except as he himself hallowed it, by a special thanksgiving in the church of St. Anthony.

With his University dignity fresh upon him, he went home for the summer vacation of 1817. He would have kept the honour hidden if he could, for the plaudits of society oppressed him, and while he was glad to see his father and mother pleased, he had otherwise little liking for the congratulations which met him at Rovereto, where a University degree had a meaning above its value. To him it was merely as the formal mark that the first stage in his course was passed, and that he was entitled to the vacation which immediately followed. This vacation implied an intermission of study ; but he took care that it brought no repose to him ; for he merely changed the subjects of study without diminishing the closeness of his application.

When about to return to Padua he reminded his parents that, having already spent a season in the

University without the vesture that should denote his vocation, the time had come for assuming it. This was a matter of far deeper significance to him than all 'the honour' connected with a Bachelor's degree. Much to his delight, the permission he sought was granted without hesitation, for no one any longer supposed that there was the least use in further delay.

Accordingly, on re-entering the Theological Faculty, he at once took the habit of an ecclesiastic. The solemnity with which he invested the act stood out in reproachful contrast with the more matter-of-course style too common amongst ecclesiastical students, even of the best ordinary type, like his cousin Fedrigotti who had already left Padua and given up his vocation. When at the University this young noble attached no importance to 'the scholastic assumption of the clerical habit,' and though a good, and, withal, a sensible youth, he thought as lightly of the seductive influences which attend worldly excitements, arguing that the cassock could confer no virtue, and social fascinations did not necessarily lead to sin. No sooner had Antonio received the cassock than he wrote to inform his kinsman of this change of dress, as a something of grave importance, and took occasion to add a wholesome warning against the dangers that beset those who deal too confidently with the allurements of worldly society :

  - To-day I wear for the first time the clerical habit. May God, who has called me to serve Him in His taber-

nacle, grant me a pure heart, an elevated mind, and a
soul full of zeal, that I may not be wanting in an office so
sublime. Pray for me, I beg of you, to this end, as I never
cease to do every moment myself, for I feel the heavy
burden that has been laid upon my shoulders. I trust confidently in Him through Whom I have entered the sheepfold. I also commend you continually to our Lord that
we may both walk together in His sight, and although by
diverse paths, not with diversity of purpose.

The students here at Padua, however much they regret
having lost you, approve, nevertheless, your new resolve, in
the event of your not having been called to the career upon
which you had first entered.

I shall be happy to hear how your studies progress. I
ardently wish you to make constant proficiency both in
knowledge and piety. Shun, more than death itself, that
which is the most pestilential of all the vices of youth ; for
nothing is easier than to fall, while nothing is more difficult
than to rise again. May the Blessed and most pure Virgin
protect you amid the many dangers to which, by the mere
force of circumstances, you are now exposed.

PADUA : *November* 7, 1817.[1]

Like St. Stanislas Kostka, he ever felt, and his
whole life proved, that 'the greater the devotion to
the Immaculate Virgin, the greater the splendour of
purity in holy souls.' Hence he never lost an opportunity of directing those he loved to revere and look
up to the Mother most Chaste—the Virgin of
Virgins. Milton, who so little understood the safeguards which Catholic piety provides for this
'brightest gem in the diadem of sanctity,' sang its
praises without supposing that it ever required more

[1] *Epistolario*, Letter xiv.

than ordinary care to keep it secure when in contact
with social defilements.

> So dear to heaven is saintly chastity,
> That, when a soul is found sincerely so,
> A thousand liveried angels lackey her.

But Rosmini, who had kept this virtue unspotted from
the cradle to the grave, never heard without great
pain that any of his young friends were thrown into
the whirl of worldly society ; for there, too surely,
would be many occasions in which the delicate
bloom of purity must run the risk of being sullied
by the breath of unbecoming conversations—many
occasions when the eye as well as the ear would have
its sensitive modesty shocked—many occasions when
social usage, without seeming to infringe any of the
proprieties, would smooth the path for the infringe-
ment of them all.

In later days Rosmini said more than once :
'When a youth is thrown into worldly society where he
has often to hear impious doctrines, wicked maxims,
abuses and calumnies against the Church and her
Ministers—when he is placed where his good habits
may be subverted and he himself gradually depraved
—alas ! how soon he gives attention to the lying
words of seducers ! How plausible they at first
seem, and, afterwards, how like the truth ! Then
how speedily he loses the Faith which he had
imbibed, as it were, at his mother's breast ! His
heart, once it is corrupted, seeks only the darkness in which he longs to hide from himself his

own moral turpitude; and this darkness—which the devil, by his agents, diffuses so densely—is welcomed with a joy not unlike that felt by the thief or the assassin, who hails a murky and tempestuous night as the safest for thefts or other crimes.'[1]

Again, on another solemn occasion we find him speaking thus : 'See the frivolous World, with its pompous raiment and flashing adornments, its immodest deportment and insipid courtesy, its loose sayings and wanton intimacies, its tables laden with delicate viands and delicious liquors, its effeminate assemblies and sensuous music, its seductive spectacles, with all else, in short, which can charm, excite, and intoxicate the senses—this World of which, as Holy Scripture says, the devil is prince, thus furnished with every variety of inciting lure, soon seduces the heart and deprives the mind of light.   Man, thus dazzled unto blindness, no longer sees the frightful abyss at his feet; and so he rushes headlong into it.'[2]

For himself, Rosmini had consistently renounced the World of which he, with good reason, thought as he did; he had renounced all the honours and enjoyments which it can offer, in great abundance, to those who, like him, had nobility of birth, vast talents, rare personal gifts, great wealth and strong consistency of purpose; he had renounced all lest he should stain his baptismal innocence and imperil

---

[1] *Rosmini's Discourses.*—Dis. 'The Light of the Holy Spirit.' London, Duffy and Son, 1882.

[2] *Rosmini's Discourses.*—Dis. 'The World and Love of Truth.'

the sanctity without which he would lose God. This was well known to his friends and acquaintances ; and therefore his warnings, his advice, his entreaties were seldom slighted and never deemed officious or out of place.

CHAPTER VI.

ROSMINI CLOSES HIS SECOND SEASON AT THE UNIVER-
SITY, AND RECEIVES MINOR ORDERS.

(A.D. 1817–1818.)

His one extravagance—Childish eagerness to purchase a valuable
library—How earnestly he entreats his parents to grant his request—His gratitude for their compliance—Fraternal advice on
the practice of Christian virtues—His great faith and humility—
His brother's visit to Padua—-How his studies progress—Preparing
for Minor Orders and testing his vocation—Receives Minor Orders
—Returns to Rovereto—Death of his uncle Ambrogio—How he
bears affliction.

THE moment Rosmini put on the distinctive garb of
an ecclesiastic, he considered himself bound to direct
his energies more exclusively to the duties of his
own college, and to follow a religious rule more
stringently than he had hitherto done. This is saying much; for the rule he already observed was as
strict as that which St. Francis of Sales used to live
up to when a member of the same University.[1]

Having grouped around him the students whose
piety he had proved, they formed a select society of

---

[1] Augustus de Sales, in his *Life of St. Francis,* gives the rule which
the young Saint had written for himself at Padua.   It much resembles
that which young Rosmini adopted, and, as Butler says, 'chiefly shows
his perpetual attention to the presence of God, his care to offer up every
action to Him, and implore His aid at the beginning of each.'

their own, and were independent of the glittering gaieties which so easily enamour young men, who seek and need occasional relaxation from the pressure of close study. Antonio's chosen companions indulged none of the extravagances to which high-spirited youths are too prone. Nevertheless, there was one 'extravagance,' so to call it, to which Rosmini yielded in those days—an extravagance that will hardly seem foolish or prodigal, in the eyes of parents who are called upon to defray heavy bills to meet the ordinary squanderings of University life.

On two occasions, since he entered the Theological Faculty at Padua, he applied for small amounts over his allowance to spend in—what? In club expenses? or horses? or dress? or convivial parties? or any personal gratification whatever? Nothing of the kind. He sought these little subsidies for urgent cases of charity, and it was in the same way that nine-tenths of his regular pocket allowance was spent. Beyond this, he next applied for means to purchase a library. There was nothing else, outside the range of 'charitable purposes,' for which the young philosopher would have appealed so energetically as we find him craving for this.

In the December of 1817 the private library of a once opulent Venetian family—the Veniers—was purchased by a Paduan bookseller, who intended to sell it again on his own account. As soon as this purchase reached Padua, Antonio was invited, as a lover and excellent judge of good books, to examine the collection privately. He examined, and was so delighted with what he saw that he longed, with the ardour of a child, to possess it. Next day he wrote on the subject to his uncle Ambrogio, who, in such matters, needed no more than the nephew's hint; but, unfortunately, the good old man was, at the time, so ill it became necessary to bring the affair directly before the father. This was a far more difficult and awkward task for Antonio than the composition of an essay on libraries would have been.

He had never before requested a favour implying such an outlay, and he hardly knew how to frame a personal petition which seemed to ask for something that was to gratify a personal wish rather than a personal want. In fact, he had to become a child for the occasion, and the three letters he wrote on the business are characterised by all the simplicity and eagerness with which a child pleads, the sedate style of the young philosopher being, for the moment, in abeyance. These three letters were despatched to Rovereto in one wrapper, and addressed to Don Orsi, his earliest preceptor in philosophy, whose affection for his former pupil had strengthened with his years, and whose influence with the parents had never decreased.

The first letter was intended for Orsi himself, to whom the delicate negotiation was entrusted, not merely because of his influence, but because Rosmini (as he afterwards informed Tommaseo) knew that if this wise Priest thought the request unadvisable he would say so, and be sure that, however much the library was coveted, its possession would give little pleasure if there were anything unreasonable in the desire to have it, or if the application were inopportune. Here is how the friendly mediator was entreated to use his influence :—

I beg you to pardon me for giving you so much trouble. But our friendship on the one hand, and your goodness towards me on the other, encourage me to do so. I enclose you a letter, and wish you to give it to my mother *with all possible secrecy.* I will tell you all. I am desirous of purchasing a library, and have written to my father, without however openly asking him to buy it for me. See if you can urge my mother, for I know what influence you exercise over her. Come now, use your eloquence with her ; I am sure you will do so.

It is a superb collection of volumes which once belonged to the illustrious Venetian family, Venier. Amongst other things there is a precious selection of Greek and Latin classics, editions, too, of great value. I should esteem myself fortunate if I had it. You remember the task you yourself imposed on me—to form a library that would do honour to our town and be useful to all our friends. I know how you prize the fair projects we were wont to plan between ourselves. Now is the time to put them in practice. I doubt not my mother will allow herself to be persuaded easily Come, like a good, dear friend, do what you can, and, in the event of success, you will then begin to see realised the desires that are common to both of us. I am delighted to find them partly realised in your case, by your appointment to the Rectorship of the Ginnasio. Great, indeed, was my joy,—my hopes are unbounded. I embrace you affectionately.

PADUA : *January* 3, 1818.[1]

The appeal to the Countess, enclosing that to his

[1] *Epistolario,* Letter xvii.

father, was couched in terms certain to gain her advocacy, without the eloquent aid so nervously sought.
Like the letter to Don Orsi, it was meant to give her
also an opportunity of withholding the subject altogether from Pier Modesto, if such a course was
deemed best. It ran thus :—

On numberless occasions I have experienced the love
you bear me, and I know that you, my dearest mother,
have at heart my welfare. Now, however, you can give me
a special proof of this your love. For eight hundred florins
I can purchase a magnificent library. Remember, God
has not given you the means you possess without a purpose.
Whatever be the issue, I shall be always your most devoted
child, and shall sigh for the opportunity of testifying the
ardent and sincere love I cherish for you. I ought perhaps
to say no more, as I have every confidence in you.

After all, what more fitting manner of employing your
riches, than in rendering happy, in this world, a son who
desires nothing save the honour of God, and the welfare
of his beloved parents. You have done a great deal
for nephews. You will, surely, do no less for a son.
If God has blessed you with riches, He has given them to
you to be employed on such an occasion. Heaven's choicest
blessings will be showered on you—upon you who use its
favours so well. In short, I fear nothing, while I hope
everything. After reading the letter you find enclosed,
hand it to my father when you think the moment favourable.

PADUA : *January* 3, 1818.[1]

The letter on which the Countess Rosmini was
to exercise her maternal diplomacy put no direct
request before the father; but trusting to the gentle

[1] *Epistolario*, Letter xv.

hints which always had been enough for uncle Ambrogio, it took this timid form :

The opening of the New Year is ever wont to give me marked pleasure, as it affords an occasion of expressing to my fond parents the genuine feelings of filial affection and respect I treasure up for them within my heart. I never cease to implore for them the blessings and graces which I firmly trust may pour from Heaven on their heads, and render them happy during the few fast-fleeting days of their sojourn on earth, and be more perfectly with them in eternity. All that I thus pray for, you, beloved father, can more easily imagine than I describe. And with my parents I always associate the name of my uncle, who well merits the love I cherish for him, because of the great affection he has shown to me. I include in the same good wishes my brother and sister, with all the other members of our family.

I have nothing new to relate to you, except a matter in which literature and the nobler studies are concerned. The illustrious Venetian family Venier, which took so important a part in the affairs of the Republic, being now in reduced circumstances have been forced to part with their library for a mere trifle. What shall I say to you ? Oh ! what books ! What rare editions ! What a precious acquisition ! What a rich collection of volumes ! How much labour and money expended in its formation ! And, mark this ! they have been purchased by a bookseller here at Padua who knows little or nothing of their worth—the person from whom I had most of the books I purchased here.

There was instantly a rush of learned men to see them. Even the Bishop, hearing of it, sent immediately to make enquiries ; but the bookseller, not having at the time unpacked the cases, did not show them to any one. I was the first to see them after they had been unpacked, and on seeing them I was astounded. I asked how much he would require for them in the gross, and learned that he would part with them all for a little more than eight hundred florins. Oh! what emotions I then experienced! It would be difficult to imagine them. And, on the other hand, how downcast I became at seeing the impossibility of making the purchase. For eight hundred florins to acquire, in one moment, a library which cost so much labour, time, and money in its formation! But I must have patience. . . .

I could not refrain from doing immediately two things, which can injure no one. First, I resolved to write and acquaint you with the matter; nor have I courage to say more : Secondly, to entreat the bookseller not to show the books to any one until I received an answer from home.

Be the result what it may, I have nothing more at heart than to be perfectly submissive to you in everything, and to give you consolation at all times. Kissing your hand and imploring your paternal benediction, &c.

PADUA : *January* 3, 1818.[1]

His request, after all, stood in no need of so much anxious urging. A youth whose whole life had been one of strict frugality, whose *personal* expenses had ever been far within the allowance voluntarily made to him, whose appeals to the bounty of his parents were ever for others and never for self, had little reason to fear that this modest petition would have met with an unfavourable reception. However, as the family library at Rovereto was already well stocked with excellent books, and con-sidered equal to any private library in that region, he thought it possible that his father—whose tastes were not literary—might look upon this purchase in the light of an extravagance. Besides, Pier Modesto was not 'lord of the manor' while Ambrogio lived,

[1] *Epistolario*, Letter xvi.

and might have had some prudential hesitation arising from his position. But, whatever private opinion the father held on the desirability of the possession, he made no delay in granting the necessary authority to complete the bargain. His grateful son promptly acknowledged the kindness in these terms :

Most esteemed and beloved Father,—I am to-day in receipt of your letter of the 7th inst. It has filled me with joy, since by it I learn that you kindly accede to my wishes respecting the Venier library. My joy, however, springs less from the favour itself, than from the signal proof you thus gave me of your paternal love, which I so much appreciate. My gratitude knows no bounds, and I wish you to accept this letter as the expression of my most cordial acknowledgments. The recollection of your goodness shall never be effaced from my heart, nor will I ever cease to pour forth my fervent prayers to God that He may shower His blessings on you ;—those blessings especially which are calculated to sanctify the soul on earth and secure its happiness in Heaven. By my behaviour I shall always endeavour to give you, in the future, as I have ever tried to do in the past, palpable proof of the respectful love I cherish for you in my heart, and of my eagerness to afford you every consolation.

I beg of you, after having read the enclosed letter, to hand it to my brother.

PADUA, *January* 8, 1818.[1]

Not a word does he here say to imply that his admiration for the library continued unabated. But, in a letter of thanks written to his mother about the same time, he thus touches the subject with the

---

[1] *Epistolario*, Letter xvii.

ardour of a bibliophile : 'Oh, dearest mother, you should see what treasures I have thus acquired! What a stroke of good fortune was this for me! Had I to procure these books in any other way, I should have to spend upon them another thousand florins at least. Make known my joy to our confidant Don Orsi ; to the rest say nothing, for I wish to astonish them on my arrival.' [1]

When the father wrote to authorise the purchase of the library he communicated to Antonio some information about the moral state of his brother Giuseppe which seemed to ask for the letter alluded to as ' enclosed.' It was therefore written promptly, and without allowing his great eagerness to conclude the buying of the library to interfere for a moment with his sense of filial and fraternal duty ; besides, the first practical return for the favour received ought not, he thought, be deferred for any personal gratification whatever. Brotherly advice on the practice of Christian virtues was a theme in which he was much more at home than when he endeavoured to formulate a request that might have the appearance o f a selfish wish. Hence, in this letter he is no longer the nervous boy gazing at a desirable prize, but once more the sedate moralist pointingout the path to virtue.

I have not written to you sooner, partly because I was immersed in my theological studies, and partly because other duties kept me busy, robbing me of all the spare moments that should otherwise have been mine. . . .

[1] *Epistolario*, Letter xix.

But of what shall I speak to you now? How shall I best give you a signal proof of my sincere and true fraternal love? My dear brother, in what better manner can true affection be known than through the desire of succouring our friends,—a desire which shows itself in word as well as deed. By this letter, then, I earnestly wish to encourage you to steadily advance more and more in virtue. May the sweet fragrance which your virtue diffuses around be a source of joy and gladness to your elders, while of good example and instruction to those of your own age. Oh! how beautiful, how lovely is virtue! It is prized by all good men, and even the wicked themselves esteem it. They who possess it find in it interior peace and consolation. Happy the household whose members are wise and virtuous. I speak, dearest bother, of Christian virtue, for no other is genuine. True it is, that the words I thus utter strike only the ear, and that it is God alone Who speaks to the heart ; yet, I confidently trust that the prayers of the good, in whom the Holy Spirit prays with unutterable sighs, will give efficacy to my words. Do you, too, raise your voice in our behalf to the Father of Lights, that He may open our minds and hearts to the truth, which, falling from the lips of holy men, may, like gentle rain, fertilise the seeds of virtue within us, so as to plentifully yield fruit that will reach maturity.

And how, dearest brother, does God distribute His graces? You must be already well aware of the manner. You know that it is not always in an extraordinary or miraculous way ; nor yet all of a sudden. How few and exceptional are the instances we have of God's despoiling us all at once of the old man, and so clothing us with the new, as to be, in a moment, re-born, as it were, and renewed in Christ Jesus. And if He has done so in some rare occasions, as, for instance, in the case of Saul, yet even with him did He not subsequently make use, also, of ordinary and human means ? Did He not ordain that Saul should recover his eyesight by means of Ananias, to whom he was sent not

only for this end, but that he might also be filled with the
Holy Ghost by the imposition of hands ?

Yes, God in most cases makes use of human agencies ;
and in how many different ways ? He speaks to us lovingly
as well by adversity as by prosperity ; as well by events
which further our own desires as by those that thwart and
destroy them ; by persons who wish us ill as well as by
those who love us. Everything, then, comes to us from this
good Father of ours Whose dwelling place is in the Heavens
above. He gives us only what is good for us, since He
loves us as brothers of His first born Jesus Christ : His
very chastisements are gifts and precious invitations of His
Grace. What then should sadden us amid the vicissitudes
of life ? Nothing but our own sins ; and even for this holy
sadness with which God justly afflicts us His infinite goodness gives us ample compensation by stretching forth His
arms to receive and clasp us to His bosom, opening to us
a refuge in His very heart, where, as it were, in an ocean of
mercy and delight, we may wash and blot away all our
imperfections and miseries.

Let nothing then, dearest brother, disturb us ; let nothing,
not even our faults, perplex or overwhelm us in this life.
But, above all, let us jealously take care that we love
the things our Heavenly Father loves, that is, our own
good, the salvation of our soul, as much interior peace as
we can have in this wretched vale of tears, and the complete bliss of that life which is eternal and unchangeable.
O God ! what ingratitude, what folly, would it not be to
close our ears to the voice of so good a Father,—a voice
which teaches us nought else but the way to acquire happiness ! Or rather what hatred against ourselves would not
this show ! I confess, dear brother, that I hear this voice in
all which befalls me, be it of a prosperous or an adverse
character ; in every circumstance in which I find myself ;
in all the discourses I listen to I hear it, whether it is my
superior, or my inferior, or my equal who speaks ; I hear it
also whether listening to the learned or the ignorant, for

God at times speaks even by the mouth of the abject and lowly.

Thus it is, my dear brother, that I give you a pledge of genuine love, urging you to be ever ready to open your ears and your heart to the constant instructions which God gives us through the medium of our fellow-men. You will thus walk in a way full of light and safety, you will be the admiration and model of your fellow-citizens, a source of confusion and reproach to the wicked, and the delight of all the good. Our beloved parents will shed tears of joy on your account. We, your brother and sister, will mingle our glad tears with theirs, and all our friends their tears with ours. And how many good souls are there not who love you sincerely? Have not many virtuous men given you proof thereof by their solicitude and anxiety for you? And for whom else can we be anxious or solicitous if it be not for those whom we love? They who merit neither love nor esteem are neglected, forsaken, and left to wallow uncared for in the mire of their own passions. Such is not your case, dear brother; for I see that when you do well all rejoice, and when you act otherwise all are afflicted and bitterly complain. Now, all this comes from love and tenderness for you. Ah! dearest brother, hide not from yourself those who love you; seek rather to know them, and knowing them to love them in return.

To me, assuredly, nothing is sweeter than to love my friends; nay more, to embrace all men in this love, to second the exertions which others make in my behalf, to correspond with them, and, if you like it, I will even say, to bear patiently with their defects. For who is wholly without defects? In bearing with others, I rejoice that I thus observe the precept God has given us by the mouth of St. Paul, ' Bear ye one another's burdens.' Moreover I hope thus to merit, in some measure, the patient forbearance of others in my own shortcomings. Nay, carrying my thoughts still higher, I sincerely trust God Himself will bear with them, and pardon me; and hence I say, with confidence : ' Forgive us our trespasses as we forgive them that trespass against us ; ' otherwise, in these words I should invoke my own condemnation.

Ah ! you already recognise in what I say the language of love, and, if it be that you do so, what may I not promise myself ? You will be a wiser and more perfect man in every way. I verily believe that no one can resist the force of love.

But I will say even more to you. I will point out to you how you may fulfil my wishes. Well then, pray God to give you light : pray very much and fervently, and then choose a learned and prudent director. Having done so, be persuaded that it is through his instrumentality God will enrich you with His graces : place yourself entirely and with all confidence in this director's hands ; take every pains to make him well acquainted with your condition as well as with all that passes within you ; let there not be a corner of your heart, how remote soever and small it may be, that you search not thoroughly, and then make your director a sharer of its secrets. Adhere scrupulously to his counsels and commands, and you will be treading a sure and easy path. These words are not the dictates of idle caprice; I have consulted men of the greatest experience and have also read the mcst instructive books on the subject, and all say the same thing. The greatest and most discreet directors of souls—-the amiable St. Francis of Sales at their head—all concur in saying that the safest road to virtue, and the one, moreover, which God requires from many persons, is that of obedience to their director.

· PADUA : *January* 7, 1818.[1]

Faith and humility were so deeply rooted in his own soul that the obedience he commended to his brother was for himself an ordinary practice. This holy obedience which non-Catholics look upon

[1] *Epistolario*, Letter xx.

as slavish, this humility which they deem a something servile, is but the regular, the easy, the
inevitable outcome of profound faith. As these twin
virtues held complete possession of Rosmini's heart
and mind, he never took any step trusting to his own
judgment. Like all the Saints he had a clear per-
ception of the utter helplessness of the human mind
when left to itself, and the total insufficiency of the
natural powers of man to procure his own happiness
or even to shield him from innumerable evils. So
rooted in his soul was the conviction that Christian
faith was a necessity of the foremost order, that 'it is
impossible to say how much he delighted to set forth
and extol the heavenly blessing of this virtue.
Whenever he spoke on the subject (which happened
very frequently) his conversation became animated
immediately; the colour rose to his face, which was
naturally rather pale; his eyes sparkled, and the tone
of his voice, conveying the emotion of his heart,
made a deep impression on all who heard him.'[1]

When this letter to his brother was posted, he
felt free to settle with the bookseller and arrange
about sending the library on to Rovereto. Shortly
afterwards, his brother got permission to visit him at
the University, as it was hoped that a few weeks
spent in Padua might prove beneficial to the invalid's
soul and body. Antonio had much satisfaction in
welcoming this dear guest at a time when most
students, similarly situated, would have deemed any

---

[1] *An Outline of the Life of Rosmini*, translated from the Italian and
edited by Rev. W. Lockhart, p. 71. London, 1856.

visit of the kind less a source of comfort than of annoyance, for it took place while he was actively
engaged in pious preparations for receiving in a
becoming manner the Tonsure and Minor Orders.
The affectionate young host, however, so enjoyed
the burden of charity that he found means of regulating his hours in a way that made Giuseppe's visit
a delight to both, notwithstanding a considerable increase in the religious exercises and studies occa-
sioned by the important step he was on the eve of
taking.   How those studies prospered can be inferred from the following letter to his cousin Fedrigotti, then at Innsbruck :—

My studies have been, so far, most successful. An
extra year has been added to the course of theology. I
have not suffered thereby, as they consider me in my third
year. The examens now take place twice a year; and,
thanks to God, I have passed the first of these successfully.
My health is excellent, and study appears to me every day
a source of greater pleasure. I have my brother with me,
who keeps me company, and we are quite happy together.

Meanwhile, I am testing my vocation, and the infinite
bounty of God confirms me, every day, more and more in
my resolve. Nay, I must tell you that, on Sunday next,
his Lordship the Bishop of Padua will confer on me the
Minor Orders, as they are called. Ah! pray for me that,
having entered the fold by the door, I may behave like a
true shepherd, and not act as a vile hireling. I, too, will
pray for you, to the end that we may both reach the same
goal—the Beatific Vision—although we pursue different
roads to arrive at it.

I must mention to you another matter which, because of
our friendship, will interest you not a little. You must
know, then, that I have purchased a number of very fine

books, and have already sent home fifteen cases, five of which are much larger than those of last year ; the rest I have still here with me. This is due to the goodness of my father, who furnished me with a large sum of money. I expended on them more than one hundred louis d'or, but they are worth twice the money. You, perhaps, have also made some purchases, which are likely to be useful, not only to yourself, but to your friends and fellow-towns-men. I know that you had excellent intentions, which, surely, have not been suffered to remain in abeyance. In case you should not have purchased any books, let me advise you to do so without delay.

PADUA : *May* 13, 1818.[1]

During the two days immediately following the date of this letter, he remained in absolute retire-ment, from which he came forth to be enrolled amongst the Clerics, and solemnly tonsured. On the next day—May 16, 1818—he received the four Minor Orders from Monsignor Scipione, then Bishop of Padua. Thenceforth he attached the title ' Acolyte ' to his name, by way of signifying his high appreciation of the dignity which belongs even to Minor Orders.

The summer vacation for that year came on soon after these events, and he returned to Rovereto where his venerable uncle lay on the bed of death. With a fond longing, the good old man awaited the coming home of the beloved young Acolyte, and when his wish to embrace him had been gratified death stepped in, and on July 10, 1818, Ambrogio Rosmini calmly slept the sleep of the just. The ' golden opinions ' he had won from men while he lived

[1] *Epistolario*, Letter xxi.

amongst them, were gently laid on his tomb by more than one panegyrist. Antonio contented himself with the tribute of fervent prayers and such outpourings of eulogy as found a vent in private letters, like the following brief note written at Rovereto on August 4 to his distinguished kinsman, the Chevalier Carlo Rosmini, Historian of Milan :

To-day you will have received a formal announcement of the grievous loss we have sustained in the death of my beloved uncle, whom I always regarded as a father, and who ever treated me as a son. May our Lord, Who is no less good when He afflicts than when He consoles us, be blessed even for this! I especially thank Him that, faithful as He is, He does not suffer us to be tempted above that which we are able, but makes with temptation issue that we may be able to bear it . . . In so much sorrow the sanctity of his death comforts me, and there is a sad consolation in the tears of all the good who have lost a friend and a virtuous citizen, and especially in the tears of the poor who sought in every way to show their sense of desolation, and have wept bitterly for one whom they revered as a father.

At no time of his life had the afflictions and adversities that wreck the happiness of most men power to disturb the peace of Rosmini's mind. For him afflictions and adversities, come whence and how they might, were as blessings in disguise which, by forcing the heart from earthly to heavenly things, bring home to us the imperishable joys we can gain in exchange for perishable ones.

CHAPTER VII.

ROSMINI'S EVERY-DAY LIFE AT THE UNIVERSITY.

(A.D. 1818-1819.)

How he met sympathy in sorrow—Religious instruction pervading all his conversations—How his recreation was spent—A collegiate society of charity—His poetry and his 'spare time'—His correspondence always conveying a lesson—How he blent pious advice and interesting news—Visit of the Emperor Francis I. of Austria to Padua—Rosmini's share in the public rejoicings—He prepares for Holy Orders—Asks permission to receive the Subdiaconate—The wish of the Acolyte Rosmini in 1818 like that of Pope Pius IX. in 1848—Stimulates his brother and sister to zeal in piety and study—Fosters his sister's religious vocation—Why he would not take the degree of doctor when ready for it, and why he put off the time for receiving the Subdiaconate—His own account of his daily life in Padua.

ON resuming his studies at Padua in 1818 our young Acolyte had occasion to exhibit some of those virtues which are best seen in affliction. He found himself overwhelmed with expressions of sympathy, for all his friends knew how deeply he loved his uncle. This condolence was met by gentle thanks, with evidences of that complete resignation to God's Will which so few can feel and so few can understand. He reminded them, as Tommaseo tells us, that the separation was no more than a brief absence from home—from that home to which the virtuous Ambrogio had gone, that home to which each could claim an heir's right of entrance, and to which he himself would, more earnestly than ever, try to make good his claim.

With new zeal he continued his religious exercises, and with enfreshened industry set to his studies, resolved to complete the University course before the next vacation.

Although he seemed to be more than ever absorbed in study or prayer, his horary still allowed times of recreation, which he willingly shared with his intimate friends. Many of those friends have left eulogistic testimony as to the fascinating conversations with which he gave a healthy glow to the leisure hours passed in their company. All describe him as a delightful companion, gifted in a remarkable degree with the art of making those who conversed with him quite at their ease, whether they were rich or poor, learned or ignorant. His favourite subjects were drawn from the store-room of philosophy ; but he never allowed a pet theme to obtrude itself when he was speaking with those who did not relish or comprehend it. His own views on any matter under discussion were held in check, where they might prove to be inopportune, or were likely to offend the honest prejudices of others.

But whatever the topic, grave or gay, he lost no opportunity in skilfully throwing in a moral lesson, or drawing forth some important religious instruction ; for religion was the one theme which he never set aside —the one theme he took care to render always opportune and never offensive.

What he called his 'regular recreation' was not always spent in agreeable conversations within chambers with approved friends, or while taking delightful rambles in quest of bracing air and scenes sacred to religion or art. Often it was directed to literary work which he regarded as a 'relaxation,' and to which he gave most of the spare moments that were not classed as 'regular recreation.'

More than once he tried to induce some of his intimate friends to join him in forming a collegiate society of charity, which might be made to utilise some portion of the 'regular recreation' time, as well as sundry odd periods in the day, for the spiritual and temporal benefit of others. But, as the fundamental rule of the society he proposed, required, first of all, the moral perfection of its own members, he was unable to bring his companions to the hard task of endeavouring to begin by making themselves exceptionally good. Therefore, the 'spare time' he wished to employ in this kind of united action, as well as much of his 'regular recreation' hours, was applied to the 'literary relaxations' just alluded to.

This literary pastime included translations from the Fathers, and essays on various subjects. St. Augustine's work *De Catechizandis rudibus* was one of the translations then and thus made at Padua, and afterwards turned to practical account elsewhere.[1] During the spare moments, too, he

---

[1] Eight editions of this little work have appeared in Italy, 'always

occasionally relieved the mind in poetry. Sometimes
the subject was sacred, sometimes plaintive, and
sometimes joyous, but always true to his dominant
piety. Now and then he published letters in verse,
like those addressed to his college companions
Appollonia and Tommaseo on the charms of solitude, study, and friendship.[1] Now and then, also,
he indulged in sonnets to honour some event in a
friend's career, as on the occasion of his fellow-
student the Baron Candelpergher taking the degree
of Doctor in Laws. This sonnet is supposed to be
the last he wrote, and, on that account, claims a
translation here, which does not, however, pretend
to reflect fully such merit as the original verses
possess :

> Man's rights, beloved friend, and sacred laws
> (Whether 'twas nature graved them on the breast,
> Or men of old, thus joined in common cause
> That greed and guilt might sternly be repressed)
>
> So well thou guardest, with such watchful zeal—
> To evil shut, God-fearing, free from stain,—
> That virtue's friends a silent rapture feel,
> While foes to virtue gnash their teeth in vain.

with ecclesiastical approval.' The first edition was published in Milan
in 1838, the second in the same city in 1844 ; the third edition appeared
in Naples, 1849 ; the fourth in Florence, 1850; the fifth in Pisa, 1854 ;
the sixth in Rovereto, 1860; the seventh in Turin, 1863 ; and the eighth
in Intra, 1878. It has also been translated into French and German.

[1] In the 'poetic epistle' addressed to Tommaseo (and which was
printed in Rovereto) occur these significant lines :—

> ' Hither and thither, whizzing up and down,
> There crowd my brain a thousand various thoughts
> Which mighty Plato woke to busy life,
> And Aristotle of the eagle eye
> Enkindled there, and blind Mœonides,
> Undying bard, aroused, or I myself
> Filch'd from the store of younger sages.'

'Tis thus, good youth, whose laureled brows attest
Fresh deeds of merit, that a man attains
Great name *above*, his truest meed and best :
So will it tide (a guerdon worth the pains !)
That the great Angel of the scales proclaim
Thy own renown to be thy country's fame.[1]

But, while much of the 'spare time' which his horary provided as a release from severe study was given to pious duties, and to literary productions of a more or less serious kind, much of it was also taken up with letter-writing. From time to time we record some of these letters as they happen to come in the regular course of our narrative, confining ourselves, however, to his familiar correspondence as that which best portrays the individual character, and shows, in his own ordinary words, what manner of man he was.

No matter what the occasion which called for a letter—no matter whether the theme was scientific or complimentary, or whether the letter itself was long or short—the spirit of religion diffused itself through all. Every sentence in some way attested an increasing recognition of God's presence, a constant

[1]   Le sacre leggi, e i dritti, o dolce amico,
Sia che natura in petto all' uom scolpio,
Sia che a fren del costume avaro e rio
Pose patto inviolabile et antico,

Tu che al mal chiuso, vigile e pudico,
Sempre vivesti ubbidiente a Dio,
Serba, e difendi, onde s' allegri il pio,
Fremendo invan, chi di virtù è nemico.

Così, o garzon, che di novel valore
Porti di lauro in sulla chioma insegna,
Si poggia al vero ed immortale onore ;

Anzi così (chè ell' è mercè ben degna)
Della patria e d' ognun faratti onore
Colei che in Ciel colla bilancia regna.

looking towards eternity, an ever-growing love of the creature for the Creator, of the redeemed for the Redeemer. The most common-place topics were deftly interwoven with pious reflections or exhortations dictated by an intense reverence for God, and they were invariably fitted to a special need.

Take, for instance, the simple 'family letter' with which his familiar correspondence for 1818 may be said to have closed. It was a response to the customary Christmas greetings of his mother; but, not content with a reciprocation of these, it passed on to give certain *advice* that may seem to be out of place or purposeless, and to mention a certain *fact* which may seem to be nothing more than an 'interesting piece of news.' Both the advice and the fact had, however, a set purpose beyond their seeming.

The 'advice' had its set purpose in this way. During the vacation which was saddened by his uncle's death, he discovered that his sister Margherita adhered, with unshaken affection, to the religious exercises which began when they 'played at monks' together in the family garden at Rovereto. He had long refrained from leading her mind in any way towards the cloister, lest her free choice should owe anything to the influence he was known to hold over her, and the grace of vocation be tinged with a human motive. But, seeing that the evidences of a religious vocation which were conspicuous in her girlhood were still so much so that her mother thought it expedient to check them, he felt it a duty to interfere for their encouragement. Hence 'the advice' which he dexterously mantled in the message the letter conveyed.

The fact or 'interesting piece of news' had its set purpose in this way : Throughout North Italy and the Tyrol the French invasion had left behind it a sediment of unchristian philosophy which so sadly tainted the public schools that many of their most promising students began to look coldly on devotion and to scoff at the relics of saints. Amongst those whose minds had thus been poisoned was a young Roveretan kinsman of Rosmini, who valued his opinion highly, and who was certain to have an opportunity of profiting by that opinion so modestly but effectively put in this letter, which the Countess was sure to read for the benefit of her misled nephew :—

I thank you, most esteemed and beloved mother, for your welcome letter of Christmas Day, to which I at once reply. My health is excellent. Indeed, I think it has been unusually good during the year. I wish you and my father, with all at home, the graces of this holy season. May the new year be replete with those blessings which fade not away, but endure even after death, when we shall be fully able to realise their worth.

Remember me affectionately to Giuseppe, and warmly recommend to him prayer, devotion, and, above all, the frequentation of the Sacraments, these being the channels through which God distributes His Graces most abundantly. Sustain my sister every day more, not less by your words than by your fervent prayers. Tell her from me that God requires much from her, and that, consequently, He will give her much, unless she should, on her part, be slow in co-operating with His Graces. Let her, indeed, apply herself very diligently to study, but far more to prayer,—especially to that prayer which comes from the depth of the heart.

I daily experience more and more the goodness of God, and though I so imperfectly correspond with it, I find it everywhere continue to manifest itself to me.

The body of the glorious St. Francis which had been lost has lately been discovered at Assisi.[1] This is a most precious relic. They say that the posture of the body is still just as it was before all trace of it was lost. The Pope has sent some persons of great weight to ascertain the truth of the matter, and he purposes to come himself to Assisi, next May, in order to celebrate, with great pomp, the exposition of the relics to public veneration. Meanwhile, he forbids anyone, under pain of excommunication, to enter the place where the body rests, and which he caused to be most carefully walled up. Let us give thanks to God who has willed to glorify His saint in this new manner.

PADUA : *December* 27, 1818.[2]

In March 1819, Padua had the honour of an

---

[1] In the year 1230 Pope Gregory IX. caused the body of St. Francis to be placed, standing upright, in a secret vault, under a magnificent new church which he directed to be built on the hill where criminals were formerly executed outside the walls of Assisi, and to this hill the Holy Father gave the new name of Mount Paradise. It was the spot which the Saint himself, when dying, designated as his place of sepulture. Three ' superb churches,' built one above the other, covered the vault, which was set within a costly chapel of marble. The body of the saint was ' never more seen from that time forth,' and its precise resting place remained unknown until it was revealed by the accidental discovery to which Rosmini alludes. A tradition amongst the conventual Friars of the Monastery on Mount Paradise held that the body would be found in a perfect state and in the same standing posture in which Pope Gregory IX. left it. The investigation made by order of Pius VII. is said to have confirmed this tradition ; but the precautions taken six centuries before were again adopted, and the casket containing the relics was once more walled away from sight.

[2] *Epistolario,* Letter xxii.

Imperial visit, which threw 'all Patavium' into a whirl of excitement. Francis I. of Austria was there on his way to Rome, and his Paduan subjects, forgetting everything but his presence, welcomed him with warm manifestations of public joy. Many of the University professors and most of the students drew away from the peaceful monotony of college life to share in the sight-seeing, if not in the exultant *vivas.*

Rosmini, however, continued his ordinary course as well as the distracting enthusiasm around him permitted. Loyalty was with him an hereditary quality, always deep and calm ; but even if he had some politic reason, like that which moved the Paduans, to display it boisterously, his strong dislike of noisy festivity would have kept him back. He was, therefore, one of the few students who held aloof from the excitement; and he quietly prayed for a satisfactory settlement of the matter which led the Emperor to Rome, while the multitude vehemently cheered, without knowing the object of the journey. There was yet another reason for his seclusion. He was just then absorbed in preparations for the Subdeaconate—for solemn service close to the King of kings—and a dignified composure seemed to him more consistent with these preparations than the impassioned delight in which the city revelled.

The local gazettes of that time tell us that the popular acclaims and exuberant merry-makings which then filled Padua for several days, confused the students' minds for months afterwards, and gave them material for sonnets, essays, and letters to the end of the season. But Antonio Rosmini dismissed the whole subject in one short paragraph, dropped casually into a letter asking his father's permission to receive the Subdeaconate :

Most esteemed and beloved Father,

Amid the many public and private occupations which duty and relaxation impose on me, it always yields me great pleasure to find a few spare moments to spend with you, by writing to you—now, at least, when I can be with you in no other way.

I hope my present visit will find you enjoying excellent health, despite the many cares which embarrass you. Would that I could render you some assistance ! I trust, however, my brother, who is so generously disposed, will supply my place.

We had the Emperor and princes of the Imperial court here lately, and, as they stayed in our street, we were, for several days, put about by the clamorous rejoicings that everywhere reigned supreme. He is *en route* for Rome, and *I earnestly wish* that all the affairs may be satisfactorily adjusted. That such will be the case I confidently hope, through the mercy of that God who will be invoked by as many saints as the Church possesses.

Regarding myself, the time at length has arrived when my age will permit me to receive the Subdeaconate. I have, therefore, to ask your kind permission to take this step, and at the same time to entreat you to furnish me with what is requisite on such an occasion. I should like to be ready for the Saturday preceding Passion Sunday. Should you happen to see the Archpriest, will you be pleased to ask him to procure the dimissorial letters for me in good time for that day, which will be the 26th inst. ?

PADUA : *March* 7, 1819.[1]

[1] *Epistolario,* Letter xxiii.

The satisfactory adjustment for which he so fervently prayed was 'peace with Christ's Vicar : ' 'the
removal,' says Tommaseo, 'from the Austrian code
of whatever laws violated the liberty of the Church,
and had been reproved constantly by the sovereign
Pontiffs.' Some thirty years later, Pius IX., in an
Encyclical given while an exile in Gaëta, expressed
himself much to the same effect. Thus, the 'earnest
wish' and 'confident hope' of the Roveretan Acolyte
was then, as in his earliest and latest years, in perfect accord with the wish and hope of one of the
most zealous chief pastors of God's Church.[1]

When writing to his mother, soon after the Imperial visit, Antonio made no allusion whatever to
it. The only subject he cared to bring before her
sufficiently explains the omission. How could the
petty gossip of worldly society interest one so wholly
devoted to thoughts of heavenly life ? Probably
the Countess Rosmini would have liked a little Court
news ; but she expected nothing of the sort when
she opened this letter, where she found what she
thought much more likely to be there—an entreaty
to stimulate his brother and sister to zeal in piety
and study :—

I am much obliged to you, both for your welcome letter
and for your solicitude with regard to the Subdeaconship.
I rejoice to learn that you are all well. From my brother's
letter, too, I have had good news, which has afforded me
sincere pleasure.

Exhort my sister not to abate her fervour, nor courage,
nor study, nor good works. Let her be assured that fer-

[1] See the Encyclical of Pio Nono, given at Gaëta, Feb. 18, 1849.

vour obtains of God courage ; that courage, having its
fountain head in God, calls forth meditation, prudence, and
study ; that study regulates action, and, finally, that wisely
ordered action is advantageous both to ourselves and others.
I am desirous of knowing whether in her meditations she
makes use of books ; for this is very necessary in her case.
Animate, counsel, and support her.   My father, I have no
doubt, will do the same.

I think it very desirable that just and holy maxims
should ring continually in my brother's ears ; for, by dint of
hearing them often repeated, they become more and more
deeply impressed on the heart.   For this reason the true
lover of wisdom is ever eager to hear such maxims, since
he is thus enabled to advance in wisdom : ' A wise man
shall hear and be wiser,' says the Holy Spirit (Prov. i. 5).[1]

The special concern he thus manifested in
what related to his sister had a special cause. He
knew, as we have seen, that Margherita's vocation
to the Religious State met with opposition at home.
She had recently made an earnest effort to join a
Teresian community (English Dames) long established in Rovereto ; but, as her parents would not
sanction the step, it had to be abandoned. This
failure, however, did not chill her ardent desire to
give herself wholly to the service of God ; so, when
drawn back from the door of a convent, where she
looked for opportunities of exercising charity in its
most perfect form, she resolved to seek means of
following her vocation for the present outside the
cloister.

Providence favoured her holy intent, and en-

---

[1] *Epistolario,* Letter xxiv.

abled her to found an orphanage, for which provision had been made by a good Priest, whose be-
quest to that end had lain neglected for some time.
To this noble work she gave her talents, her energies,
her means, her piety, but without finding encouragement beyond that which came from her brother
Antonio. However, having his support and counsel,
she felt certain (and events justified her confidence)
that God would bless her endeavours, and, sooner
or later, give full effect to her vocation.

The solicitude which his mother expressed with
regard to the Subdeaconate arose from the fact that,
though he was ready to receive it, circumstances
prevented him taking it at the time intended.
Letters dimissory could not be obtained easily,
owing to the disorderly condition in which revolutionary disturbances had left the diocese and princi-
pality of Trent, whose lawful Pastor remained long
in exile.

Antonio had arranged to take his Doctor's
degree at the University, immediately after the time
set down for the Subdeaconate ; but he decided on
deferring it until he had received the more sacred
dignity : much as he loved and respected Science, he
loved and respected Holy Orders more. Another
reason, springing from humility and charity, contributed its share to the formation of this decision.
As the fellow students who ought to have been
ready for the Doctorate before himself were not yet
in a position to pass for it, he disliked to wound
their sensibility or seem to be more advanced than

they were. This motive he sought to veil in the explanation he gave when replying, as follows, to a
letter from his father, who feared that over-study
was injuring his health :

With regard to the Subdeaconship, of which you speak,
I believe I shall not be able to receive it until next year,
for want of letters dimissory. This will enable me to
mature the matter better by a more complete preparation.
As for Doctor's degree, I do not deem it expedient to take
it this year, since, in any event, I must return for Holy
Orders. In this course I am somewhat influenced by my
class-mates, who are unwilling to take their diplomas before
next year ;—nor does it seem becoming in me to be singular. Add to this the difficulty of preparing one's self,
during the warm season, in an extensive range of study, as
well as the counsel I have received from my Professors, not
to speak of the Government regulations. However, I am
thinking of lightening my labours *then* by undergoing *now*
two of the eight examens which all must pass who wish to
obtain a diploma.

As for my method of life, I rise about six o'clock,
then study till eight, with only one interruption for prayer
and breakfast. From eight until twelve I attend such lectures as concern me ; and then, after hearing Mass in the
Church of our saint (St. Antonio) return home and continue
my studies until half-past one. Afterwards, I either take a
stroll, or discuss some point with my companions until two
o'clock, when I sit down to dinner. Dinner over, I amuse
myself for some minutes at a simple game with a friend,
or pass the time in conversation ; after which I repose for
about half an hour, and then take exercise until half-past
four or thereabouts. At that hour, I resume the thread of
my studies until seven ; spending the time from seven until
nine o'clock in recreation with some excellent friends, who
are either Professors in the University or young men of

talent. At nine o'clock, all my household, that is to say five individuals, including the two estimable young men who live with me, retire to a small room where we quietly make our spiritual reading, recite our Rosary, and then sit down to a light supper; after which we await, in pleasant chat, the hour when each one withdraws to his own apartment. Then, after having concluded night prayers, I retire to rest, and sleep the soundest sleep in the world.

I experience unspeakable delight in my studies the more deeply I enter into them; but everywhere I find a great need and a great scarcity of books. You cannot imagine what straits I am in on that account. Just fancy, I have not even an Aristotle or a Plato, books I should have in hand every moment; and you can hardly realise how much it grieves me. Well, patience; everything cannot be done in an instant : gradually we shall get into shape. Meanwhile, I mean to do my utmost in order that my well-beloved father may have no cause to repent having spent money on me, nor have reason to hesitate doing so in future. Let me tell you, by the way, that you are held in great esteem here, and many illustrious persons are desirous of making your acquaintance. But enough of this—kissing your hand most respectfully and imploring your blessing, I am, &c. &c.

PADUA : *June* 19, 1819.[1]

The simple exposition of his daily life given thus off-hand, to quiet the anxiety of fond parents, is admirable both as to what it revealed and what it omitted. What it revealed enabled them to see how faithfully he kept up the pious customs of home amid the allurements and distractions of University life ; and what it omitted included the very things which he, when at home, endeavoured to keep from all but the

[1] *Epistolario*, Letter xxv.

eye of God alone. ' He was,' says Don Paoli, re-
ferring to this letter, ' a man of universal well-doing ;
great in the discharge of the least as well as the most
important duties ; faithful in the observance of all
that belonged to his state; as perfect a man and
Christian as one subject to human infirmity can be.'

CHAPTER VIII.

ROSMINI LEAVES THE UNIVERSITY AND RECEIVES THE SUBDEACONATE.

(A.D. 1819.)

Completion of his University course—What the Paduans thought of him—How the good and the poor missed him—His first duty on returning home—His gratitude—State in which he found his Rovereto Academies—The instability of human things—How he took disappointments—What he deemed a 'great service'—He establishes a school for poor ecclesiastical students—His own preparation for Holy Orders—He receives the Subdeaconate and makes a short excursion into Venezia—How he bore himself while travelling—Sees God in everything—Returns home—His guests.

In three years Rosmini completed his University course, and returned home. Paduans, who looked merely at the studious and scholastic aspects of that course, described it as 'rapid and brilliant;' but they who were privileged to see the more sacred side of his daily life thought less of the great learning he had successfully stored up than of the great piety he had so perseveringly practised during those three years. They knew, as well as others, that he had made great progress in 'human and speculative knowledge,' but they knew better than others that he had made far greater progress in 'that knowledge which is divine and practical.' They knew, also, that the regularity of his exterior life, which challenged the respect of even the most worldly-minded, was but the ordinary reflex of the subordination of his interior life to 'the science of the Saints.'

University society, accustomed to college departures, did not, perhaps, trouble itself much about Rosmini's going away ; but the pious and the poor of Padua soon missed his sweet, familiar face, and long after felt a sorrow like that which the pious and the poor experienced when St. Francis of Sales left the same city ages before. Hence the saying recorded by Tommaseo : 'a Francis of Sales and an Antonio of Rovereto come to Padua only at inter vals far apart.'[1]

One of the first duties which Rosmini discharged, after his return home, was to write the following letter of thanks to Don Leonardi Carpentari, the estimable Priest under whose immediate care his University days had been spent :

' The paternal love that you constantly manifested towards me, during the three years in which it was my good fortune to dwell with you, the interest you took in my affairs, the confidence you were wont to place in me, treating me, who did not deserve it, as more than an ordinary friend, dispelling even your doubts on grave subjects at my words or suggestions, (though these words came from a mere youth, whose sole claim upon you was his dutiful affection)—all this, which serves to illustrate not only the goodness of your heart but the strength of your humility and affability, has won my love in a very decided manner, and awakened in me the deepest sentiments of respect and gratitude for one so

---

[1] *Rivista Cont.* Antonio Rosmini per Nicolò Tommaseo. Torino, 1855.

virtuous. If it now affords me, as it does, the greatest pleasure to express what I feel (and what I cannot but feel), judge, then, what my satisfaction would be, had I an opportunity of proving my feelings by my acts. How I long for an occasion of giving this proof! If there be any service I can render you, command me without ceremony, and so confer on me a new favour that will merit gratitude for itself.

ROVERETO : *July* 1819.[1]

No sooner was he settled once more at home, than he applied himself to the revival of the literary and charitable associations which fell into decay immediately after he had gone to the University. He had to start afresh, with companions who were quite new to such work ; for hardly any of his former associates, young or old, were any longer able to rejoin him. Some had passed to eternity, some were occupied in duties far from Rovereto, and some had lost the ardour of other days. Even Don Luigi Sonn, whose co-operation he confidently relied on, was about to leave. The changes which three short years had thus effected within a small circle, supplied him with matter for meditation on the instability of all things human. But as his heart no longer rested on human things, such vicissitudes could no longer affect him as they usually affect others. How cheerfully he resigned himself to those changes may be seen from a short letter of farewell to Don Luigi Sonn, whose continued stay in Rovereto he greatly desired. Having called at Don Luigi's residence in order to take leave of his friend, he found him absent, and then and there wrote thus :

[1] *Epistolario,* Letter xxvi.

Rosmini was here this evening, desirous of embracing you, ere you vanished from his sight. But what species of phantom you are he knows not; for, as often as he stretched forth his arms and drew them to his breast he caught nothing but—air ; so, they always returned to him empty. However, he informs you that he has embraced you in spirit ; and so closely that it will not be easy for you to escape his grasp. Nay more, he is persuaded that you will not disdain to give or receive similar embraces. Depart, then ; he permits you, or rather, he rejoices that you go, since the end for which you go is a good one. But he asks that you will not, on your departure, take with you that which you can leave behind for him without regret,— he means your love and memory. If, in this your leaving, you will remember your faithful friend, you will for a certainty be of *great service* to him. You understand of what he speaks.

Put on fortitude and constancy, and, thus armed, fight valiantly for the common cause, not to destruction but to conquest.

ROVERETO : *August* 1819.[1]

In the benevolent projects that filled young Rosmini's mind, Don Luigi had always a place ; for his sound sense, large experience and great piety, made him a prized counsellor. Although he would no longer be close at hand to continue the advice once so frequently sought, he could still continue the prayers which had been its effective substitute during the former separation. This was the 'great service' which Rosmini craved from him, as from all whose merits gave them influence at the Court of Heaven. Another 'great service' which he at one time expected from him was practical assistance in carrying

[1] *Epistolario*, Letter xxvii.

on the useful and charitable little organisations that had just been restored to working order. To these, moreover, an addition was about to be made, which caused the young Acolyte some anxiety, when he knew that his sage friend's aid was no longer available.

This addition was a school designed to prepare worthy youths for the ecclesiastical state. On his return from Padua he obtained permission from his father to use a room in the family mansion for the purposes of this school, the management of which now fell wholly on himself. Most of those who availed themselves of the opportunities his benevolence thus afforded were poor, and some, who came recommended by friends at a distance, were beholden to his generosity for their means of support while prosecuting the studies that were to fit them for some regular episcopal seminary.[1] He was their teacher, their guide, their friend whether they were rich or poor, provided their piety and their industry were such as to merit his favour.

Meanwhile, he carefully prepared himself for taking the sacred burden to which he directed the hearts and minds of others. He had a most exalted idea of the Priesthood, and drew near to that dignity with an awe that increased at every step. Although the first formal step—assuming the clerical habit— was very simple and still remote from the great office itself, he took it, as we have noticed, with a

---

[1] The Abate Barnardi supplies many instances of this in his *Giovane età*, &c. of A. Rosmini.

fluttering heart, and a deep sense of its grave import.

This sentiment grew stronger as he approached the Tonsure and Minor Orders, which he received with shrinking timidity and solemn reverence. When the time for taking the Subdeaconate came, he rejoiced at its coming; nevertheless he was, as we know, well pleased that Providence caused a delay ; for it enabled him to make greater preparations, as if all his life had not been one continuous, though undesigned, preparation. ' Full surely,' says Don Paoli, ' he entered the sheepfold by the door, because God had long since furnished him with an abundance of heavenly endowments, and gifted him, in an especial manner, with the spirit of prayer, piety of heart, innocence of soul, and untiring industry, set off by great wealth of learning.'

While he felt certain that each step which took him nearer to the Priesthood carried him farther and farther from the inheritance men of the world prize, he never, for an instant, thought of turning back ; for each step brought him nearer and nearer to the only inheritance his heart had ever craved. But, while he was ready to sacrifice everything to the glory of God, aye even all the consolation of the most precious affections, he did not therefore withdraw from any one, much less from his parents and kindred, the affections to which they were entitled : on the contrary, he preserved, increased and gave more depth to the natural affections, by sanctifying them.

The members of his family who still wished to

hold him back from the Priesthood hoped that the hindrances which the state of the times threw in his way, might, after all, exhaust his patience and induce him to go no further than he had gone. These hopes were all the stronger, as there was no good reason to expect that the Bishop of Trent would be restored to his diocese for many years ; while some thought there was reason to believe that young Rosmini would not go elsewhere for Orders. But they were mistaken ; and the reason which encouraged their hopes was the very one that led him to decide on delaying no longer the next step.

As soon as he was satisfied that the time for taking this next step had truly come, he went to Brixen, in Mid-Tyrol, and there, on the 21st of November, 1819, received the Subdeaconate, at the hands of Mons. Carlo, Count of Lodron, then Bishop of that diocese.

The new Subdeacon having devoted some days to thanksgiving and pious contemplation, started on a short tour of recreation, accompanied by Giuseppe Stoffella, his former class-mate in Don Orsi's Lyceum, and one of the early associates of his domestic Academy in Rovereto. They passed from Brixen into the Venetian province of Friuli, and journeyed through Udine down to Venice, thence, by Padua to Verona, homeward. The choice of route was made partly with the view of visiting some sacred shrines, and partly in order to call on some University friends at their homes on the way.

He remained for a few days at the chalybeate

springs of Recoaro, where he made some acquaintances who, in after years, reminded him of the fact,
when they sought from him ' the waters of truth.'
Recoaro was then a fashionable watering place more
or less familiar with Church dignitaries, but perhaps
never before made attractive by a young ecclesiastic
who secured general admiration, not by a display of
rank, wealth, or learning, but by quiet charities, retiring modesty and persistent piety.

Travelling—whether for recreation or not—
seldom interfered with Rosmini's fixed religious
duties, though it usually obliged him to set aside
his regular studies. Every morning he contrived to
hear Mass, sometimes halting for that purpose at
a village church. As he beheld God in everything
and everything in God, the ever-varying scenes
through which he passed served rather to stimulate
than to distract mental prayer.[1]

When his soul was not thus engaged his mind
turned whatever he saw to the benefit of studies that
still had God for their object. He regarded each day
of his life as a page in his history and resolved that it
should not be a blank one, but filled with good deeds

[1] ' He was accustomed to say that if it were possible man should
never cease from prayer, for it is the inestimable source of every
good, whereby man becomes, as it were, master of the very omnipo-
tence of God, Who has promised always to hear the petition of those
who humbly pray to Him. Whenever Antonio Rosmini was at prayer,
his external deportment showed that his soul was entirely absorbed in
his Creator, and no one could behold him without being moved to
devotion. . . . His religious duties held so high a place in his heart
that he would never omit any of them, unless when incapacitated by
illness.'—*An Outline of the Life of Antonio Rosmini,* translated from
the Italian and edited by the Rev. W. Lockhart, p. 78. London, 1856.

and good thoughts, with practical evidences of his love to God and man, as well as with progress in piety and progress in learning. The record was exclusively for God, though its lessons were destined to be diffused for the benefit of man, in whose interest, as dear to God, he stored up knowledge and desired to spread it.

On returning from his little tour, he was joined at Rovereto by some of the young friends whom he had visited in the Venetian provinces. They came to stay with him for a few days and see for themselves what a great deal of good can be effected by little organizations, such as flourished around his home. Two of these friends—Tommaseo and Maurizio Moschini—who were, socially speaking, probably the least of the visitors then at the Rosmini mansion, soon became its most constant and most prized guests.

CHAPTER IX.

ROSMINI AN HEIR AND A DEACON.

(A.D. 1819-1821.)

Death of his father—Finds himself to be heir general—Why he does
not expect this and why he accepts it—How he meets his new responsibilities—He prepares for the Deaconate—Arrival of the
Bishop of Chioggia in Rovereto—Receives Deacon's orders—Declines to receive the Priesthood before he is of canonical age—Goes
into a long special preparation for the Priesthood—Establishes a
class of sacred eloquence ; its advantages to himself and others—
His ordinary mode of life in those days—His eager desire to
remedy the evils produced by the false philosophy then popular.

WHILE Rosmini was away on his short excursion,
his father's health showed symptoms of approaching
dissolution, and the careful old man arranged his
worldly affairs that he might apply himself, without
distractions, to the immediate preparation for
eternity. The son was at home in time to soothe
his father's last days, with the pious attentions which
none knew better how to bestow. Exactly two
months after his beloved Antonio was advanced
to the Subdeaconate, the venerable Pier Modesto,
then in his seventy-fifth year, received the benediction of the dying and passed to everlasting rest.

The last sad offices to the dead were over, and
the fond son was still ministering consolations to his

sorrowing mother, when he was informed that, notwithstanding his being in Holy Orders, the will of
his father constituted him inheritor of all the family
possessions. This he neither expected nor desired ;
for, when he chose the Church as his spouse, he
looked upon the choice as naturally leading to a for-
feiture of his claim to more than a younger son's
portion. The custom of the country, as well as
special family reasons, led him to believe such would
have been the decision of his father. But there
were other family reasons, and higher customs, which
induced Pier Modesto to arrive at a different conclusion ; and so he framed his will in terms that
left his eldest son no option but to be his heir.

Amongst these other reasons was the fact that
Ambrogio Rosmini, from whom the estate immediately descended, fully intended to have left all his
property to his nephew Antonio, and not to Antonio's
father. However, as the good Ambrogio died in-
testate, Pier Modesto succeeded as heir-at-law ; but,
knowing what his brother's unwritten will was, he
deemed himself a trustee who was bound, in due
time, to give it full effect.

Antonio saw in all this less his father's will than
God's. To God's service, therefore, he resolved to
devote what God had thus given. Generous provision had been made for his widowed mother,
while his brother and sister had no reason to complain
of the ample allowance that had been left to them.

The loss of his father intensified the young Subdeacon's piety. Death was a subject he loved to

meditate on, as a never-failing means of detaching
his soul from the perishable things of this life, and
keeping it firmly bound to those that never die. But
there was a vast difference between contemplating
death with the eye of the spirit and viewing it face
to face as an awful fact. He first felt this difference
when he knelt by the bier of the uncle he loved so
tenderly; but he felt it still more keenly when the
tomb closed on his venerated father, and the eyes of the
flesh could never more look on that dear countenance.
The salutary effect it produced in himself was imparted to those who leant on him for the consolations he was so skilled in administering to all in
affliction.

It did not take him long to readjust the affairs of
his mourning family, and set in order the new responsibilities that devolved on himself. He made no
change whatever in the administration of the house.
His influence had so long directed it that the
change of chief was hardly more than nominal.
The management of the property he entrusted to
his cousin Count Salvadori (his mother's nephew)
who had already been the agent for Ambrogio, and
who continued to serve in the same capacity not only
while Antonio lived, but for some fifteen years after
his death.[1] When all the business affairs were duly

[1] The Rosmini retainers, whether high or low, usually spent their
whole lives in the service of the family. This was probably due to the
patriarchal relations existing between masters and servants ; some of
these retainers were descended from families that had given servants
to the house for many generations. A household register, kept by
the Countess Rosmini, mother of Don Antonio, is still to be seen in
the Parolini mansion at Rovereto, and the quaint entries in this book

arranged, he turned, once more, to his studies. These had been for a short time interrupted by the sad duties that gave a special solemnity to those divisions of his horary which nothing ever interrupted—his devotions and his charities.

Before Rosmini had been many weeks settled down to his new position, it was announced that a Venetian Bishop was expected to visit Rovereto soon, for the purpose of consecrating the church of the Holy Cross, giving Confirmation and holding an Ordination. Antonio hailed this news as a message from Providence to prepare for the Deaconate. Accordingly, he at once directed all his studies and spiritual exercises to that object. The Bishop arrived, the church was consecrated at the appointed time in May, and Confirmation given at St. Mark's and elsewhere. The church selected for the Ordination ceremonies was that of St. Mary, within which lay the ancient sepulchre of the Rosmini family.

There, on June 2, 1820, Antonio Rosmini-Serbati received Deacon's Orders, from Mons. Manfrin-Provedi, Bishop of Chioggia, the see of Trent being still vacant. On the same occasion, Minor Orders were conferred on two of Antonio's intimate friends —Bartolomeo Stofella and Antonio Gasperini.

The young Deacon, who approached his new dignity by a long retreat, had no sooner received it than he retired again for a few days, to honour its possession, as he had honoured its advent, by prayer

bear witness to the motherly care of the mistress for each of her attendants, and to the attachment of these for their ' noble home.'

and meditation in perfect solitude. When he returned to his ordinary duties, he was counselled to obtain a dispensation for receiving the Priesthood before the canonical age. There was much propriety in the advice, because—apart from his known fitness in every respect but age—the peculiar circumstances of the diocese would have made such an application in the highest degree reasonable, and the Bishop intimated that he thought the course suggested desirable.

But Rosmini looked up to the Priesthood with such a feeling of awe, that he could not be persuaded to shorten the time regularly set down for a complete special preparation. Although, from his childhood to the day on which he was urged to ask for a dispensation, he had been making intellectual and spiritual provision for 'the wonderful powers the office conferred'—although each of the steps he had already taken, with such extraordinary care, brought him closer to it in a more and more hallowed disposition—still he deemed ten months' immediate preparation as the least he could give to it.

In effect, he went into a ten months' retreat. During that time he did not, indeed, fail in the social obligations which belonged to the headship of his family ; nor did he neglect any of the responsibilities proper to his station. But he had so disciplined his heart and mind that these things never held his soul away from the one object to which he made even the most ordinary occurrences of every-day life tributary.

He himself tells us, in his Logic,[1] how, by a proper economy of time, he was able to get through with ease the vast amount of work which amazed his friends, some of whom, like Moschini, supposed that Angels must have aided him, else he would not have been able to pray so much, to study so much, to write so much, and, with all that, never to leave even the least of his domestic or other duties unfulfilled, or attended to in a negligent manner. However absorbed in studies he might be, the presence of God was never out of sight, as frequent short ejaculations of love and adoration attested. However wrapped in meditation he might be, the calls of charity to his neighbour always found him promptly attentive, for they were but a practical continuation of his prayer.[2]

In those days, his domestic Academy and its ecclesiastical offshoot more than compensated him for all the trouble he had taken with them. The estimable youths who flocked around him brought solace to his mind and heart, while the care of their spiritual and intellectual interests furnished him with an excellent means of perfecting his own preparations for the Priesthood. That nothing should be wanting

---

[1] *Logica*, p. 879. 'Life is prolonged by economising time.' To Muratori he said : 'I am able to do so much by utilising scraps of time.'

[2] ' His love of God was, as the Gospel requires, united to the love of his neighbour. He loved God in his neighbour and his neighbour in God. He desired for every one the possession of the only true good, which is eternal salvation, as well as those temporal goods which promote, or at least do not hinder the attainment of the true good.'— *An Outline of the Life of Rosmini*, p. 80.

to this end, he added a class of sacred eloquence to the course set down for his new ecclesiastical school, and undertook its direction himself. The consolation and benefit he derived from it were thus mentioned to his friend Paravia, in a letter dated April 5, 1820: 'On Thursdays I have with me a little gathering of young Clerics, and we make together some exercises in eloquence which I relish exceedingly, because charity and peace reign amongst us. And do you not deem this profit to all of us ? I assure you that I am very grateful to God for it.'

Thus, before he had received Priest's Orders, he was doing for his native diocese the services of an experienced seminary professor, and, at his own expense, closing up the dangerous gap which revolutionary disturbances had so long kept open. In another part of the letter from which we have just quoted, he gave his friend a passing glance at some of the things he was then daily doing :

'My philosophical writings are at present in repose. Charity has forced me to devote myself to sacred eloquence. I have written some sixteen discourses. I have also prepared other things for the press, but, if I once begin to publish, it is not easy to say where I shall stop. As yet, however, I have no serious thought of that. In the morning, I sometimes write verses; in the evenings I teach philosophy; then I converse with some friends and write to others ; I look after household affairs, answer letters, and see to any other business that requires my attention.' This was all he

saw fit to say himself; but Tommaseo tells us that
for the greater part of the year 1820, as a preparation for the Priesthood, he redoubled his religious
exercises and 'more rigorously than ever observed
the rules which kept him to the practices of a recluse
amid the duties of secular life.'

It was then difficult—it still is and ever will be
difficult—for worldly-minded men to understand how
a learned and wealthy young noble could toil with
such unflagging industry for others, or for the mere
purpose of reaching, in the most fitting manner, an
end that seemed to them so much 'a matter of
course' as taking Holy Orders.   His early risings,
his prolonged meditations, his frequent fastings, his
severe studies, his patient zeal and exhausting
labours as a voluntary teacher, his unwearied and
punctilious attention to the least as well as to the
most important matters connected with household
routine—all such things formed a greater puzzle to
the local worldlings than his charities, or his establishing Academies, or his abstention from the gaieties
of society, or his deep interest in the moral, intellectual, and material well-being of his neighbour.   But,
what most amazed them was that he continued to
combine all these, and yet to enjoy better health and
far more happiness than those who lived in what the
world calls 'ease and comfort.'

In the autumn of 1820, the first season of his
restored Academy was formally terminated in a way
befitting its objects.   He has, himself, left us this
brief account of the closing scenes, sketched inciden-

tally in a letter to Paravia, dated September 23, 1820 :
'We made a solemn conclusion of this year on St.
Januarius' day, which we celebrated with poetic and
other compositions.   Stofella contributed an ode,
and I a sermon.   The cheerfulness, the holy cordiality, the solidity of the conversations were admirable,
and we enjoyed ourselves much.   The order of the
festivity was this :—Don Orsi, one of our members,
celebrated Mass in the morning at the altar of my
little domestic oratory which was specially prepared
for the occasion and had as a chief adornment the
portrait of St. Philip, who is the Protector of our
Society.   After dinner, the customary discourse was
delivered, then came a prose recitation by the secretary and next followed the poetry, which each one
brought ; finally there was the *Te Deum*, after which
we had the evening's repast.'

In the letter giving these bare outlines of the
interesting scenes with which his home was then
familiar, he discussed other topics that pressed more
on his mind, which was keenly observant of the
moral and intellectual dangers of the day.   Not the
least threatening of those dangers was that resulting from an influx of the sensist philosophy which had succeeded in so corrupting literary
taste that 'society' was beginning to disrelish the
reading of anything supposed to have in it a flavour
of religion.

By way of set-off or slight check to this, he
urged Paravia to publish, forthwith, a good edition
of a little book entitled *Dio del Cotta e del*

Lemene, and made some suggestions of a practical
kind as to the best way of bringing it into note,
adding : ' Good people would all the more desire it,
since in our times most literary men are seen to
neglect authors in whom—no matter how high be
the merits of the composition—they fear to meet
with religion. The mediocre beauties of a profane
scribe are extolled to the skies, while the exquisite
excellencies of a writer on sacred subjects are
allowed to fall to the ground.'

One of the objects upon which he had set his
heart was to remedy this growing evil, and to lead
the popular taste back to the pure fountains of
thought from which the shallow but plausible sensists
had been successfully turning it away. ' Like all the
truly great intellects which God, from time to time,
has raised up within His Church, such as St.
Augustine, Boëtius, and S. Thomas Aquinas, Rosmini felt intensely the supreme utility, or rather the
necessity, of reuniting divine and human science into
one great whole, and reconciling reason with Faith, in
order to demonstrate that the works of God never
contradict each other, that Grace is easily engrafted
upon nature, and that Revelation and its mysteries
do not destroy but direct and exalt the understanding.' [1] This was the task to which God evidently called him, and to its execution, under the
guidance of Providence, he bent all his energies.

---

[1] *An Outline of Rosmini's Life,* &c.

CHAPTER X.

ROSMINI A PRIEST.

(A.D. 1821.)

The feast of his canonical majority—He draws near to the Priesthood
with fear and trembling—Goes to Chioggia for Ordination—How
he received the sacred dignity—A retreat of thanksgiving at Venice,
where he celebrates his first Mass—Returns to Rovereto unperceived in order to escape a public reception—Thanks the Bishop
who ordained him—His energy and aspirations shown by a letter
to Prince Alexander von Hohenlohe—Celebrates his first public
Mass—The day one of popular rejoicings in Rovereto—His mother
gives a grand banquet—How all this affects him—The ovations
over, he goes into retreat on the Mount—Leaves absolute solitude
for the commencement of a five years' home retirement—The
principle of Passivity as he knew and practised it—Key to the
consistency of his course—How he distributed the ordinary duties
of the day—Every hour for God—Love of gravity and of order—
The best qualities of his childhood and youth grown perfect in his
manhood.

THE feast of the Annunciation, in the year 1821,
was Rosmini's twenty-fourth birthday. He celebrated it with special solemnity, as it was the day of
his canonical majority, and close at hand was the
time chosen for the great event to which he had been
so long looking forward with trembling diffidence
and fervent devotion. ' With what deep-felt piety,'
says Don Paoli, ' with what largeness of heart and

humility of spirit, Antonio Rosmini approached the sacred Ordination we leave to the judgment of those who have been able to form an adequate estimate of the greatness of his soul.'

Much, indeed, did he fear to take upon himself an office which he deemed a burden requiring the strength of angels to bear it fittingly; therefore he drew near it, as men did of old, with an overawed heart, and with painfully scrupulous care. None had ever more thoroughly considered all the dangers which encircle an Ambassador of God—none had ever more thoroughly fenced himself against these dangers. He had so trained himself to spiritual watchfulness, he had so schooled himself in meekness and charity, that neither personal wrongs, disappointments, ingratitudes, annoyances, nor malice in any of its forms could any longer much disturb him; nor could the applause or the abuse of the world, nor the dignities or indignities of this life, any longer much affect him.

Why then did he so greatly fear? Because, like St. John Chrysostom, who also greatly feared the responsibilities of the Priesthood, he felt that he who had to tremble before God for his own sins and soul, should tremble much more 'when he found himself charged with the sins and souls of others;' because he felt that whoever had to exercise the sacred duties of this sublime office ought to possess the purity and the sanctity and the strength of an Angel, whereas he was only a man. But, when the time came, all this fear fell at the feet of the Lord Who had regarded his humility, for it was very sincere and very great.[1]

In compliance with the invitation of Mons. Manfrin-Provedi he left Rovereto so as to be in Chioggia (near Venice) during the solemn services of Holy Week. These services closed with the Ordinations of Holy Saturday (April 21st of that year), when Antonio Rosmini-Serbati was consecrated a Priest of the Church of God. No sooner did he rise up with the awful dignity fully upon him, than he felt like yielding to emotions which, in kindred circumstances, made St Basil swoon; but he was strengthened by remembering St. Chrysostom's cheering counsel to St. Basil : ' Be of good courage trusting in Christ, Who has called you to His Holy Ministry.' This gift of 'good courage,' based on Christ, was amongst the first of the heavenly favours then bestowed upon Rosmini; and as to the abundance of the celestial gifts he received from God on that occasion, 'they may be inferred,' says Don Paoli, 'from the magnanimity and constancy with which he consecrated all his life and all his means to the service of God, and the salvation of his neighbour.'

A few hours after his Ordination, he set out for

[1] ' He used to say that true humility not only shows itself before God but also before men, and he was always foremost in the practice of this exalted Christian virtue. Humility was one of those virtues that gained him the affection not only of his disciples but of all who approached him. They wondered to see a man who was raised so high above other men by his lofty intellect, his vast and profound erudition, not only making no display of his rare gifts but appearing quite unconscious of them.'—*An Outline of the Life of Rosmini,* &c. p. 84.

Venice, on a visit to his friend Mons. Traversi, then Rector of the college attached to the Church of St. Catherine. There he celebrated his first Mass, on Easter Sunday, 1821, and there he remained, as the guest of the Superior, in a retreat of thanksgiving for a few days.[1] This retirement was far dearer to his heart than the distracting festivities which the affection and admiration of family and friends in Rovereto were preparing for the immediate return of one so loved, and who had just been vested with the sacred dignity to which he ' was called as Aaron was.'

To avoid the kindly demonstrations he had been warned to expect at home, he kept all in ignorance of the day and probable hour of his return. It was generally supposed that he would come back in order to celebrate his first public Mass on the last Sunday of April; but they who thought so were disappointed. Although he reached home on the night of Saturday, the 28th of April, his return was known only to those who would respect his wish to be shielded, for a little while longer, from the too expressive

---

[1] Some say, on the authority of Don A. Gasperini, that he celebrated his first Mass at St. Mark's, Rovereto, on the 3rd of May—twelve days after his Ordination. But Don Gasperini evidently refers to his first public Mass *in patria* ; for, apart from the fact that Tommaseo knew from himself that his first Mass was celebrated in Venice, as we say, on Easter Sunday, it is not likely that Rosmini, a lover of seclusion, would have waited so long for a public occasion when he had, the while, so many private opportunities. Moreover, Don Basilio, who was in a position to test the family traditions, has assured us that there was no doubt he had said ' a private Mass in his own home on the Sunday before the 3rd of May.' It is then very probable that he had celebrated not only two but three or more Masses before that day.

kindness of his fellow citizens. He spent Sunday in the quiet of home, and gave his family alone the privilege and joy of assisting, in the domestic oratory, at his first private Mass in Rovereto.

Soon after breakfast 'on that happy Sunday,' as he informed Tommaseo, he penned a short letter to the Bishop of Chioggia, intending it to be the first written since his return home, raised to the rank which brought him

> Hard by the Throne, where angels bow and fear,
> E'en while he had a name and mission here.

That letter was as follows :—

Having reached home in safety, I feel it to be my duty to express to your Lordship, in writing, my lively sentiments of gratitude for the signal kindness and courtesy I have received at your hands.   For it is to you, my Lord,. that I am indebted for what of all things I most prize— namely, my Ordination to the Priesthood.   No treasure is comparable to that, and in exchange for it there is nothing I possess, or ever shall possess, which I could give, unless it be a soul that will ever ardently cherish the recollection of so great a favour.

But God will reward your Lordship in my behalf, and, I feel sure, you will be content with such an exchange. The many tokens of regard I met with from all the members of your household (amongst whom you deigned to receive me without any merit of mine) will also form a subject of undying remembrance.   I beg you to convey to all those distinguished personages my most cordial acknowledgments.   Your Lordship is held in great esteem here and ardently longed for.   We hope to see you, for certain, next Autumn ; and, as for me, I trust you will do me the honour of availing yourself of my home, such as it is.

O! if we had your Lordship for *our* Bishop! But may God dispose everything as He pleases!

ROVERETO : *April* 29, 1821.[1]

During the evening of the same day, though he needed mental and physical repose, he wrote one of those letters which are so characteristic of his energy and of his aspirations : no less so are the circumstances. While going to and coming from Chioggia, he had occasion to notice how nobly Catholic Germans contrasted with those who were not Catholic, and as his heart was filled with prayerful longings for the conversion of the erring ones, he poured out his feelings on the subject in a letter to the saintly Priest, Prince Alexander von Hohenlohe—uncle of His Eminence the present Cardinal Gustavus von Hohenlohe, Archpriest of the Patriarchal Basilica of Sta. Maria Maggiore, and Bishop of Albano. The letter was a long and affectionate one, written in Latin.

It conveyed not only his ardent desire for the return of the whole German race to the Church of God, but his hope that the pious Priest, through whose intercession our Lord was pleased to effect so many astonishing cures, should also be made the means of healing the wounds which error had inflicted, so that, by curing his countrymen of their heresies, he might restore them to religious sanity.

Thus, while all Rovereto, yielding to the pious affections of Catholic brotherhood, was panting, as it were, to show publicly its reverence for a young citizen who had just received Priest's Orders, there

---

[1] *Epistolario*, Letter xxviii.

M 2

was he, giving no thought to that, or to himself at all, but wholly occupied with the priestly wish to gather in the strayed sheep of his Master and have them all, like the dear children of Rovereto, sheltered within the one fold of the one Shepherd. How like Rosmini this was!—how significant of the apostolic labours that were, through all his after life, to find him so constantly and self-sacrificingly directing his every energy to the gathering in of the strayed sheep of that Good Shepherd Who had called him to aid in ministering to the flock.

On the following Thursday, the 3rd of May, Don Antonio celebrated his first public Mass in the parish church of Rovereto, amidst the reverent rejoicings of the whole town. The event made the day a kind of municipal festival. Clergy and people spontaneously united in an ovation that was meant to express their hearty love and high esteem for the young Priest whose virtues and talents had endeared him to all, and whose blessing every one was eager to receive. Don Antonio would have fled from all this had not charity obliged him, as often before on less important occasions, to surrender his own inclinations.

Not only in churches and streets, and in the dwellings of kindred and friends, but at home, the quiet he coveted was affectionately denied him ; for the Countess Rosmini, who knew well how much her son disliked to be the object of such attentions, and who had therefore seldom forced him to the sacrifice, claimed a mother's right to honour the day with a sumptuous banquet. It was not merely her son she proposed to entertain, but one who had just been made an Ambassador of God, and who happened to be her son. At her beck, relations and friends, as well as the local Clergy, thronged the palatial rooms of the family mansion : music in the garden and in the spacious entrance halls, congratulatory speeches in the dining-room, and complimentary sonnets in the drawing-rooms, gave great joy to all except to Rosmini, who took the demonstration as a penance which was only softened by the reflection that what pained him pleased others, and that, after all, it was for the priestly office rather than for himself the honour was intended.

The ovation over, several other days of con-gratulatory greetings had to be gone through, ere he was allowed to betake himself to the complete solitude for which he longed. Then he went to the villa on the Mount, where, eight years before, he had composed ' The Day of Retirement,' and where, once again, he communed all alone with God, as in the freshest days of boyhood. While thus enjoying the delightful seclusion of his favourite *Casino del Monte* he wrote to his friend Paravia, saying : ' I am more and more enamoured of this solitude which is full of God.'[1] Yes, that was its special attraction for him—' it was full of God :' that was the one charm he sought in all places and things.

Having remained a week in strict retirement on the Mount, he returned to town and commenced that beautiful home life which may be called a five

[1] *Lettre giovanili al Paravia,* No. xxvii.

years' retreat—sometimes on the Mount, sometimes at his town residence, sometimes in a rural parish whose wearied Pastor needed a substitute, sometimes in the midst of the youths who clung to him as their master and friend, sometimes with those whose intellectual, moral or physical needs sought his charitable aid, but always in circumstances that were full of God, always where he could best sanctify himself and serve his neighbour, always so as to keep unbroken the continuity of a religious retreat, and of studies which were as golden links in that continuity.   During this long retreat, the rule of life he had laid down for himself in earlier years was put into force with the utmost rigour.   This rule took its character from that 'principle of passivity' or waiting on God's Will which he thus pithily set forth in his Diary :

'I, who am a most unworthy Priest, have determined to base my whole life on the two following principles : 1. To apply myself to the amendment of my enormous defects, and to the purifying of my soul from the iniquity into which it has been sunk even from birth, and to do this without going in quest of other occupation, or attempting things on behalf of my neighbour, seeing that, of my own self, I am absolutely powerless to do anything really good for any one. 2. I purpose not to refuse such offices of charity to my neighbour as Divine Providence may think fit to offer me, because the Almighty can make use of anything for His works and therefore even of me ; and, in case He does make use of me, I purpose to preserve a spirit of perfect indifference as regards any special work of charity, resolved to perform (in so far as my feeble will is concerned) that work which may be offered to me as zealously as I would any other.'

Here we have the key-note to that consistency of character which blent the 'active' and 'passive' so harmoniously in his whole course. Here, too, we see the main spring of that comprehensive but well ordered charity to which he devoted his unwearied energies—that charity

> Which, like the perfume-giving rose,
> Possesses still what it bestows,

—that charity which embraced all for love of Christ and would not exclude even the uncharitable. And here also we find the clue of that profound humility which won from him a lifelong homage—that humility which is the genuine test of sanctity, and which caused him, like a St. Francis of Sales and a St. Ephrem of Edessa, to magnify trifling defects into 'vices.' As a sunbeam reveals the floating specs that are too minute to be seen in the clearest ordinary light, so his sensitive conscience, lit up by humility, discovered blemishes which no other human eye could discern.

> . . . O clear conscience and upright,
> How doth a little failing wound thee sore ! [1]

His life, during these five years, was regulated by a rule based on this 'principle of passivity,' that is to say, the principle of 'relying on Providence to

---

[1] Dante's *Purg.* iii. 8, 9 (Cary).

direct our steps.' Rosmini's strong faith in Divine
Providence was based on the profound conviction
that God is always watching over us with tender
care; that He never fails to manifest His Will to
those who sincerely desire it; and that they who
guide their course by the Will of Him Who is
infinitely wise, as well as infinitely good and mighty,
are sure to be called upon to employ all their talents
in a way that must, in the end, be best for the glory
of God and for the sanctification of themselves and
of their neighbour.

This principle of 'passivity' should not, therefore, be for a moment confounded with the false
system of the Quietists, for it does not mean, nor
does it lead to, inaction or apathy, but on the
contrary, as the whole of his own life proved, it
leads to an unceasing activity which shapes its course
according to the indications of Providence as seen
in circumstances. He felt that a rule based on such
a principle should commend itself to the judgment
of every one who sought to act wisely for himself
and others, for it simply enjoined that 'when you
have certain powers of action you must be prudent
in ascertaining what is the best use you can make of
them.'

The rule he based on this principle, for his
home retirement, did not differ, except in details,
from that which he afterwards formulated when
he came to legislate for the spiritual government
of a Religious Order. It provided for very early
rising, followed by an hour's meditation; then for

a quarter of an hour's study of some ascetic subject; then for a special preparation for Mass; then for Mass, followed by a long thanksgiving; then for spiritual reading, followed by a very light breakfast; then for a short walk, with a book, in the garden where he once played at monk, and now, as often as circumstances permitted, recited the Divine Office; then for a visit of consolation or piety, or the reception of some guest, or the performance of some corporal work of mercy; then for two or three hours close study, followed by an examination of conscience before the Blessed Sacrament; then for dinner, followed by recreation with his family or friends; then for a ramble in the country, his steps generally leading him where charity needed his presence; then for more study, followed by the recital of his Office, by spiritual reading and by prayer.

So, throughout the whole day, every hour was portioned off with a system that varied little from the set rules of after life; and every hour was given to God or to his neighbour for God. Twice a day he made formal visits to the Blessed Sacrament. Once a day, usually after Mass, he carefully read a portion of the Holy Scriptures (and in this way had read the whole Bible through at least seven times). He went to confession regularly every week; and, besides a rigid retreat of ten or twelve days every year, he had a rigid retreat of four days before Lent and another before Advent—all special retreats within his prolonged general retreat.

Like St. Thomas of Aquin his devotion,
fervent yet composed at all times, was most glowing
in the presence of the Blessed Sacrament. He celebrated Mass with the greatest solemnity, seldom
finishing under thirty minutes : as he hardly ever contented himself with less than twenty minutes thanksgiving, or less than twenty minutes preparation,
this grandest act of the day held him absorbed in
the Adorable Eucharist for nearly an hour and a half
every morning. Besides the two formal visits which
he afterwards paid to our Lord in the Tabernacle,
he frequently spent in the Sacred Presence some
portion of the 'spare time' which he allowed himself,
and always went there when his spirit needed refresh-
ment, or his mind was overcast. He dearly loved
to be thus, at times, all alone in the family oratory ;
but he also liked to have the family and household
join him there in the morning and at noon, and again
in the evening, when they said the Rosary together,
and lastly, before going to bed, when he gave them
the Blessing.[1]

All these devotions, the least as well as the
greatest, were performed with solemn composure and
earnestness.[2] He greatly disliked to see anything

---

[1] The 'family oratory' was originally an ante-chamber off the draw-
ing-room corridor. Rosmini's uncle Ambrogio threw down the wall
fronting the corridor, and by introducing sliding doors converted the
ante-chamber into a sanctuary, and the corridor into the nave of a
good-sized domestic chapel. When this is not used for family prayers
the sliding doors are closed. Then the nave becomes a corridor
once more, and the sanctuary the oratory. It has a handsome altar
decorated by the skilful hand of Ambrogio Rosmini, who also painted
for it a fine altar-piece representing the Crucifixion.

[2] ' His religious duties held so high a place in his heart, that he

whatever done in a hurried or slovenly manner ; but his dislike became horror when hurry or carelessness marred the gravity which should accompany every kind of devotional exercise. It shocked him much to hear prayers mumbled, or dashed off with an irreverent rapidity, as though they were the utterances of ill-adjusted automata. Nothing of this was to be found where his example prevailed or his instructions were attended to, as in his own home, where the utmost reverence and recollection made it evident that prayer was no mere lip service. 'Surely,' he used to say to Tommaseo, 'petitions to the King of kings should not be less carefully articulated or less decorously presented than those to an earthly sovereign or even a human courtier.'

While a layman, Rosmini had ever been attentive to the social duties of his state, full of courtesy to all, be their rank what it may ; but, as a Priest, he seemed to be still more attentive and courteous. He had always maintained that the gentleness and refinement of manner, which ought to characterise every well-bred Christian, should find its fullest development in the Priest. His own life illustrated what he had thus maintained. The politeness known as personal may, and often does, exist with-

would never omit any of them, unless when incapacitated by illness. Amidst so many occupations of the greatest importance, he never failed to make his daily meditation, and he spent more than half an hour in celebrating Mass. He used to divide the Divine Office into three parts, to be said at stated times, and even when the most distinguished persons came to visit him, he never departed from his rule, always leaving the company quietly in order to recite the office.'—*An Outline of Rosmini's Life*, &c. &c., p. 78.

out any politeness of the heart. But, in him, they were admirably blent together; for, with elegance of manners and the due observance of the forms of polished society, he combined habitual benevolence and a complete absence of selfishness in his intercourse with all classes. Humility and simplicity regulated all his conversations.[1]

His home was as orderly as a monastery, his household as pious and regular as a religious community; yet, no one thought the master severe or in the least degree puritanically strict. All was done so blandly, that no one had occasion to feel the depressing effects of inconsiderate rigour, and there was no want of a judicious admixture of the social enjoyments that lend to life the only charm which worldly eyes see.

In his boyhood he 'played at monk' with all the seriousness of manhood : in his manhood the play became a reality with a seriousness proportionate to the change; but he took pains to conceal the depth and force of his asceticism from the sight of all save God, for Whose seeing he did everything. In his boyhood the impulse of benevolence was strong, and he gathered his greatest delights from the exercise of practical charity : in his manhood this

---

[1] ' It happened more than once that some distinguished personages, not personally acquainted with him, attracted by his celebrity, came to visit him, and after conversing with him for some time without knowing that he was the Priest they so much desired to see, they learned, to their great astonishment, that they had enjoyed the society of the Abate Rosmini, not being able to understand how such philosophical science could be united with such simplicity of manner. They had never before seen the true philosopher and the true Christian combined.'—*An Outline of Rosmini's Life,* &c., p. 84.

impulse was still stronger, but so was the principle which directed it to the most practical purpose ; the delight was greater, but so was the seasoned judg- ment which regulated it. In his boyhood he made instruction and edification the pivots on which all his amusements revolved ; in his manhood they formed the golden hinges on which all his studies turned, and the studies were as the gateway to his only pleasure, which was 'to worship God and know His works,' for the salvation of his own soul and the well-being of his neighbour.

CHAPTER XI.

ROSMINI'S ' PASSIVITY' AS ILLUSTRATED BY THE FIRST
YEAR OF HIS PRIESTHOOD.

(A.D. 1821.)

He endeavours to establish a Society of Friends—Why the attempt
fails—Love of solitude and of association—He combines both—His
views on co-operative action for good ends—A society for the publication of wholesome literature—Doing for God and truth what the
irreligious do for the devil and error—Prefers the Latin to the
vulgar tongue for ecclesiastical purposes—Is invited to join the
Turinese society for publishing good books—What he says on the
subject—Rebukes a friend for having praised him—How beautiful
a thing it is to please God—His efforts to popularise serious subjects—Charity calls him to active parochial work—How he ministers to the dying pastor of a sorrowing flock—Why he refuses to
take permanent charge of a parish—His funeral oration on the
death of Don Scrinzi.

DURING the first four months of his Priesthood, Rosmini's attention was often called to the careless manner
in which many Roveretans went through their ordinary religious duties in public. He could not help
seeing also that some people who deemed themselves to be good Catholics were allowing the claims
of 'business' to displace those of practical piety ;
and other some were indulging in petty rivalries that
often led to bitter contentions and animosities. The
parochial clergy were doing what they could to
remedy these evils, and Rosmini, looking at all the
circumstances, considered it to be his duty to aid

them in a way that would be unobtrusive, but, if well
supported, very effective. Like all his plans for the
spiritual and moral amelioration of his neighbours,
this took the form of a Society; he called it 'the
Association of Friends.' It was to be composed of
persons who, without trenching on their particular
duties in Secular Life, should conform to a common
rule for leading a strictly Religious Life ; a kind of
confraternity seeking to harmonise, as far as possible,
the every-day interests and occupations of the world
with the regularity and consolations of the cloister.
It was to include members of all ages and conditions. They were to have for their *first* object
and constant aim the honour and glory of God and
their own sanctification ; their *second* and incidental
object contemplated the well-being of others.

But, while all the candidates who offered themselves for admission were willing enough to carry
out the secondary ends of the proposed society, and
devote themselves to works of spiritual, corporal and
intellectual charity for their neighbour, very few saw
the need, or relished the task, of looking first of all
to the complete amendment of their own lives, to the
correction of their own moral defects, so as to ensure
their own sanctification. They desired to let that
come of itself, as a consequence of the good they
might do to others. He, however, could not be induced to alter the design, and therefore the association had very few members,—in fact, it was confined
to his own household and to some young friends who
were more or less dependent on him.

As of this, so of other efforts of a similar

character, through want of associates with a spirit
like his own, his holiest projects in these days did
not pass beyond the stumbling-block which required
that spiritual charity should begin with one's self. To
all it seemed far pleasanter to try and sanctify their
neighbour at once, rather than to trouble themselves
with efforts at their own sanctification, as an essential
preparation for undertaking the same work in the
interest of others. But these discouraging obstacles
did not dismay him; for he never lost an opportunity of making new attempts at associating men
for the spiritual, moral, and intellectual benefit of
themselves and others.

It may seem strange that one who was so fond
of solitude should be no less fond of association.
But the object he sought in solitude was identical
with that which he sought in association—it was God.
Without that object neither solitude nor association
would have had any special charm for Antonio Rosmini. His purpose was to combine solitude and
association so as to make each contribute to the
strength and beauty of the other, while both, interwoven, served at once to stimulate and shield ' piety,
self-government, study and literature, for the glory
of God and good of man.' Like St. Gregory of
Nazianzen (as quoted by Cardinal Newman) he
might well say of his choice :

> And so, 'twixt these and those, I struck my path,
> To meditate with the free solitary,
> Yet to live secular, and serve mankind.[1]

[1] *Church of the Fathers*—Basil and Gregory

Rosmini's views as to the great utility of associations for benevolent and kindred purposes, and his
skill in planning and directing them, were already
known throughout Italy.   Hence, his advice and
co-operation were eagerly sought for by philan-
thropic men in various parts of the country, when
they happened to be engaged in starting some sort
of society for the well-being of their fellows.   Immediately after his Ordination, more than one appeal
of this kind reached him.   Amongst others Sr.
Battaggia, the principal of an important printing
and publishing firm at Venice, solicited his counsel
and aid in establishing a society for the publication
of good books.   In reply, Rosmini set forth his
views in a way that enables us to have a glimpse at
the state of Italian literature in the first quarter of
this century :

I am delighted to see that you always take a pleasure
in promoting the interests of religion and virtue by the art
you profess.   When things of this kind are directed to their
natural end, they acquire sterling worth, and the profits we
derive from them are then genuine.   Continue to foster and
increase these worthy sentiments.   The idea of forming
a society like ' The Catholic Society of Turin ' might
present a good opportunity of achieving much and of
gathering fruit in abundance.   A similar idea had occurred
to my own mind, suggested by my experience of the power
which books hold over men,—for demoralization if bad,
and for edification if good.   In our days this is, perhaps,
the mightiest of powers, and its activity one of the most far-
reaching.   Evil-minded men, having perceived this, have
availed themselves of it to an alarming extent.   ' Why,'
said I to myself, ' why cannot Catholics oppose weapon to

weapon, and employ for the spiritual advancement of their brethren what others make use of for their destruction? Shall we suffer ourselves to be outwitted or surpassed by our enemies in discernment and energy? Shall we allow them to do more for the Devil than we do for God? Or shall we let the love of evil display more ingenuity than the love of virtue?'

Hence it is that I used frequently to devise schemes for turning against our enemies the very means they employed against us. Many times the idea of a publishing company, supported by generous friends, has occurred to me, as a means by which the most salutary and Christian doctrines might be everywhere diffused. The moving principle of this Typographical Society should be a pure love of religion. Having this, it should brightly exhibit disinterestedness, energy, good taste, and accuracy—in short, perfection in all things. This holy union once firmly established, after having given unmistakable proof of good purpose, would assuredly meet with encouragement from the Episcopacy, the Government and all good Christians. These, if we but knew how to make its existence known to them, would naturally become co-operators in the good work;—some by their exertion to circulate and dispose of books, some by aiding in their composition, correction and embellishment, and some again by furnishing the society with the funds required to carry it on. The investment, if well directed, would appear to be a safe one; for, even in these days, there are not wanting persons who are well disposed. But everything would depend on the good sense and foresight of those who should direct it at the outset. Having had the pleasure of making your acquaintance and of knowing your high and religious tone of thought as well as your enterprising spirit and your training, I already begin to entertain hopes that what I was revolving in my own mind may now be put into execution by others.

I am not well acquainted with the Turinese Society, nor do I know what vicissitudes it may have suffered during the recent disturbances in that city. You tell me that a similar one has been set on foot at Rome. It would be well if its plan and purpose were made public. Were you to undertake a like work in the Venetian Kingdom, and were the other two firmly established and prudently directed, all three might be so combined together that, as their object is one, they might work together on friendly terms. Thus, being as it were three branches of the same stem, each one might influence and co-operate in the prosperity of the others. The affair would, in that way, assume importance. Doubtless, difficulties will present themselves, and, therefore, a wise and prudent direction is indispensable. Think the matter over, at all events, and communicate the result to me. Even the mere conception of great projects is praiseworthy.

ROVERETO : *May* 20, 1821.[1]

In the same letter, having had occasion to speak of a little work entitled *Memoriale Vitæ Sacerdotalis,* he took the opportunity of defending the use of Latin, as far preferable to the vulgar tongue in books of that class. What he then and there said derives importance from the fact that they who never knew him as he really was, have since charged him with having always deprecated the employment of Latin for this or any like purpose. Surely the words in which he expressed himself to Battaggia— and they are even less decided than those he often uttered on the subject in later years—were not such as he would have written if he had thought it desirable or expedient to dispense with the language which the Church has solemnly made its own :—

I learn from Fontana that you would have no reluc-

---

[1] *Epistolario,* Letter xxix.

tance to reprint the little Latin work (*Memoriale*, &c.) which is in use among Ecclesiastics. For my part I believe it to be an excellent book, and when better known it will have a good sale. I should advise you, however, to have it printed in Latin, which is easily understood by all. Moreover, it is the language of Ecclesiastics so long as the Church makes use of it in her sacred functions and in her decrees. We should seek to maintain it in its vigour as much as possible, in accordance with the intention of the Council of Trent, which refuses even the Minor Orders to those who are ignorant of it. Besides, as we are accustomed to hear in Latin the words of Holy Scripture and the public prayers of the Church (of which this little work is for the most part composed), which possess such strength and unction, these if rendered in Italian would seem to us shorn of their beauty and force, however excellent the translation might be in itself.

While the Venetian publisher was consulting Rosmini about the formation of a society for 'the diffusion of Christian knowledge through the press,' he was also in correspondence, on the same subject, with the Marquis Tapparelli d'Azeglio—a Piedmontese noble who had already inaugurated a kindred movement in Turin, where his great influence, learning and energy promised to make it a success.[1] In one of his letters to this nobleman Battaggia suggested the importance of securing the active support of the young Roveretan Priest whose virtues and talents he dwelt on with much enthusiasm. The Marquis, who already knew of Don Antonio's

---

[1] This marquis was the father of that Massimo d'Azeglio, who was son-in-law of Manzoni, and who is known in England as a literary man, an artist, a soldier, and as a statesman of some repute in the service of Sardinia.

zealous efforts to restore a healthy tone to Italian
literature, gladly acted on the suggestion. His invitation, which was expressed in the most cordial
terms, drew from Rosmini the following reply :—

You cannot believe how great was my consolation on
learning from Signor Battaggia that there exists a society
having for its object the promotion of the real well-being of
man and the holy religion of Jesus Christ, chiefly by means
of the publication and diffusion of good books. These are
the arms made use of but too frequently by unbelievers ;
and alas ! with such arms they far too often make serious
havoc. More than once I have pondered over the fact, and
God knows how many times I have sighed for the establishment of a society of this kind ! I even ventured to
trace it out in my imagination, but I perceived its execution to be far above my slender abilities.

To learn that such a society is already in existence and
placed upon a sure footing in Turin and in Rome,—to find
it accord in every particular with that which my own mind
was considering, so much so, indeed, that its very name is
the same as that which I contemplated—this was to me a
great and agreeable surprise. Now I have to add to all this
the favour of your kind letter of the 9th ultimo, which was
quite beyond my expectation, and in which you invite me
to participate, so to speak, in the good work.

Right willingly do I accept your invitation, and my only
regret is that I am unable to offer you or the society anything more than my poor abilities, although accompanied
by the most ardent desires. I pray you to convey
the expression of my liveliest acknowledgments to the
virtuous and distinguished members of this pious association for their goodness in thus inviting me, through your
instrumentality, to join them. Assure them, at the same
time, that though in me they will find but a very feeble
member, nevertheless they will have a sincere friend and a
warm admirer, ever ready to execute their wishes, and most

desirous to promote the glory of God and the salvation of souls,—objects which form the sole basis of their union. O how beautiful is friendship like this! How useful such a Christian alliance! such a confederation of good men !— united not only in the bonds of peace with one another but in active energy against the wicked, solely for their good !

I beg of you to make use of me henceforth freely in such matters as are within my power, since you have now truly acquired a right to my services, as well as to that sincere friendship which it is my pride to acknowledge.

ROVERETO : *July* 7, 1821.[1]

The letter to which the above was a response contained so many warm expressions of admiration for Rosmini, that his humility resented them, as it always did praise in any form. But since he could not, without violating good taste, show this dissatisfaction in the answer written to D'Azeglio himself, he hastened to give vent to it in the subjoined letter to Battaggia, who was held responsible for having offended moderation in this matter. The reproof, however, was softened by the encouraging manner in which he met his correspondent's wishes as to the practical object they both had in view :—

What could have induced you to write such a letter about me to the Marquis d'Azeglio ? I know well that I owe it to your singular partiality for me. But how did you come to represent me to that nobleman in such a favourable light ? Your letter, though couched in most kind and pious terms, speaks of things which in no way can apply to me. How am I to correspond with the high opinion which he will form of me ? Really you have said to him things that I should blush to repeat. I replied to him in the best way

---

[1] *Epistolario,* Letter xxx.

I could, or, rather, as my heart dictated. If this alone sufficed, if nothing more than mere desires were requisite, how courageously I could present myself! For God knows how ardent is my desire for His glory and for the welfare of souls. But if deeds and not words were asked of me, where should I find the requisite strength? However, I at last answered him, to the effect that as I am closely bound to himself and his colleagues by the ties of veneration and Christian friendship, I am at their disposal for what I may be worth, and that they were therefore at liberty to command me ; but that, nevertheless, they could only expect very little, since it is very little I am able to effect.

To yourself I must reply by tendering my very best thanks, good wishes and encouragement ; although, for this last, you leave me no opportunity, since you seem to be entirely swayed by that holy love which achieves great works. Yes, my dear Sir, I know not where I should find one better qualified for the work we are speaking of, either in Venice or elsewhere. Endowed, as you are, with all the requisite abilities, and being by profession a printer and publisher, does it not seem as though things had already been prepared by God for establishing in Venice the society of which we speak? As for its Director, do you think Monsignor Traversi would decline a task so noble? In my opinion, however, it is a question whether it would not be more expedient for the Patriarch himself to become its head and protector, in order that here, as at Rome and Turin, its President might be a person of high position. The list of persons mentioned by you who could give us either pecuniary or other assistance shows, assuredly, that we may have quite sufficient to start with. Come now, make a commencement.

Bear in mind its merit before God,—a merit so much the greater as the work is more wide-spread and permanent. To do good to any one individual is, indeed, a meritorious act ; but to establish an enduring source of blessings to many, and what is more, of spiritual blessings, this I deem so meritorious that God alone can estimate its worth. When you shall have made up your mind to begin, you will find in me, as I have already told you, a feeble but a faithful co-operator.

Traversi will, very probably, come here on a visit to me during the holidays, as he has himself written to say so. This will be a fitting opportunity to concert many things, if you think it desirable. Drop me a line on the subject.

O how beautiful a thing it is to do what is pleasing to God! thus preparing for ourselves a secure treasure in the mansions of eternal life! You yourself clearly perceive its beauty, and even taste its sweetness in the results of that institution which you say you have established as a refuge for a hundred little boys. Although I am not personally acquainted with it, still I must congratulate you upon it, and assure you that I share with you the pleasure you experience ; for I assume it to be a holy work, productive of much good. You would oblige me greatly by giving me some particulars about it on another occasion.

ROVERETO : *July* 9, 1821.[1]

The Monsignor Traversi alluded to was still Rector of St. Catherine's, Venice, where the Abate Rosmini celebrated his first Mass. This distinguished divine did visit him, as expected, during the vacation of that year, and willingly consented to take a part in carrying out the publishing scheme. But we may say at once that it did not prosper ; for most of those who were in a position to further the design either held aloof altogether, or entered into it with a lukewarm spirit. Rosmini himself heartily assisted with purse and pen. Leaving to others the production of such light literature as was deemed desirable for the project, he contented himself with contributing, in popular form, such works

[1] *Epistolario*, Letter xxxi.

as 'A Panegyric of St. Philip Neri,' an admirable 'Letter on Christian Education,' 'A Method of Catechising the Ignorant,'[1] and other treatises intended to popularise grave subjects, which were, at the time, very distasteful to most readers, because such subjects were almost invariably presented in a dry, dull, unattractive, or repelling manner.

On the other hand, there was an alarming superabundance of sensational, irreligious works, written with a vigour and sprightliness that was too well calculated to mislead the unwary and increase the prevailing disrelish for more wholesome literature. While Rosmini was thus helping to stem this pestiferous tide, and giving to the press little works for general use, he was also preparing for special use a new edition of a *Thesaurus Sacerdotum*, with a dedication by himself to the clergy of Rovereto, which they unanimously pronounced to be 'full of truth and unction.'

Thus he spent the first year of the long retreat which followed his Ordination, ever practically interested in all that was good, true, useful, and beautiful, and daily showing, by his ordinary acts, that the principle of *passivity* laid down by him was the principle of *activity* wisely applied. Once in that year he passed from the retirement of home and

[1] The 'Panegyric of St. Philip Neri' was composed for the members of Rosmini's domestic Academy (which was under the patronage of St. Philip), and delivered before them during the season of 1821. It was published by Battaggia at Venice the same year, and republished at Lugano in 1834, and at Milan in 1843. The 'Letter on Christian Education' was addressed to Don G. di Val Vestina in 1821, reprinted at Rovereto in 1832, at Milan in 1838, and afterwards at Naples. (The little work on 'Catechising the Ignorant' has been mentioned already in Chapter vii., with a note, pp. 125-6.)

the duties which were close to home. Charity called him elsewhere for a few weeks, and, answering her summons, he went to do duty in the old parish of Lizzana, not far from Rovereto. The beautiful village of Lizzana was originally the centre of a very extensive parish, within which Rovereto was then a churchless hamlet. But, though Lizzana remained the parish 'capital' for centuries, it never grew beyond village dimensions, whereas Rovereto, year by year, took the proportions of a town, until at last it had to be detached from its old parochial centre, and constituted an independent parish of the first class, with several dependent churches.

The venerable Pastor of this ancient parish was Don Bartolomeo Scrinzi whose society Rosmini prized, when, as a boy, he rambled through the country studying philosophy, and 'finding God in everything.' He was also one of those sages whose advice young Rosmini sought when about to establish his first domestic Academy. Age and its attendant infirmities had, for some time, deprived the venerated Pastor of power to bestow much attention on the spiritual needs of his flock. Therefore, he had frequently to depend on the charitable assistance of neighbouring Priests. Towards the close of 1821 his ailments completely prostrated him, and then he appealed to Rosmini, whose saintly boyhood had so often 'consoled him while living,' to come now, in his Priesthood, and 'console him while dying.'

The Vicar Capitular of Trent forwarded Don Bartolomeo's appeal, with a request of his own, that

Don Antonio should take full charge of the parish, at least for a few months. True at once to the principle of passivity, and his friendship, Rosmini promptly left his retirement to minister both to Pastor and flock. With tender diligence he nursed for weeks at the bedside of the dying Priest, only leaving him when the spiritual wants of the sorrowing people called him forth.

When at last the good old Priest was taken to his eternal reward, the weeping parishioners besought Rosmini to stay amongst them, and the diocesan authorities backed their entreaties with a formal request that he would take to himself the parish where he was so much beloved—a parish where his memory ' still lives in benediction.' But higher and more pressing calls forced him to decline this, although he felt bound to remain for a few months, until a duly appointed successor came to his relief.

The sermon which Rosmini preached at the solemn obsequies of his dear old friend Don Bartolomeo, so affected those who heard it that its publication was demanded. He assented, and that oration still holds an honoured place amongst his published discourses.[1] It was dedicated to Monsignor Sardagna, then Vicar Capitular of Trent (afterwards Bishop of Cremona, and finally Archbishop of Cesarea), always the firm friend of the young Roveretan divine, whose worth he had had so many opportunities of thoroughly knowing.

[1] It appeared first in Venice in 1822 ; it was reproduced at Lugano in 1836, and included in the volume of Rosmini's sermons published in Milan in 1843.

CHAPTER XII.

ROSMINI'S CALL TO THE RELIGIOUS STATE.

(A.D. 1821-1822.)

THE saintly Mme. Canossa visits Rovereto—Resemblance between
Madeline de Canossa and Margherita de Rosmini—How Madeline
conquered Napoleon I., and how Margherita conquered her father
—Mme. Canossa urges Rosmini to found a Religious Order—
How this message of inspiration affects him—He shrinks from the
thought of being a Founder though ready to be a Monk—Mme.
Canossa is persuaded that God calls him to the dignity of
Founder—She returns to Verona, sketches the plan of an Institute
and sends it to him—What he thinks of it—Difficulties in the way
of carrying out the plan—Mme. Canossa perseveres, deeming herself
the agent of God in this 'call'—He is once more invited to co-
operate with the Turinese Publishing Society—How he would
have all Christians form a universal social brotherhood—The
Household of the Faith.

IT was in the first of his five years' home-retirement
that Rosmini had the privilege of entertaining a
guest who came, like an Angel, with a message from
Heaven. This guest was Madeline, Marchioness
of Canossa, a lady who was even then ranked with
the most saintly of Italy's daughters, and who is now
(after the usual process before the sacred tribunal
appointed for that purpose in Rome) solemnly declared to be a 'venerable servant of God.' Her
visit was made to Rosmini's sister, whose charitable
zeal and earnest piety kept pace with his own. In-

deed, Margherita's work was at once the complement
of her brother's, and a spontaneous application to
Rovereto of that system of benevolence which enabled
Mme. Canossa to accomplish so much practical
good for the neglected children of her own sex
throughout Austrian Italy. The same kind of
charities which endeared Madeline de Canossa to
the poor, not only of Verona but of all Lombardy
and Venetia, had already begun to win for Margherita de Rosmini the blessings of the poor, not only
of Rovereto but of the surrounding district. The
golden chain of spiritual sympathy bound closely together these two ladies, who resembled each other in
almost everything but age; and this difference in
years probably made the tie between them all the
more potent.

There is even something alike in the incidents
that immediately preceded the formal commencement
of their respective labours,—far apart though they
were as to time and place, and far differently situated
though they were as to surrounding circumstances.
When Napoleon I. passed through Verona, not long
before his fall, he took up his quarters in the palace
of Canossa. On the eve of leaving, he intimated to
his noble hostess that he wished to requite, in some
way, her hospitality. She at once replied : ' As I
mean to recommence the work which you destroyed
by your decrees of 1810, I ask that you, Sire, give
me one of the many convents which you then suppressed.' [1]

---

[1] Don F. Paoli's *Monografia*, p. 74.

This request was also a censure ; but its brave
spirit pleased the soldier, and he immediately
placed at her disposal the convent of St. Lucia,
Venice. Forthwith, she commenced the good work
on which her heart had long been set—the establishment of an Order for the care and education of poor
children. That Order came to be known as ' The
Daughters of Charity,' and, at the time of Mme.
Canossa's visit to the home of Rosmini, its rapid
spread, with the incalculable good it effected,
were the theme of every household in Northern
Italy.

So, too, Margherita Rosmini, under less heroic
circumstances, replied to her father who had done all
he could, by parental ' decrees,' to suppress her
vocation. Wishing to give her some substantial
mark of his kindness, as a set-off to his seeming un-
kindness in opposing her attempt to enter a convent,
he requested her to name the requital. She instantly
answered : ' My father, you can afford to give me
permission and means to shelter and teach the poor
little orphan girls of Rovereto.' [1] He gave her both,
and continued to do so while he lived. On his

---

[1] *Vita di Margherita Rosmini*, Paravia, 1880. The good works
begun by her in Rovereto and carried on by herself alone up to 1821,
are still represented by a very useful institution called the ' Rosmini
Asylum,' within which the helpless children of the working class and
all manner of little street-straylings are carefully sheltered, during the
day, and piously educated. This charity is conducted by a Tyrolese
sisterhood in a handsome building erected to the memory of Margherita
on a part of the Rosmini garden, generously ceded for its use. The
structure is said to stand on the spot where little Antonio had constructed the cell in which she played at monk with him.

death, her brother Antonio not only ratified the permission but greatly increased the means. He did more : he wrote for her that admirable set of instructions on *Christian Education* which, though meant merely as a chart for his sister's local schools, remains as a guide for Christian teachers throughout the world.[1]

It was for the purpose of conferring with Margherita Rosmini on the holy work so dear to both, that the Marchioness of Canossa, in the early part of 1821, journeyed to Rovereto, where she was the guest of the Rosminis. There and then the penetrating foundress of the ' Daughters of Charity ' had an opportunity of judging for herself about the truth of the fame which popularly ' canonised' Margherita and Antonio. She took special pains, as she afterwards declared,[2] to study the character of the young Priest to whom God seemed to have sent her with the ' message of inspiration' that led him, step by step, to become the Founder of the 'Institute of Charity.' His ardent piety, great learning, orderly charity, unflagging industry, and the deep wisdom and practical nature of all his suggestions relating to the objects which engaged himself and his sister, so profoundly impressed her that she zealously besought him to quit his home retirement in order to devote himself to the organisation of a religious society for the

---

[1] It was published in 1823 by Battaggia of Venice, and afterwards reproduced in Milan and Florence.
[2] Don G. Bertoni's *Memor. di Canossa.* Venice, 1852.

good, not of a locality merely, but of the whole Church.

Such a proposal, coming from a source so saintly, stamped it as from Heaven. He was but twenty-four years old at the time, and the very suggestion of becoming the Founder of a Religious Order startled him. It is true that he had always been engaged in founding some kind of society for the glory of God and good of men ; but these efforts seemed to him as mere matters of course, within the lines of every-one's ordinary duties to God and one's neighbour. It is also true that, from the days when he and his sister played at monk in the family garden, to the day when both were conversing with the venerated Canossa on this subject in the very same garden, all his time had been spent so much in accordance with a religious rule that one might suppose he had enter-tained this idea all his life—nay, that it was uppermost in his thoughts. But no ; the one idea which stood before all others in his mind was

> Straight on towards Heaven to press with single bent,
> To know and love his God, and then to die content.[1]

To establish religious order in his own soul had ever seemed to him the safest way of 'pressing towards heaven'; but never had he allowed himself to fancy that he could best attain his object by founding a Religious Order for others. To him the

---

[1] The words are those of St. Gregory Nazianzen ; other passages in Cardinal Newman's version of the poem from which they are quoted (in *Historical Sketches*) express thoughts which Rosmini frequently puts before us in prose.

thought would have had the appearance of an ambition, not much better than certain other ambitions against which he so resolutely set himself when struggling with his parents for the right of following his vocation.

Therefore when the proposal to found a Religious Order came to him, in so solemn a manner from one so highly favoured by God, it took him by surprise. At once his humility, alarmed, threw itself around his heart, and made him feel more sensibly than ever his own nothingness. A Monk he was ready, indeed, to be for his soul's sake, and, at the same time, a co-operator in the organisation of any society for the good of his neighbour; but a Founder, as was a St. Benedict, or a St. Francis, or a St. Dominic, or a St. Ignatius, or any other of the sacred builders of religious institutes—that was a something which God, in His might and mercy, could cause him to become, but which he, himself, would not presume to think about. And, though the thought was at length placed before his mind under such holy auspices, it cost him three years of most serious and prayerful reflection ere his humility permitted him to act on it.

The saintly Mme. Canossa returned to Verona, persuaded that God intended to call Antonio Rosmini to the ranks of Religious Founders. On reaching home, determined to keep the proposal before his mind, she drafted a plan for a society which seemed to her adapted to the spiritual needs of the time. The more she considered it, the more she felt that

the young Roveretan Priest was better fitted than
any one she knew to undertake the work her
pious designs contemplated. This plan she sent
to his sister, who, earnestly seconding the suasions of
the good Canossa, placed it before him. It was, in
most respects, similar to that which the Marchioness
had found successful in her own Order. The proposed society was to be called 'Sons of Charity' and
to be composed of Priests, who should devote themselves to such spiritual work as the parochial clergy
were unable to deal with, owing to excess of population or other causes. He received this communication with reverence, studied it carefully at all points,
prayed for light, and then considered how the project
could be reduced to practice.

When he had thus diligently examined all the
bearings of the plan, he wrote to the Marchioness,
assuring her that he entered heartily into her views,
and that he was satisfied her project, if well carried
out, was calculated to produce the best results. But,
on looking around him for those who were needed
to co-operate in the work, he found reason to have
serious misgivings as to the success of his efforts to
form a society of Priests or even to begin its formation. Priests were scarce. Many country parishes
in the diocese of Trent were without Pastors, and
many Parish Priests who had charge of populous
town districts were without Curates. Moreover,
there was a marked disinclination on the part of the
Secular Clergy of his acquaintance to join a community of Regulars. While the actual state of things

furnished a good reason for the establishment of such a society as the one proposed, it held out no prospect that recruits, in Priests' Orders, could be got for the purpose. Therefore, instead of an institute of . Priests, he suggested that it should be of laymen, under the direction of a Priest. He reminded her that the most ancient and most successful religious communities had been of this kind. Although he did not quite agree with those who lamented that, in course of time, these Orders became, for the most part, communities of Priests, he felt that, in some respects, they had been more useful and more flourishing as communities of laymen. He then pointed out how the difficulty of organising a society of Priests, rather than of laymen, was much increased by the long course of studies now required for the Priesthood. While it was comparatively easy to get together immediately a sufficient number of intelligent and fairly educated laymen, years of waiting must pass by before those of them with a vocation at once for the Priesthood and Religious Life would be ready for Ordination. But, by educating young men, pretty much as Priests were educated in former times— that is, by giving them a good literary training, with a sound knowledge of Holy Scripture, and the duties of life, and by practising them well in virtue, and instructing them solidly in the doctrines of religion and morality—they might soon be made excellent coadjutors in all works of spiritual and corporal mercy, while attending chiefly to the furtherance of their own sanctification.

Having thus frankly communicated his views to the Marchioness, he concluded his letter with these remarks :—

O how advantageous would be a reunion of enlightened Christians who should bind themselves to practically assist their neighbour in all the branches of charity you mention ! Would that they might do for men what your Daughters of Charity do for women ! Assuredly, with perfect accord between them, they might afford much help to the parochial clergy in the cure of souls. I am deeply impressed with the idea, though I see so many difficulties in the way of its execution. Looking on the seculars around me, I think I see some who are well fitted for the purpose; but it is necessary for them to have such a course of instruction as may enable them to live in a religious community. They should, at least, have some intelligent notion of what constitutes community life. In order to effect this, I think the introduction of little oratories, like those conducted by the Oratorian Fathers, would be of great service. By means of these, many among the laity are not only formed in piety, but they are also accustomed to a certain regularity of life and the orderly exercise of works of charity. [1]

This letter did not in the least discourage the hopes of the far-seeing Mme. Canossa. On the contrary, it convinced her that these hopes would yet be realised ; though not perhaps in the way she at first supposed, assuredly they would be brought to pass, in some manner more to the glory of Christ and the good of His Church. Persuaded that this young Priest was set apart by our Lord for some special service of the kind indicated, Madame Canossa acted as if she felt that God had willed her to be the

---

[1] See Appendix, Letter i. (Letter xxxii. of *Epistolario.*)

immediate agent of his 'call.' Therefore she prayed heartily for the light necessary, and then allowed some time to elapse before she said anything more on the subject directly to Rosmini himself; but, meanwhile, in her letters to his sister, which were very frequent, she continued to speak of some feature in the plan as an indirect means of keeping it constantly before Don Antonio's mind.

While his thoughts were busily occupied with Mme. Canossa's holy suggestions, he received a fresh appeal from the Turinese Publishing Society to turn his attention to the active membership of that organisation. Full of the spirit which was working within him, eager to show itself in practical results for 're- ligious life,' as such, he replied to this appeal in a long letter to the Marquis d'Azeglio on the ad- vantages of such a brotherhood amongst good Chris- tians as might make the sweets of 'community life' universal.[1] He wished to have the spirit and the customs of the apostolic age restored as much as possible in these feverishly progressive days. He would have good Christians, who are to be found everywhere throughout the world, not content with spiritually loving one another, but personally knowing and cherishing one another as well. He would establish between them an intercourse of a heavenly type, far nobler than any known to mere natural society :—

A delightful friendship, resulting from that love which is the badge of Christ's discipleship, manifesting itself in

[1] See Appendix, Letter ii.

the works which are its fruits, and which serve to distinguish
the good tree from the bad.   In this manner they might be
separated from the children of the world, and so love, honour,
and aid one another that, being mutually encouraged and
consoled, by force of the union existing amongst them, their
afflictions and dangers would be diminished, while, at the
same time, a salutary restraint would be imposed on the
wicked. How many motives are there not for such a union—
pure, holy, and Christian ; I do not mean motives that have
their origin in this world, where we neither seek nor expect
repose, but motives originating in Heaven, in the charity
of Jesus Christ, and in the hope of an eternal union with
Him in the bosom of His Father.   O how desirable and
profitable a thing would it be were all treated with the same
degree of love, and regarded as equals in our Lord, to the
exclusion of all human limitations, such as spring from
blood, from country or from any special affection, without
trespassing at all on the domain of Charity, or violating the duties we have towards all men.   Thus, be our
brother ever so far removed from us, or be he close at hand,
or be he in high or lowly estate, be he known to fame or
hidden in obscurity, we should evince for him, with an
equal degree of love and tenderness, those tokens of esteem
which are his due, and from which he may reap a real advantage.

If there were once introduced among Christians an
ntercourse more cordial, more active, and more widespread,
not limiting its sphere of action to one place alone, but
extending it to many, I should expect to see the religion of
Jesus Christ rise far more majestic and beautiful, and the
world once again, as it were, in bloom—the true reflex of the
first ages of the Church, but graced, if I may so say, with a
more imposing dignity and variety, because our general
intercourse and means of communication would now necessarily produce a larger number of results, more varied, more
unlooked-for, and more marvellous.   So beautiful an idea
does not seem to me Utopian ; for, judging by the facility

we now have of mutual intercourse, and by the nature of the times themselves, it would appear to me to be a reasonable conclusion.

Either the time has already come, or come it must ere long, if things advance at their present pace, when it will be a matter of the greatest moment, not only to every Catholic but to all who cherish even a natural sense of righteousness, to stand aloof from the society of the wicked, and to have some distinctive mark that will denote the fact. Consequently, men morally inclined will feel it incumbent on them, not only to join the Catholic body, as was the case with Herr Haller; but since, even among Catholics, we have the good grain and the cockle, they will be constrained to unite in closest union with those whose exemplary and holy life can leave no room for suspicion. If such an intercourse were once established, what beneficial results would accrue to all those well-disposed persons who should take part in it! Every good Christian, as you very justly observe, would thus, when travelling (an affair now become of such frequent occurrence), be shielded from the dangers that everywhere beset his Faith ; he would always travel, so to speak, in his own house, for he would find safeguards everywhere, since he would find everywhere his Catholic brethren come lovingly to his aid.

ROVERETO : *October* 14, 1821.[1]

All these ardent longings for universal Christian brotherhood found practical expression in the ordinary conduct of the writer. The five years of that home 'retreat,' which preceded the grand life of activity reserved for him, were five years in which the 'apostolic age' was faithfully represented in Rovereto—five years in which the charity that is the badge of Christ's discipleship shone out there with

[1] *Epistolario,* Letter xxxiii.

a lustre that never once paled—five years in which he brought to maturity the virtues that had been ripening steadily from his childhood upward, and that were soon to produce such precious fruit unto God.

CHAPTER XIII.

ROSMINI'S STUDIES DURING HIS HOME RETIREMENT.

(A.D. 1822.)

He cultivates human sciences as useful to the Science of the Saints—
His domestic library—His studies—Vast extent of his reading—
His estimate of philosophical learning—How he worked to make
philosophy subserve Truth—Solidity of his acquired knowledge—
The works he wrote and planned in his home retirement—What
specially kept him in this retirement—The Divine Will regulates all
his acts—His passivity is activity for God's glory.

IN the letter to the Marquis d'Azeglio, from which
we have just quoted, no allusion was made to the
original subject of their correspondence, touching
the necessity of publishing and circulating good
books. Evidently the important matters he had
been discussing with the Marchioness of Canossa
were still uppermost in Rosmini's mind, as they were
always, in some form or other, deepest in his heart;
for they belonged to that great science to which he
made all human sciences subordinate—the Science of
the Saints. But, taking these human sciences as
subsidiary to the science without which he deemed
all else ignorance, he gave a fair proportion of his
time to their study, and to the composition of works
resulting from those studies, which included every
department of human lore. Philosophy and theology

were the departments in which he most loved to
dwell; for within them he discovered all that
illumined the science of the Saints and reconciled
human knowledge with Divine Revelation.

As in the days of his boyhood he used to lay
out methodically, on the library table, the several
books which he intended to study in turn, so, in his
manhood, he made similar arrangements, but on a
scale proportionate to his increased knowledge and
years. The old library and one table sufficiently
answered the purposes of the boy student; but
several rooms, which were so many new libraries on
the second floor of the mansion, and several tables,
scarcely sufficed for the needs of the man student.
In one of those apartments, which became a favourite
place of study, he had four bookcases filled with
the choicest volumes, including those purchased in
Padua from the Venier library. The top mould-
ing of each case bore an appropriate title in gilt
Greek characters—one was *Philosophia*, another
Encyclopedia, another *Lexica*, and another *Ephemer-
ides*.

This select library was close to the chamber in
which he was born, and to that which he used as a
bedroom during the five years of his home retirement.
A finer bookcase, larger than those in the adjoining
rooms, stood in his sleeping apartment, and was filled
mainly with ascetic and religious works. He had
planned a domestic library of ten thousand volumes;
but, though the scheme was never fully realised, few
private libraries were more complete or valuable

than that which he had then at hand, and which still remains nearly as he left it.

His studies were, as Don Paoli tells us, 'most extensive, profound, erudite and well ordered.' The vast extent of his reading may be inferred from the simple fact that in those days he had carefully studied the works of more than five hundred different authors—indeed, it is very probable that he had, even then, made himself familiar with the six hundred and twenty authors consulted for his *Logica* and for his *Diritto.*[1] Although he was no thorough linguist, he had a fairly good knowledge of all the languages necessary to his studies, and was even sufficiently well acquainted with Hebrew and Sanscrit to make these tongues available for his purpose. When he saw that philosophy was the science on which all other human sciences depended, he applied himself most of all to philosophical studies. Even from his earliest years he sought with eagerness to master and descant on everything that can come within the cognizance of human reason.

Don Paoli declares, on the authority of those 'who had known the young noble longest and best,' that Rosmini's mind was matured—'had attained its manhood'—fully ten years sooner than is ordinarily the case. Even while yet seemingly a youth in mind, as he assuredly was in other respects, he saw that the sciences generally stood in need of a com-

---

[1] The index of authors quoted in the *Logica* gives 170 names, and the index of those quoted in the *Filosofia del Diritto* gives 450 others.

plete, 'a decided restoration;' he appreciated, at their true value, the gigantic efforts that had been made by the most powerful intellects of all ages for the advancement of knowledge—the happy successes of some and the tremendous failures of others ; he perceived that on philosophy depended the foundation, the order, and completion of knowledge. He at the same time saw that this perfected knowledge did not depend on that philosophy which concerns itself wholly with matter, while ignorant of what matter is—nor on that which, groping its way by the aid of blind sense, proudly pretends that its efforts can produce truth—nor on that which, in despair, throws itself into scepticism ; but on that which, while accepting such treasures of truth as have been secured in times past, seeks to make new discoveries in order to bring knowledge nearer and nearer to the possession of the whole—the divinely beautiful Truth.

He therefore set himself to collect together the many scattered fragments of truth which had been discovered, or dimly seen, by ancient, mediæval and modern philosophers. He then undertook to reduce the fragments of truth to a body of doctrines harmoniously connected with and depending on one another. His task was greatly facilitated by the discovery which he had made in 1816, as he walked along the Via Terra, in Rovereto, when his mind hit upon that master idea which enabled him to present the system of truth in a more perfect form.[1]   But he still required to examine closely for himself what

[1] See Chapter iv. pp. 88–90.

had been done by all the philosophers who had preceded him.

Therefore he was obliged to have constantly at hand, not only St. Augustine and St. Thomas Aquinas, but Plato, Aristotle, Plotinus, Descartes, Locke, Leibnitz, Kant, Condillac, Fichte, Schelling, and Hegel, with the works of the modern rationalists and materialists. He had also, of course, to become more and more thoroughly conversant with Holy Scripture, the Fathers and the Schoolmen, though he was somewhat familiar with all these since his youth. He had to analyse carefully the writings of the philosophers, ' to distinguish the parts that were true from those that were false, and to interpret those that were obscure.' He had to remove errors, to firmly lay hold of truths even when only incidentally touched upon, and to elucidate them. He had to penetrate into the innermost depths of as many sciences as are comprised in ideology, metaphysics, and ethics. He had to examine and discuss all the systems that had been more or less happily imagined concerning human knowledge, the nature of feeling, the essence of morality and of right. He had to define clearly the supreme principles which regulate politics, to reduce to a scientific form pedagogy and asceticism ; to penetrate into the recondite depths of ontology ; and finally to demonstrate, by fact, the harmony of the truths of reason with those of revelation, ' showing that the former are the beginning and the latter the completion of the SYSTEM OF TRUTH.'

All this he had to do, and he did it within the five years of his home retirement. Nor did he limit himself to the most celebrated and accredited authors, for he sought out the truth even in those of less renown. Nay, he took note of the least known writers and the smallest productions 'down to the most diminutive pamphlets, to the constitutions of small states and to the articles in the daily newspapers.' 'Like an industrious bee,' says Don Paoli, 'he went everywhere in quest of honey, and wherever he found any he drew it forth, as must be manifest to those who are familiar with his works, for all his writings bear witness to an erudition that is very plentiful and varied—an erudition not gathered up or thrown together at random, but always to the purpose, always confirmatory of some truth either recently discovered or restored to honour.'

The solidity and rare excellence of his erudition can be readily discovered in all he wrote. It is even visible in his way of presenting the thought of any given author so as to set it forth, with the utmost clearness and impartiality, whether it be true or false. It is still more visible in his complete avoidance of all ostentatious display of knowledge; for he ever studiously keeps his own merits out of sight and prefers to appear always as a student. This, indeed, was no difficult thing for a genuine disciple of Truth, which, as Don Paoli tells us, 'is the only real teacher of all intelligences;' and from his boyhood upward, Rosmini had been one of the most industrious and earnest disciples of Truth. He often told Tommaseo, who had long watched his labours and shared in them, that, from his earliest years, he had been steadily travelling through the world of science, and as he went along he descried new regions that had never yet been explored. 'Of this fact,' says Tommaseo, 'I could myself attest the truth, if testimonies were needed from those who knew him. Even while he was still very young he used to picture to himself human knowledge as so many great trees each putting forth its branches in graceful order, all pervaded by unity of life; he used to practise himself in composing those beautiful tables in which the parent ideas are seen to generate other ideas in due succession, the prolific family growing larger and larger with the degrees of legitimate descent and kindred affinity well defined in all its parts. . . . Before 1825 he had already formed and worked out, in his own mind, the conception of the *Nuovo Saggio*, on the origin of ideas;— a conception from which so many others were to spring, each standing out by itself in the fulness of its own life.' [1]

The extraordinary extent of his reading never surprised those who knew how diligently he worked, how thoroughly he economised and regulated time, and how rapidly, yet carefully, he perused every volume, taking notes of all he read.[2] In most cases

---

[1] *Rivista Cont.* Torino 1856, Rosmini, per N. Tommaseo.

[2] Besides the notes he made apart, every volume of importance in his library bears marginal notes in his own hand.

rapid reading is little calculated to favour careful reading; but a singular quickness of eye and thought, combined with an extraordinary memory, enabled him to so systematise rapid reading that what he read was never undigested. The only obstacle to his rapid reading was some unfamiliar language. But there was no tongue so difficult as to overcome his determination to master it sufficiently for the purpose of securing the treasures it might contribute to the lore he sought. In this he was much aided by the special studies of his boyhood on language in general, on the structure of human thought, and on the laws which govern its expression.

There are those who assert that he did not go as deeply into the study of mathematics and the so-called natural sciences as into the others. If this were the case, want of full opportunity must have been the cause ; but Don Paoli calls our attention to the fact that many of Rosmini's works, published and unpublished, abundantly prove that he was 'deeply versed in the supreme reasons of those branches of learning also.' While still a youth, he gave evidence of knowing them well, else how could he have dropped, here and there, in his earlier productions, the germs of the philosophy both of mathematics and the natural sciences ? It was his intention to have developed these germs in regular treatises, 'and he would have done so,' says Don Paoli, 'had not death taken the pen from his hands.'

While the pen was held firmly in his hand,

during the five well-employed years of his home retreat, he wrote most of the minor works that were afterwards published in his *Prose Ecclesiastiche.* In those days, too, he sketched the plan of some of his greater works, such as the *Nuovo Saggio* on the origin of ideas. The subject of this magnificent production had occupied his thoughts ever since his boyhood; but it was not till his twenty-fifth year that it took the definite shape which led him to the formulation of his views in an elaborate dissertation that for many reasons ranks as the most important of all his works.

It was during this period also that he com-menced several other great works of a like char-acter, some of them suggested by current circum-stances, his mind having already stored up an abundance of knowledge well set for immediate use, whenever intellectual charity might demand it. Thus the movement for Italian unity, which sprang up amongst the Piedmontese in 1821, growing strong through North Italy in 1822, called for such a work as the *Filosofia della Politica,* and it was forthwith begun.[1] It was about the same time that he penned the opening chapters of the *Ontologia* which he left untouched for many years afterwards, as he reminds

[1] Don Paoli remembers to have seen, in 1822, the manuscript of more than one part of this work. The first portion was published in Milan on 1837 as an essay on the chief causes that lead to the rise and fall of human societies. The second portion appeared in 1839 under the title of ' Society and its End.' Four other essays, now included in the *Filosofia della Politica*—(1) on Statistics, (2) on Communism and Socialism, (3) on the Definition of Riches, and (4) on Public Amuse-ments—though written, for the most part, during the first three years of his home retirement, were not published till 1858.

us himself when resuming it—'That which we begun when still very young we propose to continue in this our far advanced age.'[1] So likewise it was in those days that he commenced the remarkable treatise on jurisprudence entitled *Filosofia del Diritto*.[2] He attached much importance to the study of this science, and tells us, in a letter written from Rovereto on June 27, 1825, to the Abate Bellenghi, why he came to take the subject in hand and how he proposed to deal with it.

Your treatise *De civili imperio* greatly interests me. It may do much good in our times, when, together with an endless variety of essays on this subject, we have an endless confusion of ideas. Let me venture to tell you that I also have given many hours to enquiries and thoughts of this kind. As these investigations seemed to me no less necessary than difficult, I have most assiduously and attentively studied the works of the most celebrated writers on the subject, with the view of clearing up in my own mind the fundamental ideas whence flow all theories of civil as well as ecclesiastical society. The pages to which I have committed the fruit of these studies and thoughts will form, if I can ever succeed in publishing them, three large volumes, which, though produced in the sweetness of peace, are probably destined to go forth as lambs into the midst of wolves.

In the First Part are laid down the rules and criteria by which to judge the value of political means. This part consists of three books, the first of which gives the rules drawn from 'the limits of society,' the second gives those drawn from the natural construction of society, and the

[1] *Teosofia*, vol. 1. Pref. No. 1.
[2] It was not published until 1841, though some portions appeared earlier in separate essays.

third those drawn from the laws followed by societies in their course.

The Second Part treats of political means themselves— finite as well as infinite—and by comparing them together it shows that religion is the most potent of all. This part is divided into seven books, each of which deals with one class of general political means; the last of these means, to which all the others tend and for which they prepare the way, being the Christian, i.e. the Roman Catholic, religion.

The Third Part discusses the way in which Princes should use this most efficacious means so that it should ob- tain the grand effect for which it was designed. This part has three books, and is occupied chiefly with the relations between civil society and the Church.

I should never have thought of undertaking such a work (which from the very first look at it seemed to me much beyond my feeble powers), had I not felt sincerely convinced that the Divine Will required it of me. Indeed, some years ago while absorbed in totally different studies I felt myself, I know not how, torn away from them, and though they seemed to me well suited to my disposition I felt constrained to leave them half finished and turn to these in preference.[1]

It was the Divine Will that kept him in the seclu- sion of home during these five years. It was the same Divine Will that drew him away from other labours, 'well suited to his disposition,' in order that he might devote himself more completely to intellec-

[1] Don Paoli informs us that the manuscript of the ' beautiful and grand work ' alluded to in the above letter has not been found ; but its contents were evidently recast in two other works—' The Philosophy of Right ' and the ' Philosophy of Politics.' The letter to Don Bellenghi shows not only the progress of Rosmini's thoughts upon those impor- tant questions, but the ease and power with which he handled the most profound subjects even while he was still very young. To successfully reproduce all the arguments in subsequent works, as he has done, im- plies very great labour and rare skill.

tual charity. All his preferences were thus regulated by the Divine Will, and whatever he studied or wrote or planned, or began or finished, had its beginning and end in his eager desire to discover and do God's Will.

The life of every man has been likened to a drama (seldom very entertaining or edifying) the scenes of which are to be viewed in reference to the main action, on which they ought all to turn or the drama will prove a 'failure.' All the incidents of Rosmini's life oblige one to view them in connection with its main purpose, for everything he did or said turned constantly on the 'main action.' This main action itself, with 'the little nameless unnumbered acts' that form an important portion of one's life, was centred in God, and, accordingly, was passive or active as either condition better fulfilled the purpose of centring on God and doing His Will. Whether he remained in solitude to find 'sermons in stones and God in everything,' or associated with those who ministered to the spiritual and corporal wants of the poor and afflicted, or stood forth to shield Christian morality from the subtle assaults of modern impiety, or to unmask the deceits of ancient error in its newer guises, the main action, with all its minor accessories, turned on the same object—the Will of God for the Glory of God.[1]

[1] ' Now, if man considers himself to be a mere instrument in God's hands, as faith teaches him to do, what can the instrument effect without Him who wields it? Let man, then, be content with allowing himself to be moved and wielded by the hand of God, and let him glory in it. It is thus that he will be able to do a great deal, on behalf of his

brethren. Let him not pretend, even in works of charity, to be, himself, the principal agent ; let him leave the first place and the glory to
the Almighty ; let him believe, with a firm faith, that God forgets none
of His creatures ; let him listen with attention, that he may hear when
his Master speaks ; and let him obey His call, whether it be manifested through the binding obligation of a commandment, or through
the requests of his brethren in need, or through the invitation of
external circumstances pre-ordained by God. If man do otherwise—
if, of his own will, or through a merely human impulse, he should interfere in things which seem to be works of charity, but which, perhaps,
are not such, or are not required of him—then, instead of benefiting his
brethren, he will do injury to himself. By not observing that commandment, " beware of men " (Matt. x. 17), or that injunction of the
Apostle, " attend to thyself " (1 Tim. iv. 16), he will forget himself, he
will neglect the salvation of his own soul, being deceived by a false
zeal of doing good to others ; so that, while he preaches to others, he
will himself become a castaway.'—*Rosmini's Discourses.* Discourse
on the Will of God, p. 40 (James Duffy & Sons : London, 1882).

CHAPTER XIV.

ROSMINI'S CONTACT WITH THE OUTER WORLD DURING HIS HOME RETIREMENT.

(A.D. 1822-1823.)

The duties of hospitality—How he made ' social intercourse ' contribute to his main object—He is recognised as the champion of
Catholic Truth against the upholders of dechristianising error—
How to write books to confound unbelievers—What he thinks of
institutions for gathering together the children of the poor on
Sundays and Holy-days—Charity always striving to do more and
more good—He goes to Padua and receives the doctorate—Is
made a member of the Accademia of the Catholic Religion—Enter-
tains the Bishop of Treviso at Rovereto—Becomes the preceptor
of a Bishop as well as of Priests—Why he declines to accept some
benefice in his native diocese, and why he accepts the office of
Synodical Examiner—His Academy of St. Thomas and his love for
the Angelic Doctor—A lost manuscript—Reproves the Italians for
not appreciating the great Aquinas—Italy and Europe holding
St. Thomas in little esteem, Rosmini endeavours to win for him
the homage that has since been decreed to him.

ALTHOUGH Rosmini's home life during the five years
following his Ordination had all the characteristics of
monastic retirement, these years were not without
little episodes which sometimes brought him into
contact with the ' outer world.' There were responsibilities connected with the headship of his family,
and he could not always conveniently or wisely dele-
gate them to others. Amongst these responsibilities
were certain duties of hospitality which he felt bound

to discharge in person : and none knew how to do so with more perfect courtesy or with truer heartiness.

But, after all, to entertain guests like the Marchioness of Canossa was no encroachment on the plan of his retirement ; it was only a special and edifying phase within it. Nor was there any departure from its completeness in sharing the spiritual toil of some overworked Priest, or visiting the sick, or consoling the afflicted, or finding out and aiding the poor, or attending to any other such ' labour of love.'

What seemed to cause a real encroachment on his retirement was the social obligation of accepting, now and then, an invitation to dine with some of his relations or friends, and of having to return the compliment. But, as he contrived to make even these occasions a means of promoting his central object— God's glory—they were like so many opportunities to vary the manner of his seclusion, without infringing its law or its motive. So, too, the sermons and lectures he was requested to deliver from time to time in some church or public institution, only lent variety to his work, without touching the sameness of its scope. The one thing which more frequently than any other called him from retirement, or rather brought his name before the public in those days, was the defence of Christian Truth from its worst foes, the propagators of the subtle errors that were then taking fresh root through Italy.

Gifted with a marvellous foresight, the young Abate clearly saw that, though the crop of mischief produced by the philosophical fallacies of the day was baneful enough as it stood, the fallacies themselves were but gathering strength for the growth of more formidable evils in the future. Hence it was that he applied himself to the composition of such books as the *Nuovo Saggio.* But, that the evils actually present might not pass current unchecked, he wrote and published immediately such essays as that 'On Happiness.'[1] Just then some brilliant literary worldlings were poisoning the minds of Italian youth with false notions of human felicity,—with ideas, in fact, that deified sensism and dishonoured Christianity.

In the principal towns of Lombardy and Piedmont Infidelity had more than one able chief, and all over the country many wily agents spread the pernicious tenets of the sensists. Against all these he set himself with such unflinching determination, tempered with so much calmness and charity, that, even apart from the solidity of his reasoning, he was soon looked upon as specially qualified to be the champion of religion ; and in that character he was constantly attacked by the foes of the Faith, and had his counsel as constantly sought by its friends. Indeed, so much was he consulted as a leader in whose guidance the friends of religion trusted, that he was almost every day obliged to write letters, such as the following, which was sent in reply to Signor Lugnani of Triest, who was desirous of knowing how best to

---

[1] It was first printed at Rovereto in 1822, afterwards (1823) in Venice, and finally, in 1828, it was reproduced under the title of *Saggio sulla Speranza* to meet some errors which Hugo Foscolo was propagating.

compose works intended to confound unbelievers, and confirm the Faithful.

A friendly letter from you would, under any circumstances, have afforded me the greatest pleasure. But, coupling, as you do, friendship and religion together, you have rendered infinitely more precious the relations between us. It is unquestionably true that there exists no more solid or sincere friendship than that which springs from, and is nurtured, perfected and sanctified by religion. Oh how deeply ought Christians to feel this truth! Should not the very consolation they experience in this most pure sentiment lead them more forcibly to band themselves together, by means of the indissoluble ties of mutual intercourse and friendship? It would assist every Christian in the increase of virtue,—it would be a deathblow to unbelievers, whose iniquitous schemes would be less successful, if there were greater union among the forces which they assail.

It is thus that I have often thought, in my own mind, envying those first ages of Christianity, when 'the Brethren,' as they were styled, were but one heart and one soul; and I am of the same sentiments at this moment, when you kindly proffer me your sincere and holy friendship. I accept it with all my heart.

You make known to me your sentiments with regard to the best manner of refuting the unbelievers of our own time. I have read your suggestions with very great pleasure. They seem to me to show a knowledge of the human heart and a sufficient acquaintance with the kind of adversaries against whom we have to struggle. I am well persuaded that there are many different classes of men—that incredulity, Proteus-like, is of ever-changing form, and therefore, that to grapple with it successfully, not only is a great variety of books required but a great diversity in their mode of treatment. I myself, with the little experience I have of the world, think I have found adversaries diametrically opposed to one another, not only in their character, but in their errors and modes of thinking. A German, for instance, must be refuted in a very different manner from that employed to refute a Frenchman. A disciple of Kant and a disciple of Voltaire are widely divergent in their way of thinking. Then, there are some who profit by pamphlets, short but trenchant and eloquent, while others, on the contrary, find large and systematic works of more advantage.

Notwithstanding all this, it is my firm opinion that, generally speaking, one of the methods most useful and best adapted for our own times is that which you yourself very judiciously propose and trace out. The special features you pronounce to be characteristic of our age are the great want of sound and solid reasoning. I will add, reasoning not too speculative and dry, but clear and easy of comprehension, supported by moral proofs and clothed in a succinct, rapid and philosophical style. There is, besides, a·great need of impartiality, discretion, and generosity of soul, of urbanity and a spirit of conciliation. These and similar qualities I deem to be necessary to our writings, if our aim be to persuade and win over unbelievers, and not simply to irritate them more and more. And does not Christianity itself suggest a certain fulness of charity, a certain degree of urbanity and shrewdness conjoined ? I must then encourage you, with all the earnestness in my power, to go on with an undertaking so ably conceived and from which, with God's blessing, you may promise yourself abundant fruit.

I know no one more competent than yourself to put your designs into execution. By doing so you will acquire great merit in the sight of God. Even if I were equal to the task myself, I should hesitate to trespass on another's sphere of action. However, my inaptitude as well as the anxiety springing from a multiplicity of affairs—amongst other things the composition of some little works—preclude the possibility of my assuming such an undertaking. Do not hesitate, then, as I am sure you will not, to enter upon the work.

Apropos of the apologetic authors to whom you allude, have you read Haller's great work, ' The Restoration of Political Science'? I have had it now for several days, but, as it is written in a language of which I have no thorough knowledge, I am reading it under difficulties. Although he treats in a great measure of politics, I have no hesitation in numbering him among our apologists, and in pronouncing his production one of the ablest and most opportune works of the day. In it you will find very well applied all your own sage observations respecting the mode of dealing with unbelievers. It is a stupendous work. The writer couples theory with experience, subtlety of reasoning with solidity, the ease and elegance of the ancient philosophers with the raciness and readiness peculiar to those of more modern times. How many beautiful observations he makes ! And on what luminous principles and reasons he rests them !

ROVERETO : *May* 2, 1822.[1]

On the same day he had occasion to answer a letter from Signor Battaggia of Venice, touching other forms of Christian charity. While the same spirit of piety pervades both these, as it does all his letters, they are different in nearly everything else, and not least in the practical hints which imply a more varied and sound knowledge of human society and its needs than long years of experience and extensive opportunities enable most men to acquire. It may be well to remember that although Sunday and Week-day institutions for the moral and spiritual well-being of poor children are now, in some form or other, common enough in our own country, they were little

[1] *Epistolario*, Letter xxxiv.

known here at the date of this letter; nor were attempts to resist the inroads of infidelity much thought of in those days, when England was still somewhat free from the malady which had already seriously infected Europe.

Your pious Institution aims at gathering little boys together on Sundays and Holy-days, thus withdrawing them from dissipation and from roaming at large through the streets, and at the same time entertaining them with instruction, prayer, and proper amusements. This being its nature, it must be very pleasing to God and profitable, in an eminent degree, to those little ones. They are withdrawn from all that imperils their virtue, and they are brought to fulfil an important precept such as is the sanctification of Sundays and Holy-days, and thus are set on the path of piety not only for those days but for the rest of the week. Well can I imagine those pure and consoling delights which you tell me you often experience. Such is the pleasure that always springs from works of Christian charity, and which the children of this world are unable to conceive, much less to relish. Fortunate, indeed, and happy are you !

True, there are times when, as you yourself tell me, you feel displeasure and anguish at seeing some of these boys not corresponding with your anxious solicitude. Now, as a matter of fact, this usually happens with charity, which is seldom satisfied; nor can it be denied that it is a difficult thing to fulfil all its obligations with due foresight and perfection. Even St. Augustine frequently deplored this fact. It is a gift which God generally bestows little by little, as is His way respecting the other virtues, and He bestows it only on those who ask it of Him in humility of heart. It so happens that they who ask it belong usually to that class of persons who, while they cease not to act righteously, are eager to do still better. They are never content, because they deem it a serious defect not to be able to reach the apex of perfection. God endows such as these with ever-increasing degrees of light, and, as we see exemplified in the Saints, they often rise to an almost incredible height of prudence, meekness and skill in winning souls and leading them to God. Take heart then, and let nothing discourage you in the meritorious career on which you have entered.

When you inform me that your projects and pious designs are not confined to this work only, you make me entertain very sanguine hopes of the future, for I know that charity is boundless. All this gives me greater confidence in speaking to you of that other project—The Turin Society. Not very long ago that excellent man the Marquis d'Azeglio sent me a long and kind letter, in the name of the Society, with a parcel of books, all of which have, I believe, been published through its agency. It is, indeed, a noble undertaking and calculated to produce most beneficial results. Whatever we may do, it is above all things necessary that our zeal be *fervent, constant,* and *discreet.* Without *fervour* we shall never accomplish anything that is valuable or useful. So we shall be wanting in perseverance, if *constancy of resolution* do not make us surmount all the obstacles which cross our path (and they are formidable) whether they come from the wicked, or the ignorant, the world or the Evil One. Finally, if charity have not *wisdom* for its guide, it will prove neither acceptable to God nor advantageous to men. In fact, then it would not be charity at all, but a meaningless name, a mere presumption, or a delusion of the enemy. Let us mature the matter fully in prayer, and in accordance with the light which God may deign to give us, whether it be by means of those good sentiments with which He may inspire ourselves or by the suggestions of judicious persons. Let us try to follow and not to forestall the designs of God, and be humbly indifferent to everything else save doing His holy Will ; in nothing seeking our own interests but His alone. These dispositions made, I trust we shall so far succeed that we ourselves shall experience, in the end, ineffable consolation. Pray meanwhile, and meditate.

ROVERETO : *May* 2, 1822.[1]

There were three occasions, during these five years, on which Rosmini consented to overstep the bounds of his seclusion in a more decided way than any we have indicated. The first of these was on June 23, 1822, when he went to Padua for the Doctor's degree, which he had long been ready to receive, but had declined to take, partly out of consideration for his less advanced classmates, and partly from a desire to give precedence to Holy Orders.[2] He was warmly greeted at Padua, not only by many personal friends among the professors and students, but by all the University authorities. He remained with them merely while it was necessary to comply with the formalities required for taking the double doctorate—Divinity and Canon Law.

Having duly received both, as one who had won them with distinction, he at once returned to Rovereto, where he had to endure yet another ovation ; for his fellow-citizens chose to consider every fresh dignity secured by him as reflecting honour on themselves. But, to his thinking, the diploma of Fellowship in the 'Academy of the Catholic Religion,' which was conferred upon him about the same time, was a loftier dignity than that

---

[1] *Epistolario*, Letter xxxv.   [2] See Chapter vii. p. 136.

which the Roveretans thought worthy of public rejoicings. Of this Fellowship he spoke as of an honour according to his heart, while the doctorate seemed to him a comparatively trifling affair—'*cosa leggiera*'—as he styled it in a letter to his friend Paravia.

The next time he passed notably far from his home retirement was in the Autumn of the same year, when he proceeded to Innsbruck, accompanied by Don Orsi, his former master, in order to escort a distinguished guest to Rovereto. This guest was Monsignor Grasser, who had been Prefect of Studies in the great Tyrolese University, where young Rosmini formed his acquaintance and laid the foundation of a life-long friendship between them. M. Grasser had just been nominated to the see of Treviso, and as he had but an imperfect knowledge of Italian he sought his young friend's hospitality and assistance while endeavouring to overcome this disadvantage. His episcopal career, which was most successful (first at Treviso, and afterwards at Verona) may be said to have taken its start, if not more, under the healthy influences of the 'sacerdotal philosopher of Rovereto.' As a young layman Rosmini had been deemed fit to prepare, and actually did prepare, ecclesiastics for the Priesthood; why then should it be strange if he, as a young Priest, was deemed fit to do some kindred service for Priests who were about to assume the Episcopal Office? Such duties as these were no real interruption to the even tenor of the monastic course he was resolved to follow, whether he was entertaining guests at home or was himself a guest in the homes of others.

Before this visit of M. Grasser came to a close, Rosmini was appealed to by the ecclesiastical authorities of Trent to connect himself officially and permanently with his native diocese. To this end M. Sardagna, then Vicar Capitular, who highly esteemed the virtues and abilities of the young Abate, and was eager to keep them for Trent, offered many inducements well calculated to successfully entice any one else. But, as these tempting offers looked too much like honouring the individual, they failed to allure one whose zeal for the Church was so pure that anything with the semblance of self-interest, instead of attracting, repelled him. However, at M. Grasser's suggestion, he consented to accept the office of Synodical Examiner, as least objectionable and not likely to embarrass him in living up to the principles he had laid down for his guidance. Moreover, it would enable him to accomplish much good, especially in connection with the little Academy for young ecclesiastics, which he still kept up in his own house and at his own expense.

This little Academy was known amongst its students as the Gymnasium of the Aquinate, because they were mainly occupied with the works of St. Thomas, for which Rosmini had always the profoundest admiration. The presence of guests in the family mansion was never allowed to interfere with the regular course of studies, nor with the formal lectures he daily gave his pupils. Sometimes the guests took part in the discussions, as M. Grasser requested permission to do while he stayed. The young professor usually strolled off to prepare the lessons in the quiet of St. Ilario (a secluded villa conveniently near the town) and then came back to read and discuss them with his disciples, or, as he preferred to designate them, 'fellow academicians.' The cream of these readings, naturally enough, passed into a formal work designed for the press, but, unfortunately, the manuscript has been lost. He has himself left us this record of it in a letter written to Tommaseo, some months later than the time of which we are now speaking :

I have begun the little dissertation on St. Thomas of Aquin, whose genius I hold to be in no way inferior to Newton's. I am writing it in Latin. At the very outset, I reprove the Italians for not appreciating the treasure they possess and the glory which might accrue to them if they but availed themselves of the riches offered to them in the writings of this peerless genius. I place the great merits of St. Thomas in theological wisdom, and then investigate the causes which have led to his being so little studied. I find them in the decay amongst us of the philosophy of Aristotle, and I endeavour to describe the good as well as evil of that philosophy. I next proceed to speak of such parts of this system as should be revived, showing that if it were restored it would appear more beautiful than at any other period. Then I do my best to give a condensed exposition of it in language suited to modern times. In doing this I penetrate as far as I can into its spirit. By such an abridgment of the Aristotelian philosophy, purged of its errors and perfected by the lofty intellect of our Angelic Doctor, I think I am appending to the works of this mighty genius the only proper means of understanding and relishing them.[1]

Thus, when not only Italy, but all Europe, looked with coldness, if not with positive disfavour, on the works of St. Thomas of Aquin, the Abate Rosmini, against formidable opposition, was vigorously striving to secure for them that place which they now hold in the estimation of the Catholic world.   Indeed, it can be claimed, with perfect justice, that the young Roveretan philosopher was one of the first, if not the very first, to insist on the pre-eminent merits of the grand Dominican ; and he was assuredly the first, and perhaps the only writer, who so thoroughly mastered the teachings of the Angelic Doctor as to be in a position to make them truly 'understood and relished.'

[1] See *Il Rinnovamento della Filosofia in Italia,* Milano, 1836, 1840 ; and *Aristotele esposto ed esaminato* published in the *Rivista Contemporanea* of Turin, November 1854 and January 1855, and by the *Società Editrice di libri di Filosofia* in 1857.

CHAPTER XV.

ROSMINI'S FIRST VISIT TO ROME.

(A.D. 1823.)

He is invited to accompany Mons. Grasser to Treviso—Quits his retirement for the third time—It proves to be the first serious departure from the monastic seclusion of home—Meets the Patriarch of Venice, who takes him to Rome—His first short but fruitful visit to the Eternal City—Becomes the friend of Mauro Cappellari (afterwards Pope Gregory XVI)—Interview with Pius VII.—The Pope counsels him to persevere in philosophical studies for the good of the Church—Is offered an important office at the Papal Court—How this perplexes him, and why he declines it—The burden of exalted friendships—Informs his mother how the time has been spent—Returns home—How news of the Pope's dangerous illness is received in Rovereto—News of the Holy Father's death—Rosmini leads the people to honour his memory—Is appointed to preach the funeral oration—Effect of his discourse on those who heard it.

WHEN Monsignor Grasser was on the eve of departing from Rovereto, in order to take formal possession of his See, he urgently requested his young host to accompany him and assist at the ceremony. Rosmini at first hesitated ; but, after he had spent some time in prayer, to discover God's Will in the matter, he came to the conclusion that all the circumstances connected with the invitation brought it within the range of the rule he had laid down for his guidance.

Q 2

It was the third time of his quitting the long seclusion following his Ordination—the third for any purpose far beyond the ordinary paths of home life. But as it led to an extraordinary extension of his journey and of his absence, as well as to scenes of exceptional distraction, it may be regarded as the first time in which his five years' retirement was seriously disturbed. Not that he failed still to carry self-seclusion with him, or to observe his monastic rule, as far as circumstances permitted, but that circumstances made it impossible for him to observe it as fully as at home. These circumstances were, however, as we shall see, of a nature to compensate him spiritually and otherwise for so unusual an invasion of the tranquillity he loved so much. Besides, they were the source of influences that had an important bearing on his after life, and thus justified the conclusion that God willed him to accept Mgr. Grasser's invitation.

The young Abate accompanied his illustrious guest to Treviso. There he had the good fortune to meet once more, and under most favourable auspices, an old Paduan friend—the learned Ladislaus Pirker, Patriarch of Venice, who had come to instal his suffragan. When the ceremonies were over, the Patriarch pressed his young friend to go with him to Venice, and thence to Rome. The terms of the invitation were such as made acceptance a duty; and so Rosmini soon found himself, most unexpectedly, on the way to the Eternal City, whither his imagination had often fondly journeyed

But, frequently as he thought of making a pilgrimage to the shrine of the Apostles, and much as he wished to carry out the desire, he would not venture to go till Providence, by circumstances, indicated the time. The indication was at length clear, and he went.

This, his first visit to Rome, was made in the Spring of 1823. It was short and somewhat hurried, but fruitful. As the honoured companion of the Venetian Patriarch he had rare opportunities of knowing people and of seeing places it was most important for him to know and see. These opportunities kept him so incessantly busy that he had no time to pen the descriptions he intended to write of what he saw, nor a moment to more than name the illustrious persons whose acquaintance he made. Amongst those whose warm friendship he then secured was a pious and learned Camaldoli monk, greatly esteemed in Rome, where he discharged the duties of Procurator General of his Order.[1] This was the Abate

---

[1] The monks of Camaldoli took their name from the once famous monastery founded in 1009 on the estate of the Counts Maldoli, in the Apennines, above the valley of Casentino near Arezzo in Tuscany. The monastery itself had its name contracted from that of the estate—*Campo Maldoli*. The founder was St. Romualdo, who died in 1027. (See Butler's *Lives of the Saints*, vol. I. pp. 208-11.) For more than 800 years this monastery was the nursery of a sanctity and learning that shed its brightness far and near. Amongst its illustrious children were—the Blessed Maldoli, one of the Counts to whom the property originally belonged; St. Peter Damian, a Cardinal and Doctor of the Church; Guido Aretino, the famous musician and inventor of the Solfeggio; Mauro Cappellari, who became Pope Gregory XVI.; Casimir King of Poland, &c. But in spite of its sacred renown and continued usefulness, in spite of the fact that its monks were 'much distinguished for their charity in years of famine, when, besides continuing their usual alms, they mortgaged the Church plate and their possessions for the benefit of their poor neighbours, and even deprived

Mauro Cappellari, who, eight years afterwards, was called to the chair of Peter as Gregory XVI. Another intimacy dating from those days was that with Cardinal Zurla; another with Mgr. Ostini, subsequently a Cardinal ; and yet another, that with the distinguished Albertino Bellenghi, whose writings on geological subjects he much admired.[1]

Pius VII. was still reigning, and though the venerable Pontiff was in very feeble health, Don Antonio had not long to wait for an audience, which proved to be of a most kindly character. The Holy Father, who had heard much about him, not only from the Patriarch but from others, was well pleased with the young Roveretan Priest, whose philosophical studies he warmly approved. He bade him to remember that much was expected from him, because he had received much, and that he

themselves of their outer garments for the same purpose,' in spite of all this the Italian Government suppressed the monastery and made it national property in 1865, ' the great extent and beauty of its forests' being an avowed reason. Some sixteen years afterwards the same Government sold the grand old home of the Camaldoli at public auction, the day of sale being, significantly enough, a Sunday, 9th of Oct. 1881. It was to stem the tide of evils which threatened results like this that Mauro Cappellari as Camaldoli monk, as Cardinal and as Pope, urged Antonio Rosmini to wage continuous war against false philosophy, and it was to a like end that the same distinguished Camaldolese, when Vicar of Christ, commissioned the Roveretan divine to found a Religious Order.

[1] It was on this occasion that Bellenghi entrusted to him the manuscript of the work entitled *Ricerche sulla Geologia*, which Rosmini read with interest and published at Rovereto in 1824. Some of the Roman journals condemned it much as the critics of Galileo would have done ; but the distinguished Professor Zamboni of Verona defended it, and its speculations are now allowed to be freely handled by every Catholic schoolboy as ' theories void of harm to faith or morals.'

must utilise his talents and his studies for the good of the Church. Don Antonio was deeply affected by this fatherly reception, 'which he recorded, not on paper, but in his heart,' as he assured Tommaseo when telling him of it.[1]

Shortly after the interview, and while the young Priest was still flushed with the joy it caused him, he received a formal message to the effect that the Sovereign Pontiff offered to his acceptance the post of *Uditore di Rota*—a mark of signally high favour, which, in the opinion of his Roman friends, was meant as the direct approach to the Cardinalate. That the Holy Father should have thought of him at all in such a manner overwhelmed him afresh; but this time a cloud flecked the sunshine around him. How was he to accept this important office without setting aside the special works of charity already begun ? How was he to take it, and carry on successfully the studies which the Pope himself had so emphatically commended ?— studies that aimed at the restoration of Christian philosophy as one of the greatest boons which Intellectual Charity could secure to men in an age of hardened scepticism.

The Patriarch, on learning his perplexity, re-minded him that the terms of the Holy Father's offer did not at all imply a command. This re-lieved him, and, having the option, he promptly asked and obtained permission to decline the high post the venerable Pontiff's favour had placed

[1] *Rivista Cont.* Antonio Rosmini per N. Tommaseo. Torino, 1855.

within his reach. Seven years afterwards, when
he had occasion to explain to the Bishop of Trent
why he could not consistently accept an important
position to which that Prelate invited him, he thus
alluded to the offers which his principles obliged him
to decline at the hands even of the venerable Pius
VII. :

I regard as one of the principal rules regulating my
course, that which forbids me to assume any office likely to
impede the doing of a greater work *already commenced.* It
was chiefly on this account and not, I hope, through sloth
or cowardice, that I found myself obliged to refuse some
most honourable posts which were offered to me in
the capital of Christendom as long ago as 1823, during
the pontificate of Pius VII., as well as on subsequent occasions.[1]

The 'sweet fame' which had preceded the young
Roveretan Priest, coupled with the advantages of
intimate association with the Venetian Patriarch,
made his stay at Rome much more honoured and
exciting than was at all agreeable to him. To visit
the sacred shrines and see the treasures of art, and
explore the venerable remains of ages long past,
afforded him great pleasure indeed ; but this had its
drawback in the fact that he was always escorted by
those whose kind attentions oppressed him. Far
sooner would he have seen all these things while
alone and unknown. He had, however, to bear the
burden of exalted intimacies, and submit to be somewhat lionised. All this made it impossible for him
to write much from Rome, even to his mother, who

---

[1] *Epistolario*, Letter clxxiv.

had from him the following explanation of his
difficulties :— .

The infrequency of my letters from Rome will enable
you to understand how much I am occupied all day in
seeing a thousand things which truly inebriate the soul. I
have hardly time left me for the saying of the Divine Office,
and for the other exercises of piety. The Patriarch, full of
activity, is indefatigable ; besides, we are overwhelmed with
visits. In short, what with one thing and another our stay
has come to an end, without my being able to write to you
as much as I had hoped.

According to our present arrangements, on next
Tuesday we shall leave for Florence, where we shall spend
a few days. Our health has been good all through. . . .
You cannot imagine how much it delights me to discover, at every turn, the art wonders uncle Ambrogio
used to describe to me in such vivid language. Few
things come so new to me, as to find me unable to say
what they are ; indeed, I can often give their history, so
deep were the impressions made on my mind by the words
of one so dear to me. Yesterday we were at Frascati
and Albano, lovely spots not far from Rome. We derived
great pleasure from discoursing on matters connected
with the antiquarian relics strewn all over these places.
But in spite of the many attractions by which I am surrounded, I yearn to find myself once more restored to
home retirement.[1]

He started for that home retirement a few days
after he had thus written to his mother. But, as in
Rome, so in Florence and elsewhere on the return
journey, his stay, though at no place long, was of
that distracting kind which little harmonised with
his private inclinations. However, since the Will of

[1] Unpublished letter, dated Rome, April 22, 1823.

Providence, and not his own, had regulated the tour—and destined him to have a more conspicuous share in it than his love of seclusion would have permitted himself to have chosen—he found therein a means of making it contribute to his spiritual as well as physical and mental advantage.

Hardly had he resumed the monastic regularity of his quiet but most industrious and useful life in Rovereto, when news came that the venerated Pius VII. was dangerously ill. Don Antonio immediately brought the members of his two Academies to combine in prayer for the good estate of the dying Pope, and for the prosperity of the whole Church. A few days afterwards came tidings of the saintly Chief Pastor's departure to eternal life, and, at once, Rosmini was busy in leading all Rovereto to unite in suffrages for the good Pontiff's soul, and in publicly honouring his memory. Every church in Rovereto had solemn services befitting the sad occasion ; and, in order that no homage due to the illustrious dead should be wanting, a committee of Priests and laymen was appointed to arrange for the celebration of a ' month's mind,' on September 25, at which the municipal authorities, with various other civic dignitaries, were to assist ' in state,' and an appropriate funeral oration was to be pronounced. Rosmini was formally requested to prepare and preach this discourse, and it was thus he came to deliver the panegyric which secured for him so much fame and trouble.

The masterly eloquence of this discourse sur-

prised those who heard it ; for, though they expected
much from the orator as to the matter, they were not
prepared for the heartiness of manner which gave
such effective utterance to what he felt and proclaimed. But what impressed them most of all was
the dauntless spirit and unanswerable logic with
which the young Abate asserted and defended the
rights of the Holy See against the aggressions,
not only of revolution but of that modern statecraft
which had then influential advocates in Austria.
When denouncing both the acts and the policy of
Napoleon—the extravagances and the principles of
the Revolution—he struck at a policy and at principles
that still lurked in high as well as low places, biding
a time to once more assault the See of Sees. A
quarter of a century later he was, himself, to witness
the new assault : it was made under changed circumstances, indeed, but its character and its dangers were
in no essential respect different from those which
he, with marvellous foresight, already denounced as
latent in the false principles underlying the political
systems of the day.

CHAPTER XVI.

ROSMINI'S PANEGYRIC OF PIUS VII. THE BEGINNING OF TRIBULATIONS.

(A.D. 1824.)

Why this panegyric calls for a special chapter—How it marks the close of calm life and the opening of storms—The greater the Saints and the more they do for the glory of God, the greater and more their trials—Synopsis of the panegyric—He is entreated to publish it immediately as an offset to current attacks on the Holy See—Why Austrian politicians opposed its publication—They fear Rosmini as an ' Ultramontane'—What he says of their course—He publishes a portrait of the Pope, and is opposed even in this— He foresees the evils which certain political factions in Catholic countries are to bring on the Church and on nations.

THE panegyric of Pius VII. may be said to have closed Rosmini's life of external peace and opened upon him that of storm ; for his bold and successful defence of the Holy See brought upon him the first of those tribulations that were, in so many other ways, to strew his path with thorns. This discourse had, therefore, all the higher value in his eyes, since it marked the commencement of a practical application to himself of the Eighth Beatitude—' Blessed are ye when they shall revile you, and persecute you, and speak all that is evil against you, untruly, for My sake. . . . For so they persecuted the Prophets that were before you.'

Seeing, then, that it inaugurated a new and most important phase in his course, it claims at our hands more than a passing allusion. But, apart from this leading motive, there are other reasons immediately connected with the views Rosmini so emphatically enunciated in this famous panegyric which make a synopsis of its contents a necessary part of any complete history of his life. He should be seen, at all points, in the clear light of his own principles, as described by himself and consistently adhered to from first to last. To be misunderstood and misrepresented was a lot from which neither a St. Augustine of Hippo, nor a St. Thomas of Aquin, nor a St. Ignatius of Loyola, nor, indeed, any great Saint, was exempt. On the contrary, the greater the Saint and the more he did for the glory of God and the Church, the more was he misunderstood, sometimes even by the zealously good, and the more was he misrepresented by those whose zeal outstripped their prudence. Antonio of Rovereto had to bear this cross of the Saints from an early day of his life, and, like all who truly loved the Cross of Calvary, he bore it meekly and patiently to the end.

I. In the exordium of the panegyric he maintains that the nature of Christian virtue is far nobler than any of which mere human heroism can boast; and that the greatness of Christian virtue has far better opportunities and more occasions for its exercise (and is actually more exercised) in the Roman Pontificate than in any other position on earth. He then takes for the argument of the whole discourse, the moral greatness of the Roman Pontiffs as seen in Pius VII.

II. He vividly describes the calamities that afflicted the Church when Cardinal Chiaramonti was chosen, in March 1800, to fill the chair of Peter.

III. He goes on to show how very difficult it must have been for the Pontiff elected in such trying times to remedy the evils that beset the Church, seeing that it was so very difficult to proceed with the election itself; and how Divine Providence selected Pius VII. as the fittest to grapple with the dangers and over-come the evils, for all that some distrusted the choice because of the monastic humility of the new Pope and the shrinking gentleness of his personal cha-racter.

IV. He dwells on the fact that Pius VII. was no sooner seated in the chair of Peter than he felt the whole weight of the immense burden imposed upon him, but without being at all discouraged.

V. He demonstrates the moral greatness of Pius VII. by an extrinsic argument, that is, by the results obtained—contrasting the state of the Church at the time of the Pontiff's death with the condition in which it was at the period of his election.

VI. He continues to prove this moral greatness by an investigation of its nature, and shows that its two leading characteristics were *wisdom* and *fortitude* —wisdom in comprehending the true position of affairs, and fortitude in acting on the conclusions thus arrived at. He then compares the fortitude of

Worldly heroes, which displays itself in enterprises full of cruelty, with the fortitude of Christian heroes, which manifests itself, chiefly, in the longanimity that patiently endures all manner of suffering however iniquitously inflicted.

VII. The better to set forth the indomitable vigour of the Pope's fortitude he begins a calm, clear, description of the persecutions raised against him —what mental anguish and what physical sufferings his adversaries forced him to go through. He then exposes Napoleon's designs on the Papal States, and how, as a first stage to carrying them out, the usurper occupied Ancona with an army.

VIII. He points out the enormity of the sacrilege attempted by Napoleon, as made painfully clear in the attending circumstances, and not least in the audacious assumption of the title Defender of the Holy See. He interrupts the narrative to give a historical sketch of the Protectorate of 'the Papal Power' which the French kings occasionally exercised, and then shows how impudent and insincere was Napoleon's pretence of imitating them.

IX. He exposes the gross insult which Napoleon offered to the Pontiff, by affirming that the Emperor knew better than the Pope what concerned the interests of the Church, and that it was on account of this superior knowledge the imperial forces took possession of the Pontifical States.

X. He indicates the profound contempt of men evinced by Napoleon, in declaring himself to be the Roman Emperor, Charlemagne's successor, and in

pretending that all the States of Italy were, therefore, his dependencies.

XI. He brings to view the further vexation
that was caused to Pius VII. by Napoleon's wicked
attempt to subjugate the Pontiff to his desires for
the enslavement of the Church, which, under pretext
of protecting, he tried to change into a human institution subordinate to the political ambition of a
despot.

XII. He lays bare the grievous insults to which
Napoleon's treatment of the Pontiff subjected him,
and not least in having sought to make it appear that
the Holy Father's unyielding attitude sprang, not
from motives of conscience, but from human interests
under the veil of conscience.

XIII. He denounces the unworthy calumnies
which Pius VII. had to endure at the usurper's
hands, and unmasks the despicable pretexts to which
Napoleon had recourse in order to hurl injurious
reproaches at the afflicted Pontiff.

XIV. He extols the firmness of the Pope, which
made him proof against all the artifices and insults
of his tormentor to coax or force him to say or do
what conscience and duty forbade; and he commends
the Pontiff's answers as firm in substance while
courteous and full of meekness in manner.

XV. He reviews the true relations of the Popes
with secular powers as well illustrated by Pius VII.,
who declared that, as ' Vicar of the Lord of Peace,'
he could not enter into any offensive alliance with
Napoleon against England, as he ought not to be at

war with any one. He shows how the Holy Father justly maintained this course to be according to the true spirit of the Roman Pontificate ; and how the example of his predecessors made it manifest that the spirit of the Holy See consists in rectitude, especially that rectitude which forms goodness and sacerdotal meekness.

XVI. He regards Pius VII. as the first Pope who was engaged in so prolonged and formidable a struggle for the defence of the spirit of Sacerdotal meekness ; and he claims that, through the conflict thus waged, the Pontiff bequeathed new glory to the Apostolic See. He then expatiates on the great merits of this struggle on such grounds.

XVII. He criticises the method employed by Nápoleon to revenge himself on the firmness of the Pope by means of fresh insults ; and explains how, in order to make the insults more effectively harsh, they were directed against the virtues which the imperial policy strove to persecute and destroy in the Pontifical States.

XVIII. He pictures Pius VII. bereft of every human comfort, while he was as ready as ever to offer consolation to all, not excepting his persecutors.

XIX. He brings to light Napoleon's attempts to stifle the veracious voice of the Pontiff, who, in the midst of his oppressions, refused to suppress the truth—a course that was utterly repugnant to the policy of his imperial gaoler, who therefore deprived him of every means of communicating with the Church of which he was the Visible Head.

XX. He relates, in detail, how the inexorable agents of tyranny tore from the Pontiff's side all his ministers one after another, and how patiently he submitted to each fresh torture, till he found himself on the eve of losing his last companion, Cardinal Pacca, when he stood up and interposed his person between this new victim and the soldiers who had come to force him away, as they had forced all the others.

XXI. Having thus fully brought to view the various forms of mental anguish that the venerable Pontiff had to endure, the orator next proceeds to describe and consider his physical sufferings.

XXII. He describes the forcible removal of the Pope from Rome, and gives an account of the wearisome and distressing journey to Savona and Fontainebleau.

XXIII. He considers the moral grandeur of Pius VII. as shown by his *fortitude* in bearing the evils inflicted upon him, and then passes on to view this grandeur as shown by the *wisdom* which regulated his conduct towards others :—First of all the wisdom that sustained him in adversity, especially that which enabled him to distinguish between what he could concede to his enemies and what he must firmly refuse to grant them ; then his wisdom in prosperity, especially in never allowing the least token of revenge to blemish his treatment of his persecutors, to whom he most generously stretched forth the arms of Christian Charity ; his wisdom in assigning their just value to things, and especially in knowing how to sacrifice mere formalities when a substantial good had to be gained; his wisdom in devising the fittest plans of operation under most difficult circumstances.

XXIV. He lays down the grounds of Public Right on which the coronation of Napoleon could be justified, and then explains how the Public Right which has *justice* for its basis was taught and promulgated in Europe, mainly by the Holy See.

XXV. He confronts the Public Right inculcated by the Popes, with the 'public right' enforced by Napoleon on the basis of a supposed public *utility*, and he lays bare the absurdity and fatal nature of this 'right,' which the sophists of modern times invented and Napoleon attempted to reduce to practice.

XXVI. He demonstrates that by his defence of public *justice*, against so-called public *utility*, Pius VII. defended the cause of all legitimate rulers and the true liberty of peoples.

XXVII. He deals with the three causes which led to the struggles of the Popes with temporal rulers :—1. The liberty of Italy, in so far as it is bound up with the liberty of the Church; 2. The necessity of supporting the moral dignity of marriage; 3. The proper maintenance of ecclesiastical discipline.

XXVIII. He insists that Pius VII. contended for all three within the bounds of Public Right, and then sets out to prove it, especially as regards the sacredness of the marriage tie.

XXIX. He enumerates the many benefits conferred on the Church by this venerable Pontiff, and
shows what his zeal for ecclesiastical discipline had
accomplished. He then descants on the wisdom of
his temporal rule, and on the enlightened generosity
which made him a munificent protector of Sciences
and Arts.

XXX. Having fully shown the greatness of the
Pontiff's Fortitude and Wisdom, he finally speaks of
his Sanctity, and proves that, in this also, Pius VII.
was great ; his public virtues possessed a special
excellence drawn from the fact that they all grew up
from the prolific and vigorous stem of this Sanctity.

XXXI. He concludes by apostrophising Italy as
a nation honoured beyond others in producing so
illustrious a son as Pius VII.

The desirability, nay the necessity, of immediately
publishing this panegyric was urged upon Rosmini,
not only by the Rovereto Clergy, but by those of
other towns in that and other dioceses, as well as by
many venerable laymen in whose judgment he had
much confidence. Accordingly, he prepared it for
the press, though not without misgivings as to its
reception by certain influential persons who were
imbued with a short-sighted policy unfavourable to
the Papacy—a policy which had slumbered in
Austria since the days of Joseph II., but had been
re-awakened by the Revolution, though under circumstances that held its supporters in check, so long
as the atrocities of Revolutionary and Napoleonic

ascendency were still fresh in the memory of the
people. But, the hostile spirit was none the less
there, and, however subdued in its manifestations, it
was potent enough to resist and trample on anyone
who might attempt to uphold the dignity and rights
of the Roman Pontiffs. When the young Roveretan
Priest was persuaded that it became his duty to con-
front this powerful and subtle antagonism to the
Holy See, he did not hesitate through fear of
personal consequences.

Already Pietro Giordani had published a panegyric of Napoleon I., and though this was at all points
unjustly and irritatingly adverse to the Papacy, it was
allowed to circulate freely through the Italian provinces of Austria. Its misrepresentations did so much
mischief that the earnest Catholics of the empire and
of Italy loudly demanded some effective off-set, such
as that furnished by Rosmini's panegyric of Pius VII.
Indeed, this funeral oration was the only discourse
or production of the time which fully met the case;
therefore it was promptly retouched and made ready
to go forth on its salutary mission. But the provincial political authorities, to whom it had to be
submitted for 'permission to publish,' looked upon
it as 'too papal,' or, as some in our time say of anything that is decidedly Catholic, 'too ultramontane.'
Hence they loitered over the manuscript for months,
and threw every obstacle in the way of its seasonable
appearance.

The Governor of Venice officially warned those
of his party in power at Vienna, that Rosmini was

a 'strong Papist having close relations with the most zealous Prelates of the Curia,' and that he had but recently returned from a journey to Rome with so pronounced a papal champion as the Patriarch of Venice. In short, this Josephine functionary sought to show that the Roveretan Abate was so intensely Catholic that he could not be trusted to express himself in the lukewarm or non-religious style which best suited the temporising and de-catholicising tactics of some Austrian politicians then in authority. Beneath all these efforts to prevent or delay its publication there ran a current of slanders that reached Don Antonio's ears through the kindness of the Prefect of the Southern Tyrol— the loyal and pious Riccabona, whose cousin had just been designated Bishop of Trent. Two years after these annoyances had begun Rosmini himself gave this account of them in a letter to his friend Mgr. Grasser, Bishop of Treviso :

I wish to tell you one thing, but in all secrecy. It is already a long time since I submitted to the Censorship at Venice a eulogy of Pius VII. This little work has had a world of vicissitudes. The Governor of Venice wrote to Vienna an angry and, at the same time, a silly report against me. The crime with which he charged me was that of being a *papist* in close relations with the Roman Prelates ! As a proof of this he adduced the journey I made to Rome with the Patriarch, and brought forward other arguments of the same decisive kind! . . . However, even at Vienna itself the report of the Venetian Governor was judged to be rash. Meanwhile, my book was returned to Venice, and once more sent back to Vienna. From

Vienna it was next time forwarded to M. Wilzek, at Innsbruck, who reported favourably on it.   The manuscript .
was also sent to the Bishop of Trent, but whether from
Vienna or Innsbruck I cannot tell. I have reason to believe that Riccabona, our Provincial Prefect, was asked to
give the Government private information about me personally.   In short, they treat me as if I were a Carbonaro !
You must allow that to a quiet gentleman whose conscience
stands clear before God and men such proceedings cannot
be agreeable.   True, all this is done in secret, and it is only
by accident that I have come to know of it; but this is
really a most unpleasant part of the affair.   Such a mode
of proceeding makes it perfectly safe for an enemy or a
calumniator to triumph always in his lying. . . .   All this,
however, cannot disturb my interior tranquillity, and I
thank God for my retired life and for the calm of my
conscience.[1]

When he found it impossible, without coming
into collision with political authority, to carry out the
project to which he was urged by so many zealous
Catholics, so many loyal citizens, and by an earnest
feeling of homage to the memory of Pius VII., as
well as by a deep sense of duty to the Holy See, he
contented himself with causing the publication of an
engraved portrait of the late Pontiff. This, at least;
could not, he thought, be objected to on any plausible
grounds.   Nevertheless, 'political expediency' did
object even to this ; for the portrait, by itself, might
suggest awkward inquiries as to the reasons for withholding the memoir.   This objection, however, did
not stand ; and so the faithful were allowed to
have a likeness of the revered Pope, which Don

[1] *Unpublished Letters*, Tom. 11. Letter cclviii. Rovereto, December 14, 1825.

Antonio intrusted to the artist and engraver, Andreès of Rovereto, who brought it out in his best style.

It pained Rosmini much to find that a time-serving political faction in a Catholic country had the power to thus fetter the action of those who defended the highest interests of the Church ; but it pained him more to know that all who dexterously assailed those interests were not only privileged but protected. He was, indeed, ready to credit the short-sighted politicians then in office with good intentions, but how could he respect the policy which covered their intentions, since it directly favoured the propagation of irreligion ? The more he contemplated the gloomy state of the times the more was he saddened at the prospects of the future. As Tommaseo tells us, he clearly foresaw that the evils which many statesmen were then sowing all through Europe, to curry favour with free-thinkers, and to affront the Church, must produce crops of bitter woe for religion, for peoples, and for governments. These forebodings grieved him sorely ; but, as he felt that it was Divine and not human power which was to succour the Church, he never had any misgivings as to the ultimate triumph of the Holy See over human weakness or human wickedness, however long and however much either or both might seem to triumph.

CHAPTER XVII.

ROSMINI'S DEVOTION TO THE HOLY SEE AND
CATHOLIC UNION.

(A.D. 1824-1825.)

He practically illustrates the holy influence of the Papacy while not allowed to openly vindicate its honour—His great devotion to the Holy See- -Distrust of secular life, and confidence in the Religious State—The cloister a harbour of refuge—The political censors will not be conciliated—Why the religious reaction following the French Revolution waned—Dangers of the future—Proposal to honour solemnly the martyrs of the Revolution—What God intended him to promote—Mme. Canossa reminds him of her ' message of inspiration '—He wishes to found a congregation for securing the perfect observance of the public services of the Church—She urges him to quit his home retirement—His efforts for the Daughters of Charity in Trent—Advises his sister to found a house of this Order in Rovereto, at her own expense—Proceeds to Modena for special studies—Advantages of union amongst the good.

WHILE a few misguided political officials were obstructing Rosmini's efforts to vindicate the honour of the Holy See, he was himself quietly engaged in illustrating, all unconsciously, the charm of its benign influences, through the many ' good works ' that surrounded his private life with the soothing, saving, blessings of Gospel Charity. Those works, having the Saviour constantly in view, never permitted him to lose sight of Christ's Church or of His Vicar. It has been well said of him that ' if ever there was

a man who understood perfectly how Christian faith
rests on the infallible and living voice of the Church,
that man was Antonio Rosmini.'

It is certain that from his tenderest years to the
day of his death he always showed the ' most prompt
and humble docility, the most tender and filial affection to the voice of the Church.' He often declared
that language could not adequately express 'the exalted idea he entertained of the office committed by
Jesus Christ to His Spouse.' Any one who reads
the second part of his *Filosofia del Diritto*, must
admit that he has taken the greatest pains, and with
much success, to set forth and maintain the rights of
the Church, 'whether resting on the dictates of
natural justice, or on the prescription of her Divine
Founder.' He was ever amongst the foremost, and
ever fearless, in defending her against the cavils
and sophistry of those philosophers and legislators
in whose eyes the State is everything and the Church
almost nothing. Unlike them, he did not believe
that 'civil society is the end for which man was
created;' for all his studies had convinced him that
civil society ' is only one of the means which, under
the direction of God's Church, are intended to assist
man in the attainment of his only end—the eternal
salvation of his own soul.'[1]

[1] *An Outline of Rosmini's Life*, &c., p. 72. It may be as well to
remember that Rosmini vindicated the rights of the Holy See with
equal ardour at every stage of his life. We have evidence of it while
he was a boy composing the ' Day of Retirement ' in 1811, and address-
ing the Rovereto Academy in 1814, when he was as firm in upholding
those rights as when preaching the ' Panegyric of Pius VII.' in 1824, or
finishing the ' Philosophy of Right ' in 1841. The same spirit of un-

But when he saw how 'the popular movements' went, he came to the conclusion that civil society was rapidly passing away from its Christian moorings, and, by mistaking the means for the end, was blindly rushing on its own destruction. He did his utmost to check these evil tendencies as one urged thereto from on High. The tide, however, seemed too strong, and, day by day, the condition of Secular Life alarmed him more and more, while the security which the Religious State afforded won his heart more and more. Hence, he sought every opportunity of encouraging his dearest friends to take refuge in this safer life, and avoid the ever-increasing snares of the world. It gave him sincere pleasure to be in a position to congratulate anyone who had made the 'better choice.' Several of his ecclesiastical friends had already given him this pleasure, and, without for a moment assuming that his influence had led them to take the course he so much approved, he deemed it a duty to wish them joy in some such terms as those used in the following letter to the Abate Villardi :—

I write to congratulate you on the step you have deliberately taken ; for it is natural for us to rejoice at the welfare of those whom we care for, and you have ever been an object of my affection and esteem. Now, if it be God who has called you to the cloister, as I am persuaded it is —(for before adopting such a course, you have, doubtless,

swerving devotion to the Papacy, and uncompromising advocacy of its inherited rights, is visible in the treatises he wrote or completed during the closing years of his life, as for example in that *Sul Matrimonio de' Cristiani*, that *Sul Diritto d' insegnare*, and that *Sulla Separazione della Chiesa dallo Stato.*

taken pains to ascertain His Will in your regard)—what more fortunate event could there be for you ? You are now at anchor in a safe harbour. Although the movement of the water be perceptible even there, you will never have to brave the heaving billows which agitate, unceasingly, the high seas of this tempestuous world. The swell, if perchance there be any, will be of short duration, free from danger, and easily steered through. You can therefore now enjoy that peace which assuredly it is not so easy to secure in the world. I clearly see—indeed, experience teaches me, —that the noise and bustle of human affairs wrest us from ourselves, and poison with a thousand drugs the chaste delights we derive from letters. Quiet and order, on the contrary, leave us leisure to make use of them, not only with delight, but also with profit to ourselves and others. I write thus with no other view than that you may see you have friends whose sentiments are in harmony with your own.

Receive, I pray you, this assurance with the same friendly spirit that prompts its utterance. I am aware that you are preaching and zealously labouring in God's vineyard, and I envy you the opportunity you have for such sweet pursuits, whilst I am unhappily immersed in innumerable cares which miserably distract me.

I have recently published a little book having for its title ' Christian Education.' I should gladly send it to you, did I but know how, in order to profit by any suggestions you may be good enough to make on it. Next Spring I purpose going to Milan and risking the publication of my ' Panegyric of Pius VII.' I say ' risking ' advisedly, for I know not how it will be received. Yet if it were read with the same amount of pleasure which I experienced in writing it (I allude to the subject-matter itself, not to the mode of treating it), I should anticipate some fruit from that class of persons for whom it was written. Good-bye. Give me a share in your affections. Employ your many

acquirements, as I am sure you do, in behalf of religion and
virtue.

ROVERETO : *Jan.* 14, 1814.[1]

At this time he had hopes of appeasing the
political Censor of Venice by adopting the advice of
the Papal Nuncio at Vienna, who suggested that it
was better to allow some few alterations in the terms
of the panegyric than to leave the enemy with any
pretexts for retarding its publication. Rosmini was
ready to comply; but on finding that sweeping
changes were demanded—changes affecting the very
principle for which he contended—it was soon seen
that, for the present, there was no use in trying to
meet the wishes of the Government.

The religious reaction following the disorders
of the Napoleonic wars was then at its height,
and thoughtful Catholics concluded that it was
precisely the time when it was not only safe but
wise to uphold the standard of the Holy See as
the symbol of Christian peace and civilisation. But,
every fresh incident connected with the attempt
to neutralise or suppress this outspoken tribute of
homage to the Papacy satisfied Rosmini, more and
more, that the poisonous principles of the French
Revolution deeply tinctured the politics of those who
controlled the reaction. The imprudent concessions
constantly made to a few noisy rationalists fostered
the germs of the old disorder for a new outbreak, at
no distant day. Statesmen, nominally Catholic, in

---

[1] *Epistolario*, Letter xxxvi.

Austria, Italy, and France, not fully recovered from the panic of the past, seemed still ready to make terms with impiety, and to such an extent that religious indifference, wearing the flimsy veil of a spurious toleration, was becoming fashionable.

Thus, though the reaction had thrown down irreligion and restored religion to its throne, the safeguards were only a delusion so long as good and zealous men, like Rosmini, were abused as ' Papists ' for speaking as Catholics should speak, while latitudinarians of every stripe were treated with special favour. Judging from this and other signs of the times, that the evil but lately overthrown threatened to recover its power speedily, unless the first fervour of the reaction could be maintained, Don Antonio did all he could to keep up what was best in this fervour. His efforts were applauded by the friends of religion in Austria and Italy, but he found it difficult to get effective assistance from men who were at once fearless and intellectual. While persuaded that the brunt of battle lay between those who depended on a philosophy which appealed to ' the sensual propensities of men,' and those who were armed with a philosophy that referred all happiness to its true source, God, and that taught men how to find God, he did not neglect to call in the aid of whatever was likely to stimulate or maintain that Christian piety without which any philosophy would be worthless.

Amongst the many suggestions he made to this end, there was one which, though far less practical than any of the others, has an interest of its own, as a 'little mirror of the man.' This suggestion recommended the solemn appointment of a feast to commemorate the martyrs of the French Revolution. The proposal was characteristic of one who had deep religious feelings, and a firm conviction that the French Revolution was the first-born monster of modern sensist philosophy—the first-born of a horrid progeny, which would endeavour to destroy Christianity, if Christian philosophy did not deprive false philosophy of its fecundity. No sooner had he thought of this proposal than he communicated it to the Abate Mauro Cappellari, just seven years before that illustrious Priest was chosen to fill the chair of Peter. Here is the letter:

With the profoundest regret, I hear of the Sovereign Pontiff's illness. May God preserve him!

For a long time I have fostered in my heart an ardent wish, and it occurs to me that the opportune moment has at length arrived for giving it effect. Therefore, I cannot withhold it from you.

I have often said to myself that it would be a glorious thing, if, now that the affairs of Spain are brought to a close, the Sovereign Pontiff were to institute a feast for the whole Catholic world in honour of the martyrs of the French Revolution. Would not this be the finishing stroke and the seal, if I may so speak, to the triumph which religion is now having over infidelity? Would not such a feast assist marvellously in procuring for those heroes the honour which is due to them? Does not Holy Church tacitly desire to see enkindled in the hearts of her children veneration of this sort? Would it not keep awake, in many, such bright and noble recollections as must serve to enflame

their fervour and stimulate their zeal in the cause of Truth ?
And, finally, would it not console the good, who have
already mourned sufficiently ? It seems to me that such a
feast, instituted with all possible solemnity, would tend to
confirm not only good religious ideas but good political
ones as well.

How fair an opening to a new Pontificate ! I have often
revolved this matter in my own mind, and, as I wish to
make known to you what passes in the innermost recesses
of my heart, I have done so after the manner of intimate
friends.   Intercede for me with God.

ROVERETO : *January* 1824.[1]

Before he received a reply from the Abate
Cappellari, there was an excellent opportunity of
discussing this subject with three distinguished
Prelates who came to share in the hospitality of
Rosmini's home.   These were the Patriarch of
Venice, the Bishop of Treviso, and Mons. Ostini,
the Papal Internuncio at Vienna.   While they all
sympathised with the pious views of their host, the
obstacles to this particular mode of giving them
effect were so numerous that they could not encourage him to persevere in an effort to put it before the
Pope.   Indeed, he had no intention of going further
in the matter than the Abate Cappellari might
advise ; and as a letter from that experienced monk,
though warmly commending the pious motives
which prompted the suggestion, did not advise
action, he allowed the affair to drop, as one which
Providence did not intend him to promote.

Turning with greater zest to the charities and

[1] *Epistolario,* Letter xxxvii.

studies that made his retirement so fruitful of good,
there came to him once more those beckonings of
Providence which indicated what it was our Lord
especially intended him to promote. He was constantly asked to supply the friends of religion with
arguments against the sophists who were busily
undermining the faith of the upper and middle classes;
he was constantly asked to co-operate with or to
direct some movement started to rekindle spiritual
fervour in the masses and to check the progress of
religious indifference; he was constantly asked to
assist organisations devoted to the relief of human
suffering in every form. As he never failed to meet
such demands as far as he could, he was constantly
engaged in works of spiritual, intellectual and corporal charity.

Amongst those who sought his aid in such things,
at that time, was the Marchioness of Canossa. The
long vacant see of Trent had, at length, received its
Bishop, and Madame Canossa requested Don Antonio
to visit the new Prelate, on her behalf, in order to
obtain from him concessions that would enable her
to extend the services of the Daughters of Charity
to Trent and Rovereto. She took the occasion as a
suitable one for renewing the subject to which she
had directed the young Priest's attention two years
previously, and again urged him to found an Order
of men that should make the league against
the common enemy more complete than it was.
His sister Margherita having already joined
the community of the Marchioness, a family tie

now bound him to the Daughters of Charity and made the holy intimacy between Mme. Canossa and himself more free, and even more sacred, than before.

In replying to her fresh exhortations touching the Order she wished him to found, he made some allusions to the importance of a Congregation which should bind itself to observe the external and public devotions of the Church in the most perfect manner possible. As the Marchioness did not quite understand those allusions, he put them before her in a letter dealing exclusively with the subject. He told her that he had long felt there was a necessity for a society which should apply itself intelligently and perseveringly to the effective observance of ' the great, the public, the fundamental devotions of Holy Church which were exceedingly dear to his heart.' He wished the spirit of all the forms and ceremonies to pervade the devotions, and not least such minor devotions as were found useful, and even necessary, especially for those who were in religious communities, and for those who formed ' the multitude.' While he admired all the modern forms of devotion, he liked best those that were oldest. ' Antiquity and authority, in matters of religion, were for him,' says Don Paoli, ' objects of deep veneration. His noble conceptions must have been most agreeable to the pious soul of the Marchioness, whose sincere respect for the young ˙Roveretan Priest increased daily ;' and so, too, increased her efforts to urge him from the retirement

of private life to the holy work which God selected
her to point out to him.

While he was pleading for the Daughters of
Charity with the Ordinary of Trent and with the
Archpriest of Rovereto, the Marchioness had occasion
to write to him frequently on that business, and
every letter contained some remark designed to
enforce her request that he would found an Order of
Charity himself. His heart was ready, but he
prayerfully waited for some positive opening that
might enable him to see the finger of Providence
more plainly indicating the time, the way, and the
place. Meanwhile, he diligently attended to the
special duties entrusted to him by his saintly
correspondent. As an effective means of promoting
one part of her object he advised her to induce his
sister Margherita to purchase a suitable house in
Rovereto, or else to appropriate a house belonging
to herself there for the reception of a Community.
He thought such a course necessary because neither
the Rovereto municipal authorities nor the Congregation of Charity for local purposes had yet taken
any steps to carry out the proposal sanctioned by the
Archpriest.

On the same day he wrote also to his sister,
saying : ' I think it best that you yourself should
do what is wanted, and so avoid giving others a
pretext for disconcerting your plans or causing you
any annoyance. Assuming that you are resolved to
spend your means in such pious works, you have
enough and to spare for doing what is required both

here and at Trent. A petty economy spoils everything, and pleases neither God nor man.'[1] The counsel he thus gave his sister was that which he was
ready to act on in what concerned himself—in fact,
that which he did put in practice when the time for
doing so came. His sister did not hesitate to follow
his advice, and the Daughters of Charity were soon
established in the diocese of Trent, without waiting
for the slow movements of secular corporations.

When he had satisfactorily concluded the
negotiations confided to him by Madame de Canossa
Rosmini prepared to leave Rovereto for a few weeks'
stay in Modena. Although this was a departure
from home, it was no departure from the purpose,
nor, indeed, from the plan of his retirement. His object
was to join some pious and learned Modenese in
certain philosophical studies for which the Schools of
that city afforded special advantages. Moreover,
the sensist doctrines which threatened so much
mischief to Christianity were then taking deep root
in Modena, and he was desirous of investigating
their growth in a nursery that favoured them.[2]

He went there in July 1824, accompanied by
a member of his domestic Academy—Maurizio
Moschini, a saintly youth in whose spiritual and
temporal welfare he took the warmest interest. At

---

[1] *Unpublished Letters.* Rovereto, December 10, 1824.
[2] In the latter part of the preceding century M. Condillac, the
subtle champion of sensistic philosophy, resided at the Ducal court of
Parma as tutor to Prince Ferdinand de Bourbon. This circumstance
enabled Condillac to make Parma and Modena a centre for the diffusion of sensistic views throughout Middle and North Italy. Modena
continued for a long time afterwards to nurture the evil.

Modena he was, for the most part, the guest of Don
G. Baraldi, a learned Priest who conducted an influential periodical devoted to religion, morals and
literature. It was in the columns of this periodical,
the *Memorie Modenesi*, that the young Roveretan
philosopher first exposed the sensualistic principles
of Gioia and others of that dangerous school.[1]
During this brief visit Rosmini carefully studied the
tactics of the enemy, and stored up a considerable
amount of intellectual ammunition for the war he
was soon forced to wage with the whole army of
sensist pamphleteers.

Immediately after returning to Rovereto he wrote
to Don Baraldi a letter in which he warmly thanked
him for the privilege of having been welcomed ' in
a circle composed of personages eminent alike for
learning, piety and refinement, and who are welded
together by the closest bonds of friendship.' ' To
speak frankly,' he added, ' it seemed to me like an
assembly of most admirable souls—a very sanctuary.
One cannot leave Modena without pain after having
known the Baraldis, Parentis, Fabianis, Bianchis and
Cavedonis—after having been admitted into their
company—after having experienced so bountifully
their courtesy, and I shall even say their intimacy.
For this reason it behoves me to be frank with you,
and conceal none of those feelings of gratitude and
admiration which I brought here with me, on leaving

---

[1] These essays were afterwards collected and reproduced in the
volumes entitled (1) *Breve esposizione della Filosofia di Melchiore
Gioia* ; (2) *Esame delle opinioni di M. Gioia in favore della moda.*

Modena. They are so deeply planted in my heart that nothing can pluck them thence.

'Pray communicate these my sentiments to all the gentlemen who deigned to bestow on me and my companion such special tokens of kindness. Although my services are of little value I may, however, be permitted to express my sincere *desire* to serve them, and to hope for an opportunity to prove my gratitude in deed as well as in word.'

Having thus recorded his thanks (and the duty of doing so was one he never neglected, even in circumstances which most men would deem too trifling for the trouble), he turned with ardour to a favourite theme—the advantages of union amongst the good. That such a desirable sodality informally existed in Modena greatly cheered his soul ; and the way he dealt with the subject in his letter to Don Baraldi was a graceful recognition of the fact that his friend was the centre of such a pious alliance :

Oh ! how precious a thing, especially in these our days, is the union of good and virtuous men, brought together as mutual friends or even as mere acquaintances. For it suffices that good men know one another in order to love one another. And without this mutual acquaintance and love how can men reciprocally assist one another and place in common their ideas, their means, and their energies, so as to coordinate the labours of the many to the attainment of some great result ? Certain it is that singly we can effect but little. If we should attempt some mighty enterprise without aid, we would have to leave it incomplete. If in these days there be any sure means of rescuing virtue from oppression, we may not hope to find it elsewhere than in the alliance of men of good-will fusing into one the righteous aims and the forces of each. The wicked alas! though ever discordant amongst themselves, are always, as you well observe, united in this antagonism to the good ; for *qui non est mecum contra me est.* The reason of this is self-evident. Virtue is eminently one, whereas all that lies outside of it is by the nature of things manifold, and there · fore essentially opposed to virtue. There is not a heart truly Christian but feels the need of Christians being united in every way, and making common cause. Without this we may possibly be sufficient for our own good, but not quite for that of others. On more than one occasion I have met with persons holding the same views as myself, and was delighted to see how Christians cherish in the inmost recesses of their hearts the same thoughts and affections, even though residing very far apart.

How full of comfort to me is this hidden, but not less perfect harmony of sentiment which exists between myself and countless others of my fellow-men, who are scattered over the face of the globe, and whose very names are unknown to me! What hope it gives me that brighter days have yet to dawn for Holy Church. . . .

ROVERETO : *August* 3, 1824.[1]

Probably it will be thought we are saying little for Rosmini's knowledge of human nature, or for his sagacity, if we claim that (in spite of the gloomy aspect of the social and political world) he cherished the hope that Christian society at large would, sooner or later, reflect the Unity and the Charity of the Church. But there is a knowledge superior to that derived from a study of human nature, a knowledge standing on far higher grounds than those of natural reason, and in this knowledge he was no less an adept than in the other. This

[1] *Epistolario*, Letter xxxix.

it was that made him not only wish, but hope and
endeavour to have Catholic society throughout the
globe as affectionately united as in the early days
of Christianity—to have it in practice as in theory
a mighty brotherhood, the far-reaching household
of Christ's family.   So far as he was himself concerned, he had already endeavoured to apply this
grand Catholic principle to his native town, where
alas! he found few to follow his example and little
to encourage the hope that the union he wished for
would ever be realised; yet the wish and the hope
continued.   His own home was for all good people,
come whence they might, what he would have the
home of every good Catholic to be for every other.
But though his neighbours admired 'the breadth of
his views,' few of them thought it expedient to give
the principle a full trial, or to remove any of the
barriers which social usage had set up against the
spirit of brotherhood that pervaded primitive Christianity.   That this spirit still lived in the Church
and swayed the souls of millions of her children
scattered throughout the world, he knew full well:
how to bring them into such an effective union as
should lead to the imparting of this spirit to all men
was what he yearned to know, and strove, while he
lived, to do.

CHAPTER XVIII.

LAST YEAR OF ROSMINI'S HOME RETIREMENT.

(A.D. 1825-1826.)

His fellow Academicians, though far apart, cling to him for advice and aid — Spiritual above temporal interests—Our true grandeur unseen to mortal eye—Conditions requisite for the Priesthood—Stern warnings to an aspirant whose motives are doubtful—Describes how the Divine Office is arranged—Rescues and provides for street waifs—Returns to Madame Canossa's ' message of inspiration '—Submits a rough sketch of what he thinks the Congregation should be—Its four leading features—The germ of the Institute deep rooted in his soul—It grows into shape, as did that planted in St. Dominic's heart ages before.

BEFORE Rosmini had completed the fifth year of his home retirement, nearly all the exemplary youths, for whose spiritual and intellectual benefit he first established his domestic Academies, were scattered far apart, and occupying various positions through Italy and Austria. The bright-minded but fitful Tommaseo was one of the few who had gone, to come back and remain a little while and then to go and return again. But, though most of his first disciples were far apart physically, they were still close together in spirit, and still proving, by an admirable course of life, the great value of their early association with the young sage whom they never ceased to love as their master and benefactor. He continued to be ' the centre of their circle,' as each still wrote to him for advice in every emergency, and to each he gave it with all the affection and frankness of old. Some of these beloved students had come from a distance and in needy circumstances, but with high testimonials as to their moral worth. This was enough for the generous Rosmini, who opened to them his home, and enabled them to proceed uninterruptedly with their ecclesiastical studies.

Amongst those thus welcomed was Antonio Bassich of Perasto near Cattaro, the most southerly point of Austrian territory on the Adriatic. This estimable youth remained until he was ready for Ordination, and when he returned home, duly consecrated to the service of God, he wrote to his benefactor a letter overflowing with the gratitude which he could not utter in his presence. Replying to that letter, Rosmini delicately avoided any allusion to the special cause of thanks. It was his custom, in all such cases, to put spiritual above temporal interests, and to take care that the 'poor scholar' who became, as it were, rich through his bounty, should think little of the personal debt, by thinking much of the superiority of the soul over the body. His answer to Don Bassich's letter of thanks will show how he managed to divert attention from little social obligations (that often press heavily on the mind) to the higher duties beyond them. In the present case, these higher duties pointed to the good work which his young friend might be the means of doing amongst the schismatics and infidels on the frontiers of Turkey—a good work always most dear to the heart of Rosmini, since it meant gathering souls to God :—

Though the distance which separates us corporally is great indeed, yet are we still, as heretofore, close together in spirit.

Oh ! God, what reason have we not thence to rejoice at the greatness of the human soul—at its immensity, if I may be allowed the expression. We should therefore set upon it a much higher value than on the miserable little framework of our body. Our bodies are so fashioned that where one is the other cannot be : and if removed but a short distance from one another, they can no longer be seen, nor do they confer that pleasure which springs from close proximity.

But praise be to God for having breathed into our natural clay a pure and subtle spirit, untrammelled by any such restriction ! And praised be God still more for having restored this same human soul to friendship with the Divinity. Restored it to friendship, do I say ? He has done yet more : He has infused into it a new and ineffable life which, however, is completely hidden in Himself, since this world sees nothing of all that greatness which we have in Jesus Christ. So much the more should we hold it dear and esteem it as infinitely precious, for through it the pride we inherit from Adam is effectively vanquished when we recognise with joy the fact that the true grandeur of our humanity is invisible to mortal eyes. The Heavens and the Earth were not formed for *our* glory, but that the Grace of Christ Jesus should have glory. And as we desire that this Grace should have victory and dominion throughout the world, it was very gratifying for me to learn that such is the case in your country.

The Author of a Grace so full of glory, I doubt not, will add force to our words. Without His aid they would resemble the noise of a sounding brass or a tinkling cymbal.

But by His help what may not be done, even by a passing breath of wind ?

The place where you are will be resorted to by Greeks, among whom perhaps Catholics will be in a minority. You will have to combat errors ; and, as a means of successfully doing so, you must study, even though by avoiding controversy you may possibly gain the end in view. Might not this object be facilitated and promoted by a short treatise, containing decisive but simple and persuasive arguments ? And would it not likewise be easy to circulate such a tract in the neighbourhood ? Beyond doubt, then, you ought to collect together, from their own lips, their most pernicious errors and grave objections, endeavouring to see, from their own points of view, the chief fallacies of their present unfortunate prejudices. The result of acquiring this knowledge from their own mouths would be better, I think, than if obtained from the books that abound on the subject. When you have advanced so far, you may count on my help in the undertaking.

The panegyric of Pius VII. is not yet printed. I shall send you a copy when it is ready. You are frequently named with affection amongst us. How much I desire that we should meet again ! But let us be content with seeing each other in the spirit. And if we meet in God, this seeing will be perfect.

ROVERETO : *December* 27, 1824.[1]

Although the youths who availed themselves of his domestic Academies were not all in need of the material assistance without which it would have been impossible for some of them to have completed their studies, all alike felt that he was their guiding genius, and all alike depended on him, under Heaven, in every difficulty. Many of them turned

[1] *Epistolario*, Letter xl.

their thoughts towards the ecclesiastical state, partly because he had chosen it for himself, and partly because the surroundings of their training inclined them that way. But while he wished to lead their minds and hearts in such a direction, he was most careful to test their vocation before allowing them to take the final step. His main object was to make them all good solid Christians; what might follow that he left to a special call. How warily he received their own declarations that they had this special call may be judged from the following letter to Giulio Franchi, a promising youth as to whose call Rosmini had some doubts, and to whom, therefore, he pointedly stated the conditions requisite for the Priesthood :—

As you are well instructed in our holy religion, you must already know that a call to the ecclesiastical state is one of God's greatest favours. You know, therefore, that no one should take this honour to himself but he who is called thereto as Aaron was. You likewise know what is immediately required from one who feels himself called to this sacred office ; that he must be fearful of himself, diffident, a lover of prayer and of mortification, fond of solitude the better to hear the supernal voice which makes itself heard sometimes near and sometimes from afar ; and finally, distrustful of his own judgment, he should submit the affair entirely to the decision of the superiors through whom God ordinarily speaks to us.

But let me ask you to consider especially that he who is called should earnestly bid farewell for ever to worldly notions and a worldly life. Then, by assiduously devoting himself to the Divine Service, and by avoiding even the shadow of danger and distraction, he must deserve more and more to obtain from God confirmation of the sacred

gift. I have already said that a call to such a state is
the greatest favour—a supreme Grace according to God. I
so said because it is not such according to the world. The
Priest has formally renounced all mundane interests. Hence
it is that the Cleric, in receiving the Tonsure, utters these
memorable words : *Dominus pars hæreditatis meæ*—' The
Lord is the sole portion of my inheritance.' So that in the
world we have nothing to expect but labours and sufferings
for the love of Jesus Christ, and if we were to look for anything else we should be simply traitors to the spirit of our
profession. On that account I ask you to reflect profoundly
on the matter before the Bishop admits you to the Tonsure
and consecrates you to God. But, what is still more, I ask
you, for the love which you bear to your soul, to beware lest
you should be so deceived as to take the step perhaps for
some human motive, such as that of being thus helped on
more surely to finish your studies ; for this would render
you guilty, before God, of a most heinous crime and deprive you of all claims to His blessing. Woe to him who
trifles with sacred things, and does not fear the Lord, who is
jealous of their honour, and avenges Himself on all who
despise them !

It is not I, but you yourself, who ought to make your
father acquainted with this grave resolution, if you have
really taken it ; for I doubt not the information will give
him pleasure. But if perchance you were induced to adopt
the course you are taking from a wrong motive, let me beg
of you to change your purpose ; and you should do so at
once, for it can do you no good to entertain such designs.

ROVERETO : *May* 7, 1825.[1]

Several of his young companions, who had
already been found worthy to carry out this ' most
grave resolution,' continued to seek instruction from
their trusted guide on almost every thing connected

---

[1] *Epistolario,* Letter xli.

with their calling. Some of them, who were serving God in remote dioceses, sent him lengthy accounts of the place and people, that he might the
better give such advice as they needed in the discharge of some special duty. Others, nearer home,
working even in sight of their own Cathedral, or
waiting for Orders in episcopal seminaries, had so
much confidence in the judgment and knowledge of
the young sage of Rovereto, that they deemed instruction from him, on any given subject, more
precious than the best that was within immediate
reach. And none applied to him in vain, for all
received from him the instruction or counsel which
they sought or seemed to want. Thus, when the
Baron Giulio Todeschi of Trent, having passed
'the sacred portal' into Minor Orders, required
some information on the Divine Office, he sought
it not in Trent but in Rovereto, and had this pithy
explanation promptly forwarded to him :—

In the first ages of the Church, as there were not yet any
Saints' festivals to keep, there were no Holy-days except
the Lord's Day. But the early Christians, remembering that
every day should be spent holily, and that the Christian
ought ever to withdraw himself from profane things to give
himself to God, had in mind to sanctify them *all* by prayer.
Hence came the distribution of the Psaltery for the seven
days of the week, apportioning to each day one of the seven
canticles of Scripture and appropriate hymns, with a lesson,
either from the Old Testament or from the Epistle of an
Apostle, and one from the Gospel, with other suitable
prayers.

After this manner was compiled the first and oldest
portion of the Breviary, that which is used on ferial days.

Subsequently many solemnities were instituted either to celebrate in a special manner the mysteries of Jesus Christ or to honour the Blessed Mother of our Lord, the martyrs, and afterwards other confessors; the first of those thus honoured being, if I remember rightly, St. Martin of Tours. In this way three distinct parts were added to the book containing the canonical hours; the movable were distinguished from the immovable feasts—the movable being those which have a certain connection with Easter. The Paschal solemnity, being fixed by the lunar year, invariably falls on the Sunday nearest to the 14th day of the March moon (owing to the difference between the lunar month of 28 days and the solar month of 30 days) and thus it comes to pass that the day which is always the same in the lunar year is not so in the solar year, which is adopted in ordinary life. Therefore, since Easter in our common calendar falls, now on one day and then on another, it brings with it all its adherent feasts in the same way that all the Sundays of the year bring with them the ferial days depending on them—that is, in so far as they have proper lessons suitable to the current festive season. For, in the course of each year, the Church celebrates the principal truths and mysteries of religion on movable feasts, the foremost of these being Easter. In this feast is centred the whole essence of the festival worship practised universally in the Church; those Saints' festivals which are not strictly conjoined with the Holy mysteries not being essential. Hence it is that the festivals which occur between these movable feasts have proper lessons of their own, adapted to the season; and they go to form this Second Part.

The Third and Fourth Parts contain the Saints' festivals, distributed on fixed days throughout the year. And there is no difference between these parts, except that the fourth, which is the last in the Breviary as now published, contains a portion of the Psalms to be recited for each class of Saints, that is to say, for Apostles, Martyrs, Bishops and

Confessors, Virgins and Widows—whether one or more be celebrated on the same day : while the Third Part contains what is proper to each Saint, such as the lesson that gives his biography or else records some other specially honourable feature of the Saint's life. Thus, to recapitulate, there will be found in the Breviary this order of contents :—First comes the common of the ferial days : that is, those days on which no Saint is commemorated ; next come the movable feasts, and with them the proper of their ferial days ; and lastly, the fixed festivals : that is, those of Saints—and in these first comes that which is proper to those Saints, and secondly that which is common.

However, why should I go on to describe the order in which the Divine Office is arranged, since you are not only well acquainted with it, but already recite it ? Nevertheless, it was incumbent on me to have complied with your request. You are then, let me add, fortunate in having now to say the Office. I feel assured that our souls can be comforted and sanctified by a worthy recital of this form of prayer, which was that of all the Saints, and is still that of the whole Church.

Not only does the entire Church sing the Divine Office, but every age of the Church has concurred in its composition ; for therein have had a share Moses, David, the Prophets, our Lord Jesus Christ, the Apostles and the Pontiffs. Indeed, so wonderfully varied is the nutriment to be found there that the most hungry soul may, if it wish, be superabundantly satisfied.

I feel indignant with those who, disliking all spiritual aliments, are scandalised at some blemishes which they think they discover in a volume that I do not hesitate to call Divine. Let us prize it dearly, and read it with relish and devotion ; for, by so doing, our spirit will ascend to God, graces will be obtained, and we shall be benefited as well as comforted to an extraordinary degree. In very truth, my dearGiu lio, we Priests have enough to sanctify us in the proper celebration of the Mass and in the pious recitation

of the Breviary. I embrace you. Communicate this letter
to our excellent Clerics and friends, and let us love one
another in the Lord. Adieu.

ROVERETO : *June 7, 1825.*[1]

Correspondence of this kind came as a relief to
the severe studies in which Rosmini persevered, no
matter what circumstances encompassed him. Works
of corporal mercy formed another real relief. These
works included nearly every variety of practical
charity, and had for subjects the needy and the suffering of both sexes ; especially since his sister was no
longer in Rovereto to personally meet the wants of
her own sex. While she remained he had no occasion to tax his generosity with the claims of poor
women, or the care of helpless little girls. But, since
Margherita had gone from Rovereto to join Mme.
Canossa at Verona, he felt bound to take up, as
far as possible, the good works to which she had
given her best energies when at home.

Sometimes he passed through the back lanes of
the town, like St. Vincent de Paul, in search of
neglected little ones, and whenever he found an
orphan, or a child whose condition was no better
than that of an orphan, he made it a duty to provide
for it. One day while he was thus engaged, a bright
little girl, whose impoverished family were unable
to care for her properly, was brought to him in the
hope that he might prevail on some wealthy friend
to bring her up as a domestic servant. He talked
to her for a few minutes, and was so pleased with

[1] *Epistolario,* Letter xlii.

her intelligent answers to questions, which much older and better-instructed children failed to grapple with at all, that he determined to give her an opportunity of developing her mind under advantages above the ordinary. With that view the following letter was at once written to his sister, who gladly complied with the request it contained :—

There is here a little girl who is eight and a half years old, of an excellent disposition, most sweet and cheerful, in perfect health, and having abilities which seem to me marvellous, as, at her tender age, she can understand very difficult things. Now, I wish that you would take her into your House, that you may bring her up. She might perhaps be of some service to you   Be it well understood that in this you should act according to the discipline of your Institute, and with the sanction of your Superiors. I shall give you what is required for her maintenance at present, and until the time that the child shows what she is fit for in after life, so that she may be placed accordingly.

It seems to me on the one hand that, being so good, she would give no trouble, but rather pleasure, and on the other hand after obtaining a pious education she might perhaps receive from God a call to the Religious State, whereby you would make a good acquisition. . . . I am wholly engrossed in my studies, to which for the present, it seems, God wishes that I should give myself; therefore, I greatly need the help of your prayers ; do not, then, deprive me of them, but rather redouble them, and not only pray yourself but get others also to pray for me.   Adieu.

ROVERETO : *September* 25, 1825.[1]

All this time neither study, nor the pious duties that relieved study, had power to keep from its

---

[1] *Epistolario*, Letter xliii.

uppermost place on his mind the holy purpose
the Marchioness of Canossa had planted there.
He thought of it constantly, and constantly prayed
for Divine Light to show him the way to its realisation. A year of special thought and special prayer
had been thus passed, without any further interchange
of views between himself and the Marchioness, when
he suddenly decided on writing her a long letter,
expounding the principles that should guide the proposed Society. She had been expecting such a letter
for some time ; but he was slow to move in the
matter, slow even to express himself on the subject,
until he felt with some certainty that the Spirit of
God urged him. In this important letter he told Mme.
Canossa that her original proposition—a Congregation of Priests—seemed to him, on the whole, to be
the best for the purpose. The structure of the
Church being the truest model for the structure of a
Religious Society, he would shape his—if God desired
him to organise one—in conformity with the plan
which our Lord Himself had adopted. Accordingly,
he drew up for her a rough sketch of the design that
sprang from her own suggestions, and gave these as
its four leading features :—

'I. The Priests gathered together (in the proposed
Order) for their own sanctification should have before
them a twofold object—the love of God and of their
neighbour. They should adopt, of their own choice,
the exercises intended to show their love towards
God and to promote their individual sanctification :
their whole desire should be to contemplate and

praise God in peace and gladness of heart. The exercises of love towards their neighbour should be undertaken at their neighbour's request, and to this request all who may be able to do so should respond.

'II. The members of the Society must depend upon their Superior in everything, and from him they should receive *the order*, in accordance with which they are to exercise their charity. There are to be no particular duties for the whole Congregation, as a body; while, at the same time, there is no duty to which its members may not be called. What the Congregation should undertake of itself is this :—to exercise charity towards its neighbours according to the calls made upon its services. All this must rest entirely with the prudence of the Superiors, to whom they who shall require the services of these Priests are to address themselves. Having taken the advice of prudent counsellors, the Superiors of the Congregation will then decide whether they have at their disposal subjects capable of undertaking the services demanded of them. In case they should have such subjects it will be incumbent on the Superiors to appoint them to these services.

'III. The rules of the Society must determine what works of charity the Superior should prefer, whenever it might happen that several requests for assistance might be made simultaneously, at a time when all could not be satisfied. The principal of these rules is that which directs the members to accept, in preference to all other offices, those belonging to the Sacred Ministry, as offices containing within themselves the most comprehensive and essential Charity.

'IV. Whoever (in that case) shall be appointed Parish Priest, etc, must thereby be also Superior of whatever portion of the Society may happen to be in that parish, or larger district. Thus, the offices of the Sacred Ministry are always to be co-ordinate with the offices held in the Society.'[1]

The Marchioness of Canossa took the earliest opportunity of assuring him that the general plan pleased her much, though she thought it likely he would see reason to alter some of the details, so as to combine his own original suggestions with those she first made: she requested him to let her see the plan which further reflection would enable him to develop and mature. One passage in his letter gave her special pleasure, as it satisfied her that the good seed she had been the means of sowing in his mind had rooted itself there ineradicably. That passage ran thus : 'Yes, I think it ought to be a Congregation of Priests. But at the same time a *desire has taken possession of my heart which probably I shall never abandon*, expecting, the while, greater light from God in order that I may know His Holy Will.' Commenting on this passage, Don Paoli says :—'A tone so decisive in a person of so vast a mind, and of such great modesty, and; what is more, of so much prayer as Antonio Rosmini was, indicates, beyond all doubt, much more than mere infor- mation to be given to Madame Canossa, and much

[1] See Appendix, Letter iii.

more than a determination suddenly arrived at.' It shows, on the contrary, if not an extraordinary inspiration, an interior movement fostered by the Spirit of God. This is confirmed by what we find Rosmini himself recording in his Diary on the very day he penned that sentence (December 10, 1825) : ' On this day I have begun to think that, as I wish to act in conformity with the second of my principles, I ought not refuse to co-operate with the undertaking to which I am invited, in case God should offer me the means for it ; but neither ought I to go in search of these means, because I should then be at variance with the first of the two principles I have chosen for the guidance of my life.[1] . . . . . I have concluded, therefore, that if God require me to found a society these two principles must form its whole rule.'

' This,' says Don Paoli, ' was the germ from which afterwards sprang the Institute of Charity.' There was nothing extraordinary either in the origin of the Institute or its subsequent development. Everything in connection with its birth and growth was orderly, but reasonable. In the same calm, prudent, prayerful way that St. Dominic matured the project of his great Order of Preachers, Rosmini drew near to the commencement of the Order of Charity. As in the one case, so in the other, there was nothing marvellous in the actual circumstances of laying the foundation—nothing even eventful ; unless we regard as such the prodigious moral evils, and the alarming inroads of error which each, in its place and time, was framed to combat.

[1] See Chapter x., pp. 166-168.

CHAPTER XIX.

ROSMINI BEGINS THE 'ACTIVE LIFE.'

(A.D. 1826.)

The spirit of association for holy objects strong in him—Difficulty of
finding suitable companions—Abundance of weeds, scarcity of
flowers—Providence beckons him to Milan—What hastens his
departure—How he smooths down a domestic trouble—Prepares
for the journey—How it affects his mother and the rest of the
family—The leave-taking—The departure—Stops at Verona to
consult with Madame Canossa and his sister—The 'message of
inspiration' once more—Mme. Canossa predicts that Providence
will clearly manifest Its will to him in Milan—His arrival in
Milan—His spiritual charges and his new friends—How Manzoni
becomes one of these—How the sensist philosophers and how
the friends of religion receive him—What he does to promote the
cause of Truth—Becomes again the guide of young ecclesiastics—
How he combines contemplative and active life—His extensive
correspondence—Still encourages the study of St. Thomas—The
'message of inspiration' now continually before him—He cannot
resist the call to found an Order—Drafts a plan and sends it to
Mme. Canossa through Don Bertoni.

THE year 1826 marks an important epoch in
Rosmini's life. At its opening he emerged from his
prolonged 'retreat' to begin the more active career
which ended only with his life. The contemplative
state and the solitude so dear to him were not,
indeed, abandoned ; but thenceforth they were to be
in conjunction with an activity that should have more
of a public, or rather less of a private, character

than hitherto—in conjunction with intellectual,
corporal, and spiritual charities that might be exercised and felt not merely within a few dioceses but
throughout the whole Church. The ardent love
of intimate association with good men, for mutual
edification and instruction, which began in his childhood, often since then sought, as we know, to find
means of formulating itself in societies of Christian
Friends and domestic Academies. But, once the
original members of these home institutions were
scattered, Rovereto had none to supply their places
—none whose sympathies ran in unison with his
own.

There was, perhaps, no lack of worthy men,
young and old, no lack of pious Catholics ; but there
was a decided dearth of companions at once pious
and cultured, at once worthy and intellectual. Few
towns of the same size could boast of more agreeable 'society' in the ordinary sense of the term ; but
this had no attractions for him. The spirit of association which was so marked a feature of his
character could find nothing to satisfy it in mere
secular society. He longed to be with those who
could live together in the world as though they were
not of it—with those who could make to themselves
a holy solitude even amid the bustle of populous
cities—with those who aimed at self-sanctification
and banished all form of self-indulgence—with those
who acted on the principle that the one thing most
necessary in this life was to be always ready for the
next.

If it was no longer easy for him to find associates of this kind amongst his immediate neighbours
—if it was no longer easy for him to find amongst
them any disciples who could fill the void made by
the departure hither and thither of the estimable
companions whose best qualities had been developed
under his sway, and whose hearts he had successfully
directed to the one thing necessary—then it was no
longer easy to find in Rovereto anyone likely to co-
operate with him in such a society as the revered
Canossa besought him to found.   In fact, he had
already trained for God the choicest flowers of his
native place, and when they were transplanted to
bloom elsewhere, he stood, as if in a lonely garden,
where flowers were few and weeds abounded.   He
did not despair of turning even the weeds to good
account, of so cultivating them that they too might,
in time, produce fragrant blossoms.   But, like St.
Francis, St. Dominic, and St. Ignatius, in face of the
same kind of difficulty, he felt that co-operation was
necessary.   Like them, also, on seeing little immediate promise of such co-operation at home, he turned
his attention to the prospects elsewhere.

In accordance with his maxim of waiting for
God's call, he resolved to allow Providence to direct
him whither he should go and what he should do.
Weeds rather than flowers abounded everywhere,
and it might be God's Will that he should labour
over distant instead of near fields.   But, whether
here or there, he held himself ever ready to answer
the call of God, as serenely and promptly as St.

Charles of Borromeo did, living and dying, 'I come, Lord, I come.'

Meanwhile, Providence, making use of ordinary circumstances, beckoned him to Milan. There he had much to expect from association with many congenial souls who invited him thither. There excellent opportunities presented themselves for going on with his philosophical studies close to those similarly engaged. Above all, there a special good work awaited him, a good work laid on his charity by Madame Canossa. When she heard of his intention to leave Rovereto, at least for a little while, she advised a visit to Milan, and the better to give her counsel effect, declared that her Community in that city, and the little children dependent on its efforts, were in need of his presence as spiritual director and benevolent father. Moreover, she had been appealed to by a Milanese Priest and two laics, who were desirous of profiting by his guidance. Surely, there was in all this quite sufficient to denote a call to Milan of a sort distinctly in harmony with the rule that governed his life. Milan was therefore chosen.

It is probable that the time of departure was hastened by a slight domestic misunderstanding. Some evil disposed or thoughtless persons had introduced a disturbing influence into the family quiet by playing on the mind of his feeble brother, who began to grumble because he, a layman, was not the inheritor of the family possessions, and because a cousin, more competent than himself, was retained as agent of the property. A few trifling incidents revealed to Don Antonio the existence of this unreasonable discontent. On inquiring into the cause, and discovering it to be one so unworthy of his brother, he affectionately remonstrated with him, and showed him how justly and generously their father had acted to all, and how there was not a shadow of excuse for grumbling at arrangements with which all had, so far, been well satisfied.

The brother soon saw his error, expressed deep sorrow, and then made an effective point of one excuse—ill health : if his physical condition had been stronger his mind would have known how to resist the sinister whisperings of mischief-makers. Don Antonio lovingly embraced him, and, imploring him not to again allow the pernicious suasions of self-seeking worldlings to overshadow his mind, requested him to share with their mother authority over the paternal home, for he intended to reside elsewhere himself. Thus was that little cloud of domestic disquiet promptly and happily dispelled for ever.

Arrangements for the journey to Lombardy were soon made. On February 20, 1826, he wrote to his cousin, the illustrious Chevalier Carlo Rosmini, requesting him to procure, in Milan, four rooms, for the accommodation of a Priest, two companions, and two servants. The companions were his secretaries Moschini and Tommaseo, and the servants, an old domestic of the family named Bisoffi, and a coachman. Considering the inconvenience and cost of stage-coach trips in those days and that region, it is

no wonder that he deemed it best to travel in his
private carriage. Apart from the greater quiet
and security of such a course, he was free to break
the journey at his pleasure. The horses were to
be sold in Milan, if he saw no reason to retain them
there.

A letter having been received, on the 24th, from
the Chevalier Carlo saying that he had faithfully
attended to his cousin's wishes, Don Antonio Rosmini next morning took leave of his family, and then
went, with his suite, to pay a parting 'visit of
homage' in that little oratory which so many
precious memories had specially endeared to him.

To no one did he hint that his absence was to be
of a permanent character, and to few that it was
likely to be for any long time ; yet, all took it as the
first step in a self-expatriation that might be relieved
by occasional returns, but no more admit of the
constant residence amongst them which his kindred
and neighbours so much coveted. The Countess
Rosmini had for years felt that this departure was to
take place, sooner or later, since her beloved son
could not be induced to accept any ecclesiastical
office in his native diocese. Months before he resolved on making Milan a temporary home, he had
prepared her with affectionate counsels which could
not fail to sustain her on the day of a separation that
was more than ordinary. But, though thus ready
and though a lady of strong good sense, the parting
filled her with a sadness deeper than she had ever
felt before.

Still more keen was the anguish of his brother, who feared that the few murmurings to which he had inconsiderately yielded might have been in some way the cause of a step that distressed them all. As for the servants and retainers of the family, 'they seemed to be,' says Tommaseo, 'inconsolable.' Could the fervent entreaties of all these have prevailed, the loved young Priest would have remained at home. But he heeded only that 'still voice' which more than once before had whispered to him the Will of Providence, and nothing on earth could hinder him going whither that directed.

Blessing all and blessed by all, he set out for Milan with his chosen fellow-travellers, on the morning of February 25. They reached Verona that night. There a delay of three days gave him an opportunity of seeing his sister and the Marchioness of Canossa. Once more the plan of the proposed religious Order was discussed between them ; once more the Foundress of the Daughters of Charity employed her pious eloquence to prove that God expected his compliance with this call ; and once more he repeated his solemn assurance that he but waited the plain manifestation of Providence in order to make a commencement. The Marchioness hinted that this manifestation would be given in Milan, probably in immediate connection with those whose spiritual interests she confided to his care ; but if not in that way, certainly in that place. She recommended him to take counsel at once with Don Gasparo Bertoni, a most devout and experienced ecclesiastic, who had founded a congregation of Regular Priests at Verona. Rosmini called on him the same evening, and, after a long interview, received much useful advice and much encouragement.

Full of the pious ardour which always followed consultations with the saintly Canossa, he left Verona for Brescia, where he spent three days, visiting the local shrines and holding converse with several learned ecclesiastics, his constant companion there being Don G. Brunati, (one of the ablest professors in the episcopal seminary), whose vocation to the Religious State was 'nursed and directed by Rosmini.'

On March 4, 1826, Don Antonio entered Milan and took possession of the chambers provided for him, conveniently near the Church of the Holy Sepulchre and 'the magnificent Ambrosian Library.' Tommaseo, in his 'Letters from Milan,' suggestively contrasted his own first desire on arriving with that of Rosmini. The wayward secretary thought of going instantly to call on some friends, while Don Antonio, gently chiding him for unseemly haste, led him and the others to visit, first of all, Our Lord in the Tabernacle of the nearest church, and then returned home to write a soothing letter to his mother.

These duties discharged, he lost no time in putting himself in communication with Don Boselli and the other two friends whose spiritual life Madame Canossa had requested him to guide. It was a most acceptable charge, and one of which he was soon

able to give a cheering report to the Marchioness;
for he found all three very well disposed to follow a
strict rule and devote themselves to the education of
youth in the little Oratories that formed so pleasing
a feature of Milanese religious life. How much
these Oratories charmed the soul of Rosmini we shall
hear presently in his own words. But before he
expressed any positive opinion as to their value, he
personally tested it, by becoming a member and
zealously assisting in the work with which these institutions were identified. His example was speedily
followed by the local patricians who had hitherto
looked on approvingly, but inactively. The practical,
earnest piety of the Roveretan was a reproach to
their lukewarmness which they were not slow to
remove.

In a short time, Rosmini had around him a large
circle of religious and intellectual friends. ' So much
learning,' says Don Paoli, ' and so much holiness of
life found joined together in a young ecclesiastic,
could not fail to attract the notice of pious, noble and
cultivated souls. Not to speak of the many clergy-
men whose friendship he won, he soon became intimate with such men as Padulli, Arconati, Castelbarco,
Casati, Piola, Vimercati, Mellerio, and Manzoni.'
Each of these had a following of his own, and all
sought to be on familiar terms with one who was
accepted as a model for all. In these circumstances,
he could not easily find the solitude he loved ; yet
he contrived to find it, though with great difficulty.
By insisting on fixed hours for general company

within the period set down for recreation, and by
using these occasions for the main purpose of his
life –turning his own and other souls to God—no
time was wasted, but much was gained for such
duties as the Pastor of a flock would consider ' works
of exhortation,' while the hours for private devotion
and study were as rigidly adhered to as ever.

His most constant companions were Count
Mellerio and Alessandro Manzoni.   They were also
his most steadfast friends.   Up to that time, Manzoni, like so many of his contemporaries, had been
floating adrift in religious indifference ; nay, he
ranked high amongst the sceptical.   Not long before
he was introduced to Rosmini, a friend happened
to call his attention to one of the Roveretan's philosophical treatises just published.   The great Italian
author having read it carefully, felt his scepticism
giving way, and exclaimed, ' Here is a *man* !'   He
took the earliest opportunity of making that man's
acquaintance, and, after knowing him for a short
time, was led back to 'the moorings of the Faith,'
became once more a practical Catholic, and thenceforth the devoted friend of his spiritual and intellectual benefactor.   Count Mellerio, whose bright piety
had never been dimmed by the philosophical vagaries of those days, was destined to be (as we shall
find) the agent of Providence in that ' manifestation ' which Madame Canossa predicted as certain
to be made in Milan.

The great consideration shown to Rosmini by
the zealous friends of religion excited the wrath of

the sensists, who were then more industriously than
ever misleading the popular mind under pretence of
directing it to what they insidiously called 'the
higher truths.' Their organ was the *Biblioteca
Italiana*, and their most active literary chiefs were
Gioia and Romagnosi. Day by day they watched
intently the course of the Roveretan philosopher, and
impatiently looked for some declaration of his which
they might twist against so vigorous a champion of
the Church. Another set of Milanese *literati*, more
modest and more chivalrous, watched him also, but
with most kindly eyes. These were the writers of
the *Ricoglitore*—young men with whom he could consistently have free intercourse—young men who fairly
represented the hopes of the future. Amongst them
were Achille Mauri, Samuel Biava, Michele Parma,
and the celebrated Sartorio. Through the pages of
the *Ricoglitore*, and by every other means in their
power, they endeavoured to raise up the ethical and
æsthetical sense of the nation, and they brought to
the effort a sincerity, an earnestness and an urbanity
which 'the old men of the *Biblioteca*' sadly wanted.
Occasionally Sartorio and his colleagues used to wait
on Rosmini in order to gather his views on the
various subjects they were dealing with, and after
the interview they assembled at the chambers of
some one of the party to record and discuss what he
had said to them.

In like manner a certain number of young ecclesiastical students, spontaneously drawn together,
petitioned him to assist their readings in the way he

was wont to do for the members of his own Academies at Rovereto. He willingly consented on discovering that they, for various reasons, were unable
to take part in the regular course of the episcopal
seminary, and obliged to pursue their studies at their
respective homes, or in a private school which they
had succeeded in establishing under the superintend-
ence of the Abate Marietti, who directed them in
philosophical and literary matters. One of these
youths was that Carlo Caccia who afterwards became
secretary to Cardinal Gaisruk, and, in time, a Priest
of the Institute of Charity.

Many such labours as these were thrust upon him
after his arrival in Milan, and, though the duties
Madame Canossa had already imposed upon him
seemed to be quite enough of themselves, he found
time for all without detriment to any. Apart from
these works of charity there were numerous special
distractions attending the first months of his residence there; nevertheless, the even tenour of the
rules that governed his home life was hardly ever
disturbed. In his apartments 'the regularity of religious observance' was kept up as strictly as at
Rovereto. Prayer and study, spiritual reading and
the composition of works on all manner of scientific
and literary subjects, went on without any marked
change in the ordinary horary. His correspondence
daily increased, and with it seemed to increase his
power of meeting the most extraordinary demands
for his advice and instruction on almost every
subject.

U 2

A few days after his arrival in Milan, he had to give a written opinion on the advisability of uniting the public Academies of Trent and Rovereto; he had to heal differences between friends at a distance; he had to state his views on certain literary works; he had to encourage those who were lagging in the studies he had done so much to promote while at home. Touching this encouragement there is a short passage in one of his letters which it may be well to quote. Don Fogolari of Rovereto, having hinted that the youths in whom 'their absent mentor' had infused a great love for St. Thomas craved a message from him, had their wish responded to in this way : ' Please to tell the friends with whom so many hours were often spent agreeably, St. Thomas in hand, that the Thomist Rosmini is still living and thinks of them frequently ; say that if he could be with them, at a bound, he would exhort them to remain steadfast in their mutual friendship, and in their adhesion to St. Thomas, of whom the study will be resumed with them some other time.'[1]

Thus, every day he had to despatch 'far and near' some reply which gave readers, far and near, a glimpse at the greatness of his heart, of his knowledge, of his humility. But, besides the encroachments which an extensive correspondence of this kind forced on his time, he had many private affairs to dispose of by the same means. Not the least of these were his numerous charities. Nearly every month, he took the trouble of reminding Don Orsi and his brother that the poor of Rovereto were to

---

[1] *Unpublished Letters*, Milan, March, 1826.

be served at his expense as diligently as if he were, himself, personally attending to their wants.

Hovering, like a bright angel, over all he did, was the grand idea which Madame Canossa had been the means of producing. It was in vain that other things obtruded—they could not shut it out of sight. It was in vain that he tried to reason himself out of it—reason brought him back to it. The more he prayed for light on the project, the more it glowed with sacred fascinations. In less than a fortnight after his arrival in Milan (and while the newness of all the surroundings, with a variety of distracting in- fluences such as we have indicated, was enough to banish the scheme from an ordinary mind) he drafted the first complete plan of the proposed Society, and sent it to Don Gasparo Bertoni, of Verona, with the following letter :—

Though I have already taken up so much of your valu- able time by the visit I paid you in person, I must ask you to allow me to address you further by letter.

The sole reason that urges me to write to you is that I may have the advantage of your enlightened counsel. I have already disclosed to you the great desire I have for some time cherished in my heart, and which I have reason to think has been implanted in it by God, of living as a Regular, in company with some Priests. I have also made known to you the general idea according to which I feel inwardly drawn to regulate this community, and you have encouraged me in the design.

Now, before beginning anything, I think of asking the advice of the Holy Father, lest perchance, all this may prove to be some illusion or other of my own, which I ought to think no more about. In my innermost soul, how- ever, I do not believe that to be the case. Therefore, I have sketched out the general idea, and enclose a copy for your perusal, hoping that you will return the plan to me here in Milan, where I am at present staying.

There will of course be some difficulty in making a beginning ; but at the commencement it would not be necessary to adhere strictly to the rule of perfect retirement, and of practising the works of charity, which I have laid down for the Society—to come into effect when it is fully established. We might at first (supposing that God were to send us good companions) establish ourselves in the neighbourhood of some church, undertaking in it the performance of the public functions on Holy-days, also the confessions, and perhaps some kind of school, which would have the effect of justifying our little reunion in the eyes of the world. Concerning all this, I should like very much to hear your opinion, and I beg of you to lend us your assistance in the undertaking ; provided that it appears to you to be the Will of God.

MILAN : *March* 15, 1826.[1]

The plan sketched for Don Bertoni was accompanied by a document containing practical ' observations ' on the nature of the Order and on the feasibility of uniting with it any other useful and pious institute. These observations were supplemented by another document giving a ' further explanation ' and showing how Superiors in the proposed Institute ' are to make a choice among the charitable works suggested to them.'[2] Don Bertoni, having carefully examined all these, consulted the Marchioness of Canossa on the scheme as thus outlined, and then returned the various papers with a general approval, and some special hints which found effect in the plan that was finally adopted.

---

[1] *Epistolario*, Letter xlvii.   [2] See Appendix, Letter iv.

CHAPTER XX.

ROSMINI'S FIRST YEAR'S STAY AT MILAN.

(A.D. 1826.)

A significant coincidence—He congratulates the Abate Cappellari on receiving the Cardinalate—Solicits the new Cardinal's opinion as to the plan of the new Order—How he and his household apply the principle of 'passivity'—What he thinks of poetry and social entertainments for the relief of sadness—' Highly wrought religious fervour' no impediment to cheerfulness, as his own daily life demonstrates—What he thinks of the Milanese—The sensist blotch on the prevailing piety—Vincenzo Monti a representative blotch—Rosmini seeks to save the dying poet's soul—Gains a victory elsewhere that promises well for the saving of souls—Works for the Daughters of Charity—His description of that Order—Madame Canossa questions the wisdom of admitting the Pastoral Office in the Order she wishes him to found—He answers her objections, laying much stress on living in *solitude with the heart* rather than the body—Danger of gloom in solitude, and of levity in society—Religion the mother to shield us from both—All his affections centered in the Church—No genuine happiness except in close union with the Church—True patriotism can belong only to the subjects of Christ's Kingdom—He would have all men fellow-subjects in this Kingdom, bound together by the sweet bonds of charity.

AT the very time Rosmini was drafting his more elaborate sketch of the proposed Order, with the view of submitting it to Madame Canossa, through their common friend Don Bertoni, an event took place in Rome of considerable importance to the future Institute and its Founder. It was on March 13, 1826, that he commenced to write out 'the plan' he had more fully matured in his mind : it was on that day, too, that his warm friend the Abate Mauro Cappel · lari was proclaimed Cardinal. The coincidence may signify little ; but it derives from circumstances an interest that makes it worth recording. As soon as authentic news of the fact reached Milan, Don Antonio sent to the new Cardinal this congratulatory note :—

It was only yesterday that the newspapers of this city informed me of your promotion to the Cardinalate by the Sovereign Pontiff Leo XII. The news, which did not at all surprise me, has filled me with the truest joy. I sincerely congratulate Holy Church and hasten to express my gladness to your Eminence, wishing that I was able to pay my homage in person rather than by letter. Allow me, at the same time to tender you my hearty thanks for the kindness which you have been pleased to lavish on the Priest whom I took the liberty to recommend to your notice. Let me humbly beg that your Eminence will continue to regard me with your usual goodness, &c., &c.

MILAN : *March* 30, 1826.

The kindly terms of Cardinal Cappellari's reply encouraged Rosmini to place before him the outlines of the proposed Order. His Eminence already had some reason to suppose that such a project was under consideration, for ' he was one of those friends who advised the young Roveretan divine to turn his thoughts to a Religious Order as well as to philo-sophical studies.' [1] It was, therefore, natural that when the Abate Cappellari took his place amongst the Princes of the Church, the young Abate should con-

[1] Tommaseo's *Antonio Rosmini*, Torino, 1855.

sult him on this matter, even though he sought rather
the judgment of the wise Priest than of the exalted
Prelate, as he intimates himself in the letter ac-
companying a copy of 'the plan' with some other
papers intended to explain the nature of the proposed Institute :—

For some time past some thoughts, awakened in me by
a holy person, have occupied my mind; but I cannot be
certain that they are from God until I am assured of it by
the opinion of some person in authority. If this opinion
were favourable, I should still desire to learn what the Holy
Father thinks. Therefore, I earnestly beg of your Eminence
to be so kind as to assist me with your advice—first with
regard to the general idea of the proposed association, and
then again, should there be need, as regards the details.

If your Eminence were to advise me to abandon this
idea, I should not hesitate a moment in dismissing it. If
you require any further explanation, you have merely to let
me know. Were I encouraged by your favourable judgment,
I should decide on proceeding to Rome, in order to receive
greater light, and to ascertain what further steps it may be
proper or necessary to take.

I do not address myself to you as to a person placed in
lofty station, but only as to a person whose kindness and
indulgent consideration I have so often experienced. For
this reason I do not hesitate to confide my idea to you, in
order to have for my guidance, before anything else is done,
the expression of your private and confidential opinion.

MILAN : *April* 23, 1826.[1]

As yet the secret of the projected Institute was
confided to very few—the few whose piety, and whose
experience in such matters pointed them out as most
competent to counsel him. But he sought the prayers

---

[1] *Epistolario*, Letter xlix.

of all his acquaintances 'for his intention.' A Novena, in which Moschini and Tommaseo joined, preceded the sending of 'the plan' to Cardinal Cappellari. Other special devotions were added to the ordinary daily exercises, and in these his more intimate friends were often asked to unite. His fasts were increased, and 'every shrine in Milan,' says Tommaseo, 'was visited that he might offer there a special prayer for special light.' These prayers seemed to be answered by an interior assurance that God approved 'the principle of passivity' on which the conduct of his life was based, and he therefore, with patience and confidence, waited for the expected indications of Providence.

Meanwhile, he continued his scientific studies, without abating the enfreshened ardour of his religious exercises. Many petty attempts were made, by the advocates of anti-Christian philosophy, to distract and provoke him; but as their efforts were timid, indirect, and clumsy, he declined to notice them. It did not fare thus with attempts to win his charity or advice; however timidly or awkwardly put before him, these were always deemed worthy of prompt attention. From various quarters and various classes of men letters continued to reach him, asking his aid in various ways. Many of these came from mere acquaintances, and not a few from perfect strangers, who wished to know his opinion on something perhaps of little importance in itself. Most men, with less than one tenth of his occupations, would refuse to give a thought to such corre-

spondents ; but his charity failed in nothing, and he
replied to the least of them as gravely and fully as
when he thus answered a Priest who ' suffered from
heaviness of heart ' and was doubtful whether he
ought not to look for relief in poetry and social
entertainments :—

I am grateful for your remembrance of me, although
you knew me but for a short time at the watering-place of
Recoaro. Your letter, with the ode, reached me at Milan.
Having perused both, it seemed to me that some tribulation
of spirit and some sadness overshadowed your mind. This
has so enlisted all my sympathy that I beg of you earnestly
to take courage, and not yield to melancholy. You well
know the good St. Philip's saying, ' In my house I will have
neither scruples nor melancholy.' Let us be piously cheerful, not with boisterous mundane joy, but with that gentle
and tranquil joy which springs chiefly from a pure conscience, and from the grace of the Holy Ghost diffusing
itself in our hearts, and producing in us resignation to the
Divine Will.

Oh ! how delightful and sweet it is to attend, with the
utmost care and goodwill, to God's service, and to correspond with the sublime duties of our vocation. I am convinced that we shall find peace and comfort when all our
cares are thus placed in what is firm and substantial, and
when we regard all the rest with indifference, as a something ephemeral. I am glad to learn from what you tell
me that you take to poetry as a pastime. You do well.
Poetry, however, can only be a trifle to amuse the wearied
spirit and refresh it for serious studies. We are not poets,
but Priests. If you follow these principles you will find recreation ; for the purpose of profiting by it, carefully avoid
all profane and secular company. For diversion, associate
only with good Priests and in decent and decorous amusements. Devotion to the most Holy Mother of God is also

a marvellous remedy against the gloom that overclouds
the mind.   The benign light of this our star comforts us in
every peril.

MILAN : *May* 5, 1826.[1]

Although he was thus exhorting others to banish
sadness, it was commonly supposed that he did not
banish it from himself. His friends in Rovereto feared
that he was oppressed by excessive study, and that
what they deemed 'an overwrought religious fervour' would destroy the cheerfulness of his mind,
as well as the vigour of his constitution.   His cousin
Leonardo Rosmini, in a humorous letter, gave expression to this affectionate alarm, and Don Antonio
replied by a sprightly description of how he and his
companions lived in Milan :—

Your letter gave me very great pleasure, not only
because it was yours, but because of its exuberant
hilarity, which is a pledge to me that your soul is serene
and gladsome.   Doubtless, you will always possess this
contentment, since you have discovered the true road to
happiness to be by virtue.   As to my own condition, I shall
briefly tell you what I can.

Know, then, that I get up early and after a hurried
toilet send word, forthwith, to my companions to be ready
if they desire to accompany me to the church.   In the
meantime, while they are hesitating, perhaps, to rise from
their soft repose, or still engaged in stretching their somewhat inert and stiffened limbs, I say my morning prayers
to our Lord, for His propitious favour during the journey
of this life.   At the termination of Divine Lauds, I go at
once to the neighbouring church, which is consecrated to
the Holy Sepulchre of our Lord.   It is a church well

[1] *Epistolario*, Letter I.

calculated to inspire devotion, not only on account of the life-sized statues over the altars—chiefly representing scenes from the Passion of Christ—but also because it is a memorial of St. Charles Borromeo, who used to frequent it. In the contiguous house, distinguished already as the abode of holy Priests, he gathered together his dear Oblates, at a time when discipline had decayed among the clergy.

After offering up the Holy Sacrifice, and partaking of the soul's celestial nourishment, the body has its sustenance administered in the shape of a moderate breakfast. Afterwards come the hours of study, which really occupy the best part of the day, seeing that they keep us very thoughtfully engaged till noon. Then, with an interval of fresh repose to reinforce the enfeebled body and also to refresh the mind, we reciprocally visit one another, like so many friars in their cells, as we have separate rooms during the hours of study. There we are occupied until four o'clock, when the signal is given to lay aside books and papers. These put in a corner, the writing-desk must give place to the dinner-table, volumes to plates, and pens to forks. And we are so attentive to the dinner bell that nobody keeps the rest of the company waiting in the refectory; whence it would seem that we are all rivals in the diligent performance of such work. . . . There remains much to say about our dinner, much about recreation, much more about our walk. But what would you? The limited space of this sheet of paper does not correspond with my desire, and so I am forced to reserve what more I might say on these 'grave topics' for a better opportunity. Meanwhile pray for us.

MILAN : *May 6, 1826.*[1]

About the same time a letter from one of his old professors, Don G. B. Locatelli, Archpriest of Rovereto, drew from him this tribute to the goodness and

----

[1] *Epistolario,* Letter li.

piety of the Milanese, whose virtues he could all the more effectually extol, as his keen sight could not avoid seeing their defects, and his impartial pen did not refuse to criticise them :—

. . . My sojourn in Milan does not displease me. Here I find religion far more prevalent than I expected, and, so far, do not think there is another city like it. The principal families are saintly. At this jubilee season, it is really impressive to meet in the streets people of every class visiting the churches, reciting aloud prayers, and performing other pious and penitential works. The alms-deeds and liberality of the gentry are very great. Asylums, churches, hospitals, and every good thing of that sort, are soon built by them. It is enough to make known the want of such a thing, and the money is forthwith obtained.

The clergy do not seem to me to be very learned, but solid and truly pious; while, as regards discipline, they are rather austere than relaxed. I find them to be extremely prudent and reserved ; diligent in their ministerial duties, they never meddle with affairs that do not concern them.

The only Religious Order is that of the Barnabites, recently restored by the Archbishop. At present, they have some young subjects, but not many trained Religious. There are some Oblates of St. Charles at Ro, and at S. Sepolcro ; but they are not recognised by the authorities. The oratories for youth, originated specially by B. Federico, seem to me to be both beautiful and useful.

The general character of the Milanese is excellent, though they are wanting in that external polish which gives such grace to the countenance, customs, manners, and dialect of the Venetians ; but in the Lombard's seriousness there is a sturdiness of temper which gives a manly tone to their affability and courtesy. Their simplicity pleases me much. Great decorum is observed in noble families, and with greater splendour than is usual among

the Venetians. At the same time, there is a certain freedom and familiarity which relieves a stranger from embarrassment, especially an awkward one, like myself. Maurizio
sends you his greetings ; and I beg of you to salute kindly
our clergy for me. I have seen Don Pietro Beltrami's jubilee
tract. For a long time no better one has been printed at
Milan. We Roveretans may be contented with our position,
when in some things we surpass even great cities.

MILAN : Sunday within the Octave of Ascension, 1826.[1]

Nearly every letter he wrote from Milan in those
days bore similar testimony to the religious character
of the people. It was a something intensely gratifying to see God so generally loved and glorified.
No matter what special subject he had to deal with,
this topic crept in, as one which had such an edifying influence on himself that he could not resist imparting it to others. For instance, when answering
a communication from Don Giulio Todeschi, that
required him to say much on a subject in no way
calling for allusion to the state of Milan, he could
not help passing aside to this grateful theme :—

This city pleases me more than any I have seen, precisely because its people are singularly pious—practising a
solid, and I will even say a robust devotion.

Everywhere around may be noticed the great works of
St. Charles Borromeo, not only in the noble edifices which
externally adorn the city, but, what is far more important,
in the good and magnificent sentiments diffused among its
clergy and people, and transmitted as a most precious
legacy from father to son. It is with these sublime sentiments that he has built an interior city and erected magnificent structures in the heavenly Jerusalem. How many

[1] *Epistolario*, Letter lii.

do not see them because they are invisible! Let us thank the Divine goodness that we see them, and rejoice greatly at such a sight. . . . Maurizio and Nicoló salute you. I shall be a little while longer absent from home, so, if you wish to write to me, you can direct your letter to this city. Pray to our Lord that I may profit somewhat by the many good examples which are here continually before my eyes, and that they may help to correct my defects. Farewell.

MILAN : *May* 9, 1826.[1]

At the commencement of the letter addressed to Don Locatelli, Rosmini incidentally mentioned the alarming condition of the celebrated Vincenzo Monti's health, an apoplectic stroke having just prostrated that mischievous personage. Monti was a dark blotch on Milanese piety—a representative blotch, in so far as the leaders of sensist philosophy were representative men. He was an adept in Italian literature of the antique sensistic school, and ranked as one of the most classic poets in modern Italy ; but his moral and political principles were so exceedingly loose that he could not be credited with having any at all. He had been equally ready to glorify Napoleon or the Austrian emperor as a god, and to denounce either as a demon, just as personal expediency suggested. . The false philosophy which Monti did so much to bring into favour at most of the Universities, made religion, as well as politics, a matter of mere convenience to himself, and to most of those who ventilated their views through the *Biblioteca Italiana.* He was the bitter personal and literary opponent of Rosmini's valued friend Cesari,

[1] *Epistolario,* Letter liii.

and the vehement supporter of Gioia and the others
who had instinctively arrayed themselves against
the Roveretan champion of Christian philosophy as
opposed to their own pernicious teachings.

Nevertheless, Rosmini, having an opportunity,
turned charitably towards this man's spiritual needs,
and, seeing that he was in the grasp of death, hoped
to fix his restless soul on the necessity of making some
preparation for eternity. The erratic old poet was
only one of the many waverers, young and old, to
whom Don Antonio acted the part of a special missionary, and among whom he did an incalculable
amount of good. Although Monti's ˊinfirmities,
physical and other, were such as promised to the
young apostle no immediate results, he persevered
in the duty, with how little hope may be gathered
from what he thus said to Don Locatelli.

Here, Monti has had an apoplectic stroke, and it is to
be devoutly wished that he would, ere it be too late, give
some external tokens of religion, demanded by his inexplic-
ably inconstant life. It is a pity that he is so deaf, as it
makes conversation painful, and renders reasoning at any
length impossible. I regard him as a man of good heart ;
but this you know is not sufficient. On the other hand,
some false friends deceive him as to his actual condition.
What is still worse is that, while he fears to die, the hope of
life is strong in him. This hope is often fatal to those
advanced in years.

While Rosmini was trying to rescue this unhappy man from the abyss on the brink of which
false philosophy left him, a letter from Rovereto
brought news of a little triumph elsewhere, that

promised to rescue many souls from some other ills which were protected by a political outcome of this philosophy. The ecclesiastical authorities at Trent were, at last, allowed to complete the arrangements Don Antonio had induced them to begin for the reception of the Daughters of Charity in that diocese. This was a victory, though a small one, over the political double dealings which made it difficult for Catholics, in Catholic countries, to use Catholic organisations for rescuing the helpless from the miseries or the dangers brought on and fostered by a state-craft having its source in false philosophy. Politicians, full of the fallacies thus generated, had come to detest any moral agencies the State did not create, and, forgetting what Religious Orders had done for civilisation in the past, sought to deprive them of opportunities to preserve it in the future. The policy of this state-craft was to crush religious societies, and to cry down, ignore or curb all religious zeal that threatened to be useful.

Owing to the efforts of this policy the excellent Order of Madame Canossa could not easily extend its labours to places where they were much needed. Many towns in Austria were in want of the services of the Order ; but politicians so misrepresented the nature of these services that people generally were led to distrust them. Thus, although the Daughters of Charity had been long and beneficially engaged in their pious work throughout the adjoining Italian provinces, even some of the Tyrolese Priests were indisposed to welcome them as cordially as they de-

served. Rosmini, who had his heart and mind fixed
on destroying the poisonous philosophy to which
this state of things was primarily due, was careful,
meanwhile, to set himself, wherever he could,
against its immediate outflow. Hence, he took
great pains to let his countrymen have correct information about the Daughters of Charity, and did
his utmost to smooth a path, at best but thorny, for
those self-sacrificing ladies. Among others who
needed this information was his intimate friend Don
Giulio Todeschi of Mezzotedesco, to whom he gave
this short but sufficient account of the Canossa Order
in the course of a letter dealing with the ordinary
points of familiar correspondence :—

Your letter commences with what is a very agreeable
subject ; for such to me is that of the Daughters of Charity.
Yes, I hope they will very soon be established in Trent.
The Emperor has given a convent to the excellent Madame
Canossa, and some Tyrolese sisters are even now ready to
take possession. It is only necessary to repair the dwelling,
which, being in a very bad condition, may cause some little
delay. All that, however, will be set right as soon as possible through the zeal of our Vicar General who has shown
himself to be full of Apostolical Charity.

What you say, as to my sister going to be Superioress at
Trent, is incorrect. She is a simple novice, who, in due
time, will be sent to that house chosen for her by her Superiors according to the needs of her Institute.

As you desire to know the general object of this Sisterhood, let me tell you that it is to take special care of a
class which is the most despised and neglected, and, consequently the most helpless in Society; and, on that
account, it is the class which is dearest to our Divine
Master—namely, the very poor ; to assist sick females in

the hospital, and if the Parish Priest wishes it, to teach
women Christian doctrine in the parish church, under his
direction ; besides, to have a school where poor girls might
be instructed in reading, writing, and in other things which
it is useful for poor women to know. They also extend
their care to the improvement of education in the villages
by receiving into the convent, for seven months in the year,
good young peasant girls of talent, with the view of educating them, so as to qualify them to take charge of rural
schools, as good mistresses, well-mannered and pious.

After caring for the wants of the poor, the Daughters
of Charity, if they have time and strength, will turn their
attention to those in better circumstances. In large cities,
as here in Milan, they do great good by gathering together
in their convent, at a certain time of the year, pious ladies
to enable them to make spiritual retreats. The Milanese
have lately, with the greatest edification, availed themselves
of this convenience.

The life then of these excellent sisters is, as their name
indicates, all charity. It is a life of active and robust virtue.
For their own spiritual support they have, meanwhile, their
Community exercises, consisting chiefly in mental prayer,
which is the secret of keeping enkindled the fire of divine
love. The virtue that I myself know these good sisters to
possess is marvellous. There is a perfect and unchanging
friendship among them, the truest purity of conscience,
together with liberty of spirit and uninterrupted gladsome-
ness. All this sweetens the most heavy labours, in the
discharge of which they are truly indefatigable.

MILAN : *May* 9, 1826.[1]

Without knowing how actively Rosmini was
engaged in what related to her own Order, Madame
Canossa busily occupied herself in what concerned
the Institute she besought him to found. As the

---

[1] *Epistolario*, Letter liii.

plan he had drawn up provided for members of the
new Order accepting the Pastoral Office in its widest
signification, she wrote to him, remonstrating against
this departure from a custom that time and experience had proved to be good. He admitted the
reasonableness of her fears; but her objections to
the seeming innovation were answered in such a way
as satisfied her that as much could be said for as
against this feature of the proposed Society.[1] He
showed that Jesus Christ had placed the germ of
all perfection in the Pastoral Ministry, and that
'there are no two things which go so well together
as the religious profession and the Pastoral Office,
professing, as both do, the perfection of life which
consists in nothing else than charity.' Having disposed of the strongest arguments that might be
urged against combining Religious Life with the
pastorate of souls, he concluded his long letter
thus :—

Pardon the freedom with which I entreat you to reflect
well on this important matter, from which so much good
may flow to Holy Church, provided what we propose is
written in the Divine Decrees. Believe me, that even the
Religious who, of his own free will, flies from the world,
would not fly from it in a spirit of perfection, if he were to
refuse to leave the delightful silence of the cloister to assist
his brethren when called forth by the voice of Charity.
Perfect flight from the world should, henceforth, be made
in spirit, after the manner of the Apostles ; and we ought
not be satisfied with a mere external flight. I am well
aware that the most agreeable life is that which finds us withdrawn completely from this most dangerous and wretched

[1] See Appendix, Letter v.

world ; but we should not seek what is most agreeable and what we like best rather than what is most pleasing to God and most useful to His Holy Kingdom. Let us then live *in solitude with the heart* ; but let us not refuse to leave it with the body, when the voice of the Superior, which should be for us as the voice of God Himself, calls us.

Milton held that '*Society* must proceed from the mind rather than from the body,' and Blair once described solitude as 'the society where no body intrudes.' The mind and the heart find in themselves all the fulness of society, as St. Bernard proved, for he was 'never less alone than when alone.' It matters not, then, where the body is ; if the mind be not there, a solitude is there in which the heart lacks not society. To train men so that they should thus live 'in the solitude of the heart' while ministering to the spiritual needs of their neighbours, would be to revive in a new way the anchoret system of Apostolic times, and establish in the midst of society, where all intrude, a solitude where no one intrudes. Rosmini attached the utmost importance to this self-retirement, even in the case of those who were not 'bound by the sweet bonds of Religious Life.' He thought it undesirable for men who were not disciplined to 'solitude of heart' to withdraw from social intercourse, lest the cares of life should lead them into a fatal gloom ; but he insisted that they must always keep the mind girt with sublime religious thoughts, lest social intercourse should lead them into an equally fatal levity of spirit.

Although the state of human society was not so

bad in his day as it has since been made by the tenets his adversaries have succeeded in propagating, he had frequent occasions to counsel those who were on the verge of moral ruin, either from dejection or frivolity. One of these occasions presented itself when he heard that Professor Bartolomeo Stofella of Rovereto had fallen a victim to melancholy, partly from yielding to family sorrows and partly from having confounded social seclusion with solitude of heart. A letter from this desponding friend gave him an opportunity of at once reproaching and consoling him in the following manner, and with the best results :—

Among the many things in your letter which gave me pleasure, the one thing that grieved me was to find you always sadly harping on these lines :—

> I love to roam alone in pensive mood,
> And slowly pace thro' dreary solitude.

Ah! pray do not always seek excuse to shun the beaten path of your fellow-men! Let human society rather alleviate and comfort you, if you have the misfortune to be in affliction and sorrow. I mean that it should alleviate you with the comfort of prudent counsels, and not merely divert you with the clatter of foolish gossippings, which not only deafen the ear but confuse the mind. The relief which one seems to take from that noisy external agitation (which afterwards leaves the soul more confused, clouded, and miserable than before) is very different from that which relieves one by shedding on man the tranquil ray of truth. This ray descending, so to speak, in the night that is then on us, dispels its obscurity and enables us to notice peacefully how agitated and confused things are in it. It likewise discloses to us the mode of reducing them to order, thus calming, as it were, the mounting billows of a stormy sea.

Yes, I understand it, you are not pleased with the life you lead. The heavy fatigues to which the school subjects you, and the many hours of the best part of the day which you are obliged to sacrifice thereto—then, the weariness which follows during the remainder of the day—many thoughts about your relations—your very health, often sickly and for the most part weak—all these things combine to agitate and disturb you. You should, however, know how to have patience—you should know how to make an offering of these troubles to our Lord, so as to turn the evil to your good. How admirable our Divine religion always is in the consolation it affords to us poor mortals! How rich it is in the sublimest reasons, the most touching affections, and the most heavenly, supernatural means to fortify our feeble hearts, and to transform almost into impassible angels, paltry men, who are full of infirmities. As for me, the more I study the matter, my dear friend, the more thoroughly am I persuaded of all this.

Our religion is a friend, or a compassionate mother, strewing flowers over all our thorns, and administering balm to soothe the bitterness of our every misfortune. She comes into us, she enthrones herself in our very heart, and from that seat diffuses, like the sun, an all-embracing serenity through the whole man, who is thus transported into a luminous paradise ;—she, as it were, lays hold of him and fastens him to Eternity. O God ! what an object of true wisdom ! In fact, if we meditated well upon eternity alone, we should better know what little value to set on all that is of earth. Eternity it is that reproaches us for having turned our affections towards some ephemeral object, whilst we should have reserved them for what was everlasting ; it makes us think with sorrow of even the least fraction of time that we have irreparably lost. Well does this teacher make me comprehend how much reason the

Saints had to charge with insanity a world that strove so
hard to possess things which would soon have to be irre-
coverably abandoned.

It is indeed madness, for the sake of such trifles, to
wage war, nourish animosities, cause slaughter, encounter
great heat and cold, and consume one's self in continual
toils and endeavours to overcome anxieties and cares ;—
for the sake of these things, let me repeat, which man must
soon give up for ever, returning naked to that earth whence
he came, without having done anything for eternity !
If this be not a deplorable madness, whatever else can
be ? God grants us time and the way to collect treasures
that endure for ever ; but we make no account of them,
preferring to waste all the precious time of life, not fearing
to find ourselves at the point of death destitute of the
many merits with which we might have been enriched ;—
not fearing to appear, devoid of any virtue, at the tribunal
of an Almighty and most just God, to render a most
rigorous account of all the graces we have lost, of all the
inspirations we have left unheeded, and of all our ingratitude towards that God who had lavished upon us His most
abundant mercies ! We know that the present life is the
allotted time for mercy ; we know that the future is reserved for justice, and, yet, with what little reflection we
allow the whole of life to pass away !—the whole of that
time in which to work out our salvation ! thus with indifference continually drawing nigh to the hour of reckoning !
What stupidity ! what madness ! it would be incredible if
experience did not show it to exist. . . . .

MILAN : *July* 16, 1826.[1]

He considered that men were most happy when,
by becoming foolish according to the principles of
the world, they became wise according to our Lord
Jesus. In his opinion, practical membership of the

----

[1] *Epistolario*, Letter liv.

Church of Christ was 'the perfection of all society,'
and the one grand remedy against the depressions
of heart with which mere human society, in the midst
of its gaieties, afflicted men.   All his intelligence, all
his sympathies, all his affections were so knit up
with the Kingdom of Christ, that there was no happiness for him except in the closest union with the
Church.   A letter which he wrote before making a
short visit to Rovereto, in 1826, incidentally shows
how profoundly he felt this.   The letter was to an
old schoolfellow, Don Giovanni Stefani, who had
been for some time in Lisbon as tutor to a prince of
the Portuguese Royal Family and had just been
prevailed on to continue in that capacity for some
time longer :—

I am glad that you remain, because I bethink me that
you will be able to benefit your young pupil. Do all you
can to make him feel the dignity of being a member of
the Church of Jesus Christ—of that immense, that divine
Society which deserves all our love, and towards which it
is right that all our thoughts should be turned.   Beautiful
is human friendship, but far more beautiful is the love of
Holy Church.   Love of family is praiseworthy, so is love
for one's birthplace or nation.   Ah! Let our love for
family, for native place, for country, be so many different
means to promote the glory of God's Church?   They
should be considered by the Christian only as parts of a
greater and higher society—that of the Church.   Since
we have received the Grace that our family and nation
should be in the Church of Jesus Christ, ought not the
part to be subservient to the whole ?

Seek to print this deeply in your pupil's mind.   Happy
will he be if he should receive the impression and carry it
with him uncancelled all his life.   Even though you should

fail to make a real impression, you will be happy to have used all your endeavours in the attempt. As regards the merit acquired before God, the effort alone is equivalent to having formed a devout son to the Church of Jesus Christ. In that way, while you will be useful to the youth, you will assuredly be more useful to yourself. . . .

MILAN : *September* 13, 1826.[1]

Rosmini's love for Christ's Kingdom on earth, if practically accepted by princes and peoples, would have thrown down the petty boundaries of national prejudice or tribal hate, to build up, in its stead, a patriotism of the most exalted kind—the patriotism of Christian Charity—the patriotism of Redeemed humanity—the patriotism that should embrace all nations as subject to the Celestial King, and thus leave mankind to that repose which a narrower patriotism must, from its very nature, be continually and brutally disturbing. Like Lord Bacon, he had ' taken all knowledge for his Province ; '[2] but, unlike Bacon, he gave the rule of this Province to Heaven and not to Earth, making it provide for the loftier and permanent rather than for the lower and transient interests of the whole human race. Therefore, like Him for Whom Bacon's Province had no set place, he took all men to be his fellow-subjects, his brethren, his neighbours, in the one grand kingdom of Christ's Charity—that Province of the New Law which comprises all knowledge and includes all men. Within this alone patriotism is a virtue of the sublimest kind. It is the patriotism of the New

[1] *Epistolario*, Letter lv.
[2] Bacon's Letter to Lord Burleigh.

Law, the patriotism of Charity, and he thus explains it to us :—

'Even in the Old Law it was discerned that the expression near or *neighbour* could not be properly understood of a propinquity wholly material (since it was quite possible that an enemy, instead of a kinsman or friend, might be living near one's house), but was intended to express a spiritual proximity, a nighness of heart, inasmuch as he who loves is, by affection, near and neighbour to the person loved. Therefore the Jew, not knowing that he should love other than a Jew, held that only the Jew was his neighbour. But Christ, loving all men, and, in Himself, rendering every man lovable, has made all in the world neighbours. Thus the Jewish expression remains true, with a new signification ; for it is true, no less by the Old than the New Testament, that "we should love our neighbour"—with this difference, however : the supernatural love known to the Old Law had not strength enough to extend itself beyond the nation ; whereas, in the New Law, by the Redemption and Grace of Christ, there were given to it wings powerful enough to carry it through all the world. The Old Law as to loving our neighbour continues, then, in force ; but there is a New Law, in which Christ ordains that "we ourselves should voluntarily become neighbours to all in the world, by loving all."' [1]

Thus the precept of Charity is at once old and new—the aim of the Old Law and subject-matter of

[1] *Rosmini's Discourses.*—Dis. ' On love of our neighbour.'

the New. In the Old Law the love which brought the Jew nigh to the Jew consisted in the natural inclinations sanctified—the affections of parents, of children, of husband and wife, of fellow-citizens and compatriots ; but, in the New, the love which brings man nigh to man is that Charity which Christ had for all men, and that which we, through Christ and in Him, have for all who are loved by Christ.

CHAPTER XXI.

ROSMINI, AWAITING 'THE MANIFESTATION OF PROVIDENCE,' ACTIVELY WORKS FOR THE GLORY OF GOD AND THE VINDICATION OF TRUTH.

(A.D. 1826-1827.)

His Milan household an illustration of the instability of mere human arrangements—Strength of institutions designed for God's glory— He goes to Rovereto with the Chevalier Carlo Rosmini and Maurizio Moschini—Calls at Brescia and Verona—Is urged to join the Jesuits—Once more at the 'old Homestead'—His mother still seeks to keep him in his native diocese—What he thinks of taking the Pastoral Ministry—Indifferent to all but God's Will—Returns to Milan with Don Fenner as Secretary—Mellerio and Manzoni meet him—His share in Manzoni's *Promessi Sposi*—How he awaits the manifestation of Providence—His estimate of human power in the salvation of souls—Why he prefers a good heart to great talent— His efforts to restore Christian Philosophy—Progress of the *Nuovo Saggio*—Literary war with the dechristianising sensists—His philosophical productions of this time—Depends on Prayer more than on Reason—Lives on earth as being always in the visible presence of God—'His conversation is in Heaven'—Philosophy and Reason would be traitors without Prayer and Piety.

BEFORE Rosmini had been a year at Milan his little household threatened such a change as furnished him with a practical commentary on the instability of the most hopeful human arrangements. Tommaseo, once more weary of living up to 'a rule of life,' sought once more the dangerous liberty of being his own master, and he obtained it. He con-

tinued, however, to work occasionally for his benefactor, but selected Florence as the seat of his
labours. There he gave himself up to preparing
his *Antologia* without much satisfaction to himself
or Rosmini. Moschini lost his health and had
'medical orders' to go back to Rovereto in the
hope of recovering it. The coachman's services
were no longer required, and the cook was soon the
only one left of the companions originally chosen to
form the Milan establishment.

If such were the vicissitudes of a small family
in so short a time, what fortune awaited a large
Community that aspired to live for ages? But his
little *dulce domum* was of human origin, mainly for
human ends, and had not been set up with all that
care and all those safeguards which must, surely,
protect an institution suggested by Heaven and
founded exclusively for the glory of God and the
spiritual good of men. This, too, would probably
have its vicissitudes in some respects like the other,
since it was in some respects human ; but Providence never yet left an institution of Its own special
creation at the mercy of human inconstancy. Knowing this, Rosmini employed every means to make
sure that Providence was the real designer of the
project suggested by the saintly Canossa. We have
already seen what these means were, and how careful he was to test their value in every possible
form. Never did the Founder of a Religious
Order more warily take every step to his object—
never more fearingly, or more prayerfully, or more

deeply impressed with its sacredness and his own unworthiness.

In the Autumn of 1826, Don Antonio decided on making a few weeks' visit to Rovereto, partly to console his mother, partly to look after family interests, and partly to have another opportunity of a personal consultation with the Foundress of the Daughters of Charity, as Verona would be the most convenient resting-place on the way to and from the Tyrol. Maurizio Moschini was to accompany him home as an invalid of whose restoration to sound health the Milanese physicians had little hopes Another companion was to be the historian of Milan—the Chevalier Carlo Rosmini—whose physical condition also required change of air. The day before they started, Rosmini dined with Manzoni at Brusuglio, where he met some of the intellectual wanderers whose thoughts he was successfully leading back to the truths and duties of Faith.

On the way to Verona he stayed for a few hours in Brescia with Don Brunati, and with some Jesuit Fathers who were amongst his warmest friends, and who, knowing that his soul was bent on the Religious State, used all their powers of persuasion to court him into the Society as offering the best field for his genius, learning and zeal. To no one did he yield in love and admiration for 'the true children of St. Ignatius;' but the voice that spoke so constantly within him did not prompt him to join them, and he faithfully followed its whisperings to proceed elsewhere.

At Verona he remained a day, the greater part of which was given to prayer and consultation with Don Bertoni, and an interview with Madame Canossa and his sister on the subject of the Institute. His sister was no longer merely a guest studying the educational system of the Daughters of Charity, but a novice practising 'the way of perfection' as laid down by their rule, and on the eve of taking the vows. Having stored up in his mind and heart the hints and consolations that came from his conferences with these holy people, he continued the journey to Rovereto. There a hearty reception greeted him on all sides, the 'welcome back' being of that kind which one usually associates with a return after long absence. Once more, the fond mother and devoted retainers were comforted by his presence. Once more, the little domestic oratory had its morning Mass. Once more, the poor gathered in the courtyard of the palazzo to receive alms from his own hands. Once more, our Lady's shrine on the Mount had its most fervent votary. Once more, the deserted library had its industrious master to utilise its contents. Once more, the public Academy hailed its brightest member, and listened to his learned disquisitions. Once more, the hospitable mansions of his kinsmen and friends thronged with guests eager to show their respect for one who 'cast gleams of sanctity on their gladness' and who never refused to recognise the reasonable claims of social intercourse.

This visit to Rovereto, however, was short; but

in that stay of a few weeks, the untiring energies of Don Antonio accomplished a great deal for the moral and intellectual benefit of himself and others. His mother, though now more seasoned to the thought of his permanent absence, made yet another effort to persuade him that he ought to remain with the parochial Clergy of his native diocese. Not trusting to her own reasonings, which were purely those of the heart, she sought the aid of friends whose virtues and talents had most weight. Few of these were ready to promote her wishes in this matter, for they saw more clearly than maternal sentiment permitted her to see, that her son was already doing an Apostle's duty, not for one parish or one diocese but for the whole Church. One of the few who consented to do as she desired was Don Giulio Todeschi; he did so, however, in such a timid, indirect way, that Rosmini hardly suspected the drift of his advice as to 'taking upon himself the Pastoral Ministry.' Therefore, he made but a passing, though a sufficiently expressive, allusion to the subject in the following letter :—

Your letters are always dear to me, because there flows from them an oil which is so fragrant that its odour affects the innermost sense of the soul and thence diffuses itself thrillingly ; because, in short, they always contain the name of our Lord and Redeemer. Oh ! with what truth and reason St. Bernard said that to him would be insipid the book in which he did not meet with the most lovable of all names —the name of JESUS. So, indeed, it ever should be ;— every thing which is not seasoned and signed with this name should be tasteless to Redeemed men. Unhappy me ! I am not worthy to pronounce it. . . .

At Milan, there are many oratories for young men
which are exceedingly useful. I used to go to them on
festival days, when able, and, although I gave short discourses and spiritual conferences when asked, I was really
there more to learn than to teach. But, as you have very
well said—for all that I regard with so much pleasure
exercises relating to the welfare of souls, our Lord has not
called me, as yet, to this sublime ministry. I am thoroughly
persuaded that He has, with good reason, kept me a step
backward, as one may say, from His 'Inner Sanctuary,'
for so it seems to me I should designate the Pastoral
Ministry.

I certainly do not desire, or at least wish to desire,
anything more than the fulfilment of God's adorable Will.
And can I desire anything, except to serve my Lord and
my God in that way wherein He wills me to serve Him?
'For what have I in Heaven ; and, besides Thee, what do
I desire upon earth?' Most happy should I be were I, at
once, to become a faithful, and not a wicked and perfidious,
servant as I now am. It appears to me, or I am mistaken,
that I am indifferent to any kind of service (be it low, contemptible and small, or great and laborious), which our
Lord may require of me,—all, yes truly, all would seem
the same to me, provided only one thing followed—that I
was at last a good and faithful servant.

Ah! my dear friend and brother in Christ, urgently
pray to our Lord to give me this grace,—I desire nothing
more than this. . . .

ROVERETO: *September* 30, 1826.[1]

Owing to the unsatisfactory state of Carlo
Rosmini's health, Don Antonio returned to Lombardy before winter set in. He took with him as
secretary, in place of Moschini, Don Andrea Fenner,
and, on their arrival in Milan, this clergyman was

[1] *Epistolario,* Letter lvi.

announced in the public journals as 'corrector of the press to the Roveretan philosopher.' Count Mellerio and Manzoni were the first friends to call on Rosmini immediately after his return.

Mellerio, who shared his confidence as to the projected Religious Order, was anxious to know how the affair prospered, and what further light God had vouchsafed to give him, directly or through Madame Canossa. Rosmini could only assure his friend that the plan was matured, and that the good Marchioness continued to name Milan as the place where God's Will would be further manifested to him.

Manzoni, who shared his confidence as to the scientific works in which he was engaged, sought his counsel with regard to some of his own literary labours. Who can tell what effect these literary consultations had on the *Promessi Sposi*? It is pretty certain that some of the manuscript and all the proof sheets were submitted to Rosmini, and, though it is not very likely that he meddled at all with the polished diction of Manzoni, there is reason to believe that he left the impress of his hand there, for many turns of thought, many pointed reflections, many moral adornments that enrich the work have a strong Rosminian flavour.

The year 1827 found Rosmini calmly waiting for the special indications of Providence which Madame Canossa told him to expect. He went on assiduously providing for the spiritual weal of the pious souls committed to his charge. His charitable deeds in connection with the Milan Oratories increased.

Although the publication of his philosophical works, combined with his studies, occupied more time than usual, his amazing activity of mind and body enabled him to continue without interruption all the aid he gave to those who laboured for 'God's little poor,' or who strove to win back to Christ such souls as had been led astray by the seductive teachings of false philosophy. How much he prized this co-operation in the salvation of souls we already know : yet, he valued little mere human power in these efforts, as he took occasion to tell his sister Margherita in the following letter :

I am glad that your sisters labour, as you tell me, so cheerfully, and I doubt not you ardently desire to imitate them. A soul saved to our Lord is, assuredly, a great gain. But this is not human work. Man can only reach the ear in an ineffectual way ; but it is God changes the heart. In this affair, therefore, we are not only ants, as you say, but even much less. However, it is an infinite Grace, which also demands our gratitude, that God vouchsafes to accompany our useless efforts on the *exterior* man, with His secret operation on the *interior*. In this way, He is pleased to make man what may be termed a co-operator with His Divine Son, which is the greatest, and, yet, the most humiliating dignity that man can think of. I say the most humiliating, remembering from Whom he receives it, beneath Whom he must humble himself, not only on account of his own nothingness, but again through gratitude. . . .

MILAN : *January* 4, 1827.[1]

A curious little short-lived controversy which sprang up in these days had Rosmini for its centre. His genius was admitted by the bitterest of his

[1] *Epistolario,* Letter lvii.

assailants, the champions of sensistic irreligion; but some of them insisted that he valued genius more than goodness of heart, whereas his friends claimed that he looked on genius as a possession infinitely less desirable than a good heart. Not only in Milan, but also in Rovereto, there were those who contended that his practical charities, which kept pace with his intellectual works, were rather due to his genius than to his heart, inasmuch as the heart was, according to them, directed by the genius and not independent of it. Others declared that, being a genius, he was bound to regard a good heart, which is no uncommon possession, as far inferior to a possession that was very rare; still others held that if he had merely a good heart men would not admire him as much as they did, though they might love him no less. Don Orsi of Rovereto, who undertook to get Rosmini's own view on the subject, put the inquiry somewhat in this way : 'Which is preferable, an excellent intellect with a perverse heart, or a feeble intellect with a good heart?' The reply was prompt and conclusive :—

My solution of this question is, you must already know, your own. The following seem to me to be the principal reasons :—

1. Talent is a gift ; the use of it is an act of our own. Now, of itself, talent does not help us to employ it well ; it may rather tempt us to use it improperly. The heart, on the contrary, inclines us to make a proper use of the talent we possess. Hence, the endowment of the heart is more valuable, because it is that which disposes us to do well those acts which proceed from ourselves. It is, in short

virtue ; and we all know that only virtue can entitle a man to praise, as belonging to himself.

2. Talent, if badly employed, does not make us happy. The heart, on the contrary, by inclining us to virtue helps us to obtain happiness. Experience furnishes us with continual proof of the fact, and history illustrates it. Setting aside the arrogance of the philosophers of Greece and other nations, Solomon, Origen, and Tertullian were brought to unhappiness by their talents.

3. Jesus Christ never praised the gifts of mere intellect, but always those of the heart.

4. Great intellect is a property even of the Devil,— that is to say, of the most wicked of creatures : not so the heart.

5. Men love a good heart more than high intellect. Hence, even the world considers great geniuses as being dangerous. They usually have many enemies, while those who have a good heart are loved by everybody.

Having satisfied your questions, I hasten to close this letter. Greet all, especially your dear brother. It seems to me that, through Divine Grace, I labour more than usual. I see clearly that it is the will of God that I must still be far from you. Before the work I am engaged on is completed, at least four years must elapse. The labour seems to grow under my hands. The Lord truly spreads flowers for me over the rough paths, all along which I find the ruins of gigantic geniuses. Adieu.

MILAN : *January* 27, 1827.[1]

The labour alluded to in the above letter aimed at nothing less than the complete restoration of philosophy. It was, indeed, a formidable task, and that portion of it on which he was then specially engaged—*The new Essay on the Origin of Ideas*— was destined to open a most important epoch in the

[1] *Epistolario,* Letter lviii.

history of science. Therefore, it would take a long
time ; and, although he had been for many years
occasionally working at it, four years more of constant labour would hardly have sufficed to complete it,
if he was not a man of unflinching industry. But, in
order to give, meanwhile, a sample of the knowledge
he meant to propose for the restoration of philosophy
he began to publish at once (1827) in Milan the first
volume of his *Opuscoli Filosofici.* This volume
contained several essays. Two were on *Divine
Providence,* and discussed the limits set to human
reason in its pronouncements on God's dealings with
man, and also defined the laws which govern the
distribution of temporal good and evil ; another was
on the *Unity of Education*; and another on the
Idyl and the New Italian Literature.

'The writers of the *Biblioteca Italiana,'* says
Don Paoli, 'were still waiting with ears erect for
what the young Abate, who had recently come
amongst them, would have to say for himself.'
Well, they heard him and one of them threw down
the gauntlet; but the Roveretan would not take it
up, ' as it was the challenge of a polemic who could
not be serious.' Rosmini 'contented himself with
writing in the preface to the second volume of the
Opuscoli, and on the same page, the objections of
the assailant side by side with the replies of the
assailed.' In this way, every impartial reader might
see, at a glance, that Rosmini was attacked mainly
because of the fancied prejudices which it was then
customary to attribute to such ecclesiastics as ven-

tured to demonstrate the harmony between the truths of Reason and those of Revelation. It was on this occasion that he said in a letter to Don Orsi, 'The article in the *Biblioteca Italiana* has made me laugh. They say it is by Gioia or Gironi.' In the same letter to Don Orsi we find an interesting scrap of information as to the progress of the *New Essay on the Origin of Ideas*: 'Since my return to Milan I have written more than two hundred pages of the work on which I am engaged, and at least one hundred and fifty of these are large-sized pages. Nevertheless, I can find time for rest, and for holding conversations with some few friends. One of those whom I see the most frequently is Manzoni, whose company I enjoy very much.'[1]

The second volume of the *Opuscoli* was already in hand, though not immediately published. In it he recast and enlarged the treatise on *Happiness* which he had published at Rovereto in 1822. Its new title was *An Essay on Hope*, and its object to nullify the desolating teachings of Ugo Foscolo. Among the other treatises in this volume was *An Examination of the Opinions of M. Gioia in favour of Fashion*, and the *Exposure* of the same author's philosophy. Both essays were intended to counteract the sensistic views then in vogue, and both won much fame for the author throughout all Italy, where Gioia's writings had hitherto held an unchecked popularity.

Gioia was perhaps the most attractive of the

---

[1] Unpublished Letter, dated Milan, January 23, 1827.

Italian authors who at that time held a far-reaching influence, most hurtful to truth and sound morality. In fact, his dangerous renown was so great that every new writer was expected to do it homage. But the Roveretan Abate, instead of highly commending, strongly condemned it, by laying bare the hideous character of the tenets on which it was poised. Gioia made pleasure the idol of man's worship and the sole principle of ethics ; he took from the ' transmontane utilitarians ' the most ruinous maxims of political economy, and presented them, in his many books, under the alluring garb of a popular style, which was made very effective by a bold, derisive smartness borrowed from the French writers of the last century. All this was far too well calculated to captivate unwary readers, and, as a matter of fact, it had already ' corrupted the heart and intellect of the flower of Italian youth.'

Rosmini fearlessly struck at the strongholds of this baneful system, and the celebrated writer who defended it was so enraged that he could at first find no other reply than what Don Paoli calls ' a torrent of abuse.' But he came to regret this, and it is very probable that he owed to our Christian champion's writings the nobler sentiments which he manifested at the close of his life ; for ' he felt it his duty to publicly declare that he died retracting and detesting his errors.'

The more Rosmini thus laboured successfully to overthrow error, and the more his works became the theme of much public discussion and no little praise,

the more thorough were his humility and his dependence on, and confidence in, God. This is very evident in all his letters of that time, whether they were
written with much deliberation or thrown off as hurriedly as the following note to the Baron Don Giulio
Todeschi :—

I am here immersed in studies. I thank God who
gives me strength for the work. Every day I more and
more understand the Divine Will. I must remain here for
some time yet. How pleasant it would be for me were I
so placed that I could converse personally with my good
friends,—with my good Giulio.

I beg and entreat of you to recommend me warmly to
our Lord. Would that I had a spark of that fervour which
you mention in your dear letter ! Would that I had drawn
profit from the recent Christmas solemnities, during which
Jesus came to visit us ! Had not my heart been harder
than stone, certainly I ought, as you say, to have been
duly softened and melted with grief for my faults, and with
gratitude to the Divine goodness. But, it was not so, my ·
dear Giulio, it was not so. I am always as heretofore—
nay worse. *Non peccator, peccatum sum.* I am comforted
only by the thought that it is when our misery is extreme
that the Divine mercy shines forth more resplendently.
God will not deny Himself one of the greatest of His
glories, which consists in raising up children to Abraham
from the very stones. Let us unite together earnestly in
prayer—in prayer continuously ; let us detach ourselves
more and more from all earthly things ; and let us at
length live in the way we shall wish, at the moment of
death, that we had lived.

Oh ! what happiness ! To live on earth as if we were in
Heaven, and could say—our conversation is in Heaven.
· What contentment ! To be able to hope that Christ liveth
in us. ' I live ; but now not I, Christ liveth in me.'

This is the one grand object of my desires and the most soul-absorbing of my aspirations. But what afflicts me is to think of the distance I still am therefrom! How I resist and oppose the Divine Grace!

I embrace you in the Lord. Writing thus hastily I scarcely form intelligible letters. Adieu. Love me in our Lord, in Whom I also love you.

MILAN : *February* 4, 1827.[1]

Rosmini's constant endeavour was to live on earth as if he were in Heaven—as if he were always in the visible presence of God. He often declared to his intimate friends that ' if he could have followed his own wish, and if duty to his neighbour had not forbidden it, his whole life would have been spent in meditation and prayer.'[2] But, as we have had occasion to see more than once, he continued to make ' duty to his neighbour,' whatever form it took, a continued act of prayer. Not only his works of charity, in every shape, but his recreations and his ordinary acts of social intercourse, as well as all his studies and all his writings, were of God, for God, in God. Fond as he was of *philosophy*, and highly as he valued *reason*, he looked upon both as certain to be dangerous traitors, if Prayer and Piety did not shield him from their treachery. His private and public life thus put into practice a lesson that can be well described somewhat in the phraseology of a distinguished British scholar :[3]   Philosophy may be

---

[1] *Epistolario*, Letter lix.

[2] Don Francesco Barone, *Orazione nei solenni Funerali dell' Abate Rosmini*, Torino, 1855.

[3] Sir Wm. Drummond, Preface to *Academical Questions* (speaking of Prejudice and Reason).

trusted to guard the outworks for a short space of time, when Prayer and Piety perchance slumber in the citadel, but should Prayer and Piety fall into a lethargy, Philosophy will quickly erect a standard of its own. Prayer can dispense with Philosophy, but Philosophy cannot dispense with Prayer. Each can support the other, and if they act in concord they are invincible. 'He who will not reason is a bigot ; he who will not pray is a fool, while he who dares not is a slave.' It is thus he felt ; and it is thus that the Truth held him from bondage—held him in 'the freedom wherewith Christ has made us free ;' it is thus that he lived on earth as if he were in Heaven, and could say 'our conversation is in Heaven.'

CHAPTER XXII.

ROSMINI CONTINUES THE WARFARE AGAINST THE FOES OF REVELATION.

(A.D. 1827.)

He refuses to be a Jesuit, but urges others to join that Order—Beauty of the Religious State—What he says of the 'livery of St. Ignatius' —How delicately he avoids influencing anyone to join the Order he is himself founding—What he thinks of surrendering one's own judgment to that of Superiors—Two possible exceptions to the rule —What he deems the surest means of bringing hearts into close union with God—The Science of the Saints applicable to all states of life, but not alike safely or easily practised in all—Religious Life the port of refuge from worldly storms—Necessity of mastering human affections to reach this port—Himself as an example of triumph in this—Shows his sister that true union of hearts cannot be, except in God—Explains the principle of obedience as laid down in the Jesuit Rule—Agrees with St. Thomas as to the mode of choosing a Religious Order—Commends a compendium of medi- tation by a Jesuit—Sorrow for the death of Carlo Rosmini, the historian—Patience in affliction—The war against the propagators of anti-Christian philosophy—Teaches the leaders of irreligion how to conduct controversies—The world, as it is, must needs have evils —Opposes godless education and foreshows its dangers—Men led by sensist philosophy are most intolerant— Virtue and truth, being a check to human passions, are detested by the champions of irre- ligion—He is evidently 'called' to resist the inroads of sensistic error—All philosophy mere vanity without religion—The Gospel shines above all human systems—Revelation and true philosophy perfectly harmonious—A great and pious historian's prayer to God answered in the person of Rosmini.

ALL Rosmini's friends knew of his tenacious affec- tion for the Religious State ; but few of them knew anything of the special call that kept him back from joining any existing Religious Order. There was, therefore, nothing unseemly in those who were thus ignorant of the true condition of affairs freely employing all their influence to support the invitations which some Jesuit Fathers were pressing upon him to enter the great Society.[1] But, though he would not become a Jesuit himself, he embraced every opportunity of leading others to choose that Order, when he found them inclined to the Religious State, or hesitating as to a choice in it. Amongst those whom his counsel thus 'directed to the rule of Ignatius' was the estimable Don Brunati of Brescia, who, on having resolved to quit Secular Life, communicated his decision to Rosmini, as to the prompter of his course. Don Antonio replied :—

Your letter brought me news that was not indeed surprising, but very agreeable. What surprise could your resolution give me, since I was already aware that your heart was burning with the love of God,—was, in fact, all His ? For me, it is not more marvellous to see a man who is imbued with such sentiments, drawn to the Religious Life, than to see fish attracted by the bait or a bird by its food.

Be comforted, then,—' Be strong and of good courage' (Deut. xxxi. 7), because our Lord so loves you as to create in your heart such holy desires. Yes, yes, nothing is more beautiful, nothing more advisable than to fly from this world and take refuge in the safe port of Religion where one is sheltered from the stormy waves that submerge all else.

---

[1] Tommaseo (*Rivista Cont.*) says that this influence came mainly from some of his personal friends in the Society at Innsbruck ; but the Fathers who happened to be staying at Brescia and Verona were its immediate means.

Nothing is more desirable than to make a solemn consecration of ourselves to our Lord in this secure harbour. Then we enter as it were our nuptial couch. Oh how fragrant are the pure roses wherewith all there is strewn! How magnificent is this nuptial couch in the eyes of the faithful!—aye, even the magnificence of Solomon's couch loses in comparison! I believe you to be blest, then, in these espousals, to which our Lord has been pleased to elevate you.

But, my dear friend, can I any longer conceal from you what I have for a long while jealously kept as a secret in my heart? No; not after the confidence you have reposed in me. Well, then, know that I also have come to a similar determination ; that is to say, I have resolved to quit the world and to enter the Religious State.

But, you will eagerly ask whether I think of wearing the livery of Ignatius? I so greatly love his livery that I could cover it with kisses : it is the livery which (if I may licitly say so) belongs to Christ's Pretorian guards. However, God calls me to something else ; and you know how attentively His voice should be listened to and how faithfully followed. I am, as I have said, called to something else ; but still to the Religious State. In being of Ignatius you do not cease to be of Jesus, to whom I shall belong, also, I hope ; and, therefore, we shall be in the service of the same Captain, and, in Him, we shall love one another as fellow-soldiers under the same banner.

Perchance you would like to know more. I may tell you all when next I see you ; for the present let the intimation I have given you suffice. Not, however, that I know the time set by our Lord, for the accomplishment of this project, any more than you know it. Therefore, let us together pray, and pray unceasingly ; for, from Him alone all must come. Embracing you I tell you, once again, to pray.

See with how much delicacy he refrained from

saying anything about the Order he was himself on
the eve of founding, lest personal affection should
turn Don Brunati's thoughts from the Society he had
already recommended, to that for which he might,
without impropriety, have induced him to wait. He
excelled in the power of thus blending considerate-
ness and self-denial, because he excelled in true disinterestedness. No less skilful was he in the art
of removing difficulties such as Don Brunati raised
with regard to ' the obedience which demanded
the surrender of one's own judgment to that of
Superiors.'

You wish to know my opinion upon the duty of sub-
jecting one's own judgment entirely to the authority of
another, as is the practice in the Society of Jesus. St.
Ignatius was well aware of the strength which his Society
would acquire, if he established in it the greatest uniformity
possible in all things, and thence also the greatest agreement in doctrines. I do not deny that there may be some
cases difficult to overcome. Yet, generally speaking, the
submission of the understanding is the first requisite of a
good Religious. All other virtues, even though heroic, can
be of no advantage to him, unless he knows how to obtain
the mastery over himself, in this particular, so as to sacrifice his own views to the authority of his Superiors. This
it is which, in a body composed of many members, pre-
serves unity and the blessings of harmony.

Now, this is not impossible in ordinary cases ; commonly
speaking the things on which our minds are prone to differ
from others are not self-evident. Therefore, not having
evidence on our side, it becomes simply an effort of self-love
to affirm one's own opinion as certain, instead of leaving it
open to doubt. But from the moment that one doubts
one's own opinion, it is no longer difficult to embrace that

LIFE OF ANTONIO ROSMINI.

not he who had a really humble opinion of himself naturally act thus ?

I confess, notwithstanding, that in this matter I should
have a great difficulty in two cases (which, however, seem
to me very rare) and these are :— 1. If in some opinion
which I have adopted, I find, after having divested myself
of all self-love, such evidence as there is, for instance, in a
mathematical demonstration.   2, If I find that the opinion
which I am desired to embrace is evidently *false*.

In these two cases, it is impossible for one, nay one ought
not, to give an internal assent, but to retain one's own
opinion—without, however, causing disturbance in the Com
munity, if one should not succeed in convincing Superiors
of its truth.   These cases, however, are, as I have said,
extremely rare.   It is almost always our self-love which
gives to our opinions a greater degree of certainty than
really belongs to them.   A man who has become truly
humble and foolish, for Jesus Christ, seldom finds a case
like this ; but, it is not altogether impossible, and I admit
that it would be somewhat embarrassing.   The Religious, in
short, should be thoroughly predisposed to lay aside his
own opinion, and to embrace that of others ; but, he ought
to add to profound humility, and to the inward contempt
of self, a tender and unswerving love of truth, in obedience
and in charity.

MILAN : *April* 9, 1827.[1]

From his earliest years, it gave him intense
pleasure to try and bring hearts into close union
with God ; and from his earliest years he felt that
profound humility, passive obedience, active charity,
constant prayer, and complete self-denial were the
surest means for this.   Hence, whenever he found
pious men, like Don Brunati, eagerly in quest of close

[1] *Epistolario*, Letter lx.

union with God, he pointed out the gate to the cloister and exhorted them to enter, that they might take the safest path to what they sought.

Frequently, however, he was appealed to by those who craved this union, without being in a position to adopt the Religious State. For them, too, he pre-scribed 'the science of the Saints,' with instructions as to how each one could shape his course by it, no matter what his state in life may be. But he knew full well that as surely as the man who chooses to walk through fields infested by venomous reptiles has far less chance of escaping danger than the man who prefers to take a well-protected path, so they who endeavour to attain union with God, while surrounded by the many allurements of the world, have far less chance of reaching it than they who seek it through the shelter of the cloister.

Therefore, although he could not hold out the same assurances of security to those who strive to draw very near to God through the embarrassments and excitements of the world, he none the less encouraged all to persevere in the struggle to per-fection, even amidst the worst distractions of social life ; for he knew that many Saints had practised the most heroic virtues, even when brought daily in contact with the most hideous vices, and he knew that the noblest self-sacrifice was sometimes found where self-interests most abounded.

He did not shut his eyes to the fact that even those who had passed into 'the port of refuge,' as he loved to call the Religious State, were not free from some of the most dangerous worldly influences, so long as they had not the completest detachment from all human affections. But study and experience had long since convinced him that, while complete detachment from human affections was essential to thorough union with God, this detachment was infinitely less attainable in Secular than in Religious Life. He could speak with all the more authority on this subject since he had, himself, mastered human attachments as effectively as if he had been all his life a cloistered monk. Now, it had cost him much to tone these attachments down, for his nature was of the most affectionate kind. No son, no brother, no man had deeper love of kindred and country and home and friends than he ; but he earned the Grace which made this natural love absolutely subordinate to the love of God. So much had he subdued even its most legitimate manifestations, that his sister, of whom he had ever been very fond, and whose heart Grace had also long since detached from mere human affections, could not help, in a moment of womanly softness, reminding him that she was entitled to a sister's love, as if he had for a moment forgotten it. In reassuring her he took care to let her understand that it was only in God true 'union of hearts' could be preserved :

For your last letter I thank you all the more, as it was a blooming one, like the season in which we are ; like that, too, it invites us to raise our thoughts towards the ineffable goodness of the Creator, who continually loads us with

benefits. Yes, let us be grateful to Him ; let us think continually of Him ; in short, belong to Him entirely. Is not
this the only happiness of our hearts ? I know it is thus
your heart speaks. It is thus I feel that mine speaks, by
the Grace of our Lord, to which I respond imperfectly.

There can be nothing more delicious than this union of
wills and affections which I trust exists between us. I
infer from a certain passage in your letter, that you suspect
that my affection for you has decreased. Even if I desired
it, I could not but love you ; and I love you with more
than a brother's affection. The infrequency of my letters
should not make you doubt : attribute this to my affairs,
and to the defect of negligence which I have in many
things of secondary importance. As regards my soul,
believe it to be full of affection for you. I often remember
you before our Lord, and it gives me great pleasure to
speak of you, or to hear tidings of you, especially when they
come direct from yourself. This is natural in me ; but, I
hope it is also rooted in our Lord, as I wish all my affections to be. I hope likewise that it will make it all the more
dear to you, to find that we meet together in our Lord in
perfect unity of heart. He is the true centre of the greatest
love, of the greatest alliance of hearts: nay, He is the only
centre, the ocean of love. . . .

MILAN : *April* 14, 1827.[1]

Rosmini's remarks on the submission of one's
own judgment to that of Superiors did not quite
satisfy his Brescian correspondent, in so far as the
principle of obedience seemed to be applied amongst
the Jesuits. Don Brunati, therefore, wrote to him
again, intimating a wish to choose another Order, and
asking his opinion of the Benedictines, with special
reference to the one difficulty which continued to

[1] *Epistolario*, Letter lxi.

be an obstruction. Still desirous of holding him to
the original choice, Rosmini met the whole case in
this manner :—

Confidence in God is what alone can assure us as to many
things in which, without it, we should be ever wavering and
in suspense. This need of intrusting all to God has been
vividly brought home to us by Jesus Christ, on more than
one occasion, as when He taught us to pray with the petition
'And lead us not into temptation.' Only God can preserve
us from occasions such as those in which the strongest
virtue may be exposed to danger,—occasions which are
to be found even in Religion but much more in the World.
It is for this that it has been said of Jesus Christ Himself—
'He hath given His angels charge over Thee, to keep Thee
in all Thy ways.' The same may be said of all those who
are one with Christ, or who fully trust in Him. We are
travellers on this earth and we know not whither we are
going—whether into places full of dangers and difficulties
or into those that are easy and safe. Confidence in God is
the only thing that can fully reassure us, in the midst of
all uncertainties ; and this must, in my opinion, remove
from the soul all anxiety about the point in question.

Moreover, the precept of St. Ignatius is not so absolute
as some might suppose ; for, when enunciating it, he adds
'as far as is possible' (*quoad id fieri poterit*). Thus, in the
1st Chapter of the Third Part, speaking of the preservation
of the novices in the things useful for their souls, and for
their advancement in virtue, he says this :—' Let all the
brethren, *as far as possible*, hold the same sentiments and
language, as the Apostle teaches.' So, also, in the last
chapter of the Constitutions, where he teaches the way in
which the whole body of the Society ought to be maintained
in vigour, and increased, he touches on agreement in
doctrines, but ever with the same clause—' as far as this is
possible.' It is, of course, true that all this moderation
would be of no avail under Superiors who were over-

exacting ; but this, let me repeat, is not to be feared from
God's mercy. Even if He allowed the danger, it is certain
that He would give to the Religious who hoped in Him the
means of deliverance from all embarrassment. In fine, I
believe that there is no reason why we should have any
hesitation in giving ourselves to Religion,—that being an
act most agreeable to God, who never allows Himself to be
outdone in generosity.

As for what you say touching the Benedictines, I can
give you no other advice than that you should mature the
affair by long and frequent prayer. I have always derived
much pleasure and consolation from the last article of the
Second Part of St. Thomas's *Summa*, wherein he proves
that, *as regards entering into Religion or not, one should
never take counsel, not even with one's friends; because, to
enter Religion is a thing so evidently good, in itself, that it
requires no counsel ; but counsel is necessary, in order to
choose which among the various Religious Institutes is the
one most suited to us.*

Read this article, for it appears to me to be full of the
Spirit of God. It will give you the same consolation that
it has given to me. For the rest, do not allow yourself to
be influenced by inclination towards, or aversion from, any
particular thing or any particular office. Do you think
yourself qualified for preaching, or for the confessional ?
Leave that for your Superior to decide, and put yourself in
a state of perfect indifference to all, so as to be ready even
to preach, to hear confessions, or to do anything else for
which you are less inclined by nature, or fitted by habit.
It appears to me that the first and principal requisite, in
order to know the Will of God, and to make a good choice,
is to establish one's self in a state of full and perfect indifference to all things.

O most beautiful indifference ! so much recommended
by the Saints ! This is that virtue which removes all the
obstacles to the Divine illuminations. It is only with this
that we can hear, in our hearts, even the softest whisper-

ings of our Lord ; in Whom continue to love me, and to Whom commend me in your prayers.

MILAN : *May 4, 1827.*[1]

This letter had the desired effect; for Don Brunati soon consoled his director with the assur‑ ance that the indifference he recommended 'had reconciled him to the resolution of trying to practise holy obedience in the Society of Jesus.' In order to carry out this determination he was about to leave at once for Rome, in the company of Mons. Ostini then Internuncio at Vienna. Rosmini, well pleased with the result, made the expression of his congratulations the medium of commending 'an epitome of Christian meditation' which ought to be specially acceptable to one who was about to take a long journey for the purpose of joining the Order whence this little lesson emanated :

What an excellent opportunity you have of making the journey to Rome with the excellent Ostini! I should envy you, if it were my time to go. Happy you, if, at the end of your journey, you hope to find, not only *the Gesù*, but *Jesus* ! Oh! if this were our whole desire ! At least it should be so, that we may all be absorbed in unity.

I was reading. a few days ago, a beautiful and instruc‑ tive lesson, in the life of that admirable man Father Caraffa, who was the seventh General of the Society of Jesus. He there says that he used to meditate on three letters—one *black*, another *red*, and a third *white*. These meant :—his own sins, the sufferings of his Saviour, and the glory of the Blessed. In these three points I really seemed to see a compendium of all Christian meditation. By the black letter, we may learn to know ourselves, and

[1] *Epistolario*, Letter lxii.

direct our endeavours to the purification of our souls ; by
the red one, we can excite ourselves to imitate Jesus in the
mortifying of all our human nature, without excepting any
portion of it ; while by the last, or white letter, we are
admonished to resist the discouragement and anguish of
soul which the sorrow for our sins and the greatness of our
sufferings might otherwise bring upon us ; imitating, also,
in this, Christ who, when joy was set before Him, endured
the Cross (Heb. xii. 2).   One may say that such is, likewise,
the substance of that admirable book *The Exercises* of St.
Ignatius, which I always keep close by me. . . .

MILAN : *June* 3, 1827.[1]

Shortly after the date of this letter, Milanese
literary circles—indeed all circles of society in the
city of St. Ambrose—had cause for mourning.
The popular historian, Carlo Rosmini had just died
rather suddenly.   Although he had lived 'like a
recluse moving amongst men,' the news of his death
cast a gloom on the whole city.   He had never
married, and the onlypassion to which he was said to
have ever yielded was that for literature ; but for all
that he freely allowed himself to be captivated by this,
never, in the course of his long life of 70 years, did
the charms of literature blind him to the beauties
and the obligations of religion.   On the contrary,
he made the beauties of literature so dependent on
the intrinsic charms of religion that without them he
would have found little attraction in literature.   No
home in Milan was without some expression of
regret that the venerated Chevalier had been taken
away ; but none missed him so much as his cousin

[1] *Epistolario*, Letter lxiii.

Don Antonio, and their intimate friends Count
Mellerio and Alessandro Manzoni. In a letter to
Luigi Sonn of Rovereto, Rosmini thus feelingly
mentioned the loss they had been called on
to bear, and made it the occasion of counselling
patience in affliction to his correspondent, who was,
at the time, troubled with trials of his own :—

I have received the two letters which you sent me.
The answer that I make to you is brief, as befits a man
whose mind is depressed and embittered by sorrow. The
reason you have already heard. Last Saturday a terrible
stroke deprived my cousin and friend Carlo of life—at the
very hour in which the family vainly expected him home to
dinner. His loss, which is deplored by all his friends
(whose great grief attests how much he was loved), has also
most acutely pierced my heart. The wound is only soothed
by reflecting on the Divine Mercy, and on the goodness of
that soul which has departed, and which was wont to live
in the body as if any hour were to be his last.

Such was his purpose, as I have heard him many times
repeat. I have written on this subject to my brother and
mother.

Keep yourself, I pray you, comforted and cheerful.
This I hold to be the best counsel and the best medicine
that can be given. You very properly call the malady
which afflicts your throat—sad. I feel all the force of that
word, because a like malady troubled me last year, and in
such a manner that every day blood came from my throat ;
and I am not yet quite free from the inconvenience.
Cheerfulness of mind and a thorough submission to the
Divine Will (which is ever full of a love and a pity beyond
our comprehension) is a marvellous moral antidote, that
has its influence also on the body. Cheerfulness imparts
to our body a movement and vitality that is indescribable,
and this helps the circulation of the blood, loosening it, so

to say, from that stagnancy from which this kind of ailment seems to proceed.

MILAN : *June* 5, 1827.[1]

All this time the intellectual contest between Rosmini and the propagators of dechristianising philosophy went on, without allowing him many long intervals of rest. On all sides, and in every form, the Italian champions of sensualism and infidelity attacked him in and through his works. Foremost in every assault were Gioia and Romagnosi. The latter assailed him with special virulence, for having attempted to disturb the sensistic notions then floating about as to Divine Providence in relation to the distribution of good and evil. The treatise in which Rosmini successfully vindicated the Catholic view of this most important question was intended to destroy, at the very root, all the objections advanced on behalf of irreligion. There could be no better proof of the importance of his Essay, or of the good that it had done and was certain to do, than the violent abuse it thus forced from the enemies of religion.

It was in reproducing this, with the other two essays which form *The Theodicy*, that Rosmini arranged in the preface all the objections made by Romagnosi, face to face with the answers which the true Christian had to offer. He clearly showed how all the objections sprang from ignorance of physical cognitions ; he entered fully into the grand problem of the nature and origin of evil, and demonstrated that the possibility of evil is inherent in the nature of limited

---

[1] *Epistolario,* Letter lxiv.

beings, and that to expect a world without evils of
any sort, is to expect from God contradictions and
impossibilities ; he proved that when evil and good
come, finally, to be weighed one against the other,
the good will outweigh the evil to an extent that
could have been possible in no other way than that
which the Sovereign Goodness and Wisdom of the
Creator had ordained. The treatise is, therefore,
highly metaphysical ; however, like the rest of that
great work, the conceptions are so sublime and
original, and the style is so vigorous, that the reader
is not fatigued by the aridity usually found in
abstractions, but finds his soul raised above the
world and thrilled with the loftiest and most refreshing sentiments of truth, of wisdom, of religion.

Hoping to induce his adversaries to see the
necessity of moderating the rancorous spirit which
seemed to animate them, he published the famous
Essay on the Etiquette of Literary Men. This had,
at once, a salutary effect on the popular mind ; but,
for that very reason, it exasperated his opponents.
The quiet but telling censures which it dealt out
to literary offenders so well fitted those who led the
cohorts of irreligion that they were furious—Gioia
especially so.

Now, Gioia had more than once fiercely resented Rosmini's criticisms on sensistic philosophy.
He even went so far as to abuse personally the
editors of the Modenese periodical in which his own
opinions were first calmly examined and charitably
exposed by ' the Roveretan philosopher.' Nay, he

stepped out of his way to revile all those, especially ecclesiastics, who stood out for 'Faith in Truth and in God,' stigmatising them as 'Ostrogoths' and 'obscurantists.' A long appendix to his *Galateo* was made the means of reiterating all his errors and his invectives against the severe morality of Christianity. Rosmini felt obliged to reply once more to the sophisms and aberrations of this antagonist, and he did so in a way that set before literary men the genuine mode of conducting controversies.

Not only in Milan but also in Modena and Florence, the press was kept busy at the essays which the defender of Christian truth poured forth against the teachers of error. As Florence was then the head-quarters of the pamphleteers who were stoutly advocating the establishment of *Godless Schools*, it was there that he published his admirable essay on *The Unity of Education.* The forcible reasoning of this treatise told well against the irreligious tendencies of those days, and was the first strong barrier erected against the policy which has since taken a fatal hold of our own country. He explained clearly the first principles on which the whole theory of education depended, and demonstrated, in a way that was both new and irrefragable, that religion is and must be the beginning and the end of all education. He then applied himself to solve the problem of so harmoniously combining individual, domestic, national, and cosmopolitan education that the egotism neither of the family nor

of the individual should prove an obstacle to the
development of the national spirit ; he showed that
the spirit of nationality, on the one hand, should set
no wall of separation between those beings who,
having been bought by the Blood of Christ, know
no longer any distinction of Jew or Greek, but form
one single brotherhood ; and that the vastness of
the cosmopolitan and national circle, on the other
hand, should not impair the sentiments of citizenship,
or of the family or of the individual.   In short, he
laid down the principles by which to answer all the
gravest questions on education — questions which the
profoundest thinkers of our days are still agitating
without coming near any satisfactory solution.

   Although this warfare for the best interests of
religion pressed heavily on his time, he found it
covenient to continue the *Nuovo Saggio on the Origin
of Ideas*, as well as two other important works—the
Philosophy of Politics and the *Philosophy of Right.*
Day by day, he felt more and more deeply that God
called him to lift philosophy from its ruins and make
it subserve all the purposes of Revealed Religion.
It was the solemn consciousness of a vocation which
every incident in his life, and the counsel of his holiest
and sagest friends confirmed.   ' I feel within me a
voice *commanding*, a force impelling me to this
duty,' he wrote to Tommaseo.   ' In the first of my
Philosophical Essays I have traced some outlines of
that science which is always before my mind, like an
ever-present picture the sight of which greatly cheers
me.   I pray you, nay I conjure you, to assist me in

what I am thus endeavouring to do. Spread abroad the good principles, and help to recall men from the intellectual lethargy into which they have fallen ; raise them up from matter to spirit. I know well what fortitude is required in order to withstand the total mental prostration that is produced by the crushing weight of our mortal body. But all Philosophy is mere vanity if it be not subservient to Religion—if it only inflate us instead of edifying and humbling us. This danger of pride, which is so apt to mix itself up with the natural speculation of the understanding, is the only thing that sometimes alarms me ; but I get rid of this false fear by placing an unbounded confidence in the Grace of God.'[1]

In the preface to his works, he tells us that he saw the Gospel shining above all systems, 'like the sun untouched by the clouds of the atmosphere of earth,' and he felt certain that though heaven and earth should pass away the word of God should not pass away. He knew, indeed, that 'divine Wisdom has no need of any philosophical system for the salvation of men, and that it is in all respects perfect in itself. But he knew also that 'no dissension can arise between Revelation and a true philosophy, for truth can never be contrary to truth,' since it is most simple in its origin and never inconsistent with itself. He considered that 'the errors, the prejudices, and the doubts which arise from the imperfection of reason, and which interpose so many

[1] Unpublished Letter, dated Milan, November 8, 1827.

obstacles to the full assent that is due to revealed truth, may and ought to be solved and dispersed by reason itself. He remembered that the Catholic Church, 'especially in the last Council of Lateran, invited and excited philosophers' to apply their studies to this duty. But the duty had been long neglected, and, as a consequence, false philosophy 'invaded every human institution, art, and science,' producing a hideous perversion 'in the mental and moral life of individuals, families, and nations.' Influenced by this false philosophy, 'the passion and the base calculation of material interests, gradually became the only counsellors, the only masters of men's minds, 'which were left open to every prejudice and ready to give their immediate assent to the most extravagant propositions, or to withhold it from the most plainly demonstrated truth,' on any trivial pretence.

Men thus misled even plumed themselves on being enslaved to the most preposterous opinions, and therefore disdained a nobler subjection. They became 'credulous even to absurdity but incredulous even to evidence.' While they claimed the right to legislate for all the world they began to be, themselves, intolerant of any law. They trampled on their duties while 'intoxicated with their own judgment.' Their deeds showed treachery and selfishness, while their words seemed to glow with philanthropy. Embracing irreligion, they willingly lost themselves in shameless licentiousness. 'Finding virtue and truth a check to all this, they cast them aside as inventions of superstition' or at least as things which had no proven existence.

Human society, thrown on the current of false philosophy, had been thus drifting rapidly towards the fatal reefs of irreligion, when Rosmini arose,—evidently called forth by Heaven,—not merely to warn men of the dreadful dangers ahead, but to guide them back to the safe channel of truth—nay, to the source of all truth, God Himself. The duty was one which none but the most gifted could undertake. It required an intellect of surpassing power, as well as learning of the most extensive and the profoundest kind, and a moral character as perfect as man can have. Above all these it needed 'a call from on High.' It is hardly possible to follow the career of Rosmini, examining it by the light of his words and deeds, without feeling that he possessed all the essential qualifications in a remarkable degree.

Yet he greatly distrusted himself. Like St. Thomas of Aquin, St. Dominic and St. Ignatius, in their time and place, he shrank from his 'special call;' held back by humility, though impelled to the work not only by mysterious interior monitions, but by the firm conviction that, in order to resist the ruinous inroads of error, it was urgently necessary to bring reason into the closest possible union with Faith, and Philosophy into the most perfect harmony with Theology.

In fact, he was forced by Providence into the struggle for Truth and for the Church of Truth, as if to represent the Almighty's answer to this prayer of the illustrious Abbé Rohrbacher : ' May God raise up a man to finish the work which He inspired Boetius to begin, a man like him in genius and in virtue, who shall luminously arrange all human sciences and show their accordance with that which is Divine, and shall appear to the Church the perfect model of a true Catholic and a true philosopher.' [1]

[1] Rohrbacher's ' Universal History of the Catholic Church,' Book xiv.

CHAPTER XXIII.

ROSMINI RECEIVES THE EXPECTED MANIFESTATION
OF PROVIDENCE.

(A.D. 1827.)

His health at this time—How he came to know the Abbé Löwenbrück—Attractive qualities of the Abbé—Contrast between him
and Rosmini—Gospel prudence and human enthusiasm—Hopes
and aims—Löwenbrück's first lesson in religious Passivity—He is
given 'the models of all charity'—The indications of Providence
at length plainly visible—How Monte Calvario, Domodossola, was
found to be chosen by our Lord for the new Society—Löwenbrück
is sent to Domodossola—His report satisfies all—Why the plan of
the new Institute was not shown to the Abbé until he was at
Calvario—Rosmini foresees what awaits him as Founder and
Philosopher—Löwenbrück's objections to the plan fully answered—
Testing the spirit of the Abbé—Rosmini seeks to have no associates
but those manifestly sent by Providence—Löwenbrück's restless
spirit checked by Rosmini's wonderful calmness.

WHILE obeying the call to do battle for intellectual
charity Rosmini did not neglect the call to serve the
interests of spiritual and corporal charity. With
prayerful patience he waited for the special indications of Providence which Madame Canossa led
him to expect at Milan. The month of May 1827
had just passed, and his earnest supplications 'for the
intercession of the Mother of Divine Grace were
accumulated in Our Lady's presence.' June came,

and with it the first rays of ' the promised manifestation.'

Humanly speaking, he was in no condition to give them a fitting reception, because the bright month found him suffering from the first serious symptoms of a physical malady that afterwards afforded him frequent opportunities of practising exemplary Christian fortitude.[1] But, spiritually speaking, he was in the best possible state for recognising and following the monitions of Providence, in whatever form they presented themselves. The form in which they actually did present themselves was, as we shall see, by no means dazzling, or even such as ordinary men would take to be very notable. On the contrary, it came in such an apparently tame and commonplace manner, that most men would pass it by as indicating nothing.

We already know that during Rosmini's stay at Milan, the Count Mellerio was his most constant visitor. On the 7th of June, this nobleman called, as usual, to see his friend, whom he entertained with an account of a certain Abbé Löwenbrück, whose outspoken zeal for religion had made his residence in France no longer acceptable to many in that

---

[1] Up to the twenty-fifth year of his age, Rosmini had enjoyed such perfect health that, in after years, he often referred to it as supplying a means of estimating the delight of living in the state of original innocence ' before Adam bequeathed the curse of the fall to the human race.' He inherited from the Rosmini-Serbatis what Don Paoli calls ' ancestral inflammation of the liver.' This family malady did not show itself in him until 1822, when the symptoms were very slight. In 1826 it declared itself more decidedly, and in 1827 took an acute form which never afterwards left him wholly free from its tormenting presence.

country or agreeable to himself. The French
Minister at Turin furnished him with letters of introduction to some of the noblest personages in Milan,
Count Mellerio being one of those thus favoured.
The Abbé belonged to Metz in Lorraine ; but he
had come to Italy directly from Rouen, where his
unsparing denunciations of certain vices that were
not only locally but nationally popular, earned for
him an enmity which endangered his personal safety,
and forced him into temporary exile. Rosmini was
much interested in Count Mellerio's description of
the persecuted Priest's sufferings, zeal, and intense
desire to be associated with those who should systematically devote themselves to the winning of souls
to God.

Not the least of the qualities which commended
the pious stranger to Don Antonio's heart was this
eagerness to organise, or aid in organising, an institute for resisting the forces of modern impiety.
Judging that the best way to begin was with a congregation of missionaries 'for the improvement of
the clergy,' he had planned an Order of that kind.
Mellerio, well knowing that such a disposition would
attract to each other his old and new friends, proposed that they should dine with him together, as
soon as Rosmini's health permitted. Although still
unwell, Don Antonio would not allow his health to
be an obstacle in the way of an immediate meeting.
Accordingly, he arranged to spend the following
evening (June 8) at Mellerio's house. There he
met the Abbé Löwenbrück, whose exuberant

358 LIFE OF ANTONIO ROSMINI.

eloquence was all directed to topics that never failed
to fascinate Rosmini. Before they were long
together, the Roveretan Philosopher and the French
Missionary learned to esteem each other more even
than their host had hoped.

Although no two men seemed to be less alike,
there were so many links of sympathy between them,
so many turns of thought common to both, and,
above all, they had such a sameness of purpose, that
the dissimilarity of their natural character formed
no barrier to a warm friendship. Both were equally
zealous for God and the Church ; but Löwenbrück's
zeal was somewhat oppressively evident, and little
under control. He was all aglow with energy, an
energy that had in it much that might pass for 'extravagance of spirit.' Feverishly restless, full of
stir and bustle in everything, he was eager to rush
forth and conquer the world to God, without pausing
to ask if anything more was necessary than an enthusiastic will, a perpetual activity of tongue, and an
unwearied roaming through the highways and by-
ways of the world, pressing all to 'the feast of the
Lord.' He would preach to men in and out of
season, and whether they could understand him or
not, as he relied quite as much on the effect of enthusiasm as on the force of reason.

Rosmini's zeal, on the contrary, was subdued,
partly by its own intensity and partly by a long
course of discipline which enabled him to divest it,
at will, of whatever had the appearance of disorder
or singularity. He was invariably calm and self-

collected. Although never wanting in true energy, and often moved by strong impulses, he was never carried away by excitement, never fidgetty, never worried. Therefore he had none of the vagaries, none of the checks to perseverance, which spoiled and sometimes neutralised the zeal of the other. No less eager than Löwenbrück to win all men to God, he measured the means at every point, and fully realised the magnitude of the task and the insignificance of the agents. Hence, though he was always vigilantly looking for the occasions of doing good to others, and always sedulously working for the salvation of himself and his neighbour, he never took a step forward without first coolly convincing himself that God's Will directed him, and God's Grace guided him to the object. Unlike Löwenbrück, he trusted not at all to the aid of mere enthusiasm, but, in everything, to the co-operation of reason.

Now, this marked diversity in character, instead of serving to keep them asunder helped to draw them together; for the one saw in the other qualities which he seemed himself to need, and, since both alike strove for the glory of God and the good of men, there was fair promise of such a beneficial exchange of gifts as might impart strength and harmony to their united action. At all events, it is certain that Rosmini hoped much from the evidences of mental and physical activity, as well as piety, which he discovered in Löwenbrück.

Count Mellerio contrived to leave them interchanging their views without fear of interruption,

and before they separated for the night he could perceive that they had come to an understanding which
promised well. Next day, they met again to compare notes and discuss several points of difference as
to the best means of accomplishing the purpose which
they both had in view. As the Abbé's bubbling
enthusiasm had simmered down to an edifying moderation, after a night's reflection, Rosmini reasonably
concluded that its extravagances were within easy
reach of control.

It is, indeed, true, that the fervent Lorrainese
was still far more eager to bring all the world, forthwith, into the path of truth and virtue than to bring
himself, first of all, within any set rules for his own
sanctification. But when Rosmini insisted on this
indispensable preliminary, Löwenbrück's overflowing
zeal subsided quite enough for him to see that he
must begin with his own soul, before he could be in
a true position to labour effectively for the souls of
others. His recognition of this fact, though tardily
given, led Rosmini to hope that, in a little while, he
would prove to be as docile as he was already
energetic.

Within the first three days of their acquaintance
they had prayed together at every shrine in Milan,
and visited the Carthusian monastery of Pavia, discussing, the while, every form of institute or congregation for religious purposes which presented itself
to the fertile mind of the Frenchman, who was still
eager to establish a society of missionary preachers.
He drew highly-coloured pictures of the means and

results ; but the other could not discover much that was practical in the means, or better than visionary in the results.

Rosmini did not, at once, communicate the details of his own well-devised project, further than showing how certain features of his companion's pro-posals were embraced in it, and how some others were inconsistent with the set purpose of self-sancti-fication as the first requisite, or with the principle of dependence on Providence, both of which formed its cardinal points. Löwenbrück soon saw that, com-pared with Rosmini's fixed and luminous policy, all his own plans were dim and driftless ; he soon came to admit that mere human expedients (however good), when they sprang from mere human impulse (however ardent and pure), were not sufficient for the grand purpose on which his soul was bent. Recog-nising this, and knowing how vacillating all his own emotions were, he decided on surrendering his zeal to the guidance of a master mind, that put no confidence in mere human impulse. Therefore he resolved to become a disciple of Rosmini, and learn from him how to apply the Science of the Saints to the organisation of a society for forming Saints and doing the work of the Saints.

The first lessons he received taught him to take the Following of Christ as his text-book, and our Lord as the model on Whose life his own life should be shaped—the pattern of perfect Charity, in all its phases. Amongst those who had success-fully taken this course, St. Thomas of Aquin was set before him as the model of intellectual charity, St. Augustin as the model of universal charity, St. Ignatius as the model of governative charity, and St. Francis of Sales as the model of charity in the details of daily life.[1] It was a new study for the restless Abbé, and so long as he applied himself to it the superabundant natural benevolence which incessantly tossed him to and fro, without allowing him to produce any good results, was kept within wholesome bounds.

Finding himself spiritual, and, to some extent, temporal director of this new friend, as well as of two or three pious Priests, who were also desirous of seeking perfection under his guidance, Rosmini felt that the time had come for giving effect to the project which had so long held a firm hold of his mind and heart. Neither St. Francis, St. Dominic, nor St. Ignatius had a more numerous or more piously importunate set of subjects to start with ; and the circumstances — whether as regards the individuals or the times— were no less pressing or encouraging in his case than in theirs. It seemed to him that the 'indication of Providence' which the saintly Canossa told him to wait for in Milan was plainly visible. He was ready to act on it ; but, as yet, Providence had not pointed out the place of commencement. Many consultations were held on the subject with his intimate friends ; but none of

---

[1] Another version of this names St. Augustin as the model of intellectual charity in all its forms, St. Francis of Sales as the model of 'interior spirit,' and St. Ignatius as the model of exterior and interior government, in all that relates to the 'body of the Institute.'

them knew of an abode, or locality even, where the
Founder and his first associates might most conveniently retire, to take further counsel with God
'in complete solitude.' There was no spot near
Milan like the mountain retreats around Rovereto;
though, even if there were, he would require some
special evidence that the place was chosen by Providence for the purpose in view.

With calm earnestness, he sought light from On
High even as to this. No anxiety was visible in
him, no restlessness, but a tranquil biding of his
time for some distinct sign of God's Will. All the
members of his little family united, twice a day, in
fervent prayer for this sign, and he obtained, through
Count Mellerio, the prayers of many devout Milanese
for the same intention.

One day, as Rosmini and his household were
thus engaged Don Luigi Polidori (intimate friend
of Count Mellerio, and brother of Cardinal Polidori)
unexpectedly entered, having come from St. Celso
expressly to make a communication which seemed
to be an answer to their supplications. When the
little devotion was ended he informed Rosmini that
while offering up the Holy Sacrifice for their object
that very morning (it was June 13, 1827[1]) his
thoughts were suddenly carried to the summit of
Monte Calvario, over Domodossola, and a something
seemed to speak in his mind saying, 'this is the
place.'

Count Mellerio joined them while they were

[1] The Feast of Rosmini's 'patron,' St. Anthony of Padua.

conversing on the subject, and as he was a native
of one of the Ossola valleys, and had a noble mansion in Domo, close to the sacred Mount, he was
more than delighted with this announcement, which
but anticipated one he was himself about to make.
He, too, had had his mind directed to Monte
Calvario, during his morning prayers for their
common intention, and he had actually come to
give Rosmini a sketch of the place. It was already
'a sacred place' which the clergy of Novara frequented for their spiritual retreats.

After they heard Mellerio's description, all
agreed that the spot was exactly such as met the
conditions they had separately thought best, not
only for the commencement but for the perpetuation
of the work contemplated by the proposed Institute.
That very evening, it was decided to send Löwenbrück to Domodossola, he being the least occupied
and the most robust. His immediate business was
to examine the condition of the house, ascertain
what steps were necessary to its possession, and
report generally on whatever might interest and
inform those for whom he acted. He went at once,
duly provided with letters from Count Mellerio to
persons having authority or influence in the locality.

The impetuous Lorrainese lost no time on the
journey or in making his investigations, for within
three days after he had left Milan his first report
was received. It was so favourable, nay so enthusiastic, as to the fitness of the place, and at the
same time so hopeful with regard to possession,

that Rosmini had no longer any doubt as to God's
Will in the matter. Then, for the first time, he
thought it prudent to place before Löwenbrück the
whole plan of the proposed Institute. The distractions of Milan were a sufficient reason for having
withheld the details of the project from such an
excitable person, while he stayed there ; but everything favoured a thorough study of the whole
design while the Abbé was on the Ossolan Calvario,
in sight of the sacred memorials of the Passion, and
amid the sobering solitude which he described so
rapturously. A draft of the plan was therefore sent
to him, and with it the following letter :—

I hasten to send you the plan of that Institute to which
God seems to call me. Read it; think over it; take
counsel about it with our Lord. What consolation it
would be for me if you, also, had a similar call. The
mercy of God would 'shorten the times.' I should never
have thought that the realisation of this calling was so
near its commencement. If you find that your spirit
accords with mine, I should take this discovery as a token
given me by God that His hour is already come. *I know
well what awaits me*—'and how am I straitened until it be
accomplished' (St. Luke xii. 50).

1 beg of you to meditate attentively on all that I have
set before you in that paper, and to probe your spirit, in
order that you may see whether it is in harmony with
mine. Let me repeat that, if I find it to be so, I am ready
to begin forthwith. As I have already told you in conversation, one obstacle in my way was the work which I am
engaged in writing, and which I believe to be in accordance
with God's Will. But, having taken further counsel with
our Lord, I find this impediment is no longer so strong as to

cause me to postpone the commencement of the enterprise explained in my letter, the moment God offers me the occasion. One should never neglect an occasion offered by God, and it will, therefore, be my duty to reconcile the prosecution of that work with the duty of organising the new society.

The principal end of the proposed congregation is, as you can see, to form the Priest on the pattern of Jesus Christ. Nothing that is found in this pattern should be excluded. It is a question of putting before one's mind the pattern of the Priesthood in the fullest and the most perfect sense, and, therefore also, the pattern of the greatest sacrifice. It is a question of being able to say, in the closest union with the great High Priest, I sanctify myself for them (St. John xvii.). What a sanctification is not this ! What vows of blood are not ours !

The place described by you for the commencement of the work appears to be admirably suited for it. It would seem as though Providence had prepared it for us. O how incomprehensible are Its judgments ! and how unsearchable Its ways ! From how far Divine Goodness takes Its measures ! combining and weaving them together, in one tissue, for the formation of that plan which has been pre-ordained 'from the foundation of the world !' My dearest Brother in Jesus Christ, I leave you in *osculo sancto*. Let Mary be our mother, that we may ask our Lord to look on the children of His handmaid. May the glory of Jesus in His Church be our good upon the earth ! So be it ! Amen for ever !

Pray for your unworthy brother.

MILAN : *June* 16, 1827.[1]

He had often said to Mellerio and Tommaseo what he here repeated to Löwenbrück—' I know what awaits me' ; and often had he assured them that his soul was distressed until the burden, the

[1] *Epistolario*, Letter lxv.

Cross, which our Lord intended for him was on his
shoulders. He seemed to foresee clearly the trials,
the disappointments, the sufferings, he should have
to endure as the Founder of an Order, and as the
champion of truth. The personal vituperation which
the propagators of irreligion poured upon him, gave
him a foretaste of what he would have to bear as
the restorer of Christian philosophy. He was, indeed, already committed to the struggle with them,
and eager to carry it on, no matter what vexations
it might cause him. But the principle guiding his
course led him to see that God's Will required him
to take up new crosses—to pass on to the foundation
of the Institute and to the acceptance of the discomforts and sorrows, which that, too, might bring
upon him. Therefore he promptly prepared to leave,
for a time, the literary and scientific labours he so
much loved, in order to assume the other labours in
which the French Abbé was desirous of aiding him,
and to which all his most trusted friends were urging
him.

In replying to Rosmini's letter, Löwenbrück
showed that he had carefully read the sketch of the
new Order, and that, in the main, the plan commended
itself to his adoption. He would have liked it better
had it provided more for ' dashing forward,' than for
proceeding staidly, or had it made ' missionary enterprise and preaching ' its leading, if not its exclusive
work. Although the Abbé was well disposed to
have charge of a parish, with the right of roaming at
will beyond the parochial bounds, he doubted the

wisdom of uniting the Pastoral Office with that of Superior in the Society. To his thinking, there were many practical difficulties in the way of making a union of these two offices workable. But for the rest, he seemed eager to be associated with the new Institute, and expressed himself in most hopeful terms as to its future.

Rosmini, without delay, wrote an elaborate answer to his objections, but before touching them assured the Abbé that his ardour in the matter was consoling. 'I take it as a new proof of our Lord's Will. As I have told you, I am quite ready. For the present, however, we are not in a position to come together; several things must take place before that, and of these the two principal are:—*First*, that we prove our spirit a little longer in God's presence by prayer, and, as to ourselves, by an epistolary correspondence, in order to ascertain whether our minds are in accord, and whether it is one and the same spirit calls us. *Next*, that we receive the blessing of the Holy Father, in order that, from the very outset, we may be incor‧porated with the Church—a thing especially requisite because of the special nature of the Institute. While waiting for all this, we should keep ourselves united in spirit, if not in body ; beseeching the Lord of mercies to unite us in body also, when and how it pleases His adorable Will.' [1]

He then replied, at considerable length and with his usual clearness, to the objections raised against the union of the Pastoral Office with that of Superior in

[1] See Appendix, Letter vi. (*Epistolario*, Letter lxvi.).

the Order, and concluded thus :—'You must bear in mind that the conjunction of the Pastoral Office with that of Superior in the Society is such a characteristic feature of the Institute I have planned, that if we were to exclude this feature it would no longer be the same Institute, but another. Before despatching this letter, I show it to our excellent friend Count Mellerio, who salutes you. I have the greatest confidence in him, and hope, as you well remark, that he also is an instrument for good in the hands of our Lord. I rejoice that you find the mount over Domodossola so well adapted for our purpose. The description I have heard of it makes me, too, of that opinion. Much as I desire to see it, I must wait yet a little longer.'

By thus loyally following the monitions of Providence, in small things as well as great, he meant to prepare a fitting nursery for the Order which God desired him to found. Through loyalty to the same principle, he continued to exhort others to correspond with the grace of their vocation, without once attempting to use his influence for the increase of his own spiritual family. They who came to him, like Löwenbrück, or who were already spiritually dependent on him, like those recommended to him by Madame Canossa, he looked upon as having been sent by Providence. Other excellent subjects, like Don Brunati of Brescia, needed only a hint, and their call to the Religious State would have become a call to join the Order he was organising. That word he would not utter, lest man, rather than God, should sway them. In this he was, possibly, too punctilious ; but so were such great Founders as St. Francis and St. Dominic.

Just as he was on the eve of setting out for Domodossola, he received a letter from Don Brunati, to say that he had completed his arrangements for entering the Religious State. The writer so expressed himself that Rosmini had merely to say 'join us,' and Don Brunati would have gladly done so. But, instead of such an invitation, he sent the following letter as a voucher of their separation :—

I have thanked God for the Grace which He has granted to you, in calling you to a perfect life. The consent obtained from your Bishop is a seal on the reality of your vocation. How many obligations towards God has not one contracted who has received from Him such special Graces ! He who understands their high value can only feel himself con-founded, and, as it were, annihilated in the consciousness of his having nothing whatever to give in return for so great a gift. Happy you who feel this greatness which is so humiliating! How delighted I shall be, if you allow me to embrace you before you set out. I wait for you with impatience. Do not tear yourself away from me,—perhaps for a long time,—without letting me see you.

I thank you for the Mass you said for my good cousin. Our Lord has, I firmly trust, taken him to Himself; and in doing so he wished, as you say, to show how liable human things are to fail us at any moment. Every day we receive such lessons, if we had only understanding to profit by them.

It may be that, in a few days, I shall go on a visit to the birth-place of St. Charles, and perhaps even to Mount Varallo, where, by devout meditations, he prepared himself for death, or rather for a second birth. Would that you were with me ! How delighted I should be to be able to make this little excursion with you before our separation. Wherever you be, I shall ever love you in the hearts of Jesus and Mary, where friends are inseparable and friendship is immortal. *In osculo sancto.*

MILAN : *July* 3, 1827.[1]

Don Brunati's intimate knowledge of the region through which Rosmini was about to pass, on his way to Domodossola, would have made this dear friend a valuable companion ; but he was certain to discover the object of the visit, and such a discovery might interfere with the choice he had already encouraged him to make. Therefore, when they met in Milan, Rosmini advised him to proceed without unnecessary delay to his destination, and then took leave, without allowing him to suspect that he who so earnestly counselled adhesion to the Jesuits, was actually engaged in founding an Order of his own.

Meanwhile, Löwenbrück, having succeeded in renting two rooms of the old house on Monte Calvario, got permission to rescue them from ruin, and make them somewhat more fit than he found them for human beings to dwell in. But, when he had given orders for the necessary repairs and seen the men at work, he soon became tired of superintending them ; all the more, as he was not allowed to carry out some extravagant plans of his own. Then his constitutional impatience led him to complain of being left so long alone at Monte Calvario. Anything resembling solitude was little to his taste, and after a month's rambling through the lonely hill tracks

[1] *Epistolario*, Letter lxvii.

around Domodossola, always ' in search of souls to be saved,' he longed for other company than mountaineers, whose language he did not understand, and for other sights than wood-girt gorges, foaming torrents, and snow-capped mountains. He therefore entreated Don Antonio to call him back to Milan, or join him forthwith at Calvario.

The restless Abbé was unable to understand how thoroughly Rosmini held all his own movements free from mere human impulse, and how completely a supernatural composure restrained his natural desires. Much as he wished to be at Domodossola, he wished more to be sure that he went at the right time and in the right way. Fearing to take any step precipitately, he made even the least of his preparations with prayerful sedateness.

Löwenbrück would have him hasten to open the house at once, and set the proposed Order in motion without more ado. It was not thus impetuously that Antonio Rosmini ever began anything. His hand was to the plough, and all his thoughts, with all his acts, were directed imperturbably forward. It was not human but divine influences that led him on or held him back. God ' had already made known to him many things.' We have his own words for this remarkable declaration, and he who wrote them was one of the humblest and most dispassionate of men. He added, ' I should be an unfaithful servant were I to speak otherwise, or not to follow what I believe to be God's Will in this undertaking.' [1]

---

[1] *Epistolario*, Letter lxxvii.

CHAPTER XXIV.

ROSMINI'S FIRST VISIT TO MONTE CALVARIO,
DOMODOSSOLA.

(A.D. 1827.)

Receives a 'permit' to pass into northern Piedmont—Travels in sight
of scenes sacred to St. Charles Borromeo—Muses on that Saint's
birth and life—Stops at Stresa in front of the Borromean Isles—
Grieves that no memorial of the Saint there embodies practically
the great lessons of his life—How he is himself destined to supply
the want in that very place—Passes on to the foot of the Simplon
—Sketch of Domodossola—The Sanctuary of Monte Calvario—
His first visit to the Sacred Mount—What he saw and thought on
the way—The *Via Crucis* and its chapels—The Ruins on the hill—
The magnificent valley of the Ossola—How what he beheld
affected him.

TOWARDS the end of July 1827, Rosmini had completed his arrangements for making a first visit to
Domodossola. Owing to the unsatisfactory political
relations between Sardinia and Austria he had some
difficulty in getting a regular passport from Lombardy to Piedmont. It is very probable—indeed it
has been asserted as a matter beyond doubt—that
the party influences which hindered the publication
of his panegyric on Pius VII., still fettered his
course in this as in other respects. Be that as it
may, every obstacle was at length overcome by
means of a special 'permit' to travel in the Lake

District, within which lay the places he desired to visit. Count Mellerio, not content with giving him a formal introduction to Cardinal Morozzo, took the trouble of writing privately to that eminent Prelate, in order to secure for his friend a most kindly reception. Manzoni and others also offered to furnish him with letters to persons of distinction in the diocese ; but he would have none that did not specially relate to his object, and Mellerio's to the Cardinal sufficed for this.

On July 30 he was at Novara. Cardinal Morozzo happened to be absent, but his representative cordially welcomed the Roveretan Abate, and was in a position to give the necessary permission for himself and Löwenbrück to do what they proposed in the remotest nook of the diocese. Next day he passed on, by the public coach, to Arona on the Lago Maggiore. Travelling thence alongside the magnificent lake, over the fine Simplon road (Napoleon's one real gift to Italy), he had an opportunity of meditating on the life of St. Charles Borromeo in sight of scenes intimately linked with his memory.

Just outside Arona he beheld the ruins of the grand old castle where the Saint was born, and probably thought of the miraculous light that suddenly filled the room in which the event took place, as a light foreshowing how the holy nephew of Pope Pius IV. was to dispel the moral gloom which had settled down on all that region.[1] Not far from

[1] Don Vincenzo De-Vit, in his *Life of St. Charles Borromeo*

the old castle he saw, in the colossal statue overlooking the town, a grateful recognition of the
Saint's triumph over the darkness he had battled
against for a quarter of a century. So onward,
mile by mile of the journey, he met with some
pleasing vestiges of the great Prelate, whose sanctity
seemed to tint the natural beauties of the lakeside
scenery, lending it supernatural hues that shone
more resplendently than all else he saw ; for Rosmini beheld all things more with the eyes of the
soul than of the body.

When he was in full view of the famous Borromean Isles, the charm they imparted to the strag-
gling villages skirting the lake was not lost on him ;
but he thought less of that than of the absence of
some permanently useful memorial to commemorate,
near by, the Saint's practical charity. He knew that
the patrician glories of the Borromean family were
splendidly preserved in the palatial villas and
gardens of the Isles, but where were the glories of

(*Il Lago Maggiore*, vol. ii., p. 192), tells us that on the night of this
Saint's birth 'a great and extraordinary light was seen by many
shining upon the chamber where the child was born. It foreshowed the splendour of that marvellous sanctity which he was to
attain.' Pope Paul V. in the decree of Canonization records that 'this
light was like a glowing white zone, about four feet wide, and extending from the turret of the castle to the bastion, exactly from east to
west, so as to encircle the room in which Charles was born.' Cesare
de Cucchetti, whose father was captain of the guard, and who was
himself in charge of the fortress on the occasion, described on oath
the appearance of this wonderful light in the terms adopted by the
Pope. His testimony was confirmed by all the guards then on duty.
Like declarations were solemnly made by several domestics who, on
that occasion, had to rise before dawn in order to discharge their
respective offices in the household. (*See* Prof. Antonio Sala's *Vita di S.
Carlo*, p. 3, Milan, 1858.)

the *Saint* fittingly represented or expressed in the hamlets and towns on the shore? It is, indeed, true that local traditions embalmed them, and an altar, here and there, in the village churches enshrined them; it is also true that, here and there, along the lake coast in front of the Isles, there dwelt pious Priests and people who were as ' living monuments to the spiritual revival ' which St. Charles had been the means of effecting. But, for all that, as Rosmini stopped a few minutes in Stresa, close to ' the beautiful Isles,' he could not help saying to himself, as he afterwards said to Madame Bolongaro, that he missed from the scene some serviceable and significant testimony to the purifying labours of St. Charles.[1] The colossal statue near Arona was well enough in its way; but better still, and more to the purpose, would have been a college or an asylum near the parish church of Stresa, on the wooded beach, or on the green mountain side behind the quaint village, which had then a mean, unthrifty appearance, notwithstanding ' the wealth of natural charms ' that encircled it.

He found time to visit the noble parish church, which the piety and generosity of the Bolongaro family had enriched and beautified. What he saw there pleased him much, but seemed to make more evident the want he noted—that, so close to scenes hallowed by precious memories of a great Saint, there was no special institution to practically embody and transmit the grand lessons of so grand a life.

[1] *Rivista Contemp.* Torino, 1856.

How marvellous are the ways God! Ere long, the deficiency which the pious traveller deplored was to be supplied by himself, almost in spite of himself. Ere long, Providence would cause to be erected in that very place, overlooking the Borromean Isles, a noble college bearing Rosmini's own name, and giving to the locality a memorial of sanctity quite in keeping with the heart of St. Charles. Ere long, that poor village was to grow prosperous, materially and spiritually, through the influence of him who was then contemplating its condition, without for a moment thinking that he would ever have any personal connection with it.

But, as highly favoured servants of God have been permitted, sometimes, to see into the future, perchance the saintly Roveretan had been thus privileged? Had he, then, some premonition that for years he should himself reside in Stresa, to renew, after a manner of his own, the battles of Charity which the illustrious Borromeo had spent his life in fighting? Had he an interior presage warning him that he should pass from earth to Heaven nigh to the spot where he then mused?[1] Did he, perhaps, foresee that his body would repose in a shrine on 'the green mountain side' behind the village?—a shrine surmounted by a white marble statue of masterly design and exqui-

---

[1] The little albergo or inn at which Rosmini alighted, while the coach delayed for a few minutes at Stresa, stood near the Palazzo Bolongaro. He much admired this fine villa, then the only important one in the locality. Fifteen years afterwards it was left to him by will; he dwelt in it for some time, and in it died. It is now the palace of the Duchess of Genoa.

site finish ?—a shrine enclosed within the elegant
church of a commodious and stately college ?—a
shrine that was to associate him and his name with
St. Charles Borromeo, B. Catherine of Pallanza,
B. Arialdo and other holy personages whose lives
had shed the lustre of heaven on the region of the
lake ?—a shrine to which pious pilgrims would
resort, not only from the country of the Borromean
Isles but from the far off Isles of Britain ?   No ; we
take it that he foresaw nothing whatever of this ;
for he was thinking not of himself at all, but of God
and of what St. Charles had done for the glory of
God, and of what should have been done to identify
this place with that glory.

Full of such thoughts he resumed his seat in the
coach and continued his journey through the picturesque valley of the Toce, on to the foot of the
Simplon.   By evening he was in sight of Domodossola, an interesting little town of Swiss-Italian
character, 'peering through the foliage of sylvan
embowerments.'   Had he been well acquainted with
the local topography he might have easily recognised
Monte Calvario, on the crest of 'the sacred hill,'
long before he got a glimpse of the town over
which 'its steep cliff kept watch and ward.'   But
though he noticed a ruined tower on the hilltop,[1]

[1] This castle which, from the original name of the mount, was called
Mattarella or Matterello was already in ruins and deserted towards the
middle of the seventeenth century, when two zealous Capuchin friars,
who were preaching in Ossola, formed the design of exhorting the in-
habita·ts to choose the hill as a most suitable place for the erection of
the Stations of the Cross.   By this means, not only the people of the

and thought the site admirably fitted for the purposes of a Sanctuary, he knew not yet that he was
admiring the spot chosen by Providence for the
commencement of the new Order, As he entered
the town the sun had sunk behind the western
mountains, which threw out deep dreary shadows
wrapping all the place in gloomy shade ; but the
Roveretan was familiar enough with such sunsets to
see a balmy brightness within the gloom and to
deem the general effect 'nor too sombre nor too
gay.'

The town stood raised somewhat above the
valley level, on a plateau to itself facing the immense
rotunda formed by the Lepontian Alps, known of old
as Alpi Attreziane. Before the construction of the
Simplon Road (in 1810) Domodossola was an
obscure village ; but it had, even then, a dignity
superior to the many other hamlets that dotted the
bosom of the great valley, or the bleak sides and
the woody dales of the surrounding mountains.

town and district but strangers from a distance might be enabled to
assemble and publicly meditate on the Passion of our Blessed Lord,
and thus increase their religious fervour while gaining the spiritual
favours and rich indulgences which the Church has attached to this
devotion. The design was communicated to some rich and pious
people of the locality, who approved it and resolved to erect, forthwith, a sanctuary which should faithfully represent the sorrowful
stations of our Saviour's awful journey from the house of Pilate to the
spot on which the great Sacrifice was consummated. No sooner was
this decided on than steps were taken to obtain the property, including the ruined castle, from the King of Spain. The Governor of
Milan, who held the Province for the Crown, supported the movement,
and Mount Mattarella was ceded for the purposes of a Sanctuary and
became *Monte Calvario.—Vita di Don Luigi Gentili* per Francesco
Puecher. Lugano, 1850.

This dignity centred in the fact that it retained the name by which the whole province was known— *Ossola*—and that its parish church was popularly styled *the Domo*, to distinguish it from the other 'houses of God,' which were thus declared to be its juniors, if not its offspring. Gradually, the mountaineers came to speak of this village quite as often by the name they gave its church, as by the name it had inherited, and so, in course of time, the two designations were made one—*Domo-d'-ossola*.

After the completion of the Simplon Road, the village began to lose its obscurity and its littleness; for its position as the first 'posting stage' on the Italian side of the Alps opened up an era of expansion, and secured to it the custom of many travellers who, otherwise, might never have taken the trouble to visit it or the magnificent and ever-varying scenery of the district. The population speedily increased, and at the time of Rosmini's visit was about 2,000. The finest house in the place belonged to Count Mellerio, and was remarkable rather for size than beauty. As its noble owner preferred to reside in a more southerly latitude, this mansion was applied to purposes of education for the benefit of the neighbourhood—a course, by the way, to which the 'absentees' of that region were not more partial than those with whom we associate the title in our own country. But Mellerio was an exceptional man in most respects—one of those men in whose nature all the elements of good were so cultured by religion, that nothing which was unproductive of good had a chance of growing up in his heart.

When Rosmini arrived at the diligence office, he found Löwenbrück with Mellerio's agent waiting to welcome and conduct him to the lodgings they had hired in the town for his short stay. These lodgings were near the handsome parish church— the Domo—whither he immediately went to make a visit of homage and thanksgiving. As the 'thick shades of night were fast approaching,' it was decided not to go up to Calvario until next morning.

Meanwhile, he heard once more all about the history of the Mount, known of old as the Matterella—how the tower and keep were erected, in the eighth century, by Lombard adventurers resolved to lord it over the inhabitants of the plain; how the Church came to convert that fortress of barbaric tyranny into a stronghold of Christian mercy; how it served for generations as an episcopal palace; how the Capuchin Friars (whose monastery lay half concealed on the hillside) had long ago won for it a sacred character, and consecrated it to a commemoration of the awful scenes connected with *the* Calvary; how the Bishop of Novara, in 1658, officially decreed that it should be known, ever after, as *Sacro Monte Calvario* ; how Signor Capis of Domo, influenced by the eloquence of the Capuchins and assisted by the pious people of the district, commenced, in 1760, to build along the winding path to The Mount, regular chapels, instead of the little pillars formerly marking the successive Stations of the Cross; how the place came to lose all its ancient material splendour without losing any of its 'sacred spiritual character.'

That this character survived all else was to Rosmini's thinking one of the most suggestive facts in the history of The Mount. Its formidable keep and the episcopal palace were gone, and represented by no more than battered ruins. The mighty men who once wielded power within its walls, and the proud ones who lived in state there had not left even their names behind. Mellerio's agent could tell him nothing trustworthy about them; for the best legends of the locality failed to supply more than confused mythical information ; and there was no other. Had Don Antonio ever read Spenser's *Ruins of Time* he might have recalled this passage :—

> How many great ones may remembered be,
> Who in their days most famously did flourish,
> Of whom no word we have nor sign now see,
> But as things wiped out with a sponge do perish.

It is not thus that it fares with the 'sacred spiritual character' which can withstand the ravages of time and outlive all greatness that is merely human. This character clung to The Mount, and, as enduring as its rocks, lived on through storm and calm, without any essential change. A palace and a stronghold the place might still be deemed, but of a sort in keeping with the sacred character it never lost—that associated with Calvary.

Having obtained permission to celebrate an early Mass in the parish church, Don Antonio was ready by 7 o'clock in the morning to accompany the Abbé Löwenbrück and Signor Chiossi (Mellerio's agent) to The Mount. When they emerged from the trees, screening the street in which Rosmini lodged, the Sacred Hill was fully in sight and seemed to be but a short distance off; in fact hardly outside the boundaries of the little town. This, however, was an optical illusion, for many thriving fields and little vineyards lay between the town and the base of the hill ; but the side first in view, being 'as steep and perpendicular as the ' Tarpeian Rock,' so cheated the eye as to leave the impression of close proximity.

The better to reach The Mount they had to take a road which appeared to lead in a different direction. Having walked on for a few minutes, through a dreary waste made by the floods of the Toce, they came to a great archway known as Pilate's Gate. A little beyond it, in a field to the right, they saw a large wooden cross and pillaret marking the spot where once stood the first of the chapels dedicated to the leading scenes of our Lord's Passion. Don Antonio was informed that when Napoleon invaded this part of Italy, the little chapel was used as a powder magazine, and the desecration ended in an explosion which left not a trace of the structure. Passing away from this sad memorial of a sacrilegious invasion, they were soon in front of a chapel constructed with more elaborate care and on a larger scale than any of the wayside sanctuaries abounding in the neighbourhood. It was the first still standing of the regular series of chapels erected, as Stations of the Cross, at convenient intervals, on either side of the steep, zig-zag ascent to The Mount.

This chapel, facing the level road that led straight from Pilate's Gate and the town, seemed to end the highway, so abrupt was the change of course towards the Mount, instead of continuing the path away from it. In a few moments they were at the next turn, or rather sharp angle of the road, where a pillaret marked the site of a chapel of which not a vestige remained. Mellerio's agent said that there had never been more than a pillaret at this spot; but others are of a contrary opinion. There the real ascent of the hill began; there the road seemed once more to lead away from The Mount; there it narrowed and became more rugged and steep, but pleasantly lined by umbrageous forest and chestnut trees all the way up. Soon they came to another chapel, where they paused for prayer and rest. Thence on and up they went, slowly and prayerfully, Rosmini (as he afterwards told Tommaseo) all the while musing on the various scenes of the Passion, and blessing God for having invited him to a place in so many ways admirably fitted to commemorate *the* journey to Calvary.

Thus going on and on, up and up, now in the direction of The Mount, now as if moving away from it, slower and slower at each stage of the constantly rising roadway, they saluted chapel after chapel until at length the flattened summit was reached and they entered what was for them the crowning chapel of all—that of the Crucifixion.[1] Here they remained for some minutes in prayer, after which they joined Canon Capis, the Rector and (to all intents and purposes) lord paramount of Matterella—that is, of The Mount and its appurtenances. His dwelling was near at hand —the house in which Löwenbrück had a room, and for the full possession of which they came to treat.

It was a nobly placed, poorly constructed, and miserably neglected abode. The site, however, and

[1] It was a small but elegant octagonal church, its portico and piazza paved with stone. Above the high altar was presented to the contemplation of devout pilgrims the image of the Crucified, larger than life, having at its feet the virgin Mother, the beloved disciple, and the penitent Magdalen. Right and left on either side a chapel was built, in one of which was represented the deposition from the cross ; in the other, the Sacred Infant, flying from the arms of His blessed Mother to embrace the cross presented to Him by an angel from heaven in the name of the Eternal Father ; a tender allegory full of truth. In the Cupola, Christ risen from the dead, clothed with light and bearing the standard of victory, floated in the air. Around the Church in the angles of the walls were placed statues of the prophets David, Solomon, Isaias, Jeremias, Daniel, Micheas, Zacharias, and Aggeus, each having over his head an inscription taken from his own writings in allusion to the great mystery. The square niche over the high altar, in which was placed the crucifix, was closed by a red silk curtain ; this when thrown back disclosed an ample choir, as large as the church, its walls and vault stored with representations of mysteries relating to the Crucified Redeemer. From the right side of the sanctuary a small corridor led to a narrow stairs which descended to a chapel under the church and facing a garden ; this chapel was called the sepulchre, because in it was represented the vault in which lay the dead body of Christ, covered with a transparent veil, supported by adoring angels at the head and feet.—Puecher's *Vita di Don L. Gentili.*

its associations were all that Rosmini could have desired.[1] From every point the view was enchanting; but to him it was most beautiful for being so rich—

In those deep solitudes and awful dells
Where heavenly-pensive contemplation dwells.

All around him were the lofty Alps; some in the distance retaining their glistening snow domes, others nearer refreshing the sight by the rarely tinted verdure with which they were clad to their peaks, and greeting the ear with gurgling strains that came like weird music to make the prevailing stillness more marked and solemn—the music of numerous little torrents foaming down to the immense basin of Ossola, where the Toce took up the silvery streamlets and carried them to the Lago Maggiore.

[1] At the left side of the Sanctuary was the sacristy, through which you passed into a stone-paved corridor conducting to the cells, used by those pious persons, priest or lay, who might wish to retire there in order to make a spiritual retreat. Another part of the house was assigned to the Rector of the Sanctuary, whose duty it was to reside there in order to preserve everything in decent order, and perform the sacred offices in the church. From this building you passed to the place where the Castle of Matterella stood. Of this castle there still remain (after building the Sanctuary, the Chapels and the Capuchin Convent from its materials), a large wall which traverses the entire width of the summit, and a square tower which rises from a rock at the highest point of the hill, the remainder of which is covered by a coppice and garden. From here a vast and magnificent view is obtained of the town of Domodossola, of many villages with their churches and campanili, scattered about the sides of the surrounding hills, of the winding course of the Toce, of the devastating torrents Bogna, Divena, Isomo, and Melezzo, of the openings of the neighbouring valleys, of the snow-capped Alpine peaks, of fields and vineyards, meadows, marshes and sands.—Puecher's *Vita de Don L. Gentili.*

Passing beyond the house through the battered walls of the tower and keep—crumbling memorials of mediæval state and power—Rosmini was soon beneath the shady trees of the garden terrace, on the crest of the lofty cliff overlooking the whole valley. If he had not been from boyhood familiar with magnificent scenery of a like character, the view then before him would have had as over-whelming an effect on him as it had on the French Abbé. 'When I first stood there,' said the charmed Löwenbrück, 'I was like one spell-bound and could not speak.' Rosmini could speak, and his words were those of the Royal Psalmist, 'O magnify the Lord with me, and let us extol His name to-gether.'

What he saw greatly delighted him, and none the less that the whole seemed to be a beautified and hallowed enlargement of scenes which recalled the view from a favourite hill above Rovereto. 'While he looked out on the vale of the Ossola, from the appointed nursery of his spiritual posterity, it was hardly possible for him to avoid thinking of it in connection with the nursery of his ancestors.'[1] Apart from this, we infer from fragments of con-versation preserved by some of his earliest and most lowly-placed associates, that the view at first ap-peared to him much as it did to the fancy of a later visitor—like a vast saloon in nature walled by mountains ; its carpet a diversified vegetation 'streaked with streams and fertile fields and bare

[1] Tommasseo, *Rivista Contem.*, 1855.

C C 2

marshes, over which rippling surges on countless
pebbles chafed ' ;

> Its roof the sky untainted,
> Sun, moon, and stars the lamps that give it light,
> Clouds, by the Celestial Artist painted,
> Its pictures bright ;

its furniture villages gemmed with cupolas and cam-
paniles that seem to be for ever brightly reflecting
the praises of God.

Beneath him lay the town of Domodossola, looking more diminutive than it really was. But,
making every allowance for the height at which he
stood above it, there was little in its extent and less
in its elegance to compare favourably with the view
of Rovereto from the sanctuary of the mount he loved
to visit when at home. Nevertheless, there were so
many features of resemblance between both mounts
and both views that he had no difficulty in blending
the cherished memories of the past with the prompt-
ings of the present. Although Domodossola presented no such city-like appearance as Rovereto, the
grandeur of its natural scenery was more marked,
more imposing, and far more cheering ; while, as for
monuments of Christian piety, these were as numerous and as various in the valley of Ossola as in his
native vale of Lagarina.

Having satisfied himself that all he saw more
than justified the brightest descriptions of the place,
Rosmini returned to the church for a few minutes to
pray. He then accompanied Canon Capis to discuss matters connected with the repair and occu-

pancy of that portion of the establishment which
they had consented to rent. It was with much
difficulty that favourable terms could be obtained—
indeed, it is only by a stretch of courtesy that the
terms actually agreed on can at all be called favourable. However, they were the only terms he
could then get, and, as he had made up his mind to
begin on this Mount, they were favourable in so far
as they gave him an opportunity of carrying out his
purpose. The Canon was quite ready to have
Rosmini and his friends as tenants-at-will, and to '
permit them to spend as much money as they
pleased in repairs and improvements, but he was
indisposed, at that time, to give them much accommodation in the dilapidated buildings, or to concede
anything likely to lead to a permanent hold on the
place. Nay, he was not willing to allow them even
the privilege of walking when they pleased in the
gardens, unless they chose to pay for it. These
were by no means hopeful features in the business;
but Rosmini felt so sure that God had called him
there and designed the place for the objects of this
call, that he was content with the agreement, and
confidently left the rest to Providence.

The most ruinous portion of the edifice was
forthwith hired for a few years, at a substantial
annual rent, and a kind of limited partnership established as regards the garden. Then certain favours
were obtained as to the use of the chapel; and an
arrangement made for sharing in the spiritual
labours of the district. Löwenbrück, after much

persuasion, consented to remain and see to the partial restoration of the structure in accordance with plans suggested by Rosmini, who had to leave for· Rovereto to provide the means necessary for the work. Meanwhile, in order to relieve the loneliness of which Löwenbrück complained, a useful companion was found for him in a Franciscan lay brother named Peter. This kind old friar was one of those who were driven from their convent in Domodossola by the cruel decrees of 1810, when that and many other religious houses were suppressed. He sought shelter on the Mount, where he had, at length, an excellent chance of assisting another to bear discomforts and solitude with a pious composure never wanting to himself.

Although Löwenbrück had been previously told that this visit was to be merely a 'flying' one, he hoped Rosmini would have remained long enough to have made himself acquainted with all the hamlets in the neighbourhood, and to have joined in a preaching tour among the mountaineers. The wish was characteristic of the Abbé, and its discovery gave Rosmini an opportunity of once more explaining the special objects for which they had chosen this solitude, and of once more commending to his attention the principles of the proposed Institute which set so high a value on the orderliness of charity in all its forms. He warned him to control a zeal that was only wasted, since it was not likely to be productive of any good so long as he was unable to speak in the language of the people. More-

over, the mountaineers were, on the whole, very
pious, practical Catholics, whose spiritual interests
were not neglected. For the rest, he consoled him
with the assurance that their separation should not
be a long one, and that when he returned they should
act together in any missionary duties to which they
might be called. He then reminded him of what he
had said in a letter written from Milan on July 6, to
this effect :—

Next Lent I shall come to reside in Domodossola.
We shall spend Ash Wednesday in fasting and prayer
together. From the very outset Jesus must be our pattern,
in the work which only He can carry to perfection. Probably I shall bring with me a good companion, and we
shall thus be the better able to comfort and support one
another with the words, 'Where two or three are gathered
together in My name, there am I in their midst.' O happy
mountain solitude where we are to be united in prayer
and in the fast of our Lord ! He then will teach us all
things, and remind us of what we have hitherto heard from
the Church ; but these things would remain as though
dead and forgotten, if the Paraclete, 'which the Father
sends in the name of the Son did not quicken them into
life.'

Lent (he continued) will be the best time for writing the
constitutions 'according to the pattern which will be shown
us on the mount.' Should the six weeks of Lent not suffice
for the work, we shall continue it until Whitsuntide.
*I firmly believe that God has already made known to me many
things.* I shall set them before you, that you may judge
whether they are from our Lord. I should be an unfaithful
servant were I to speak otherwise, or not to follow God's
Will in this undertaking. I proceed slowly, indeed; not
through coldness but through fear. I have no wish to be
beforehand with God, nor to be tardy in following His

Will ; but I fear the first defect more than I do the second. However, God is good, and has given his Saints repeated calls, even to the third time, often urging them on with goads too sharp for their resistance. Surely, He Who has given language to man knows how to speak Himself. He Who has made babes eloquent cannot fail in making His own utterances clear and effective. Let us well employ the time that remains for us between now and February 20— let us employ it in attending to the voice of God, and in making more and more certain our holy vocation.[1]

As a means of restraining Löwenbrück's eagerness to go forth preaching to people who did not understand him, Rosmini besought him to devote much of his time to the study of their language. 'While I am away,' said he, 'putting in order my temporal affairs, do you endeavour to acquire some knowledge of Italian, so that, on my return, we may be able to interchange our thoughts more easily than we can at present.'[2]

Before leaving, Don Antonio got many promises from Löwenbrück that he would do his utmost to follow the advice given to him ; that he would endeavour earnestly to overcome the spirit of impatience and discontent which sprang from an excessive and ill-regulated ardour ; and that he would, with all humility, accommodate himself to circumstances which Providence had so evidently designed for the spiritual well-being of both. Many disappointments, annoyances and hardships were, doubtless, still in store for them ; but if the call they had

---

[1] *Epistolario*, Letter lxviii. See Appendix, Letter vii.
[2] *Cronica Contempor.*, Torino, 1856.

answered had come indeed from God, they should be able to bear all without a murmur ; nay, to welcome all their trials as favours.

Löwenbrück took these admonitions in good part, as he was wise enough to understand that the friend who thus gently pointed out his faults and their remedy, not only did him a true service but paid him a high compliment. For Rosmini it was always an unpleasant duty to censure any one, and, when he undertook the task, he assumed, as in this case, that the friend censured possessed many excellent qualities, else he would be incapable of listening, calmly and profitably, to the mention of his failings. He and Löwenbrück then parted, the one full of promises of amendment, and the other full of hope that the promises would bear fruit worthy of the object they both had at heart.

CHAPTER XXV.

PREPARING FOR MONTE CALVARIO.

(A.D. 1827.)

He returns to Milan—An invitation to Rome—Why he does not
accept it—Löwenbrück's phantasies—How Rosmini rebukes them
—Man's nothingness—The first thing to be done on the Mount—
Count Padulli to represent Rosmini in Rome—Visit to Verona—
Madame Canossa's gratitude to God for granting her petitions—
In Rovereto once more—Moschini's illness—The means for preserving the spirit of the Institute—Prosperity should make men
humble—The Exercises of St. Ignatius his special study—Bad
health no hindrance to his twofold vocation.

ROSMINI returned to Milan on August 5. He was
so full of the object which had led him to Domodossola that he determined to remain in Milan no
longer than was necessary for setting in proper
order, and entrusting to competent hands, the charitable and literary works with which he was identified
in that city. This done, he would proceed to
Rovereto, to complete arrangements for making a
home on the dreary Mount. Count Mellerio and
the few others who were acquainted with the purpose of his visit to Monte Calvario had the satisfaction of hearing from his own lips a most interesting
account of all he had seen and done there. What
he felt and hoped with regard to the results of his
visit was freely discussed with these friends. Al-

though the obstacles still in his way seemed to be numerous, and were set forth by him in the strongest light, his pious counsellors were persuaded that, as God so evidently designed the place for the purpose and directed the steps that had been thus far taken, He would prosper the holy enterprise to the end.

Amongst the letters which had accumulated during his short absence, was one from Canon Silvestri Belli entreating him to visit Rome, where the interests of Christian philosophy claimed his presence, and where many friends were desirous of giving him a cordial welcome. Had this invitation reached him two months earlier, he would have found it so much in keeping with what might have then seemed most expedient that it would have been difficult for him to have declined it. But the Will of God was now so apparent that he could not be drawn aside from the path to which It plainly pointed. This path led not to Rome, at present, but to the rugged hill, where, as he foresaw, many severe trials to the flesh and the spirit awaited him. When he should have taken all the steps required of him at this juncture, it may be that God's Will might guide him to Rome; but, until then, he must not think of moving in that direction, and so he told Don Silvestri :

Every time you speak to me about going to Rome you arouse in my heart a great temptation. You must know that I have long had an intense desire to go, but I have always resisted it. You will ask me the reason why.

It arises from the rules of conduct which I have embraced. I should be disquieted and inconsolable if I could believe that I had done my own will rather than the Will of God. On this account, I am thoroughly passive with respect to deliberations of that sort, feeling assured that if God requires any thing of me He will make it known to me in an unmistakable way.

You cannot imagine the tranquillity produced in me by living in accordance with this rule. The Lord disposes all things with sweetness, and it is·this sweetness that one enjoys in following God's arrangement of events. However, I may tell you that my journey to Rome seems to me a settled thing, though I do not yet well know the time in which I can accomplish it :—perhaps sooner than I expect.

Let us pray, my dear friend, let us pray with one accord, and let the centre of our thoughts be Holy Church, for which I beg of our Lord to allow me to die.

MILAN : *August* 6, 1827.[1]

Rosmini had been barely half-way on his return journey to Milan, when the Abbé Löwenbrück began to set at naught some of the sage counsels he had received. He did not, it is true, violate them in the letter so much as in the spirit; for, while he felt bound to abstain from exhibiting his zeal in preaching to the poor mountaineers, who did not understand him, he felt free to talk confidentially with· some of the better instructed people of the neighbourhood, telling them wonderful stories about the grand designs of the Abate Rosmini. Löwenbrück was not a poet ; yet his active imagination was constantly giving to some 'airy nothing a local habitation and a name.' As if to atone for what

[1] *Epistolario*, Letter lxix.

were to him the substantial miseries of the present,
his plastic fancy built up a splendid future for the
bleak hill on which he lived, and made Rosmini its
genius. He spoke of his talents, of his learning, of
his wealth, of his influence and of his plans, in terms
so exaggerated that Mellerio's agent deemed it a
duty to warn him of the impropriety of such a course,
and to communicate with the Count on the subject.
Mellerio promptly let Don Antonio know what his
agent had reported. When thus informed, on
August 9, Rosmini wrote to Löwenbrück a long
letter couched in kindly terms, but still stern
enough to check the phantasies of his too enthusiastic friend.[1]

I fear (he said to him) that your temperament,
perhaps a little too ardent, has prevented your observing
that prudence which I have so much recommended to you,
and of which we have such great need. It has come to my
knowledge that you have overstepped this prudence by
saying things which have no foundation whatever, and
which, even if they had, it would be wiser not to speak
about. I do not believe that you intended to deceive, for
I have confidence in the sincerity of your soul ; but I am
greatly afraid that you have deceived yourself by convert-
ing into a reality some fair idol of your imagination. For
the love of our Lord ! let us be cautious and prudent, and
let us say rather too little than too much ; especially as to
things which may be favourable to our undertaking. This,
my dear friend, is of great importance to us. Words
indiscreetly spoken or written may be fraught with immense
danger to the work which God seems to wish at our hands.
We shall have to answer for this to Him. Every im-

[1] See Appendix, Letter viii. (*Epistolario*, Letter lxx.)

prudence we are guilty of may gain for us the title of unfaithful servant—*serve nequam*—which God avert.

He then explained to him, once more, the spirit according to which he sought to regulate his own course, a spirit 'which should ever animate our Society, if it please God to give us associates.' This spirit was to keep them thoroughly persuaded that, of themselves, they were nothing, that all their natural abilities were, of themselves, powerless to do even the least thing pleasing to God, or of the least use to their own or their neighbours' souls. How then could they, of themselves, give increase or glory to the Church of Jesus Christ ?

Jesus, Head of the Church, is He who, alone and un-aided, does all. He has no need of any one, and He is so jealous of His glory that He unfailingly confounds those who presume that they are, of themselves, able to accom-plish anything for His glory or for His Church. Convinced of this, the Christian should not only not think himself necessary, but he should continually regard himself as being the unprofitable servant he indubitably is. There-fore, not being necessary, he should never have any anxiety or solicitude about doing great things ; nor should he act in the things of God as an adventurer or enterpriser, as men do in the affairs of the world, when seeking to make themselves famous or powerful. In the things of God we should do just the contrary.

As Löwenbrück was much concerned for the afflic-tions of the Church, and seemed to think that the petty persecution which had sent himself into exile, identified him more than others with those afflic-tions, he found therein an excuse for many of his excesses. Rosmini besought him to be perfectly tranquil with regard to the vicissitudes of the Church.

Be sure (he wrote to him) that Jesus Christ still lives; that He has all power in Heaven and on Earth ; that He does all that He wishes, and that nothing happens without being ordained for His greater glory—for His more complete triumph. What then remains for the Christian to do ? To work out his own sanctification, to purify his own conscience, to bemoan his own sins, to acknowledge his own weakness, to recognise his own nothingness, to pray, and to consume himself in the fire of unbounded love.

Rosmini next dwelt on the duties of a Christian as regards undertakings beneficial to his neighbour or useful to the Church, and showed, at some length, how the principles of the proposed Institute met every condition required for accepting and duly performing these duties. He concluded that part of his letter thus :—

Let us be candid, let us be sincere. Candour will enable us to embrace the good actually before us, without giving a thought to any other. Sincerity will not permit us to speak of more than we know and that our Lord desires us to know. Let us not aspire to do *great* things, but simply to do whatever God wills us to do.

With regard to the 'great things' to be done on The Mount—the 'great things' of which sanguine Löwenbrück had talked so much—Rosmini quietly disposed of them in this way :—

What are we going to do, my friend ? Nothing more than to make a retreat of forty days, nothing more than to observe fast together after the example of our Divine

Master. This we know; or at least we think we know it, because it is a thing close at hand, and circumstances appear favourable to its accomplishment. Do we know more than this? Nothing which we are in a position to communicate to others. Let us then be contented and not speak about things we are not certain of. If we were to die to-morrow, we should leave nothing unfinished; for we are every moment fulfilling God's Will. If we talk of doing anything in the future God will punish us for it, as we shall have been unmindful of His words. Lent, indeed, may reveal to us something else; and when the time shall have come for doing that something, the time will have come for speaking of it. Far, then, be from us all human artifice, all exaggeration. We should never wish for anything by such means, since we wish to do only that for which God provides us nobler means.

He wound up these admonitions by reminding the Abbé that when they were about to part in Domodossola they agreed to propose, each to the other, a subject for their daily meditation. In accordance with that agreement, he proposed to Löwenbrück the subject of man's nothingness and absolute dependence on Providence. Then, with a humility which he sincerely felt and always acted on, he requested that his friend would, in turn, propose a subject for his meditation, adding:—

If at the same time you administer a brotherly reproof for some defect that you may have seen in me, during the time we were together, you will confer on me a great benefit. Meanwhile, think over what I have written to you, and be reserved as to our affairs when speaking or writing to your friends, and especially careful to avoid building on future expectations which are without any present foundation; for all this would be contrary to the

spirit of truth, of simplicity, and of confidence in Divine
Providence. Besides, it can do us no good, but rather
much injury.

Löwenbrück made no immediate response to
this letter ; but Mellerio's agent, without knowing
that any such remonstrance had been sent, reported
a marked improvement in the proceedings of the
Abbé. After a week's delay Rosmini again addressed
him :—

Let us trust in God, and let us hold fast to the maxim
which I explained to you in my last letter, to which I am
anxiously awaiting your reply. Let us not take the least
step which is not founded in the prudence and truth of our
Lord. I repeat to you, let us not ambition to do great
things, nor take trouble to ourselves about the future. Let
it be the Lord Who leads us, nay Who impels us, as it
were, at every step ; so that we may not move a foot
without having solid grounds for hoping that it is *not man*
who moves us, but Jesus Christ *in man.* O happy are we
if we walk with such caution ! Thus are we dead to ourselves, because our life is hidden with Jesus Christ in
God. ' I live ; not I, indeed, but Christ liveth in me.'

I love you much, my dear friend in the Lord : peace,
patience, and perseverance be to us. We know not what
we are doing ; nor even what we are asking for. ' We
know not what we should pray for, as we ought,' saith the
Apostle. Where then can we put our confidence ? Listen
to what follows—' But the Spirit Himself asketh for
us with unspeakable groanings ; ' and again, ' He that
searcheth the hearts knoweth what the Spirit desireth,
because He asketh for the Saints, according to God '
(Rom. viii. 26, 27). This, therefore, is our duty, that the
Holy Spirit pray in us, according to God, begging for all
that concerns holiness. The rest will be done by God,
who searches the bottom of our hearts, to find if they are

well disposed. What will He do then? He will show us what we ought to do, as well as the way, and the time, and the place in which He pleaseth that we should do it. Then we shall do what we do understandingly; for God will have set His light before us, and we shall no longer do anything of ourselves, but God will do all in us.

To Him be glory for ever. Amen.

MILAN: *August* 16, 1827.[1]

About this time Count G. Padulli, one of the few who shared in the secret of the projected Institute, came to him from Verona bearing some encouraging messages from the Marchioness de Canossa. As Padulli intended to visit Rome in September, it was suggested that he might act there somewhat in the capacity of an agent for Rosmini. With that view, the following letter to Cardinal Capellari was handed to him :—

Availing myself of the opportunity presented by the visit of my excellent friend Count Giovanni Padulli, to the capital of the Christian religion, I take the liberty of placing before your Eminence the first volume of my minor philosophical works, recently published.

In accordance with your sage counsel, I have warmly recommended the affair of the Institute to the prayers of pious persons, in order that, if the work comes from God, God Himself, working in His servants, may carry it out. It is a great consolation for me to have always remained passive, and to have taken no step in it without having been, I will say, compelled to do so by the clear Will of God. On the other hand, I could do nothing else; for, I feel in myself an extreme insufficiency, and a certain shrinking from what may happen to me, if indeed God has ordained it.

[1] *Epistolario*, Letter lxxi.

Padulli will be able to tell you, by word of mouth, some particulars about the affair ; for he is one of the very few who know anything of it.

I hope that the light your Eminence will communicate to me concerning the two papers, which I sent you by means of the Consul Alborghetti, will bring me comfort. I have great confidence in your Eminence, and I foresee that the affair will be more yours than mine. Thus importunate am I ; and yet, because of my passivity, I am slow to do anything if others do not move me.

MILAN : *August* 17, 1827.[1]

On the following day Rosmini (accompanied as far as Verona by Count Padulli) left Milan for Rovereto. He passed through Brescia without resting there, as on former occasions. At Verona, however, he stopped, as usual, to consult with the Marchioness de Canossa and his sister. When he had given to them an account of the little flock entrusted to his care at Milan, he alluded to the steps he was now taking for the organisation of the Institute, and reported all that could interest them with regard to his visit to Domodossola. The Marchioness, filled with gratitude to God for having thus plainly indicated His approval of 'the call' she had been the means of giving, requested him to join herself and his sister in their Oratory to praise and thank God, and to beseech Him to strengthen His servant for the completion of the work thus auspiciously begun.[2] Her joy was all the greater because she had been so many years urging him to the course which he had at last been obliged, as it were,

---

[1] *Epistolario*, Letter lxxii.   [2] Bertoni's *Memor. di Canossa.*

to take—so many years praying for this result, so many years hoping to see him committed to the great duty. Her entreaties had prevailed, her prayers had been answered. Henceforth, her prayers and hopes would be directed, with all the greater confidence, to the success of a Society with the origin of which God had so intimately associated herself.

After a short visit to the homes of Don G. Bertoni and Count Padulli, Rosmini proceeded to Rovereto. His mother and brother expected him ; but, as they knew that his return was connected with some business arrangements for making his residence elsewhere more permanent, their happiness was not unmixed ; for all that, his presence brought, as usual, joy to all, and he himself felt, as fully as ever, the sweet pleasure he always experienced in the bosom of his family. Moschini's continued illness was the only thing to cast a saddening shade on the joy of being at home once more. No gloom, indeed, found its way into the sick chamber of that saintly youth, who was full of happiness at the near prospect of going to God ; but all who loved him—that is, all who knew him—could not help feeling heavy of heart when they saw death stealthily approaching to deprive them of one so worthy of their affection, one so young and so full of promise in everything good. Rosmini did not escape this sadness ; but, though he had greater reason than all others to feel the loss that was impending, he had more strength to contemplate it with resignation.

The customary home welcomes were not quite over before he set about regulating his temporal affairs, with special reference to the great spiritual work to which he had been called.

A private letter from Domodossola to Count Mellerio was forwarded to Don Antonio, and reached him the day after his arrival in Rovereto. It relieved him from some misgivings as to the preliminary steps taken; for it gave proof that the Abbé Löwenbrück had profited by the reprimand, to which no direct reply had as yet been sent. A letter from the Abbé himself, which was received at the same time, touched on other matters, and was mainly confined to the expression of some doubts as to whether the plan of the proposed Institute sufficiently provided the means best calculated to preserve the spirit of its foundation. Rosmini immediately answered these objections :—

. . . . Coming, in the order of time, so long after all the others, this Institute will be able to derive profit from the lights of all; so that it will be found to concen-- trate, in itself, what the Holy Ghost has distributed amongst the different religious Orders, as regards their means of preservation. As he who has the more enemies should have the more support, so, in times when the Faith is attacked from very many quarters, there should arise a Society which will be armed at all points in its service. But be it always understood that the natural frailty of the men composing any such organisation must never cease to be an object of fear; for, there is no man who can be sure of himself. To prove this, God allowed that all the religious Orders should more or less deviate from their primitive spirit; so that no flesh might glory in His sight.

Every assembly of men is corruptible, save the Church of Jesus Christ; for Jesus, with tears and vehement entreaties, obtained this exception from His Father, as a special favour. Therefore, the Church is the work of God and not of man, and it is the only work founded on the Divine Word, which is the firmament of the spiritual universe, according to the saying—' Heaven and earth shall pass away, but My words shall *not* pass away.' That apart, as we do not confide in human councils, I hope, my dear friend, that God will give us lights to form an Institute as strong as is necessary, and endowed with powerful means to preserve itself in our Lord and in His Holy Spirit, for the time to come.

I do not wonder that the Institute should appear to you somewhat indefinite and diffuse, because of its great extension ; for I have not had time to communicate all things to you as minutely as I shall yet do. You will then see that this indefiniteness exists, if I may so say, only in theory : in practice, the Order is sufficiently restricted to ensure solidity. Its definition, reduced to a few words, would be the following :—An Institute in which the members, especially the Priests, endeavour to perform, with the greatest perfection, all the duties of their own state, in order to be an example to others, and who, there-fore, must strive to attain to the highest degree of holiness. And since Charity towards others, preached with evan-gelical prudence, enters, as a part, into their own sanctifica-tion, they must attend to its exercise also, in the order prescribed by charity itself. Consequently, they are first to practise spiritual charity towards Priests, as being the more excellent charity, seeking before all the sanctification of these.

To descend to particulars : We-shall unite ourselves together in prayer and in study, which will be the two duties undertaken in the choice we ourselves have made of the interior life. And to what will our study be directed ? According to the discretion of our Superiors, it will be directed to acquire a profound knowledge of our sacerdotal state, in order to be able to impart this knowledge to others. Should a Superior, for instance, see amongst us members qualified to give spiritual retreats, he will direct these to prepare themselves for such duty ; and thus will be realised this branch of the sanctification of the clergy.

But it is impossible for me to express myself clearly in a letter, without writing a treatise. It is, therefore, better to remain for the present in tranquillity of spirit, persevering in prayer, and wholly committed to the hands of Divine Providence; following all the lights which It will give us.

ROVERETO : *August* 24, 1827.[1]

While Rosmini was steadily following the lights which Divine Providence set before him in Rovereto, Mellerio and his Milan friends, guided by the same light, were using all their influence to remove exist-ing obstacles, and to bring the favour of ecclesiasti-cal authority to the aid of the new Society. · Their efforts promised success in every direction. When Mellerio (who was on the eve of visiting Domodos-sola) pictured to him the brightness of the prospect, Rosmini hastened to remind him that prosperity should always make men have more and more humility in themselves, and more and more confi-dence in God.

Thanks for all you have done; and these will not be the last thanks that I shall have to offer you, since I always avail myself of your valued friendship. I am rejoiced at the leave granted by the Archbishop. Our friend sent me a copy of his letter. All the rest, so far, goes on well;— nay, to a nicety, as you express it. So much the more

[1] *Epistolario*, Letter lxxiii.

should we work out our salvation with fear and trembling. The thorns have not yet appeared. God will treat us with this tenderness, as long as we are spiritually infants. Knowing this to be God's mode of treatment, prosperity should be a motive for our humbling ourselves.

However, in our humiliation let us be joyful, and let us with open and free hearts (for free we are) enjoy God's gifts, without thinking of aught else. ' Eat those things that are placed before you, without thinking of the morrow ;—continuing always in the giving of thanks.' It seems to me that the thought of being children of so good a God should afford us great consolation. Even if we fall short in something, He is neither exacting nor insistent, as men are ; but readily forgives and compassionates us, looking at the heart, 'for we have an advocate with the Father.'

In spirit and in truth, there is the law of Christians ; let us not impose upon ourselves intolerable burdens ; but let us be humble and offer ourselves to our Lord that He may do with us what we have not been able to do ourselves. Verily, He alone makes the yoke sweet and the burden light. Of ourselves, we are unable to lift a straw from the earth. I have said this for my own consolation ; for it is a consolation for me to speak with my friends of these things,—with friends to whom, as I know, the voice of the Lord is not new, nor are His words unwelcome.

ROVERETO : *August* 30, 1827.[1]

We have had occasion to say, more than once, that Rosmini never allowed travelling or visiting to interfere much with the regular course of his studies ; for these had charms which were second only to the religious duties he loved to practise under all circumstances, and with a never-failing strictness.

---

[1] *Epistolario*, Letter lxx.

Hitherto his studies were directed rather more to philosophy than to asceticism, though the spiritual element pervaded all his thoughts, no matter what he studied. During this visit, however, his studies were turned almost exclusively to asceticism as such. The reason for this must be obvious. He was occupied in clearing the ground for the foundation of a religious Order, and these were the studies nearest akin to the object. The text-book he then used at home was the 'Exercises of St. Ignatius.' A thorough study of this prized volume was carried on by him, for the most part near the bedside of Moschini, who loved to linger over every line, and draw forth spiritual honey from every sentence. The effect of these exercises on that dear patient, the brilliant light which his remarks often threw upon certain obscure passages, made the little volume doubly precious to Rosmini.

It was while he was much absorbed in these studies that he had the consolation of receiving from Löwenbrück a submissive letter—the first containing any direct allusion to the shortcomings which had been so gently censured. The Abbé was penitent, and ready to admit that no man was quite so good as he ought to be, not even his mentor. Rosmini replied :—

It was only yesterday that I received your two letters. I have returned thanks to God that you are in perfect accord with me in the sentiments I have explained to you ; for this has been a fresh proof to me of what I had already expected, and I am glad that I have not misunderstood

you.   Be assured that I love and esteem you, and sincerely
hold myself as unworthy to be your servant.   One thing I
desire and yearn for in our Lord is, that it may never come
to pass that any success we may obtain should lead us to
trust in ourselves, and to take even one step of our own
motion, without having first consulted the Lord ; for 'all
flesh is grass, and all the glory thereof as a flower of the
fields.'

I see from your letter that you are well aware that
every man is imperfect, and that I myself am so in particular.   This gives me great confidence and courage.   For,
I firmly trust that you will be disposed to sustain me, and
to bear with my innumerable faults.   Of this I have great
need, and, for the love of Christ, I earnestly conjure you to
give it to me.   So much the more do I need it, since, as I
told you, weakness is what may be called my habitual
state, and it gives me great consolation to see that my
brethren bear with me.

I am passing these days in familiarising myself with
the ' Exercises of St. Ignatius.'   It is a book which seems to
me all the greater the more I meditate upon it, and I hope
that it will be of much use to us, as it was of the utmost use
to the infant Company of St. Ignatius, being very efficacious
in gaining the heart to virtue,—nay, to the very highest perfection.   If these Exercises no longer produce as great effects
as formerly, it is, perhaps, because the method prescribed
by that man of God, who was deeply versed in spiritual
things, is no longer so closely adhered to as formerly.   In
this as in all other things, men wish to innovate through a
presumptuous hope of doing better.   Hence it happens that
the ' Exercises of St. Ignatius ' have become so enfeebled
and nerveless as no longer to obtain that sure effect which
could be secured by the rigorous method of the Saint.
But of this more when we are together.

Let us persevere in prayer, by means of which we shall
obtain all things through Christ.   I am unceasingly occupied about our association ; and, although my health is

very weak and my infirmities are many, I, however, fear
nothing.

How much I prize those words you wrote to me, ' For
when I am weak then I am powerful ' (*cum enim infirmor
tunc potens sum*). Then, indeed, it is that we hope in God,
when we feel that we have nothing to rely on in ourselves.
We have need of experience. ,The knowledge of the mind
is too cold and inefficacious of itself, without the knowledge
gained by experience, which was the knowledge of the
Saints and of Christ, according to the Apostle's words :
'From those things which He suffered He learned
obedience.'

ROVERETO : *August* 31, 1827.[1]

Although Rosmini was much troubled at this
time by ailments which constant application to study
and ascetic habits fostered, he usually described them
as slight physical attacks intended for his spiritual
good. But his physician, Dr. Ramondini, looked
upon them as likely to bring about serious consequences, if proper precautions were not soon adopted
and persevered in. The doctor warned his patient
of this, adding that if he so diminished his labours
and austerities as to leave himself much more leisure
of mind and body, his constitution was hale enough
to justify hopes of a very long life ; whereas, if he
decided not to follow his advice, or if he perchance
neglected it, some years of suffering were in store for
him, to be followed by a comparatively early death.
This frank opinion of a skilled physician did not in
the least alarm Rosmini. He regarded his studies,
austerities and infirmities as alike from God for God.

[1] *Epistolario,* Letter lxxv.

In obedience to his physician he consented to take the waters of Recoaro from time to time ; he also agreed to use mercurial frictions, and to neglect nothing which might, in that way, be prescribed for him ; but his confidence in God soared above all human remedies. He felt persuaded that, however much he might have to suffer, God's Will required that he should not pause in the work before him, and that, whatever he might have to endure, or however soon to die, this work should be finished before our Lord would call him hence. It was the two-fold work of his vocation—the restoration of Christian philosophy and the foundation of the Institute of Charity.

CHAPTER XXVI.

PREPARING FOR MONTE CALVARIO.

(A.D. 1827.)

His mother's new efforts to keep him at home—The Cross his only love—He sustains others against the assaults he has himself to meet—Provides for the work on Calvario—Löwenbrück and the water supply on the Mount—External circumstances indications of God's Will—The poverty and mortification proper to the new Institute—The ornamental and the necessary—Mellerio's visit to Monte Calvario—Two Bishops visit Rosmini at home—Moschini's illness—The Cross our only treasure—How to win it—Golden rule of humility—Man's nothingness—Death of Maurizio Moschini—Rosmini knows of it miraculously—His eulogy on Moschini.

ALTHOUGH the Countess Rosmini had reason to know that her son's presence in Rovereto was connected with arrangements for making his abode elsewhere more permanent, she was not without hopes of changing his purpose. She knew that the Bishop and Clergy of Trent were eager to keep him amongst them. She knew that the people of Rovereto desired him to remain at home. She had many relations and friends in elevated positions, who, for the good of the diocese, would be glad to promote her own fond wishes. Therefore, while he was industriously providing the means, and settling his affairs for an absence of long duration, she was as industriously bringing all those influences to bear on his course.

Monsignor Luschin, Bishop of Trent, supported by the representations of Monsignor Sardagna, its former Vicar Capitular (and at this time Bishop of Cremona), entered cordially into his mother's views. Forthwith the rectorship of the diocesan seminary was pressed upon him, and other posts of dignity and responsibility were placed within his reach. All these offers were accompanied by arguments based on the great need of his services, and appealing strongly to the claims which his native diocese had upon him. But God had already so plainly indicated the work set for him, that no inducements, no blandishments availed to turn him in the least from the path in which he was moving. The miserable home, with its certain privations, on the bleak hill above Domodossola, was now dearer to him than the most stately residence and enticing comforts that could be associated with ecclesiastical preferments.

It is, however, but right to say that none of those who tried to persuade him used arguments addressed to his personal interests under any guise. They all knew how worse than vain, how very offensive to him, any attempt of that kind would be. Far more to the purpose were the educational wants of the diocese, and the urgent calls from more than one populous parish for such aid as he could beneficially give. He replied to the Bishop, as to the others, that he was ready to abandon Milan and Domodossola, and his special studies, and all other undertakings, the moment he was convinced that God's Will required him to do so. It would be more agreeable to himself to stay and labour where they asked him ; but after prayerful reflection he came to the conclusion that God's Will demanded the sacrifice he was about to make. Some of his zealous tempters, who appealed mainly to his natural affections, were made to understand that unless such affections be sanctified by Divine love they cannot be good or useful.

While his family and friends were thus importunate with every variety of affectionate lure, he was himself engaged in supporting another against somewhat similar assaults. This was Count Padulli, a widower who had resolved to tear himself away from the endearments of home in order to be more completely in the service of Christ. Rosmini, when passing through Verona, on his way to Rovereto, visited the Count's family, and had then an opportunity of forming a decided opinion as to the greatness of the sacrifice his friend was making. The fond dissuasions that beset Padulli were in many respects so like those now brought to bear on himself, that the following letter to that nobleman may be taken as the echo of his own answer to his own tempters :

The tender affection you manifest for your children is natural, and will become a means of promoting their true welfare ; because, the sentiments which accompany your affection show that your natural love is sanctified by a more exalted love,—that is, by the love of our Lord Jesus crucified, in Whom we should love all things. This love of Jesus sanctifies the natural affections, so directing them that they do not blind us, but rather assist us to accomplish all that we find to be good for others. Human and natural affections, of themselves, do not understand what is good ; but affections governed by the love of Jesus know what is truly good, and make use of human things to render thanks for the attainment of that true good outside of which there is only the appearance of good.

How rationally you act in resolving to place your whole self at the feet of Jesus crucified ! From Him you will receive strength to discharge the duties of your present state, and to accomplish your holy vocation. From Him you will receive light to direct, in the path of holiness, the children given to you by our Lord, until our Lord Himself crowns His own work: for He never abandons any one who confides in Him.

You feel some misgivings arising from a consciousness of your own weakness. And, in truth, so long as we think only of ourselves, any fear is reasonable. Poor, indeed, is man when abandoned to himself. But let us give thanks to our Lord, because (as you very properly remark) when we abandon ourselves to God He then gives us His own courage and His very strength. I cannot but urge you to be always more and more impressed by this truth. All the study of the Christian's life consists in two points :— ' In the knowledge of ourselves, and in the knowledge of God.'

The thorough knowledge of these two things produces in the Christian two effects opposed to each other, and both immensely great. Self-knowledge brings with it the greatest fear and the greatest discouragement, while knowledge of God, on the contrary, infuses an unlimited hope and an indescribable courage. Let us take care that one of these two feelings is never separated from the other in our hearts.

Wherefore, dear friend, let us fear, let us tremble, but, at the same time, let us have full confidence. We must remember that we not only do wrong to God by presump-

tion, but also by diffidence. Neither temerity nor pusill-
animity can befit a Christian.

Is not this a happy condition, that we not only can
have courage in all the circumstances of life, but also that
we are obliged in conscience to have it ?   O the unspeakable goodness of God!   He takes offence at our being
disheartened.   He exacts from us a courage as great (if
that were possible) as His own,—an infinite courage. Who
would impose this obligation except God?—except a God
infinitely good and infinitely powerful to help us? Let us,
then, with the Apostle, say in our distresses : 'If God be
with us who is against us ? '   But the Apostle adds, ' How
is one to know whether God wills to be on our side ? '   He
answers: Have you not a manifest sign given by the
Heavenly Father who did not spare His own Son but
gave Him for us all ? And if he has given us His Son, how,
then, has He not, with Him, given us all things ?   As He
has given what is more, can He refuse what is less ? What !
will He not give all the graces necessary for the circumstances in which we find ourselves ?

Assuredly, then, you do well in placing yourself and
all you have at the foot of the Cross ; since, according to
St Paul, this is the pledge that has been given us by the
Eternal Father, and the sure guarantee that He will also
grant us all other things ;— nay, it is the fount of all the
graces that we need.

I exhort you, therefore, to be courageous in the Lord,
and to fear nothing in all that you are going to undertake.
Banish every doubt and discouragement, by one sole glance
at the crucifix, whence flows all our strength and wisdom.
Nay, you should make it a duty of conscience to have
courage, because it is certain that Jesus takes care of the
Christian who entrusts himself and all he has to Him.
Let us, therefore, not incur the reproach which Christ
made to His disciples, when they were still unconfirmed :
' Men of little Faith, why do you doubt ? '   All turns out
well for those who commit themselves entirely to the hands

of Him who disposes of all things. Let us not be scandalised at any thing. Let us not hesitate. Let us work
with holy daring, with liberty of conscience, and with
faith.

When you are in Rome I will write to you something
more particular. For the present enough. Let us live
from day to day with joy, in prayer and thanksgiving.
May our common mother Mary assist us !

ROVERETO : *September 7, 1827.*[1]

With a 'holy daring' that had regard to nothing
beyond the Will of God, he continued the business
for the settlement of which he had come home. All
the money which could be conveniently transferred
from his Rovereto agent was forwarded to Milan,
where Count Mellerio kindly undertook to see it
duly banked. A specified annual amount was fixed
on as a future contribution to the same fund from
which he was to draw as occasion required. The
home charities he had founded, or habitually assisted,
were not allowed to suffer because of these arrangements. A sufficient sum for immediate use was
sent, through Mellerio, directly to Löwenbrück, of
whose proceedings the reports were still favourable.
The Abbé himself wrote frequently, and gave hopeful accounts about himself and the works he directed.
One of his greatest fears had just been so suddenly
and completely dispelled that he took the circumstance as denoting God's marked approval of the
undertaking. The incident is too characteristic not
to be mentioned. Löwenbrück was very fond of
good water. Now there was a very insufficient

---

[1] *Epistolario,* Letter lxxvi.

supply of water, and the quality of the beverage was not good. He had a nervous dread of the supply running dangerously short some night, while all day he was afraid that it was slowly poisoning him.

Although excellent water abounded in the neighbourhood, and was visible in almost every direction, the murmur of little brooks and greater torrents perpetually announcing that it was not far distant; nevertheless there was much difficulty in getting the necessary quantity for the purposes of the house. A good spring-well of the purest water was known to be near the deserted Capuchin convent; but through neglect of the most ordinary means to keep it clear of natural obstructions it was no longer easy to reach it, and the water, flowing into pools and streamlets through the little marshes beyond it, was impregnated with vegetable matter that made it neither palatable nor wholesome. To fetch better water from other streamlets severely taxed the carriers, who had to go down some distance to a ravine, and then, laden with full buckets, make the steep ascent to the hilltop. The water thus brought was not of the best; and as it did not long preserve its freshness, this trying little journey had to be repeated several times during the day. The anxious Abbé had devised all manner of ingenious schemes for overcoming these difficulties; but not one of them was found practicable.[1] His nervous fear was

[1] Through the skilfully directed efforts of Don Luigi Lanzoni, the present (1882) General of the Institute of Charity, all the difficulties

at its highest point, and despair of being able to improve matters had set in.   While praying for relief, Brother Peter suddenly came to him to say that 'the blessed spring' near the convent was found to be accessible, that its water was 'the purest and best in the world,' and that it could be delivered at the house more readily and regularly than any water under the old arrangement.   Investigation soon satisfied him of this, and the pious Abbé took it as a distinct manifestation of God's special favour.   As full of confidence as he had been shortly before of fear, he made much of the circumstance in a letter to Rosmini, who, when replying, barely alluded to the incident, passing quickly from it to the fact that external circumstances must always be, for the man of God, indications of the Divine Will.

I have received your kind letters, and have delayed answering them, because I saw all things going on so well that I did not like to multiply letters without necessity. Thanks to our Lord for the water He has provided for us. Both from yourself and my friend, I learn that the works are going on.   May God be blessed !

Here, I am much occupied with our most important business.   God grant that my labours may be of service for that which is the true foundation of every thing,—the formation of our spirit.   To-morrow I go to meet the Bishop of Trent, who is coming on a visit.   I cannot do less than ask his blessing on the work before he leaves us ; but this will be in strict secrecy between ourselves.   I also

which Löwenbrück's plans failed to touch have been completely mastered, and the home on Monte Calvario is now supplied in the greatest abundance with excellent water brought by pipes from Monte Cuculo.

expect shortly the Bishop of Treviso, a friend of mine in whom I have great confidence. But let our trust be in God alone. The favour of men never gives me encouragement without at the same time alarming me. Ah! wretched me! were I to put my confidence in them! God grant that I may die rather than that I should trust in man, or in human things. I beg of you to remember, in your prayers, to beseech from God the grace that we may hope in Him *alone*, and that we may only see in external circumstances the words which He directs to us as a means of manifesting His Divine Will. Only that, and nothing else. Let us attach no weight to them, just as we attach none to the mere voice or writing of a king, but only to his will as expressed in or by them. In this way we shall be entirely abandoned to Divine Providence, without offending by presumption or rashness ; for we have a fixed rule to follow, namely *External circumstances as signs of God's Will.* It is for this reason that, without these signs, we remain in the Contemplative State, and that thence (by means of these signs, and not of our own will) we prudently pass into the Active State, as I have explained in the short Latin description of the Society. This, it seems to me, is the road of peace and tranquillity ; this is the sure way either to silence what St. Peter styles 'the ignorance of imprudent men,' or to bear, with gladness, persecutions to which we have not given occasion, and which are, therefore, really 'for justice sake.'

I am longing to embrace you, and am eagerly looking for the dawning of that 20th day of February which is to find us together. Ah! may God grant that all be for His glory! May God grant that we really come together in His name! and that there be established in us this ground of our hope : 'I say to you that if two of you shall consent upon earth concerning anything whatsoever they shall ask, it shall be done to them by My Father Who is in Heaven ' (Mat. xviii. 19). Let us find ourselves met together in God. Let us two be as one, that we be one in Christ, as

Christ and His Father are one. Oh! ineffable oneness! Oh desirable consummation! May our Lord absorb and consume us in Himself! He is as fire, He can receive sacrifice, and He does receive it, if it comes from the heart, if it is complete.

ROVERETO : *September* 24, 1827.[1]

Notwithstanding the means of consolation that the Abbé found in his improved water supply, he was still far from reconciled to the position of things. He could not yet bring himself to bear privations with heroic resignation, while the thought of having to endure them continually, and as a matter of course, gave him a good deal of uneasiness. Fretted by misgivings thence springing, he became rather petulant, and complained much about trifles, such as not receiving letters more frequently from Rosmini, or not getting permission to purchase furniture of a kind likely to relieve the dreariness of his mountain home. There ran through his letters so many traces of doubt as to his own vocation to the life they proposed to lead, that Rosmini decided on testing them by alluding pointedly to the principles of poverty and mortification which members of the new Institute ought to practise.

Your letter of the 15th inst., which I have just received, shows that you are somewhat anxious on account of my silence. Although such anxiety must be now removed by the letter which you should have received from me since your note, nevertheless I hasten to send this to corroborate the other. Have no doubts, my dearest friend in Jesus Christ, have no doubts. Assuredly, you would neither

[1] *Epistolario,* Letter lvii.

hesitate nor imagine the possibility of any coldness on my part, if you knew how much I loved you, and how much I felt indebted to you for your cares and labours : although they are borne for your neighbours, they still appear to me as though done for myself alone.

I am full of ardour, my dear friend, but I am, at the same time, feeble. God will strengthen me. After all, the only reason why I have been remiss, in the correspondence between us, was merely that of not wishing to needlessly multiply letters ; since, the less we write the better, perhaps, for the secrecy of the affair. Besides, there was really nothing requiring an answer from me. I beg of you to bear this in mind every time that my letters seem to be slow in reaching you; for that may occur again, and I do not wish it to be taken as a sign that I love you less, or that our common affair has become distasteful ; but only that I have not thought it necessary to write to you immediately, or that I have no leisure to do so.

Ah ! how I desire to be with you ! I have myself no doubt whatever of the oneness of our spirit : may this be God's work ! Let us trust in Him only, let us abandon ourselves to Him, without presumption. External circumstances should be to us as signs which we must use for interpreting His Holy Will. Let us not do our will but His, and do it in all peace, tranquillity and patience. Patience is necessary for us, and it is that virtue which Christ has taught us by His life and by His death.

I have been considering about the furniture, which must be made in accordance with that kind of poverty we intend to profess. For this purpose, I have written down a few short rules expressive of our external poverty. I beg of you to examine them, in order that you may see whether the poverty I have described as the most suited to our object be really that best calculated to obtain it. If these rules are approved by you they may be of service, by guiding us in the selection of furniture for the house. All this should breathe but one spirit :—edification, and a contempt for mere human comforts; so there should be nothing which might allure or distract our mind (which ought to be wholly occupied with God), nor the affections of our heart (which ought to be full of God alone).

From these few rules you will see that in my opinion the greatest poverty possible ought to be observed in the house and in its furniture, especially in the cells. The principle whence springs my way of thinking is what I have expressed in the first rule—'That it is very profitable for us, on looking around, to see everywhere an extreme poverty of ornamentation, in order to remind us that we were born naked, and that naked we must return to Christ; but, at the same time, that nothing should be wanting which may either instruct us or help towards our perfection.' We should not be subjected to too many privations, whether voluntary or prescribed by rule ; simply because we ought to make an oblation of ourselves in charity. Therefore, we should not be deprived of the necessary strength, since all our forces should be spent in this. Hence it is that I have said,—'it is not *conveniences* which ought to be deficient, but only all *ornament.*' And by conveniences I do not understand those things which help us to be indolent, but those which help us to be the more active ;— for, there are these two kinds of *conveniences*. It is for this same reason that I do not think it advisable to prescribe any general corporal austerities, but only to provide that those the Church ordains for all the faithful be well and devoutly observed. I leave it, however, for each one to do, in particular, whatever the spirit suggests to him ; subject to the approval of his Confessor or Superior ; provided, also, that he does not diminish the strength which should be wholly spent *in the love of God* by the prayer proper to the state he has chosen, and *in the love of his neighbour*, by the charitable offices undertaken at his neighbour's request and assigned him by his Superior. This forms the second state of the Society.

I shall add nothing more, except that I embrace you in

our Lord, in Whom I wish us both to be made one and altogether absorbed.

ROVERETO : *September* 29, 1827.[1]

About the time that Löwenbrück had digested the contents of this letter, Count Mellerio arrived in Domodossola with money and advice for the Abbé. The money was welcome, but as the advice did not coincide with the 'hermit's' views of what was at once most comfortable and desirable for the hermitage, it can hardly be that it was very welcome. Nevertheless the amiable Abbé gave no signs of disrelishing it. Indeed, he appeared to be so heartily taken up with the work entrusted to him, that Mellerio saw no reason to suspect the presence of any form of discontent. Therefore, when he wrote to Rosmini a report of his visit, he described Löwenbrück as, on the whole, satisfied with his lot, though somewhat weary of being alone, for Canon Capis seldom favored him with his company, and the society of Brother Peter was hardly to his liking, since the old friar was prone to be rather too much of an admonitor.

Rosmini did not reply with his usual promptitude to Mellerio's letter. The Bishops of Trent and Cremona were, at the time, his guests, and the illness of Moschini had just then taken an alarming turn. Here was a combination of obstacles pretty certain to fritter away his time and over-task his strength. When not personally entertaining his illustrious visitors he was by the bedside of his

[1] *Epistolario*, Letter lxxviii.

dying secretary, ministering most tenderly to the numerous little wants of body and soul which no one else there had such skill in discovering. With the Bishops he had to discuss new forms of the old arguments to induce him to remain in the diocese. Thoroughly tired of this topic, as of everything that related mainly to himself, he used to seek relief in frequent visits for a few minutes to Maurizio, with whom he talked on a subject that never wearied him —the sufferings of our Lord, and the joy of those who died consumed by His love. After a few days' stay the Bishops left for Trent, and he accepted an invitation to visit them there, if possible, during the following week. Meanwhile, other distinguished guests claimed his hospitality, and it was the middle of October before he had leisure enough to acknow- ledge the receipt of Mellerio's letter :—

This letter you will receive late for too reasons : First, on account of the illness of the good Maurizio, who appears to be on his death-bed, if God does not interpose His power. He received the holy viaticum a few days ago. What a consolation it is for me to see him so well prepared for the great journey ! He reposes in the hands of God with an enviable tranquillity. If God should now take him to Himself, I hope, confidently, that it will prove to be a favourable moment.

The other reason was a sudden arrival of Prelates. Two Bishops were here at the same time, and I had to keep them company almost the whole day. Afterwards, other guests arrived who have made me lose a great deal of time. May God forgive me, as I hope He will.

I am extremely pleased with the visit you have paid to Domodossola, and all the more as it seems you made it

somewhat against your will. I am especially gratified by
the news you give me of the hermitage and of its hermit.
God can do all things, and He is the more wonderful the
more He works alone. When I think I see God working,
so to say, more of Himself, then I have greater courage,
as His Will seems to be thus more manifest. How merci-
ful He would be if He were to look kindly upon our undertaking! If I am horrified when I look within myself,
what will God see in me with that glance which can discover depravity even in angels?

I take your friendship and kinship with the minister
Brignole—of whom you say so much in so few words—as
another token of Divine Providence and of God's mercy.
How willingly I shall make his acquaintance, for which
you offer me such an excellent opportunity.

I thank you for all your kindness and friendship.
Would that I could prove to you in some way the gratitude I feel!

ROVERETO : *October* 14, 1827.[1]

An unexpected improvement in Moschini's condition gave some slight hopes of his recovery : it
also supplied the attending physicians, and the
Countess Rosmini with a good pretext for renewing
their request that Don Antonio (whose own health
needed much care) should visit the sick chamber less
frequently, and shorten the times of his stay there.
He yielded when the saintly patient joined in the
advice, and reminded him that the regular correspondence was probably in arrears, since he, the
secretary, could no longer assist in it. Two days
sufficed to dispose of the unfinished correspondence.
Amongst the letters then despatched was an impor-

[1] *Epistolario,* Letter lxxix.

tant one in Latin to Prince Alessandro von Hohenlohe ; it besought the prayers of that holy Priest for
the new Institute, and gave him full information of
all that had been done in the matter, and of all that
was in progress and in contemplation. There were
communications to be sent off touching literary and
scientific subjects, others on business, and others on
social topics. All these were dealt with more con-
cisely than usual, but in a way that well befitted the
occasion. As the letters in which Rosmini most delighted—those on purely spiritual subjects—presented special attractions under such circumstances
as found him housed with the dying, he took the
opportunity of pouring out his soul's thoughts on
these without stinting the expression of them.

There were many letters awaiting reply, especially those from the little flock he had left at Milan,
which gave him the opening he desired. To all he
expatiated on the Cross as the treasure of treasures.
Suiting the mode of application to each of his correspondents, he pointed out the defects they had to
overcome, the humility they had to practise in order
to win this priceless treasure. Some of his friends
objected that as no one was without defects of a
more or less grave character, no one could secure
the treasure hidden in the Cross. He replied that
to be fully conscious of defects was the first step to
be rid of them, and a sincere consciousness of our
defects was evidence of that humility through which
the treasure had to be reached. He reminded them
that St. Benedict set down the following as the

seventh cardinal degree of humility, and St. Thomas of Aquin commended it as a golden rule : ' Sincerely to esteem ourselves baser and more unworthy than every one, even the greatest sinner.' [1] St. Augustine maintained that no one could 'without presumption, pride, and sin, think better of himself than of the worst of sinners.' [2] St. Ignatius of Loyola, as every one knows, when surrounded by marked tokens of God's special favour, used to speak of himself as ' the most miserable of sinners,' and sign his letters ' Ynigo, little in good.' Of the many letters which Rosmini wrote in those days, on various phases of this subject, one to Don Boselli of Milan is given here, not because it is the best, but because it is the shortest, and as illustrative of the man as the longest could be.

For your kind remembrance of me I am thankful, and I also thank Signor Francesco, our friend in the Lord. He writes to me that he is wholly taken up with gold and gems,[3] as if he would suggest a pleasing contrast between the state of his body and that of his spirit, with the favourite symbol of which I am well acquainted ; it is the Cross, and therefore rather of wood than of gold. He holds the very same sentiments that your letter leads me to deem yours. Ah ! how great is this treasure ! How precious is this wood ! May our Lord enable us to comprehend its inexhaustible wealth ! Therein we shall have all wisdom, all perfection, all good, all fulness of joy, and stability in the fulness. And if this should not be ours immediately *in fact*, we shall have it *in hope*—in a hope

---

[1] St. Bened., Reg. c. vii.   [2] *Vide* St. Aug. *de Virginit.*
[3] This Francesco kept a jeweller's shop in Milan.

that confoundeth not—a hope that is better than fact, because founded in faith ; and this has a merit far superior to the reward, if the reward could be considered as entirely separated from the merit.

That which you say about defects in the practice of our little religious exercises, should humble, without terrifying us, and may be even encouraging. Our Lord permits this effect of our nothingness, that we may see the more clearly how, of ourselves, we have not power to lift a straw; and *our* religious exercises are really but as a straw, or even less, when contrasted with what holy men in the past have done by the help of the Lord. I not only see that I am infinitely the most imperfect of all, but I feel it thoroughly, and my heart suggests that, in His goodness, God will always act thus towards us ; until, in this school, we shall have learned to despise ourselves—in a word, to know ourselves.

Let us beg of our Lord to give us this precious know-ledge of ourselves, joined with a knowledge of His good-ness, in order that we may not be dismayed. Jesus is able to shed upon our minds the enlightening rays that show us the two pivots upon which all knowledge turns—that *we* are nothing, and that *He* is everything. This knowledge will conduct us to the complete sacrifice of our whole selves, because, recognising our nothingness, we will arrogate nothing to ourselves, but consecrate all to Jesus. Then we shall have complete tranquillity ; then external things will not be strong enough to disturb us, since we shall have our foundation in the truth—because that which is nothing can neither be disturbed nor mortified by men. Nothingness is incapable of being anything, and He Who is everything cannot stand in need of nothingness. When we shall have become as nothing to ourselves, there will have then ceased in us every agitation and anxiety, all precipitancy and over-eagerness. We shall then allow God to extract from our nullity what He pleases, and we shall always readily obey His creative Will alone, just as all

things obey it. Let us learn from these to know that
Voice and not to resist it.

O ! blessed is that human passiveness which, becoming
as plastic as wax, is easily impressed by the spirit of God !
I mention these things, because of my own defects, for I
am more full of evil than others. I conclude entreating
you to pray unceasingly that our Lord provide for the
wants of Holy Church, and give to His divine Son a glory
infinite ; causing Him to reign in all men and in all things.

Prayer ! prayer ! prayer ! that is our need. We know
the means. Jesus has told us what it is. When we fail to
make use of it—whose is the fault ?

ROVERETO : *October 7, 1827.*[1]

The improvement in Moschini's health seeming
to continue, Rosmini consented to go and spend a
day with the Bishop of Trent as promised. He left
on the morning of October 21, intending to return
next day. When he took leave of his young friend,
promising to be with him again on the morrow, he
was greeted with a peculiar smile, which seemed to
say, ' You know not what shall be on the morrow.'
Monsignor Strosio[2] assures us, on the best authority,
that while Rosmini was driving back from Trent,
the following afternoon, he suddenly turned towards
his companion in the carriage and exclaimed, gazing
at something near them, ' Alas ! Moschini is dead.'
He then leaned backwards, and without uttering
another word remained in profound meditation until
they reached the door of the house in Rovereto, when
he asked, in soft mournful tones, ' Is it long since
he departed ? ' The hour named in reply corre-

[1] *Epistolario,* Letter lxxx.
[2] *Difesa della fama e della vita di A. Rosmini.*

sponded, to a moment, with that which Rosmini's companion had carefully noted on hearing the exclamation ' Moschini is dead.'

When the faithful Moschini was duly laid in his grave, lamented by all who assisted at the solemn ceremony—lamented, even though they were all persuaded that he had gone where the Saints reign with Christ—Rosmini had nothing more to detain him in Rovereto. He would have left ere this (for the affairs he came about were already settled to his satisfaction), but he foresaw that his beloved secretary was on the eve of going to God, and he wished to be near him up to the last. Before starting for Milan he sent to Count Mellerio this brief notification of the loss they had to deplore :—

The good Maurizio has been withdrawn from me, in his visible presence, since the 22nd of this month. Our Lord was pleased to spare me the pain of seeing him depart within my arms. I was absent from Rovereto only one day, on a visit to the Bishop of Trent, and it was on that day God took him from me.

Blessed be God ! with Whom, I have no doubt, he now is in bliss ; still, I ardently pray for his well-regulated soul, lest, after all, there should remain any blemish to wipe away—it is so easy for us to defile ourselves in the mire in which we here are.

. I beg of you to notify your friends of this sad event, for I would ask the charity of their prayers also.

ROVERETO : *October* 31, 1827.[1]

Shortly afterwards Don Antonio returned to Milan, where Moschini had made many personal

---

[1] *Epistolario,* Letter lxxxi.

friends whom his admirable life had greatly edified,
and to whom the history of his death, impressively
told by Rosmini, became a source of new and lasting
edification. Not only they who had been intimately
connected with him, but all who knew how much
Rosmini loved him, felt it a duty to express their
condolence in a more or less formal way. It was in
reply to one of these—Signor F. Arrivabene of
Mantua—that Don Antonio penned the following
terse eulogium on his saintly secretary :—

I was about to write to you as to the death of our
Maurizio, when I found myself forestalled by a letter from
you, full of words to comfort my sorrow, because it was
full of my sorrow ; that is, of a grief like unto mine, resulting from a common friendship, and which seems to vent
itself in the relief of another as in its own. However,
yours is sorrow for a distant friend, while I bewail the loss
of one who was constantly at my side, a companion of my
studies, and I will even say my partner for a long time in
every woe and weal of life. I have known intimately, and
have admired, the virtues of Maurizio ; I have seen them
increase almost daily. They have grown, I should say,
under my very eyes, after that manner in which they are
always accustomed to grow in a good man. I should have
wished to have drawn as much profit from his example as
I did from the assiduity of his labours, and from his assistance in literary affairs. I saw him taken off in the full
bloom, when he already promised the richest fruit. He
had a sound mind, virginal, like his heart, and well regulated, like his life. He did not seem to be of this earth
nor of this age. How many things did not his lofty spirit
already embrace ! With what avidity did not that soul
hold fast to the good and the beautiful, whenever he saw
them, wherever they presented themselves ! How many
holy projects had he not already conceived ; had he not

already matured in his mind ! How many things had he
not already taken in hand ! Perhaps they were too much
for his fragile constitution ; perhaps that which the more
endeared him to us—his indefatigable ardour for good—
helped to deprive us sooner of his presence.

Grateful for your expressions towards me, who have no
higher merit than that of having been the friend of your
friend Maurizio, let me offer myself to you in place of him,
if I can be of any service to you.

MILAN : *December* 8, 1827.[1]

It is the special privilege of those who have lived
saintly lives to retain their holy influence after death.
Maurizio Moschini was often fondly styled, by his Rovereto friends, 'a lamp of the sanctuary.' When he was
no longer on earth, he became, to all who had known
him, as a star in Heaven to brighten their paths and
guide them over the course he had passed. His
youngest brother, Felice, who had come to assist in
nursing him during the severe illness he bore so
patiently to the last, soon felt that if sufferings like
Maurizio's were as a rod, it was a rod resembling
Aaron's which blossomed beauteously and produced
the fruit of unending peace. Ere long Felice took
his brother's place as 'a lamp of the sanctuary,' and
he was not the only youth of those days whose career
the example of Maurizio benignly swayed : it still
sways the course of many a timid and weary pilgrim
in this ' vale of tears.'

Possibly, as some have asserted, Rosmini's grief
for the loss of young Moschini was mixed with a
little natural disappointment that his trusted secre-

[1] *Epistolario,* Letter lxxxii.

tary should have been taken away from him just as the Institute was about to begin its existence,—that Institute for the foundation of which Maurizio had so heartily prayed and worked—that Institute amongst whose first members he so eagerly longed to be numbered. Doubtless, Rosmini had counted more or less on this member, and probably thought much of the special good one so rich in virtues was likely to accomplish. But they greatly misjudged Rosmini who supposed that he ever set his heart on the aid of any man, however good and gifted. He trusted so little to mere human co-operation, as such, that its withdrawal for whatever reason, and however suddenly, little troubled him, even when this withdrawal seemed to seriously threaten or actually disconcert his best plans ; not that he was wholly insensible to the feelings of disappointment thence ordinarily arising, but that he was so wholly reliant on Providence, that these feelings were deprived of power to distress him. He felt, indeed, sincere joy at the prospect of seeing realised Moschini's ardent wish to be one of the first members of the new Order, but the joy was centred in the sanctification of that dear friend's soul. This sanctification having been secured already, and by the very means which the Institute was to employ, there was nothing left to give Rosmini real disappointment, nor was there anything to grieve him sorely, except some feeling akin to that which caused our Lord to weep with those who wept at the grave of Lazarus. For the rest, though Maurizio was not spared to participate, on earth, in the opening exercises of the new Order, his intention had already for a long time consecrated him to it, and he was expected to do his part in Paradise. Hence his brother Felice was justified in describing him as 'the first Envoy of the Order to the Court of Heaven,' Felice himself most worthily representing this envoy in its ranks here below, when these ranks were, at length, solemnly ranged with the noble companies forming the regular army of the Church Militant.

END OF THE FIRST VOLUME.

* 9 7 8 3 7 4 4 6 9 4 6 7 4 *